ASIA
HAND

Other titles in the Vincent Calvino series:

Asia Hand

A VINCENT CALVINO CRIME NOVEL

CHRISTOPHER G. MOORE

Black Cat
New York
a paperback original imprint of Grove/Atlantic, Inc.

Originally published in Thailand by White Lotus in 1993

Printed in the United States of America
Published simultaneously in Canada

ISBN-13: 978-0-8021-7073-6

Black Cat
a paperback original imprint of Grove/Atlantic, Inc.
841 Broadway
New York, NY 10003
Distributed by Publishers Group West
www.groveatlantic.com

10 11 12 13 14   10 9 8 7 6 5 4 3 2 1

For Jim Gulkin and Owen Wrigley

ONE

MONKEY SHINES

THREE days into the Year of the Monkey, around midnight, Calvino perched on a stool at the Yellow Parrot jazz bar. He was killing time. Pratt, his police colonel friend, was running more than an hour late. The private investigator instinct made Calvino ask himself some questions. Then he stopped. Bangkok was Pratt's town, his beat; he was running a little late, that was all there was to it. Calvino's attention drifted until it focused on a twenty-something Thai waitress who pulled all male eyes within a twenty-yard perimeter. She glided like a bee, dancing from bottle to bottle, pouring drinks. She was packaged in a pink silk dress wrapped like mist around the waist and hips. It was the kind of dress that wore a woman. Her earlobes and throat were fitted with gold pieces; more gold bracelets encircled her wrists. The gold was a statement that she had successfully mined the Bangkok night for her precious metals. She emptied the last shot from a Chivas Regal bottle as a Thai man in a business suit held a mobile phone to his ear and smoked a cigarette.

The waitress waited for some reaction from her customer. She leaned over the bar, smiled at Calvino, and then turned back to the customer.

"*Hum hiaw*," she said, using a Lao expression, which immediately suggested she had sprung from peasant stock in the northeast. The Japanese businessman on the mobile phone laughed, and then washed away his smile with his drink.

Hum hiaw—the condition of a penis that even though suitably stimulated remains placid—was an emotional stinger aimed to puncture

1

the male ego. She scored a bull's-eye. The customer winced as his ego recoiled into an outburst of nervous, hollow laughter. Then he ran a finger along the edge of the gold bracelet on her left wrist, touching a three-inch scar.

He shook his head. "*Hum khaeng,*" he whispered. He was hard, he was telling her. But she grinned as if she wasn't buying it.

"*Hum hiaw,*" she insisted, then pulled her hand away and swept to the other end of a bar, where another customer was holding up an empty glass.

When a Thai woman stared you in the eye and said, "*Hum hiaw,*" she was passing on a piece of confidential information, some personal intelligence. She had disclosed that she was from the region of Isan and that Lao (as opposed to Thai) was her native language—a Thai from Bangkok would have said, "*juu hiaw.*" And a woman in a Brooklyn bar would have said, "Can't get it up. Can't get it to stay up."

In the Thai language, this was said as a joke to foreigners. *Pood len.* Talking fun. Most of the time Thais liked to play with language; it was fun.

"You'd never say that to a Thai boyfriend," Calvino said to her. "He'd box you."

The smile disappeared from her lips and she turned from the Japanese customer. "*Farang* know too much, not good." She'd suddenly lost her sense of fun. Reminding her there were two sets of rules: one for the locals and one for the foreigners wasn't appreciated. Her Japanese customer bought her another drink, and she drifted back into conversation with him, making a point to ignore Calvino.

Calvino knew that most jokes, even in Thailand, were like a fingernail rubbing a tender spot of despair or fear. Inside this world the hard were favored. Bangkok allowed them to show their stuff—to score, flash money, buy affection and respect; to accumulate followers who looked to them for protection. In these ways, Bangkok was no better or worse than Brooklyn. The same nocturnal raids, the same get-ahead and stay-ahead paranoia, the same strong arms and big swinging dicks building an empire out of force. He glanced at his watch again, then over at the large crowd by the door. There was no sign of Pratt's shrewd eyes sweeping the room, looking for Calvino at the bar.

Overhead a string of dozens of yellowing New Year cards fluttered. *Hum hiaw,* thought Calvino. The cards flapped aimlessly and limply as the overhead fan blade rotated. Another Chinese New Year had come and gone. He liked the idea of a twelve-year cycle—everyone was some kind of animal, depending on the year they were born—a pig, horse, rabbit, snake, dragon, and several others. This year brought another animal—the monkey. If you were born in the Year of the Monkey—and if you believed human beings fell into one animal cage or another, as determined by the laws of this zodiacal zoo—then you bought the idea that a person born in the Year of the Monkey was clever, compassionate, and sex-mad. Monkeys weren't *Hum hiaw*. People born in the Monkey Year were great lovers, always ready and willing.

Calvino sat forward and watched the waitress measure a shot from a bottle of Johnnie Walker Black, and he wondered what animal she was. Her Japanese customer with the mobile phone had gone. She drained the last drops into the last shot from the bottle; it had been a Chinese New Year bottle from Pratt. The odds were he had another two cycles of the monkey before he took the inevitable journey to that big jungle in the sky.

A slight shudder passed through Calvino as he watched the waitress, gift-wrapped and available on the installment plan Bangkok style, drop the dead bottle into the garbage. He arched an eyebrow as she looked up at him; and she arched one eyebrow in response. Monkey see, monkey do. One of the New Year cards broke free of its moorings and sailed in a rough tumbling action onto an ancient out-of-tune piano a few feet in front of Calvino. Several members of the Thai jazz combo—Dex's Band—had wandered back from the break and the guitar player was warming up with a few riffs on an acoustic guitar. All night two white women in their mid-twenties had sat curled up like cats beside the piano. One of the women had a pair of large white thighs that rippled from her short hot-red skirt like paste from a tube stepped on by a jackboot. She reminded Calvino of Judy, his first cousin in Brooklyn. Judy had the habit of sitting with her skirt hiked up and other members of the family would notice and tell her she had nice legs. Judy believed she had nice legs too. But legs were like wine: They didn't travel all that well from west to east. Some of the old hands had an expression for girls with Judy's build—an elephant chicken. Every band attracted the groupies it deserves, thought Calvino, sipping his scotch.

Dex had been warming up on a tenor sax. He was one of Pratt's arty friends who had taken on a hip Western name. Jazz and saxophones were the things Pratt and Dex shared. They talked about jazz like guys into sports talked about leagues, teams, and players. Dex and Pratt were players. For Pratt the sax was a serious hobby, but his job was a different world—he was a cop attached to the Crime Suppression Unit. Pratt had supported and encouraged Dex's career, which was about to take off: He had signed a recording contract with a label out of New York. Pratt had been invited to the Yellow Parrot for a party after the bar officially closed. It was Dex's last night as a local celebrity before heading into the big time of jazz in Japan and Europe. His first big tour. And Pratt had asked Calvino to drop in and say good-bye.

Only tonight, Pratt was running late and had missed the first session. On the break, Dex came over and leaned against the bar next to Calvino.

"Pratt says you got him involved in the pro-democracy movement, and now you're ditching the masses to become famous. You would make a good American," said Calvino.

Dex smiled. "Pratt says that, man?"

"Democracy will survive without you, Dex," said Calvino.

"You're forgetting we live in a country where people don't always survive politics," said Dex.

"Becoming famous is an insurance policy against getting yourself killed," replied Calvino. Dex had received threatening phone calls telling him to stop supporting troublemakers. Pratt took the threats seriously, as did Calvino, who phoned a friend, an entertainment lawyer in L.A. named Tommy Loretti, and got Tommy to have Dex booked for his first international tour. Tommy put together five hotel engagements; that allowed Dex to leave Bangkok a hero instead of under the threat of armed attack. The people on the other side of the democracy movement had their own idea on how to handle troublemakers like Dex.

"I wanna thank you for helping, Vinny. Pratt said—"

"Pratt said I helped? Forget it. You gonna believe him when he can't show up for your farewell performance?"

Calvino twisted in his chair and looked straight ahead, picking up Dex's big, mournful eyes in the bar mirror. Dex had a large fleshy head; his hair was shaved except for a long Apache mane that divided his head into two lumpy spheres. "Stay cool, Dex. Playing jazz is an art form."

"So is dying in your own bed when you're an old man," said Dex. He laughed and leaned in close to Calvino. "Pratt's not gonna stand me up on my last night, is he?"

"What do you think, Dex?"

"No fucking way, man. Did I tell you some film people were in the other night asking if I was interested in a film role?"

"Japanese?"

"Americans," said Dex. "Bad timing, I guess."

"What goes around, comes around," said Calvino.

"So they say. I'm still waiting for the 'come' part," cracked Dex. Nice, thought Calvino.

A few minutes after Dex strapped on his tenor sax and began the second session, a cop in a brown spandexlike uniform, a hat with the plastic bill pushed back, a .45 riding high on his hip, made his way across the crowded room, seemingly toward Calvino, whose head was visible above the horseshoe-shaped bar. Dex's last night brought in a standing-room-only audience, but the young officer had no trouble parting the sea of fans. *Farangs* and Thais crammed together over their drinks, craning their necks for a glimpse of Dex and his band. The officer pushed through a huddle of expat single white women: thirtyish, bored, indifferent, and distant, with diamond-hard faces set off by shark black dead eyes. The kind of eyes of someone who'd survived a head-on collision with life. It was as if the seal holding the soul inside had burnt out and the life force had leaked out, then boiled away into steam on the tropical heat of the night.

He watched the officer inch closer. Calvino felt the officer had been sent for him; and he wished it would take him an eternity to reach the bar with what could only be a piece of news he didn't want to hear. Calvino ignored the officer for a moment and locked onto the faces across the floor. People with money and toys who had jaded out too soon. In Bangkok, to survive meant finding the right path to that final state. The worst cases were expats who had jaded out too soon; and a few had skidded off the road beyond jadedness. They filtered into the Yellow Parrot hoping that Dex's tenor sax might revive them for a few hours, or for another night. The man threatened with death still came out to perform in public. He drew a kind of executioner's crowd on his final night, thought Calvino.

The police officer squeezed in beside him as Calvino's arm slowly lifted his drink. The cop watched him drink. As the empty glass was lowered, the cop slid a name card along the bar. Calvino glanced at it without exchanging a word. No word was necessary. It was one of Pratt's cards. In engraved gold lettering, "Col. Prachai Chongwatana," and below the name Pratt's handwritten message: "Lt. Somboon will escort you through security."

The waitress with the dance of the bee asked if Calvino wanted another drink. Calvino looked up from the card at the bartender and shook his head, and then lifted off his stool with a glance at Lieutenant. Somboon.

"We got far to go?" Calvino asked the young officer.

"Across Soi Sarasin."

Was this some kind of a joke? Pratt had sent this guy to escort him across the road? Calvino looked hard at the cop, then decided to leave it, play it later. He let the cop sweep a path through the crowd. He winked as he caught Dex's eye, his cheeks bulged as he blew hard into the sax. Dex lowered the sax and let the acoustic guitar player take over. He watched Calvino leaving the bar with the uniformed officer. There was something in the way that Calvino moved, a level of aggression, a swift, determined, hard stroke in his step. He had the look of a man trying to kick down a door before someone on the other side could hurt him. Dex had crazy ideas. It was his last night. People had threatened to shoot him. He closed his eyes, puffed his cheeks, and did what he knew best, played his sax.

❖

A wind had broken holes in the gray ceiling of accumulated pollution, revealing the moon and stars. Taxis and *tuk-tuks* parked, let out and picked up passengers. The crowds spilled from sidewalk tables, mingling in twos and threes into the street. Opposite the bars was Lumpini Park. Some said Lumpini Park was the lung of Bangkok. Others said it was more like a lung in an emphysema patient. At the side gate to the park, two uniformed Lumpini district station cops stood guard and saluted as the police lieutenant escorted Calvino through an outdoor restaurant. The place called Mom's restaurant was closed, and as his police escort led the way through the dark, narrow lanes of tables, Calvino thought about the author of *The Man with the Golden Arm,* Nelson Algren. He liked Algren's three principles for living: Never eat in a restaurant named Mom's, never play cards with a man named Doc, and never sleep with a woman whose troubles are greater than your own. Calvino prided himself on never having played cards with a man named Doc.

A ground fog swirled at ankle level above the concrete patio. Plastic chairs stacked upside down on the tables threw ghostly, elongated shadows. A moment later, they came out of Mom's and onto a paved road. Twenty meters beyond the shoulder of the paved road, a paddleboat churned through the water. A spotlight swept the shore and stopped on Calvino, who kept on walking toward the light. The splashing stopped as the boat docked against a wooden wharf, where dozens of plastic hulled boats were tied alongside one another.

"I have the *farang*," said Lieutenant Somboon to the two officers in the paddleboat.

They said nothing, as they shone the light into Calvino's face. He had put on the sunglasses that made him look like a blind man. One officer spoke into the walkie-talkie, and a couple of minutes later they had turned their boat around and pulled away toward the center of the lake.

"Maybe you should take off your sunglasses before you get in the boat. You might step wrong. Then we have *two* bodies," said Lieutenant Somboon, stepping into the lime green boat with number 34 painted on the side. It rocked to one side, splashing water.

"Whose body you got out there?" asked Calvino, folding away his sunglasses and looking at the lake.

"Ask the colonel."

"I will. But now I'm asking you," said Calvino.

"Get in. We go now," Lieutenant Somboon said, ignoring the question.

"An old Patpong line," said Calvino. The joke didn't dislodge the look of distrust on the lieutenant's face. Being assigned to escort him from the Yellow Parrot to a murder scene must have been costing Lieutenant Somboon a load of face, thought Calvino.

Calvino eased off the wharf in the dark, touching a foot into the molded seat cubicle next to the one occupied by the lieutenant. He hated the look of a dead body submerged underwater—it often looked like a French fry pulled out of a Coke bottle. He sat crumpled up, wishing he were back on dry land, listening to Dex's sax. The Chinese New Year moon had a small slice missing, as if an axe had shaved it. The pinkish fog rolled out from the empty outdoor restaurant, following Calvino across the lake. The boat moved out as they worked the bicycle pedals on the floor of the boat. Soon the wharf disappeared as moonlight rippled across the lake, leaving the shore in darkness. As they paddled closer to the center of the lake, a number of boats were circling around a common point. He could hear officers speaking Thai and directing spotlights at an empty boat. As they pulled up, one spotlight swung around and illuminated the paddleboat. An officer in Pratt's boat reached out bare-handed and steered Calvino's boat alongside.

"Why is it I think you wanna spoil my evening?" asked Calvino.

He followed Pratt's eye line to the left, where a large black tarpaulin covered the form of another of the toylike plastic boats. He stared at the tarp, thinking about Calvino's law: People were divided into two groups—those who sought protection and those promised protection. Tarpaulins were invented to cover the bodies of those whose protectors had let them down. He watched as the tarp was pulled back to reveal the identity of the body.

"Whatcha got, Pratt?"

With a pole, Pratt peeled the tarpaulin back from over the face as water ran off the sides.

"A dead *farang*. Jerry Hutton. An American. Twenty-eight years old. The kid you helped a few days ago."

"Shit, Pratt. I should have gone with him. Christ, I had this feeling something was wrong."

Calvino, feeling sick, leaned over the victim's boat. It was Hutton. Maybe five-eight, stocky, a moon-faced kid with a receding hairline. He could have passed for forty with his gut. Hutton was from Scranton, Pennsylvania. His old man had worked in one of the steel mills when America still made steel—until he was hurt on the job and went on permanent disability. His parents were divorced, his mother an alcoholic. Hutton decided working in the mill wasn't for him. He went to community college and became a mass communications major. Then he found there were as many mass communications majors as ex–car plant workers. But Hutton never gave up his dream of becoming involved in show business. He became a freelance cameraman, working off and on—mostly off—in Chicago. Then left for Thailand. He hustled a few TV news assignments for the Europeans. Enough to break even in a slum. Hutton lived in a two-room slum with an ex–Soi Cowboy bar *ying* named Kwang and assorted members of Kwang's upcountry family in a complex of sweatshop shacks hammered together from stolen condo site lumber. The slum was next to Calvino's apartment. They were neighbors. Co–slum dwellers on a backwater soi that flooded every rainy season, driving the snakes from the sewers and the rats to the high ground. He had lasted three years in Thailand before being fished out of the water in the lung of Bangkok.

Calvino stared down at the body. "And you thought Vinny might have an idea how his neighbor ended up dead in Lumpini Park Lake."

"Something like that," said Pratt. "It is the same guy?"

Calvino nodded. "One and the same." He turned and looked straight at Pratt. "You're thinking that just maybe that Chinese guy on Sukhumvit whacked him. Forget it. Not a chance."

Colonel Pratt smiled. "Khun Sompol threatened to kill him. He lost a lot of face in the accident."

"Chinese don't kill you for running over a couple of cooked ducks and spilling their rice."

Colonel Pratt looked away, sighed, shaking his head. Who knew why anyone goes about killing another person. The papers always classified a murder as either a business or a personal conflict. A clean, uncomplicated vision of why people murdered others. Some of the time, the vision didn't fit. Like with Hutton, thought Pratt.

Calvino reached down to close Hutton's eyes; they had gone dead-battery flat, and the image of the women at the bar listening to jazz flashed through his mind. He caught a glimpse of some pressure marks on Hutton's neck. When Calvino rose again, Pratt held out a necklace of small wooden penises with water dripping from the tips.

"What do we have here?" Calvino said, taking the necklace. He turned, held it against the light, then recognized it.

"Amulets," whispered Colonel Pratt, as the scratchy sound of walkie-talkies broke the silence.

"Upcountry Thais wear them. Rice farmers from Isan," said Calvino.

"But not *farang*," said Colonel Pratt. "Or am I wrong?"

"It's either a fashion statement or an attempt to keep your dick from going limp. Or in this case, a murder weapon."

"Was he depressed? Could he have drowned himself? Maybe it was an accidental drowning. A boating accident. We don't know he was killed."

"Look at the marks on the neck."

"He hooked himself on the boat. The marks are from the necklace. He tried to surface and couldn't."

"He was going to a meeting on a film," said Calvino. "He was excited. This was gonna be his big break. His dream come true. He wasn't depressed or worrying about his dick."

Calvino twisted one of the wooden penises over on his palm. He guessed the length as no more than two inches, with a circumference of about an inch. Seven anatomically accurate cherrywood penises, each indicating a skilled craftsman's perfect knowledge of wood, not to mention a surgeon's skill in circumcision. At the base of each wooden penis a hole had been drilled and a tough piece of water buffalo hide threaded through it. A black-headed nail had been hammered into the tip and protruded like the lidless eye of a bug. Calvino cupped his hand around three or four of the amulets and shook them; the penises rattled like a snake ready to strike. Encased inside the hollow penises, a tiny lead pellet was sealed.

"He had one of those women who used *Hum hiaw* every third sentence," explained Calvino. "A ballbuster ex-bargirl type."

Colonel Pratt smiled as Calvino lowered the necklace into his hand. "What about this business meeting?"

"The film was about this kind of superstition."

"You have a name?" asked Colonel Pratt.

"He was closemouthed about it."

Pratt rattled the amulet and dropped it into a transparent evidence bag.

The amulets connected the believer who wore them to the supernatural. It was another kind of protection system for people short on faith in their human protectors. Amulets granted access to the invisible forces, the ones from the spirit world that kept cocks hard, people safe from evil, accidents, enemies, and the hungry ghosts in check. A wooden cock was a sacred thing, a supernatural phone system allowing dialogue to be carried on between the spirits and humans; only Hutton had found the line engaged when he needed to make the call.

Pratt had been right about the marks on his neck. Maybe he had drowned himself by hooking himself under the boat. But Calvino knew the kid and didn't buy the theory for a moment. To him it looked as if in a world haunted by a life-and-death struggle, Hutton had been a loser; in a world where no one ever survived for long,

Hutton had spent his last moments on earth in Lumpini Park, fighting to breathe, as someone held him under, marking the time and watching the bubbles grow thinner and finally the water still as the breathing stopped and the pinkish fog and Chinese New Year moon cast a last anguished flicker on a surface as clean and still as glass.

TWO

THREE DAYS EARLIER CHINESE NEW YEAR'S DAY— HUNGRY GHOSTS WANDERING

DEEP inside the odd-numbered soi running off Sukhumvit Road, Calvino lay curled under a wrinkled sheet, his pillow covering his head. A line of sweat coiled down his chest. But Calvino was somewhere else in the fold of music piped from an old jukebox playing "One Night in Bangkok." He was in a large hall with castlelike walls and a vaulted ceiling. He sat beside Daeng, a bar *ying* he had bought out in the pre-AIDS years of what seemed like a century ago. She wore a black bikini top, a G-string, and red high heels. Thing was, Daeng didn't stop working after the plague hit. The last year of her illness, Daeng shrank into skin and bones inside her crumpled sheets. She was all alone; no family or friends had gone to see her. She had become a nonperson who had died before she stopped breathing.

"You look great," said Calvino, not believing his eyes.

"So are you gonna buy a girl a drink or what?" she asked.

"And since when did you talk with a Brooklyn accent?" asked Calvino, sitting at the bar which came out of nowhere.

"Whaddya think dead people talk?" She shrugged her shoulders and screwed up her face and stuck out her tongue. This was vintage Daeng.

"Remember today's Chinese New Year. Free duck on Sukhumvit this morning. Not you, homeboy. This freebie is for the dead. You don't qualify, *Hum hiaw*. How you like my new place? No scorpions in a million light-years. Look, hotshot, in case you didn't know it, in this kinda place, I can give you a good sting, set you on fire, if you know what I mean," Daeng said, hooking a leg around Calvino's waist.

Calvino knew what she meant.

When she was eleven years old a scorpion had crawled inside her shirt as she pulled it over her head; it stung her left breast. The tiny mound swelled and ballooned into a woman's breast. A lopsided baby-woman, who walked through the village with one huge tit. Her mother's sister, a Patpong dancer on a weekend in the village, saw the firm, large breast and stored the image away for later. Such a breast was a prize.

When the sting had left would the real breast emerge like the scorpion breast? At fifteen, Daeng was in Patpong, her scorpion breast long gone, but resurrected on that site and on the opposite side were two perfect, firm, ripe melons.

"Let's go for a walk," she said, sliding off the bar stool.

"So we going all-night or short-time?" asked Calvino.

"That kinda depends on you."

He followed her through a large, bunkerlike complex of a building. Calvino was the only person on Daeng's guided tour; he saw no one else. She pointed at several dozen *farang* heads, which had been mounted like trophies on the rough stone wall. The *ying* gestured toward the head of a middle-aged man; a smile was etched on the dead face. As Calvino moved in closer he recognized the head. "Mr. Templey," he said. His eighth-grade math teacher. Daeng was silent. A spider's web of spit was suspended between Mr. Templey's slightly parted lips, creating an unbearable degree of tension as to whether the threads, which appeared to hinge his lips together, would break.

"That one bought me a motorcycle," said Daeng.

She pointed her foot—the ultimate in Thai insults—at another mounted head. "That one always gave me one hundred baht for cab fare."

Ten feet away Daeng stopped beside a mounted head, and nodded with a slight upward movement of her chin. Calvino stared at this mounted head. He was looking eyeball to eyeball at himself.

"And this one tried to pardon me. But he came too late."

A burst of firecrackers woke Calvino; his eyes snapped open. He looked in the dresser mirror, dripping with sweat and feeling like he had journeyed to the far side of hell. He blinked and fell back on the bed with a groan, his arm wrapped over his eyes.

Ever since Daeng's death, he'd dreaded Chinese New Year. He felt her presence. She had found some way, against all rational thought,

13

to come back for the free food. If anyone could have made the trip, it would have been Daeng, thought Calvino.

Around ten in the morning on Chinese New Year's Day, in the Year of the Monkey, the street action had been slow and easy. A couple of Isan teenagers cleaned fish in the back of the restaurant off Sukhumvit. They tossed heads and guts into a bucket. Flies buzzed around the lip of the bucket. The sun filtered through the dust and exhaust, hitting the street with a dull, dirty urinal white color. At the top of the soi, four or five dogs, licking their balls and begging for food, lounged in the shade of a noodle vendor's street tables. One of the local drunks, his red eyes floating in watery slits and his gray, uncombed hair in knots, kicked back, unscrewed the top of a small bottle of Mekhong whiskey, and drank straight from the bottle. Behind him, inside the car lot, an attendant whipped a peacock feather duster against the side of a navy blue secondhand Benz, twisting the dust into whorls. The rent-a-guard, in a blue uniform which matched the upholstery of the Benz, leaned over the iron fence and ordered a bowl of noodles. The guard and drunk exchanged hard looks; they hadn't spoken for a week after a shouting contest involving a gambling debt.

The Chinese merchants had set out the annual ancestral feasts on covered tables. From the top of the soi, the food tables stretched in both directions on Sukhumvit. It was part of the Chinese ancestor worship ritual. The placated ghosts arrived before noon every year in front of the same shops like salmon swimming back upstream. Jerry Hutton wheeled his 400-horsepower specially imported racing motorcycle to a stop. One of the boys cleaning fish looked up and admired the bike. The guard stared over his bowl of noodles. The soi had many eyes, which tracked who came and went, who belonged, who was from the outside, and who consumed the women, drugs, and alcohol and underpaid their maids. Hutton cranked the hand throttle. The bike responded with a loud jet-engine roar; this was the kind of racing machine which required constant maintenance. Hutton was proud of the fact that there were no more than fifty of the bikes in Thailand. The bike attracted attention in the neighborhood. Everyone knew the short, fat *farang* mounted on the huge, roaring machine, his face hidden behind a red helmet with a pitch-black visor.

Hutton was hurried and distracted. He had worries pressing on his mind—work problems, domestic problems: the usual load of urban anxiety. He had an important meeting with an L.A. film producer who was staying at the Dusit Thani Hotel on Silom Road. Before he had finished breakfast, Kwang had thrown a bottle at him. It shattered against the wall. She wanted money. He said he was broke. Four unemployed teenage relatives from upcountry scattered for cover as Kwang ran to the kitchen sink and picked up a kitchen knife from the dirty dishes. She broke a couple of plates as she pulled out the eight-inch butcher's knife. He was running half an hour late, delayed by his fight with Kwang. As Hutton looked up and down Sukhumvit, he thought about that blade, about being broke and late for his meeting. He couldn't make a right turn onto Sukhumvit from Soi 27, so he did what all the local Thai motorcycle taxi drivers did: He lifted the front wheel of his bike onto the sidewalk and hit the throttle. In his mind, he was going over possible locations with the producer, schedules, and transportation of lighting equipment. He was thinking about the knife attack.

The phone bill had arrived and he was thinking about a couple thousand baht of long-distance calls, the unemployed members of his extended household. He was thinking about how to get his house back from Kwang's endless number of underage hookers who had suddenly become unemployed.

"You say no money, then I sell my pussy, okay?" Kwang had screamed.

"You like whoring?"

"You call your Kwang a whore?" She looked around at her relatives slinking away as she had suddenly lost her face. "Before you buy my pussy. Then you not call me a whore." She had the knife now.

"I didn't call you a whore."

She cut the air with the knife. "You think Kwang a no-good whore. Fuck you, *farang*."

Hutton rode his bike down the sidewalk, his thoughts on Chinese New Year and the tradition of throwing firecrackers to scare away any lingering ghost before the offerings of food were removed from the tables and carried inside the shophouse for the family dinner. Hutton knew he was in Bangkok, but this was also a Chinese city, and on Chinese New Year, they turned Bangkok into one huge Chinatown. He gathered speed as he passed a row of shophouses on Sukhumvit. Opposite was a huge billboard with a smiling thirtyish Thai-Chinese male with an expensive hairdo, a five-iron slung over one shoulder, and his free hand resting on the shoulder of a boy. It was a family advertisement for units in the Royal Worcester Condo Project out by the airport. Another real estate project named after middle-class English porcelain some land developer had seen advertised in an airplane magazine.

At eye level, on the street, a real-life middle-aged Chinese male in a cotton golf shirt and gray slacks touched the flame from a cigarette lighter to a string of firecrackers. He hadn't seen Hutton tip the wheel of his racing bike over the far curb—he was watching a chubby Chinese kid in short brown pants dart from the backseat of a new Honda and run across the pavement. Hutton's eyes were also on the kid, who had appeared out of nowhere, right in his path. The Chinese merchant threw the string of exploding firecrackers without looking; they locked inside the spokes of Hutton's front wheel. This was the Year of the Monkey and the monkey was full of tricks. Hutton jammed hard on his hand brakes and the bike did what it had never done before: It jerked hard and sharp, veering out of control. The bike skidded and he flipped through the air. Hutton smashed the ceremonial table. The Chinese boy whipped around—his face red, screaming and tears of fear swelling in his eyes—ran back on his short, stubby legs, and leaped headfirst into the car. Hutton had crashed his newly painted lime green bike through a ritual wooden table set in front of a shophouse, which was a flower shop.

The table was loaded with burning candles, smoking joss sticks, two fat glazed ducks on plates, a bottle of imported German wine, a large wicker basket of fruit, several plates of vegetables, petals from lotus and orchids, a roasted whole chicken the size of a newborn baby, and red banners with gold Chinese lettering wishing everyone prosperity and happiness in the New Year. After the impact, loose packets of Chinese paper money scattered in the wind and floated over Sukhumvit. Nothing from the table survived the crash intact. Every February on the day of the full moon Khun Sompol, like all good Chinese, had helped prepare the table for the spirits of the dead. Ghosts were invited to dine at his table. It was a family day. The chubby kid in the new Honda was a nephew. All the other relatives were inside his house, shifting their bare feet, waiting for the food to be brought in so the feast could begin among the living. Instead they poured out onto the sidewalk.

16

Hutton had spilled headfirst over the handlebars, flipping onto his back in the middle of the table. The back wheel of the racing bike was still spinning as Khun Sompol, his flushed face pivoting, surveyed the massive damage. A bomb could have done little more. The brace of ducks and the enormous chicken had bounced like rubber toys, leaving pieces sprawled across the sidewalk, over the curb and into Sukhumvit Road. Khun Sompol watched in horror as the back tires of a bus hit one of the ducks dead center, flattening it like in a cartoon. The duck grease trail streaked another twenty meters before it disappeared into a faint smear in front of the car dealership. An urchin who lived in the shacks alongside a nearby high-rise construction site scooped up the monster chicken in his thin arms and ran off like a three-million-dollar-a-year running back breaking to the end zone. A small hit-squad-sized group of motorcycle taxi drivers in red vests at the mouth of the soi began laughing just as Khun Sompol emerged from his flower shop. They liked it that a *farang* had given the Chinese merchant a hard shot.

Khun Sompol, his mouth open in disbelief, shook his head after a full inspection of the wreckage. Hutton, dazed and in shock, raised himself up and then collapsed on wobbly knees. He leaned forward, pulled off his helmet, and blinked, slowly moving his neck. He worked his jaw, his fingers, hands, and legs before brushing off the remains of what appeared to be shattered cauliflower lobes.

"Man, who was the asshole who threw the goddamn firecrackers?" asked Hutton, looking around angrily.

That was the start of Jerry's serious trouble with Khun Sompol.

"Why you not drive in the street?" asked Khun Sompol.

This was the start of Khun Sompol's decision to get revenge and recover his face from Jerry Hutton.

"I could sue you," said Jerry. "Look at my bike."

Khun Sompol had not only lost all his food for the family celebration; he had lost his face—*sia naa*—before his entire family. Not one member of the family could have any doubt that a *farang* on a fast motorcycle had wiped out the honor of Khun Sompol—not to mention the offense caused to his dead relatives. Khun Sompol trembled with rage. He clutched and unclenched his hands, clicked his tongue, and assumed the peculiar smile of an executioner preceding a public execution in Beijing. Kwang holding the butcher's knife flashed through Hutton's brain. He was having a bad day in paradise.

Hutton shakily rose to his feet and walked around his bashed motorcycle. The right side of the gas tank was smashed in, several spokes in the front wheel were bent or broken, and the rearview mirror was broken and hanging by a metal thread. He thought of Oxley, the L.A. film producer, his pal (so he claimed), waiting for him. Guys from Hollywood like Oxley had an attitude about local hires—*farangs* who lived in Bangkok had the reputation for being second- or third-rate. Hutton fiddled with the brake handles. He kick-started the engine; it fired, spurted, and flamed out.

"Shit. Someone fucked with my brakes," said Jerry, moving his neck from side to side as he checked the cable and found a cut in the line.

"Why you make this?" asked Khun Sompol. The ropelike veins popped from the side of his neck.

"Why you throw firecrackers?" Jerry asked, looking at a large scratch along the side of his motorcycle.

Two motorcycle cops did a U-turn on Sukhumvit, cut across the central median strip, and stopped beside Hutton's bike. Broken motorbike, *farang* driver, and angry Chinese merchant all added up to a payday. The officers smiled as Khun Sompol, in rapid-fire Thai, recounted Hutton's act of terror aimed at his family, his dead ancestors, and the war damage inflicted by this one-man assault team.

"Khun Sompol wants to press criminal charges," said one police officer, taking Hutton to the side.

"And I want to press charges against him. He threw a bomb at me. He tried to kill me," said Jerry.

The police officer smiled. "You have any witness?"

Hutton glanced over the cop's shoulder at Khun Sompol's huge family, and swallowed hard. "Fuck. So that's how it's gonna play. Okay, how much does the sonofabitch want?"

"Better if you talk polite," said the police officer. "Khun Sompol demands payment of fifty thousand baht," he added without missing a beat.

"He's gotta be crazy. For a couple of overcooked ducks and a chicken he was feeding to the ghosts? That's two thousand U.S. dollars," said Jerry. "I've got five thousand baht of damage to my bike. Is *he* gonna pay *me*?"

"It's up to you," said the police officer.

Hutton understood the code phrase. Pay the damages or go to jail. "Tell him I ain't paying."

"I think you make a big mistake," said the cop, who was no longer smiling.

❖

ON the second floor of the Tonglor district police station halfway down Soi 55, Hutton leaned one shoulder against the steel bars of his cell. With a two-hundred-baht deposit, he had been allowed to make one phone call. He told the police he wanted to phone the American Embassy; but he knew that was a waste of time and instead phoned Vinny Calvino, who lived in the building next door. Once or twice a month he had given Calvino a ride on the back of his motorcycle to the top of the soi. "It's Jerry. Jerry Hutton. You know, I live in the shack at the end of Soi 27," came the sound of Hutton's voice into Calvino's half-awakened state. Calvino remembered him.

"I'm in trouble. I'm in Tonglor jail. Can you help me?"

"Don't sign anything," said Calvino.

"I'm an American. I grew up on all those cop shows. I ain't signing anything."

In the holding cell next to Hutton were twenty-nine prostitutes aged fifteen to forty-seven years who had been hauled in on a dragnet sweep of the streets the night before. The police had nailed them as they walked the street near a coffee shop on Sukhumvit. The working girls were being held without bail for forty-eight hours. Another election was coming and the word had come down to clean up the streets. The politicians had sent the message to the cops, who understood the medium.

Calvino was led to the cells by a police officer. Hutton, his hands gripping the bars, was giving several of the girls an English lesson.

"I want a lawyer," Hutton said slowly.

The girls slowly repeated his words. There were some hard-core women who chanted back, "I a layer want." They giggled, looking at Jerry's reaction, and followed his eyes to Vincent Calvino.

"Hey, Vinny, God am I glad to see you." Hutton turned to the girls. "This is my lawyer."

"I layered him once," shouted one of the streetwalkers. The other women laughed and rushed to the bars.

"Hey, Toom, baby, how you doin'?" asked Calvino. "You're lookin' good. Better than the usual political prisoner."

Her hair was matted, dirty, covering one eye, her makeup was smeared on her face, and her clothes—like those of the other girls—were rumpled. She had the city jungle look on the first day of the Year of the Monkey. It was going to be tricky, Calvino thought.

"So am I outta here?" asked Hutton.

"After you cough up three thousand baht for Khun Sompol," said Calvino. The police officer started to unlock the door to Hutton's cell.

"Pay him? Why? Because some asshole fucked with my brakes? They owe me. I'm the one who nearly got killed. What did he lose? Three dead birds. My bike's wrecked, and now I gotta pay three thousand baht. I don't believe it."

"Believe it. And change your attitude. Hostility doesn't play all that well with the Thais. So keep your voice down, and smile, even if it kills you. Smile. You got that?"

There was a long pause.

"It's not fucking fair," protested Jerry Hutton, standing in the open door of his cell. He wore heavy leg irons around his ankles. His face looked pale and puffy.

"Okay, you're in Dinkwater, P-A. It's Christmas Eve, the whole family arrives at your house."

"My parents are divorced," said Hutton.

"Don't interrupt me," said Calvino, catching his train of thought again. "You gotta look at it from their point of view. All you can think about is your bike. I understand that. But think of how they see what you've done to their special day. Think of yourself back in the States. It's the twenty-fourth of December and your family has gathered and they're singing "White Christmas." Now this Chinese guy roars across your front yard, gets off his bike, and pisses on the Christmas crèche. Your parents, aunts, uncles, sisters, brothers, cousins, and neighbors watch this foreigner taking a leak on the baby Jesus, Joseph, Mary, the Three Wise Men, and their fucking plastic camels. Then this Chinese guy tells you in broken English to fuck off, that he didn't do shit, he pissed on the crèche because some white asshole doctor screwed up his medicine. The Chinese guy wants you to pay him. Because you're white, his doctor's white. So there must be a connection. How would you take that rap on Christmas Eve?"

20

Hutton said nothing and had started to calm down. He stared at the floor.

"A few hours later, you cool down. Even then, ask yourself, would you take a hundred twenty bucks from the Chinese guy to put that right? No, you would want that piss artist's balls. Now you can get out of here for the same price, or go back into your cell and Khun Sompol can serve your balls to his dead ancestors."

Hutton had to get out or he would certainly lose his freelance job on the American film. This was his chance, his big break. Was he going to let his pride get in the way? Kwang was right—he should have had the money. He had something to prove to her and to himself: that he could make it. And he liked Calvino and knew what he had said was right. And he had got the cops and Sompol to agree to a compromise. They settled for three thousand baht.

"Tell you what, why don't I advance you the three thou, and on payday you pay me back," said Calvino, having a good idea what piece of pride had it hold on the kid.

THREE

DEAD-END HOWL

IT was past two A.M. when Calvino and Pratt walked back to the Yellow Parrot. The "Closed" sign was in the window. But Dex and two other guys hung in the jazz time zone, waiting for Pratt; they knew that, sooner or later, he would show up. It was an article of faith: Time inside Thai friendship never bumped against deadlines. The bar had emptied, leaving behind the floor trash of the jaded crowd. Calvino walked around the back of the bar, poured himself a drink, and leaned over the bar.

"Hey, Khun Winee, what was it you said about democracy?" asked Dex.

The question caught Calvino by surprise. Dex had been thinking things through during the interval.

"Democracy is having a difference of opinion with those in power without getting whacked," said Calvino.

"Right, man. Got it," said Dex.

After Hutton's death he wanted to add something to it. But he kept his modification to himself: Democracy or dictatorship, you ran up against the wrong people you still had a good chance of getting whacked. Voting and debates didn't have much to do with what happened on the street. Flatbush Avenue or Silom Road. People got themselves killed for forgetting their place in the monkey colony.

Pratt hooked the harness of the tenor sax around his neck and Dex blew on the alto. Together they made a clean, fine mist of jazzy blues, the kind of jazz people play when they want to make a stand against the rough corners, some fear traveling at the speed of a runaway train.

Neither Calvino nor Pratt had said anything about the kid fished out of the lake, but Dex sort of guessed it was something like that. People vanishing in the night. People had threatened to make him vanish. So they played and didn't bother with talk.

Calvino watched Pratt jamming with Dex and two other members of the band. No one in Dex's Band talked very much. The music had pushed all the words out into the night. Jazz cut out the bullshit of words; it was the realm of pure feeling. Language was left to weave and stumble from one lamp pole of desire and fear to the other, never being able to quite stand up. Endless talk among people afraid of failing, who shielded themselves behind superficial bar chatter. There were only two ways to get sober: jazz and silence, thought Calvino. Silence without thinking. After seeing Hutton's body, this was the kind of silence he needed. He threw the scotch straight down, savored the slow burn, and then refilled his glass. Calvino's law: You can't get lost if you don't know where you're going. Hutton didn't know where he was headed. He was another *farang* rambling around the walls of the City of Angels, thinking he could make it. Another *farang* who had no idea where he was going.

That's why Calvino drank—he thought he was no different. Just as lost with no way out. He drank to cleanse his mind of all the bullshit, all the clutter of conflicting feelings and thoughts. Calvino thought about Hutton's body in the lake. His wet, matted hair; the way the water drained out of his mouth and ear as the cops flipped the body onto a stretcher. Hutton's body on the way to the Police Hospital morgue. The official cause of death would be drowning. That's what would play in the newspapers. Pratt's theory was drowning by misadventure. But the marks on Hutton's neck suggested that Calvino's theory of murder might be right. The *farang* could have been strangled by a necklace with wooden penises, and then his body hooked under the boat to make it appear to be an accident. If so, the killer was a professional. An autopsy would determine if Hutton had water in his lungs. What an autopsy wouldn't reveal was what Hutton was doing in a rental boat in the middle of the lake after the park had closed. Or whether he had gone alone.

No witness had come forward and none would. There were blades lurking on the edge of silence, spinning, moving beyond the ear and eyes, deep in the night. Giving in to fear was standing still, listening, waiting; but Calvino had lived long enough in the mean streets of

Bangkok to understand that once faith in oneself had been surrendered to those forces, there was nothing left to cut but flesh and bone and that alone hardly mattered. You broke through the code of silence or let it break through you, thought Calvino. The Italian mob guys had their *omerta*. Silence or death. But what they didn't tell the *paisan* was that silence *was* guaranteed by death.

The choice was facing fear or turning tail and running.

It was better to ram your head through that propeller of silence; count to ten, then pull back, scream, and shout, and if you could still hear your voice, then your head was attached—you'd survived a battle. But winning a battle wasn't winning the war, and that was something you could never pull back from. It was always in your face.

❖

THE taxi dropped Calvino at his front gate. The taxi lights swung around the dark, narrow concrete path which passed for a back soi, and in so doing, for a moment, illuminated some broken-down vehicles: a taxi, the shell of a car body, an old truck with worn tires, plus stacks of rusty bed frames. Hutton had once said it was like living on an Indian reservation with palm trees. Junk accumulated against the concrete retaining walls. Then the taxi was gone. Calvino felt the crunch of pebbles under his shoes as he stood at the gate. The darkness was broken by a bramble of overgrown banana, bamboo, and palm trees. The big old truck plugged the dead end like a bathtub stopper. Hutton's death had hit him hard. He looked out at the lights attached to the distant cranes. They had been encircled for a couple of years with the towering unfinished concrete structures. Towers swaddled in green netting which hung to the ground like a loose-fitting fishnet stocking on a one-legged elephant chicken. Thoughts of Cousin Judy in the '60s, of cowboy-and-Indian TV shows drifted through his mind. He had stopped drinking before he was drunk. That was a mistake. To come back to the soi sober after identifying Hutton's body.

As he continued toward the row of wooden shacks at the end of the soi, he thought about Kwang. She was alone in the world again. He had known her before she lived with Hutton. He guessed it made sense for him to tell her. What kind of sense he didn't want to examine too closely. Maybe the truth was, Calvino didn't want to be

24

alone either. Establishing contact with Kwang was doing himself a favor, he thought. There was a village worth of poor upcountry people cubbyholed at the dead end of the soi. Even these poverty-stricken and worn-out peasants looked down their noses at women like Kwang. She had once worked the bars. That cut her connection with a certain moral world. She could never reoccupy the world which belonged to other women; nor could she be accepted back by the lowest of the low.

Kwang heard her neighbors' maids, squatting along the side of the soi as she rode past, whisper among themselves, "*Ee dork thong,*" the golden flower girl—but literal translation disguised the launch of a nasty, vicious, cruel, and mean piece of slang, meaning "whore." "*Karee,*" she heard other voices say. Wherever she went there were variations, but the meaning was the always same: "whore." In the eyes of the other Thais, such women were banished, like the *farangs,* to the world occupied by eternal outsiders.

People fell into the common mistake of thinking all girls like Kwang were whores, prostitutes. But the labels never quite fit what happened in Bangkok. As he walked to her shack, he thought about the time he had spent with Kwang. He didn't really know her, but he knew enough about her life. She made more in a week than her family upcountry made in a year planting rice. With four years of village school and no future except planting rice, she'd rented herself out like fast food, a convenient take-out goody. Calvino had seen a hundred Nois before he'd strated working the sexual coal face of the night. Some had taken the first chance to marry a *farang,* raise a family, and pretend their old life happened last lifetime or to someone else. Others found a *farang* and left the street—though not permanently; it was more like a remission, or a suspended state of animation, which would last a few weeks, months, or years. But always, like a dog which had sucked eggs, they would be back in the henhouse one day. It was in their blood. His reading of Kwang was that she was one of the girls who would never forget the taste of the raw egg.

Kwang was—at twenty-two years old—Hutton's chick; she was hired out to a *farang.* In street language, she was a *mia chow,* or rental wife, a woman on the layaway plan, a golden flower plucked by a *farang.* He had seen Kwang pedaling her beat-up bicycle with the metal basket on the handlebars. She was either going to or returning from the market. She was dark-skinned, wore plastic sandals, tight red shorts, a low-cut top, and the dead giveaway: a two-baht gold chain that bounced around her throat, catching sun rays to blindside the judgment-bound neighbors. Kwang wore a mane of long black hair, and the muscle definition showed in her thin, tapered legs as she pedaled along the narrow soi. She pulled back her shoulders, hiking out her large breasts, which along with her wasplike waist displayed a balance-sheet bottom line well into the region of extraordinary profit. But no Thai would ever confuse her for a neighborhood maid. In Kwang's case, it was hard to believe a *farang* who knew the scene would have made such a mistake. But Hutton knew the scene and made the mistake. That was the depressing part of it. He knew but couldn't stop himself.

Anyone could see it a mile away—that lack of a reserved, docile, shy look; instead her face carried the confident, aggressive stare of an upcountry girl who said, "Fuck the peasants. I am okay. I'm making it." Kwang had quickly developed a street attitude—call it body language, it was in her carriage, the way she held her head high, the way her eyes lingered for a second longer than necessary, the way she clocked men on the street. And the way she held a knife.

Her look screamed, "I'm here, baby. You comin' with me or what?" Calvino remembered the look. He remembered the body.

He descended deeper into the shadows. Light would soon slice a razor-thin fissure, an opening against the dark sky. He knew that he wouldn't sleep until he saw her, and told her about Hutton. He wondered how Kwang would take the news. She had worked the bars a couple of years before Jerry had taken her off Soi Cowboy. In whore years two years in the bars was worth a couple of civilian lifetimes. Whores lived in a wormhole world of danger, pain, risk, injury, anxiety, and threats. The possibility of death lurked daily. The *yings* risked unintentionally ordering off the menu an overdose, beating, or stabbings. Once in a while, one got shot or thrown off a balcony. In all likelihood Hutton had been another mark; another piece of thread through the needles she used to patch together her life, and if it broke, there was always more thread where she found the last spool. Such women didn't become widows; they simply went back on their back.

One of the soi dogs crawled out from under the truck, showed its teeth, making a low guttural growl as if it were half mad. He recognized the skinny brown soi dog with the wild, fearful eyes, bony ribs, and the hacking smoker's cough which vaguely sounded like a bark.

The dog always barked at him. It was a tradition. In the mornings it lay beneath the vendors' carts on the soi, and barked as he passed. For years, the same dog had seen him. The dog had a wounded bar *ying*'s attitude of rejection turned to bitterness. Given the possibility of reincarnation, he sometimes wondered what offense he had given this creature in another life. Soon another dog joined in the barking. Then a chorus of dogs barking. Soi dogs operated like a forward listening post, he thought. Calvino turned in to a yard, took a narrow path past an elongated structure, and then, at the end, followed a boardwalk in front of a row of old shacks. He saw Kwang's bicycle leaning below the window of the last shack. He figured she was sleeping under the rusty corrugated roof. It was dark and hot, and from where he stood, Calvino could no longer see the moon.

He almost turned and left.

Death looked the same from a telescope as from a microscope; and whether it was viewed from far away or close-up, no one disputed the conclusion that the end game never changed. Silence was how it ended.

He knocked on the door of Jerry Hutton's building. A light went on inside. In a matter of seconds the lives inside would be forever changed. There was the faint sound of anxious voices whispering in Laotian. Children's sleepy, whiny voices. Then Kwang quickly opened the door. She stood framed, the light of a naked 40-watt bulb hanging from the ceiling behind her. She clutched a large kitchen knife. Her hair was tangled and her free hand balled into a bony fist. Calvino's presence had startled her.

"I think Jerry come," she said, in Thai. Her eyes narrowed. "Maybe he drink too much. And police take him again. So now you come. Why? You want to tell me he's in jail again?"

Calvino shook his head. He had a feeling Kwang was lying about the reason for the knife. The left side of her face was swollen as if she had taken a shot. But he wasn't sure; her face was in the half-shadow.

"Jerry's not in jail. Something happened to him," he answered in Thai. "Something bad."

She slowly lowered her knife hand. If he had to guess, it was likely Kwang and Hutton had had a fight. She had been waiting at the door to settle the score. It fitted the profile. Weapon ready at four in the morning. In those early hours before dawn, when her man had still not returned, the answer pressed down hard and heavy, like a pillow suffocating a victim, like a man sucked under a paddleboat in a lake. In Bangkok, the odds were high the AWOL *farang* was screwing a hooker in a short-time hotel room with floor-to-ceiling mirrors on the wall. Every man knew the purpose of the knife in those circumstances; it was to cut off the reprobate's penis and throw it to the ducks. No more *Hum hiaw,* thought Calvino. No more *hum.*

"Can I come inside?" asked Calvino. He saw her indecisiveness. What was it that Calvino wanted? "You want to know about Jerry, or you want to read it in the newspapers? It's up to you."

Kwang never took her eyes off him. She swallowed hard, nodded, and backed away from the door. Calvino slipped off his shoes, and stepped inside the room. The murmurs of children echoed back. Mosquito nets hung like clumps of spiders' webs from the ceiling. More than a half-dozen Isan peasants from six to early teens leaned up on their elbows on bamboo mats. The perfumed smell of stale mosquito coil smoke clung to his nostrils as he entered deeper into the room.

"Where all these kids come from?" asked Calvino, switching into English. The chances were slim that any of the girls could follow a conversation in English. They were too young to have worked in the bars. If the prisoners in Tonglor were political prisoners, then these girls were political refugees, hiding out until the police crackdown was over. They were putting in their time in a dead-end slum with Kwang as their role model.

Kwang cocked her head to the side and lit a cigarette like a veteran of the bar wars. "My cousins can't work on Soi Cowboy. Cops tell them, 'You don't have papers, go home. Not eighteen, no work in bar,'" speaking in English as the faces stared between Kwang and Calvino in incomprehension.

"Jerry's dead," Calvino said, watching her eyes. "The police pulled him out of Lumpini Lake. They say he drowned."

She blew out a long column of smoke. "Jerry's dead?"

Calvino nodded, scanning the eyes of Kwang's too-young-to-whore, too-old-to-cry cousins squatting on the floor. Kwang flicked the ash off her cigarette, surveying her accumulation of relatives—dependents who looked to her as their patron. In a patronage system, everyone had a patron somewhere. Kwang was their luck of the draw. They waited for her to translate what was being said, what was about to happen to their lives. She ignored them and turned back to Calvino.

"You joke me. Why you joke me, Vinny? I think you his friend. Before, you my friend, too. Or you forget Kwang?" she asked. She made a quick, slicing motion with her knife hand. Calvino caught her by the wrist and she dropped the knife.

"Kwang, I get this feeling like you're bullshitting me."

"Not bullshit you."

"Like someone checked in a little earlier tonight?" he asked Kwang, as she started to cry. "Left you with a black eye."

"You hurt me. Let me go."

Calvino kicked the knife away and released her arm.

"What did the *farang* want?" asked Calvino, trying to draw her out. "The one who came tonight."

"He say, he want Jerry's story."

"That makes no sense. What kind of story?"

Kwang shrugged. "I say, I don't know what story he means. He don't tell me. Ask Jerry, I tell him."

"What time did the *farang* come here?"

"One, two hours ago. I forget."

"What did the *farang* look like?" asked Calvino, as Kwang turned away from him.

She looked over her shoulder. "Like *farang*."

That was bar *ying* talk—over a beer and a bowl of peanuts with music blasting in the background all *farang* customers were interchangeable. The *ying* equation matched the *farang* hard-core customers' attitude that all bar *yings* were another commodity to be harvested, enjoyed, and discarded. Only guys like Hutton looked at Kwang as an irreplaceable human being. But Hutton was dead.

"Why did the *farang* hit you?" asked Calvino, looking at the swelling on the left side of Kwang's face.

She glared at him and at her knife on the floor. "He say I talk a lie." Suddenly she was weeping and had collapsed to her knees on the floor; when the tough act had folded it had happened in an instant. Kwang was in trouble, and a couple of her cousins ran to her side. "Jerry not dead," she wailed in English. "You talk a lie." The relatives, without knowing fully what had happened, joined in the chorus of howling. The entire house echoed with loss and sorrow. Hutton's death had violated Calvino's law: The *farang* wanted a one-on-one relationship and his *ying* wanted a sanctuary for her family. Hutton's death was a kind of corporate loss, like a large company had gone bankrupt and its workers had been left without a paycheck. He had been the real patron. The death of a patron was a cause for major alarm because no one would be protected until a new patron could be found.

The rent had been paid through the end of February. By the first of March, Kwang and her band of relatives would be thrown onto the streets of Bangkok. A few days later they would have targeted another Hutton, another source for securing food and shelter. They were survivors. They would survive in the street in a way Jerry Hutton never could. He had been welcomed in their lives as a *farang* patron; but that was all—they had never needed him, he'd never been a necessity. Huttons were a commodity. They came, left, died, killed themselves, disappeared, or went crazy.

In Brooklyn, Calvino remembered there being a different kind of illusion about life and death, need and want, family and strangers. America was populated by people who confused month-to-month living with living good, with living forever. As if the fact they had paid the next month's rent punched some immortality ticket. You can't die if you've paid for the whole month, an uncle once said. No Thai or *farang* who existed below the waterline of poverty in Thailand ever enjoyed the luxury of that conceit.

❖

CALVINO had left Kwang's shack and was halfway down the narrow path between the shacks and an eight-foot-high concrete retaining wall when he noticed something. The black unnamed stuff found at the end of telescopes and microscopes: silence. He crouched low on the boardwalk. He had no choice but to walk into the dead end. Why wasn't the dog which hated his guts barking? He stopped and slowly removed his .38 Police Special. Someone was waiting for him at the dead end. The hair on the back of his neck bristled as if a noose had suddenly dropped around his neck. Pure instincts kicked in. He felt the silence like an anchor strapped to his chest. He slipped off the safety catch and dropped down on one knee. He couldn't see the old truck from his position. It was still pitch dark. The dog should have picked up his scent. He edged along the boardwalk until he reached the end of the shacks. Then he quietly slipped through a door into an elongated building made of corrugated junk metal. It was a sweatshop: twenty girls sewing shirts, pants, blouses, and dresses for fancy shops which fronted on Sukhumvit Road.

With his lighter, he swung a skinny arc of flame across a narrow room filled with tables, sewing machines, patterns, scraps of fabric, and stools. He saw the forms of girls sleeping on mats. He killed the lighter and walked in the dark. He groped through the room until he found a door which opened onto a footpath behind the soi. He slipped out and waited, focusing on a spot no more than twenty feet ahead of him. He watched for a couple of minutes, then picked out some movement. When he looked again, Calvino saw in the half-shadow a figure dressed in combat camouflage; the man was leaning over in the firing position, his eye cupped into a night sniper's scope mounted on a high-powered rife. The sniper braced himself over the hood of the old truck. The chances were above 50 percent the sniper was wearing a bulletproof vest.

"Drop it, asshole," he shouted, from a position directly behind the sniper.

The figure froze, then rolled off the hood, swinging his rifle around into the firing position. Calvino squeezed off three rapid shots at the head. The sniper's head jerked as the first round ripped through his forehead, the second round slammed into his upturned chin, and the final round pierced his throat. There was no return fire, and after a long minute, Calvino left his cover, holding the .38 Police Special out with both hands, and cautiously approached the sniper. He kicked the sniper's rifle away from the body before kneeling down. The flame from Calvino's lighter passed over the dead man's face. One entry wound in the chin had blown away part of the face. Calvino put the sniper's age at late thirties. His long blond hair was soaked in blood. On the top of his head was a bald spot. In one pierced ear was a diamond earring.

The sniper had a strange death mask—what was left of the face, anyway—creased with deep ridges and wrinkles and large, rubbery lips. This wasn't the face of the average Bangkok gunman, who was Thai, small, lean, and young, with raven black, short hair swept back into a duck point from high-speed rides on motorcycles. Calvino searched the sniper's pockets. He turned them inside out but each one was empty. The dead man looked like an extra from central casting hired to play the part of a man whose face had been raked with .38 slugs.

Calvino stepped away and stumbled into another body. This one was a dog. The back haunch lay beneath the old truck. It was the body of the soi dog which had not barked. He pulled the body out and held out his Zippo. The dog's throat had been slit open leaving a gapping wound; the body had been dragged forming path of blood. The upper lip pulled back displaying canine teeth. He'd never seen the teeth close up. They could have inflicted serious damage. Its open eyes were glassy, a thin layer of blood in the left one. The expression was nothing like he'd remembered. The fierceness replaced with a sad, puzzled laughter as if the dog had caught the punch line of a bad joke.

But he owed this ownerless mutt. Through its silence, the dog, which Calvino had believed for years had hated his guts had unwittingly become his patron. By dying in defense of his territory, the animal had spared Calvino's life. Call it karma. Death always closed one circle just as it opened another. Glancing over at the dead sniper, he hoped that dog after crossings over to the next life, had a chance to get some payback against the man who had so brutally had killed him.

FOUR

WAR CRIMES

LESS than a week after Hutton's death, Calvino's neck ached and his eyes were bloodshot from the hours he'd spent glued to the TV news. Years had passed since he had watched a TV. It was as he remembered. An image seduction box to view a selection of the unfolding daily catastrophes from the far corners of the earth. Hutton had been fed into the box. Calvino studied what came out the other end and did not recognize the kid who lived in the slum next door. TV wasn't about reality so that part didn't much matter. TV was more about people who had forgotten what it meant to be alive, substituting pranks, wisecracks, and posturing as alternatives for how to experience the world. It was like watching a thunderstorm without ever getting wet. Hutton, the third-rate expat cameraman, had caught compelling images of violent human thunder, and the images floated like angry clouds across the screen. Calvino massaged the back of his neck. His skin felt as cold as ice. This was what it was like to be one of the dead people.

CNN replayed the execution videotape again, as they had done for hours. The camera followed each act of brutality and death, building the suspense—will they die or will they live? Hutton had brilliantly worked the jungle canopy and clearing for all it was worth. The camera lens teased the scene, letting the drama unfold from a Burmese soldier's gesture, then zoomed in for a close-up: a mask of pure terror etched on the face of a boy who has realized—as the audience has—that he is condemned; there will be no salvation. Then it happens. Fast. *Akkkkk. Akkkk.* The jazz of war weapons sweeping a target. Mindless, lethal, permanent. The boy drops in the dirt. A TV Land big moment: the gunfire. Then the body. Hit the reverse button on the VCR, and the body pops off the ground like a puppet on strings. Hutton had filmed the sequence. Hutton was famous. He was also dead.

Calvino had some questions about the clip, and each time he played it on Pratt's VCR he also asked himself about the day he bailed Hutton out of Tonglor district police station on Soi .55. Why hadn't Hutton told him he had documentary footage? Hutton's rap had been about Hollywood, a feature film, scripts, and a second-unit team. What Calvino had pieced together with Pratt was that the action had taken place some fifteen miles north of Mae Hong Son along the frontier with Burma. The executions took place near a Karen rebel camp. Hutton's camera made a few establishing shots of teenage soldiers shouldering AK-47s, grenades strapped on their belts, smiling and joking like they were performing a show-and-tell at school. Some of the soldiers were sixteen-, seventeen-year old girls in jungle fatigues. Then Hutton jumped from the camp and panned the thick mountainous jungle terrain. The camera zoomed in close on the figures standing in a clump in a small clearing.

Three young men—late teens to early twenties—stared into the camera, with sweat and blood streaming down their faces. The one in the center had the rough, handsome face of a high school quarterback. A hero, someone who defeats the bad guys, gets the girl, and rides into the sunset. But that's the movies, of course, thought Calvino. Anywhere else, the trio might have been college kids jumped by a mean street gang for crossing into their turf or for staring the wrong way at a gang member's girlfriend. Calvino watched the faces of the frightened Burmese students, thinking about what must have gone through their minds at that moment. And what had been inside Hutton's head as he had filmed the scene. When Hutton looked through the camera he would have picked out that their eyes were yellow from malaria, their lips swollen and cracked. One licked the blood from his upper lip and swallowed, his head twisted toward the camera. A Burmese soldier in combat fatigues with an infantry unit badge on his shoulder, his AK47 rifle raised, stood slightly to the right of the men. Here was an unpredictable, violent psycho, thought Calvino the first time he saw the guy. The soldier suddenly raised his rifle butt and crashed it into the ribs of one student, who, coughing and spitting, doubled over in agony. From the sound bite, Calvino counted two, three ribs cracked. The student spit blood. One of the ribs might have punctured his lung.

Another square-jawed tough guy with a three-day beard strutted into the frame wearing the uniform of a Burmese Army officer. The officer, his lips a sneer of hate, interrogated them. He shouted obscenities and threats in Burmese. His boot slammed into the student who had fallen to his knees, catching him in the stomach. Then he drew out his service pistol, extended his arm, waited until the student looked up, aimed, and fired a single .45 bullet into the student's forehead. The boy's head jerked back, then he collapsed, his blood flowing into the dirt. The camera zoomed in on the lifeless face leaking brains and blood, and as it pulled back the two remaining students were in complete panic. They cried and pleaded for their lives. The Burmese officer gave an order. It was followed by the crack of rifle fire. The grunt executed the order and a second student dropped like a side of meat from a butcher's hook. The soldier approached the body and flipped over the dead student with the toe of his boot. Another upturned dead face appeared on the screen, then the grunt turned and smiled at his commanding officer.

The remaining survivor fell to his knees. He raised his hands above his head as if trying to surrender, then he slowly formed them into a *wai,* a gesture of grace, respect, and devotion. The Burmese officer screamed at him and then fired three shots into the boy's face. Afterward, the officer lit a cigarette and sat in the clearing. There was a self-satisfied, happy expression on his face. He ignored the clump of bodies in the clearing no more than twenty feet away. The Burmese soldier opened a tin of fruit with a knife, and together the two men ate pineapple slices as if they were on a picnic. A minute later, the soldier and officer were on their feet and had been joined by another half-dozen soldiers, who looked at the bodies, joking, laughing, and then rolled them over, to loot the dead of watches, wallets, and amulets.

Hutton's video had played on television networks around the world. He was finally famous. Protests were lodged, meetings held, politicians and commentators outraged. Hutton's video had been the first demonstrable evidence of Burmese Army atrocities along the

Thailand-Burma border where the Karen and Burmese students from Rangoon faced off against the Burmese Army. TV had all kinds of people screaming from their armchairs for revenge. "Barbaric, cold-blooded murders," the CNN reporter had called the executions.

A CNN news update showed Rama IV and Silom Roads in Bangkok. A reporter stared into the camera as he spoke about Jerry Hutton. A photo insert of Jerry Hutton appeared in the top right-hand corner. "Jerry Hutton, the cameraman who risked his life to take the startling footage of Burmese Army war crimes, was later found dead in Lumpini Park Lake. Bangkok police at first speculated that Hutton had accidentally drowned." Another photo insert appeared in the top right-hand corner. It was the face of the sniper who had tried to ambush Calvino as he had emerged from Jerry Hutton's slum apartment.

"But not long after Hutton's death," said the reporter, "Jerry Hutton's soundman, Roland May, a thirty-eight-year-old American citizen, was found shot to death in the fashionable expat neighborhood in Bangkok. May had been shot through the head in an execution-style slaying. The executioner's signature is nearly the same as appeared in our earlier footage of the student killings. Earlier today we spoke with Colonel Prachai Chongwatana about Hutton's and May's murders."

Then the reporter disappeared and a clip of an earlier interview with Pratt appeared on the TV.

"Do you have any evidence that the Burmese government may be behind the deaths of Jerry Hutton and Roland May?" asked the reporter.

"We are exploring all leads," said Pratt.

"Could you tell us if the Bangkok police have made any arrest in the case of the two dead Americans?"

"No."

"How many suspects have you questioned in the case? And what are their nationalities?"

Pratt stared into the camera, his head tilted, and smiled. "We are in the middle of a full-scale investigation. Any comments at this time could make our job more difficult and put other lives at risk."

"Who else is at risk, Colonel?"

But Pratt had already turned away from the camera and disappeared through a door.

As the clip of Pratt ended, the TV screen switched back to high-lights of the execution of the Burmese students.

❖

CALVINO should have been dead. His last-minute decision to knock on Kwang's shack and break the news that Hutton was dead had saved his own life. He told himself he should be worried. He told himself he should be dead. And finally, he told himself that it wasn't over—someone would be coming at him, picking the time and place. Mean-while, they would let him stew about it; that constant worry that it might come any minute now was effective in softening up a target. It was an old trick. The *farang* who had paid the surprise visit to Hutton's apartment, and beat up Kwang, might try and come back. Pratt had some Tonglor district police posted in the neighborhood. But no one was going to wait forever for someone who might never make a move. Kwang and her tight band of underage relatives had given no intention of leaving the soi soon. They were at risk.

Calvino, after returning from Pratt's house and the TV viewing, paced the broken floor tiles of his slum apartment. Pratt told him to stay put until they could find out from the street—the bamboo telegraph—who had a stake in Jerry's death. This was what Pratt had meant but couldn't say when he'd stared into the CNN camera and said that other lives were at risk. What did the fucking TV viewing world understand about the real world of risk, thought Calvino. Calvino's law on homicide: In reality, waiting for a wiseguy to make his move was a nightmare without any TV commercial interruption or remote to change the channel.

He ran through the execution sequence and the aftermath in Bangkok which followed. May's mistake in killing the soi dog, his warning, the shots he fired, the bullet holes in May's head, the dia-mond earring and the bald spot on the top of the head. CNN had called it a signature-style killing from the Burmese border. People could find connections in any random killing if they looked hard enough. Each time Calvino finished thinking through the entire or-deal, he came away with the strange gut feeling that May had been operating according to a plan that had gone right. That the joke had been on May. And if it had gone the other way? The sniper's bullet had split Calvino's face in two—then what? It had all the hallmarks of a double-contingency, highly professional plan with the usual back-ups. It had been perfectly executed. No matter who was killed that night in the soi, the planners would have had a victory.

Calvino's head hurt and he needed a drink to nurse the pain. He had promised himself not to open the new bottle of Mekhong that Mrs. Jamthong, his maid, had bought, until after five. He had promised Pratt he would stay inside. So he lay on his bed, the TV turned to CNN, the volume down, thinking and trying to decide who else might be at risk. Kwang and her relatives were likely to remain safe. Otherwise, they would have been killed the same night as Jerry Hutton was hit. By killing Roland May, he had saved someone else the price of a hit. But who'd benefited? According to the news reports, May was the only other person to have been with Hutton on the day the execution-style killings were shot. And he was dead. It was too tidy, convenient, rational, and above all too maddeningly simple: no loose ends. It was what a TV audience would love—an absence of complications.

The Year of the Monkey, thought Calvino. Then something clicked. An update on CNN—the film rights to the Jerry Hutton story had been sold by Hutton's father, an ex-GM steelworker in Scranton, Pennsylvania. Film rights, shit. Why not phone someone real tricky, he thought. Tommy had mentioned he was doing deals. So Calvino picked up the phone, thinking Tommy would know the personalities behind the movie-of-the-week deal based on Hutton's life. Tommy was out. He phoned back and left a second message. Finally around two in the morning the phone rang and it was Tommy on the other end.

"You know what time it is?" asked Calvino.

"Lunchtime," said Tommy Loretti. "I got your message. Two of them. Is long distance free from Thailand, or what? Or did you rob a bank?"

Calvino checked his watch. The bars were just getting out. Lunch-time was a foreign concept in Bangkok, where people commenced eating at first light and finished about the time they fell into bed. He shifted onto his elbows, turned on a light, peeked outside. The cops were still at the gate. Then he explained some of the background but left out a few details, such as killing Roland May in self-defense.

"What in the fuck are you doin' in Thailand, Vinny? You phone about some sax player targeted by right-wing death squads. I get him out of the country. Now I get a dozen messages about some murdered kid. What's going on over there? Ain't people got anything better to do than exchange threats to whack each other?"

"I want to know about film deals," said Calvino.

"Yeah? You working on something?"

"I've got something in the works."

"Keeping it close to your chest. Just like in America."

"This film has a lot of social realism."

"That can be big money. So what do you wanna know first? How much or who was the buyer of this Hutton project?" asked Tommy Loretti. He hadn't changed much from when he was a nerd in Calvino's neighborhood in Brooklyn and Calvino had protected him from getting his ass kicked going to and from school.

"Enough already—who's the buyer, Tommy?"

"The rumor is that Hutton's family got themselves involved with a sleazebag lawyer who doesn't know dick. Word is that this greaseball got old man Hutton to sign an option with a director named Jesse Tyler. The guy's been around since the early seventies doing mostly low-budget features. Tyler's over there in Thailand now making something called *Lucky Charms*. He's done a TV series on vampires that didn't go anywhere. Now he's got two films. The word is Tyler got a one-year option on the cheap. Chump change is what he got. Ten grand tops. And the lawyer pocketed half of that. It's a bullshit number —anyone worth the commission could have gotten ten times that. And a purchase? If the movie gets made we're talkin' half a mil. They've got *War Crimes* as the working title, and a script."

"I thought you made a pledge to stay out of organized crime," said Calvino.

"People in organized crime would never survive in this business," replied Tommy Loretti.

"Okay. Just for the record. Nothing like a film deal can happen that fast," said Calvino. "Not without something or someone making it happen. Say the Burmese Army popped Hutton. But why not whack him on the road back. He's on a bike, in no hurry. They had a hundred chances to take him out. So why did they wait until he's back in Bangkok? Doesn't make sense. The Burmese generals have their goons in Bangkok. Yeah, one of them could have done it. But I got this bad smell, Tommy."

Loretti laughed. "Vinny, you don't know how the stink smells here anymore. This is L.A. That Hutton kid shot what may be the best live war film of the century. Then he gets himself zapped. People in this town would eat their own children for a property like this. A story like *War Crimes* goes not just fast, but at the speed of light. The film will be in fourteen hundred theatres by Christmas. The producer's casting Hutton's part as we're talking, for fuck sakes."

"What producer?" asked Calvino.

"A guy named Oxley. He's an old Asia hand; knows the terrain and how to get things done. He's done films with Tyler before."

Calvino thought about the angle, and continued.

"The military is running the show in Burma. They got the world looking inside their backyard. Since when does a dictator want bad publicity? Now they've got people saying, 'Hey, these guys are real gangsters. Not even Al Capone shot students in the face and all that,'" said Calvino. "You see that film?"

"Everyone in the fucking world's seen this film."

"How did you feel seeing those Burmese students blown away?"

Loretti paused. "What are you saying, Vinny?"

"I ain't sayin' anything. Have you heard me say anything, Tommy? But I got this question buzzing around my head. In the old neighborhood, you ever see any setup like this go down on video?"

"It ain't the same. Who in the fuck ever had foreign correspondents covering Brooklyn? You sometimes forget that you're living in Southeast fucking Asia. Hutton captured something he wasn't supposed to see. Like the guy who videoed the cops beating the shit out of Rodney King in L.A. The whole world watched, thinking, This is America?" asked Tommy Loretti.

"That's what I'm saying. Anytime the whole world agrees on what happened by watching TV, you gotta think that maybe, just maybe, it's fucked up," said Calvino. "Besides, Burma isn't Los Angeles, Tommy."

"What goddamn difference does it make? When it's on tape, you can't deny what happened."

Loretti had a point—his was probably the fullest, most accurate answer anyone in the United States could give. Whoever had set up Hutton had counted on this lack of feeling for nuance. "An old Asian hand"—that was Loretti's description of Oxley. Old hands knew the superficial image of Thailand as jungles, rice fields, faceless peasants, water buffaloes, drugs, bar *yings* but saw through it. But for the rest of the people in the States nothing much else stuck in the memory cells for more than five seconds before it burned into an ash of forgetfulness. And what was forgetfulness but another kind of silence? Calvino guessed an old hand might have gone through this thought process—taking into account TV, the American ignorance about Southeast Asia—and banked on the assumption that no *farang* or Thai had the will to search beneath the deeper layers of silence and ask out loud exactly why Jerry Hutton had been able to shoot such a scene. Calvino had seen people killed in real life and in the movies. There was no connection. In real life, it was fast—no special effects, over before it happened. But movies had actors, directors, angle shots, and special effects. What Hutton captured was too special-effects-like to be real. But the students had died. It had been real death.

❖

JESSE TYLER's seventeenth-floor suite at the Dusit Thani overlooked Lumpini Park across Rama IV Road. Day or night, his eyes stared down at the glasslike surface of the water, and the mist clouds above the fountains which gave the lake the appearance of a par-five fairway on a golf course with a wicked dogleg to the right. His Toshiba laptop computer was plugged in and on the screen was a call sheet for the following day's shooting of *Lucky Charms*. Fresh-cut orchids and roses were in abundance, overflowing on every table. Tyler, a little over six foot, tanned, green-eyed, was dressed in a tailored silk shirt from Chiang Mai, tan slacks, and penny loafers with no socks. A pair of glasses with a slight blue tint and wire-rimmed gold frames were pushed back on his head. His blond ponytail was tied with a piece of white silk. He passed for mid-thirties but after midnight in the shadows he looked closer to his mid-forties. He leaned back in his chair, hands folded behind his head. He reached over and scrolled down the page on the computer screen.

Jesse Tyler didn't bother to look up as Calvino entered the suite, escorted by two production assistants: a couple of imported *farang* tough guys with two-day beards, weight-lifter upper torsos, and grade-school reading ability. They looked like off-the-rack rental bodyguards from a Hollywood security firm. The standard California muscle-heads who had seen too many wiseguy films and concluded that enough attitude could convert them into mobsters. Earn them respect. Calvino's law: In case of intimidation, never pull a gun unless you

41

intend to use it, never ball your hand into a fist unless you intend to throw it, and never threaten violence unless your target is in range. The muscle squad Tyler had sent to meet Calvino in the lobby broke the rules. Tyler was checking him out; making a point. But this was Bangkok and Tyler was just another asshole in a hotel suite with a couple of wannabe tough guys.

"Mr. Calvino is here to see you, Mr. Tyler," said one of the assistants, the one with the shaved head, chewing gum. The second assistant, in an L.A. Lakers T-shirt, stood on Calvino's other side cracking his knuckles.

"May be no one told you. But this is the Year of the Monkey," said Calvino, staring at the two bodyguards. "And I am starting to think you've celebrated by sending me a couple of gorillas."

"Fuck you," said Shaved Head, spitting his gum into a cupped hand. His head may have looked like a monk's but he sure didn't talk like one.

Calvino watched Knuckles double his hands into a fist and take a step forward. Big mistake. He was off balance, and Calvino, shifting his body, came around with the heel of his shoe and slammed it into the bodyguard's knee. The impact made a dull crunching noise, like taking the leg off a cooked chicken, and Knuckles screamed in pain. Calvino let Shaved Head rush him. Another big mistake that came from watching too many movies. Calvino dropped him with a single sharp ramming stab of his elbow into the goon's jaw. There was a loud crack of bone shattering and Shaved Head went down, his eyes rolling back and leaving blank white spaces. Both men groaned on the floor. Tyler continued to stare intently at the screen.

"You can leave Mr. Calvino and me for now," said Tyler.

"He broke my jaw," said Shaved Head. His words slurred as he spit blood.

"Danny, go have your jaw checked," ordered Tyler. "And help Mike while you're at it."

Mike, the guy with the damaged leg, was in too much pain to say anything, but rolled around with his injured knee held between his hands, tears pouring from his eyes.

Calvino leaned against a chair, watching the knuckle cracker slowly rise to his feet. He limped within a foot of Calvino. He stood there, his eyes wet, his nose running, his chin quivering. The intimidation was gone. Pure hatred and anger fueled with pain had replaced the tough guy expression. Holding his right leg, as he hobbled to the door he said, "Fucking asshole, I'll 'get' you."

"American TV noir smart-ass talk. This is Bangkok. It don't work here. You ain't gonna 'get' anyone," said Calvino.

Tyler looked impressed as his two bodyguards called production assistants slowly moved across the suite, dragging themselves like a pair of road animals sideswiped by a car. But Tyler tried not to show that he was impressed. He kept his eyes level with the computer screen.

"They say Stalin always spoke in a low voice. Just above a whisper," said Calvino in a slow whisper of a voice. "When he was in the room no one talked. They all listened. He never shouted or screamed. He didn't need hysterics. He killed millions and never raised his voice. Some say Pol Pot never raised his voice. A quiet man. These rent-a-guard outfits don't know any history. And without some knowledge of how the industrial-scale killers carried out their business, you're bound to make mistakes," said Calvino.

The bodyguards had left before Calvino had finished speaking.

"What do you think works better?" said Tyler, opening a script on his table. "This is the bad guy at the sacred shrine. He turns to the hero and he says, 'If you violate the promise, then you die.' Or, 'If you remove this necklace, nothing can save you.'" Jesse Tyler spoke with a hint of a southern accent underlying some studied and added-on-later California vowel tones. The effect was like listening to Philip Glass music.

Calvino thought for a moment. "Why don't you have the bad guy say something like, 'Seven wooden cocks do a war crime make.'"

Tyler turned around in his chair and slowly lowered his tinted glasses. He considered Calvino, who was six-two, dark-haired with flecks of gray at the temples, a two-day growth of beard, and dressed in a crumpled charcoal gray suit and red-striped tie. Calvino dropped a necklace of wooden penises on Tyler's desk.

"A little too Shakespearian," said Tyler.

"You know, I've got a Thai friend who has forgotten more Shakespeare than most *farangs* will ever learn. But the main point is, on the street, I hear you're making a new feature—a film called *War Crimes*."

"Whose street in Bangkok has that news?"

"L.A. streets got ears on every corner. Or so I hear."

"Mr. Calvino, what is your "connection," if I might ask?"

Calvino smiled. He liked this idea of "connection." All of L.A. was based on some variation of this word; it rolled like thunder across every sound set, studio, and agent's office.

"Jerry Hutton was my neighbor."

Tyler raised an eyebrow. "Hutton's an American hero. We've got a line on an A-list actor to play his part in *War Crimes*. Don't ask me for names. Trust me." He sighed, looked at the back of his hand. "Pity about the Burmese killing Jerry. He was a nice kid."

"He's been dead less than two weeks, and you're casting his part?"

"His footage of the execution is history."

"That's a good definition of history. What happened two weeks ago."

This brought a smile to Tyler's face. "Are you in support of the Burmese Army?"

"And who the fuck are you, Senator McCarthy? When you live here, you understand that defending the Burmese government is like defending Hitler. And Hutton's film might make a difference. But I'm more interested in your connection with Hutton, a second-unit guy hired for *Lucky Charms* who ended up with the execution film and dead in the lake." Calvino looked out the window at Lumpini Park Lake.

"You are so right about how fast things move, Mr. Calvino. Who in the fuck knows what is really important, what really lasts?" He rose from his desk and headed to the well-stocked bar. "Would you like a drink?"

Calvino stared long and hard at the bar. "An orange juice."

The answer seemed to impress Jesse Tyler. This meant he had done his research, thought Calvino.

"Jerry was working for you," said Calvino in a deadpan voice as the orange juice was handed to him. He looked out the window at Lumpini Park.

"Of course Mr. Hutton was an employee. I liked him and he made a contribution. We hired him as a location scout. But am I bleeding inside, torn up, losing sleep because he's dead? Of course not. He was a freelance cameraman, the kind of guy who was scraping by on the margins. He stumbled onto a once-in-a-lifetime situation. He got lucky. He wouldn't have died if it hadn't been for his film footage of those executions, but now he's famous, part of history. Maybe part of the lore of Indochina as 'the man who exposed an act of pure evil.'

We plan to make a lot of films here. And we could always use someone like yourself. I mean someone who knows Bangkok. An old hand."

"Like Oxley?" asked Calvino.

The question caught Tyler off balance. It wasn't a name that he'd wanted to think about.

After a long pause, he whispered, "Yeah, like Oxley."

Tyler came across as bloodless and cold; but there was something too controlled in his delivery. The way he watched Calvino without staring, the mini-speeches which seemed to have been memorized from a politically correct script approved by a corporate committee.

"I'm curious. About *Lucky Charms*. This necklace has been troubling me. I figured it might have been used on the set," said Calvino.

Tyler glanced over to the table where several bound copies of the script were visible. Calvino followed Tyler's eyes to the stack. The title of the script on top stood out with its bold letters: *Lucky Charms*. Tyler was teasing him. "Catchy little title. You ever eat them as a kid? I loved them. There was always a toy in the box. I looked forward to that toy as much as eating the cereal," said Calvino, fishing the wooden cock out of his pocket and tossing it to Tyler, who plucked it out of midair. Calvino watched the director slowly turn the amulet over in his hands, the wrinkles spreading out from his eyes as he smiled.

"It looks like one of our props," said Tyler, rolling the wooden penis between his fingers like a cigar. "Jerry probably borrowed it from the props manager."

Calvino caught it as Tyler tossed it back. "Hutton was wearing it when the police fished him out of Lumpini Park Lake." Calvino rapped his finger against the windowpane. "If you follow my eye line, you can see exactly where the police found him."

Tyler looked away from the window.

"But you didn't come here to show me Lumpini Park Lake," said Tyler.

"I want to see the script for *Lucky Charms*."

"Out of the question," said Tyler without missing a beat. "No one sees a shooting script except for the production people and cast. It's never done. Never."

"This is Bangkok, Mr. Tyler. A place where things that are never done happen just about every day. In this city there are *farangs* who seek protection and fail. Their rent-a-muscle goons let them down because they don't know the situation. Then these *farangs* go home, fall on their ass, or disappear in a lake. Like Hutton. Or maybe Hutton had a patron who let him down. It's possible. But I can't make up my mind, so I thought you could help me."

"Ask the Burmese. They had every reason to kill him," said Tyler.

"You're not listening," said Calvino, then he dropped his voice to a whisper. "I'm asking you. Not the Burmese. I want to see the script. I ain't gonna show it to your competition, I ain't gonna steal the idea or characters. I just want to know what Hutton was working on. And then once I know that, I will ask the Burmese."

Tyler thought about this, his eyes darting from his computer to the table. He let the phone ring. His jaw clenched and unclenched as if he was remembering the bodyguard who had been chewing gum before Calvino broke his jaw. He looked straight through Calvino like he was exactly the kind of bastard he hated but knew that it was nearly impossible to defeat short of giving him what he wanted or killing him. He walked over to his worktable and pulled a bound copy of the laser-printed script out of the pile and threw it at Calvino. "You got one hour to read it. Here. Now. And then you go. Understand the ground rules?"

Calvino took the script, sat on the sofa beneath the window overlooking Lumpini Park, and opened the first page of *Lucky Charms*. He had never read a script before. A "Reader's Note" was paperclipped to the top and contained an explanation:

"In Thai culture amulets protect the wearer by giving him or her access to supernatural power. An amulet is often a Buddha image. But it can be a tattoo on a man's neck, arms, chest, belly, or back. It can be sacred writing on a shirt. Or an amulet can be a wooden penis. The wooden penis varies in size from an average ballpoint pen to a small rocket launcher (which opens numerous possibilities for the special effects department). The smaller variety are worn by men around their waist or neck. The wooden cock, like any amulet, is sacred. The cock protects from evil, accident, enemies, those who would injure or take away life. Amulets are the dialogue of redemption in a world haunted by the acting out of the life-and-death struggle."

At the bottom of the note were the initials J.H.

Calvino lifted the note, and read the opening paragraph of the script:

FADE IN:

EXT. NIGHT. BANGKOK

An attractive American woman in a short skirt gets out of a hotel limo. She is in her mid-thirties, inhales hard on a cigarette, then flicks it into the night. She's dressed to kill. She moves with the kind of radar accuracy of a SAM missile homed in on a target. The doorman smiles as he opens the lobby door. She walks down a flight of steps, across the lower lobby, through another door, passing the lit swimming pool.

A deep, evil darkness cloaks the American as she leaves the hotel grounds and enters a kind of green, lush tropical garden.

Candles are lit and illuminate a strange outcropping of objects.

CLOSER.

This is a private ceremony from the American woman's POV. There is a group of four or five middle-class Thais near what looks like an altar. The objects take form and shape. They are phallic images —some painted, some draped with flowers. One member of the group is playing a string instrument, and there is a strange, otherworldly music breaking through the night.

An ancient holy man—a shaman—with dark skin and Asian eyes, and dressed in white clothes, a hood covering his old shaved skull, emerges from the shadows. His gown is covered with strange blue and black ink writings, serpents, dragons, and penises. As he comes out the music stops. The group forms a small circle in front of the altar as the shaman slits the throat of a pure white goat. An arc of blood spurts out onto a phallic pole.

The holy man lifts his hands up as if in prayer. A young Thai woman steps out from the group. She looks scared, her hands shaking. The old holy man uses his fingers to smear the goat's blood on the woman's forehead, then he opens her silk dress, exposing her naked body. With his index finger and forefinger, he draws a wet bloodline from her neck and down between her large breasts, then circles her pubic hair. The woman bends to her knees and kisses a series of phallic objects.

STILL CLOSER.

From the American woman's POV, the old holy man raises his knife as if to strike the young, nubile girl.

THE MUSIC "ONE NIGHT IN BANGKOK" INCREASES.

The American woman screams. The members of the ritual group look around, trying to find the source of the scream. One Thai man pulls out a handgun. The shaman disappears into the shadows. And the American woman recovers, turns, and runs into the darkness. Gunshots ring out into the Bangkok night.

❖

TYLER finally answered the telephone.

He looked at Calvino as he listened.

"Russ, of course I'm happy that you're happy. I'm glad you liked your overtime. Yeah, Toom is a sweet girl. When I sent her up to your room last night, I said to myself, Russ is going to be one very happy boom operator on the set. No more problems about overtime. No more problems. You want her again tonight? I don't see any reason not to. If you want someone different, let me know. You're doing a good job. Be good."

Tyler hung up the phone. Calvino was deep into the script at the window. He flipped the pages of the script without his eyes or attention flagging. Tyler saw himself with a problem. One that was not going to be as easy to fix as sending a prostitute to the room of an L.A. guy who'd forgotten the last time he'd had sex. All Tyler had ever wanted to do was just make films. He wanted to keep to the creative side, and each time he heard Oxley's name mentioned, he knew there were going to be complications. He wished he hadn't heard Oxley's name from Calvino. It was going to be a difficult shoot.

FIVE

THE COLOR OF DEATH

CALVINO stretched, slowly shifted from his back to his belly, one arm hanging over the bed. Something brushed his nose and then tickled his lower lip. His eyes opened in the dark, his heart pounding in his chest. He'd had a nightmare, dreaming someone had intended to kill him and succeeded. He opened his eyes. He should be dead. Killed in mid-dream. Still his heart boomed in his chest: the fear of waking to a stranger's touch. The tightrope walk between dreaming and waking when the edge of what has floated between those two worlds is blurred. Slowly, without moving position, Calvino hooked his arm over his head and straight into his holster, which lay on a table beside the bed. He lowered the .38 Police Special into the firing position, and switched on a lamp. Between small, delicate pink toes, the nails painted black, was a single, shaggy peacock feather. It was embroidered with a feathery dull blue wide-open eye. The kind of feather someone would pluck from a maid's duster. She wiggled her toes, fanning the feather over Calvino's nose and giggling.

He stared straight ahead, then blinked, closed his eyes, his mind racing. The woman in his bed was naked, and part of the sheet covered her face. His mind couldn't place the giggle with a face. He stared at the feather between her toes. The woman continued to lie as if frozen in an odd, contorted position, like a circus performer suspended in time and space. He had not made a practice of remembering women by their feet and toes. Shifting his .38 from one hand to the other, he rose to a sitting position. His eyes stopped at the wooden penis around her waist—it had a wooden monkeylike creature prostrated, with hairy arms and legs wrapped around the base of the penis. The string was threaded through a hole in the monkey's ass. His eye line followed down the slender body until he pushed away the sheet and saw her face. She had been in this bed before. She leaned up on her elbows, brushing away her long, black hair, which had fallen over her face. She stared back from the end of his bed, giggling and running a finger around the inner edge of a two-baht gold necklace.

"Are you going to shoot me?" Kwang asked.

"You could get yourself killed doing such a stupid stunt."

She threw her lower lip into a pout. "You're not happy to see your little Kwang?"

Kwang got her answer in the way he looked at her. She tried her next best bait. She lay with her feet pointed toward his head, her legs stretched open like a pair of scissors. Her legs were firm from all the bicycle riding to the top of the soi and other physical activities at which she excelled. This movement was not having the desired effect either. Calvino had run enough laps around the sexual track to merit an honorable mention in a couple of bars. He'd learnt that like all long distance runners, pacing was everything, and that a second wind before crossing the finish line might guarantee victory but it was always appreciated.

"You not like Kwang?"

Calvino's hand brushed against her toes as he removed the peacock feather and ran it down the bottom of her foot.

"I haven't decided," he replied.

"You can touch my pussy, but you can't touch my toes," said Kwang, pulling back her legs and grabbing her knees.

This was a new line, thought Calvino. Why was it that the dreams in Bangkok were never as strange as the reality? Why was it the same women reappeared years later and acted as if they had never left? Where else in the world would a naked woman sneak into a man's bed and proclaim, "You can touch my pussy, but you can't touch my toes"? No one could invent such a line; it could only spill out in real life. Calvino's law: When it came to touching a *ying*—whatever you touched you paid for. It was connected to another Calvino's law: The only free sex is the sex you pay for. Remembering those two rules kept a man alive, kept him from losing his mind, his money, and his sense of humor.

Calvino turned the feather over and touched Kwang's thigh. She recoiled as if she had touched ice. He asked himself if Hutton had

had some kind of a strange ticklish fetish, spending his money on feather dusters. He had a vision of Kwang crawling on catlike paws over the interconnected rooftops between the slums and his apartment building; she darted along the corrugated roofs, weaving through the dead, matted leaves and rubbish, avoiding the sleeping soi dogs below, until she reached his tumbledown building.

"How did you break in?" asked Calvino.

She shrugged, her lips in a pout. "Easy. Kwang go up the stairs. Window open, and climb out. Very easy to go through. I go to your balcony, and open the door. You are sleeping, and I want to sleep, too. So Kwang very quiet girl. I think maybe you a little drunk. I think you are mad at me if I wake you. So I sleep a little because I'm bored waiting for you to wake up. Kwang very tired. Thinking, too much. It gives Kwang a headache. Then Kwang say, Okay, you sleep enough. Finished."

She had come for a reason, thought Calvino. When a *ying* suddenly showed up or phoned, the reason was money; she was broke and looking to score a payday. With Kwang toying with her gold baht chain, upside down in his bed, she had the look of a woman who had a formed a business purpose requiring an immediate cash payment.

"I not come for boom-boom. Kwang wants to show you something special."

"You got something special to show me?" he asked.

She nodded, hopped off the bed, and walked over to the handbag hanging over a chair. "I think maybe you want," she said, coming back to the bed. She squatted down in front of Calvino without any hint of shyness. The naked squat made Kwang a definite candidate for hard-core status. Most girls wrapped themselves in a towel or sheet once the lights had gone on. Not Kwang, her eyes large and unblinking as she saw the interest Calvino showed in what she had given him.

Calvino flicked through about a dozen black-and-white photographs. Hutton was in each photograph. Roland May was in about half, and a third man Calvino hadn't seen before—because if he had, he would not have forgotten him. Calvino studied the third man: late twenties, about the same height as Hutton. He was stripped to the waist, displaying muscles upon muscles, a cartoon hulk pumped up with steroids. His pale skin was covered in tattoos—skulls, eagles, swastikas. A postmodern neo-Nazi'roid warrior. In a couple of shots, his tattooed arms hung loose through a photojournalist's vest. In another he gave the camera the finger. His cheeks and eyes were hollowed-out black craters, like someone who had done a ton of drugs on top of the steroids, had seen too much front-line action, had too little sleep. A narrow tuft of black hair, moussed. Along one side of head, his hair had been cut to form the word "BERLIN." What the Karen or Burmese would have made of this space invader look wasn't evident from the photo. A guy like that would have stood out almost anywhere. How in the hell had he ended up tagging along with Hutton, who had humped it up to the border scouting locations? The motto of the jungle was "Melt into the Foliage"; this guy had been listening to a different drummer, and had no intention of melting into the animal kingdom. Here was a man who groomed to be noticed at a distance.

The Mohawk/graffiti hair and clothes would have earned him a pass to clubs featuring windowless doors with metal studs and doormen packing guns on the Lower East Side of New York, thought Calvino. This mystery man was the sole survivor of the trio who smiled into the camera. Each shot was taken against a dense backdrop of jungle and a river; Calvino guessed it was the Moei, which formed the frontier between Burma and Thailand. Some of the photos were of war-zone scenes. Sleeping Dog Mountain, with one of its faces having been blown away by artillery shells, loomed in the distance. There had been massive fighting on that mountain every dry season. In one of the shots next to the river, Hutton wore a green combat helmet, an AK47 slung over his right shoulder: a picture postcard from a war no one had noticed—until Jerry Hutton's video footage of the executions appeared on TV screens around the world. The helmet was not jungle green; it was from a spray can, the kind of freaky neon green intended to attract an audience. Someone wearing such a helmet could be picked out as a target moving through the jungle a hundred meters away.

"Who is the funny-looking guy?" asked Calvino, fingering the outline of "BERLIN" sculpted below his Mohawk.

Kwang bent the photograph around. "Karl," she said with confidence and without any thought or hint of reflection.

"His family name?" he asked.

She shrugged.

"What country is Karl from, Kwang?"

"Europe."

"Europe's not a country, Kwang. Try Denmark, Austria, Germany, England," said Calvino, stopping at "England" so she could let the sound of each country register.

"Karl's *farang*."

"I know, *farang* is *farang*. But try and remember his country."

"Germany. Maybe."

"You ever see Karl?"

"He's a Cheap Charlie," she replied.

"But did you ever see him?"

"Maybe once, twice."

Meaning that Karl had likely gone short-time with Kwang behind Jerry Hutton's back—while Hutton was on assignment, or when Hutton was going short-time behind Kwang's back. Calvino was getting nowhere fast so he moved the story ahead a couple of frames. Or perhaps she was playing a game so well that she was controlling Calvino's emotions without his knowing she was pulling all the right strings and bringing him around just where she wanted him.

"Who else wants the photos, Kwang?"

She smiled like a pro recognizing a businessman who understood the function of market forces.

"The *farang* who come. He hit my face, and he very angry with Kwang. He say, 'You have pictures from Jerry?' he say to me, angry, angry, and I say, 'Kwang stupid girl, he tell me nothing.'"

Calvino snapped the photographs down on the bed like playing cards. He nodded at the wooden penis with the grasping monkey.

"How much for the pictures and that?" he said, pointing at the penis dangling from a string around her waist.

Kwang sighed, tilted forward, and looked at the photographs.

"Ten thousand baht," she said. "Not so much, I think."

Calvino pulled out three of the photographs and tapped the end of the wooden penis with his fingernail, making the metal ball inside rattle. "Five thousand baht," he offered.

"Can."

She nodded, removed the string from around her waist, and dropped the wooden monkey headfirst into Calvino's outstretched hand. He clenched his hand into a fist, looking down at the three photographs he had selected.

Kwang scooped up the five-hundred baht notes, and with the efficiency of a bank teller counted them twice, and aloud; each time the number came out to ten. She folded the notes into a tight roll, reached down to the floor, picked up a T-shirt, pulled it over her head. Printed on the front in large yellow letters was the word "Saigon" and below, in large blue letters, "Vietnam." In between the words was an advertisement for Saigon Lager Beer in a lime green color.

"Why didn't you sell them to the *farang*?" he asked as Kwang pulled on a pair of oversized red gym shorts.

"I not tell him a lie. I not know Jerry had pictures. My younger sister she tell me Jerry hide them. She see Jerry lift the floor and put Nescafé jar inside. So after *farang* beat me, she tell me, 'Older sister, how much money you give me for what *farang* want?' And I tell her fifty baht. She say okay, and she show me where Jerry hide pictures and monkey-cock."

Calvino looked at the object that many believed was sacred and vested special powers—sexual prowess—in the beholder who believed. A believer would never call such an object a monkey-cock.

"*Farang* who hit me say, 'Okay, whore-girl, I want pictures, and I want monkey-cock, too.' Kwang hate him very much. I think he has a black heart. Animal heart, too."

She wrapped her arms around her chest and rocked back and forth. She suddenly looked scared.

"If the *farang* comes back, give him these pictures," said Calvino.

"No give," said Kwang. "Sell, can do. Ten thousand baht," she said, trying to put on a brave face.

"Better yet, Kwang: Get out of Bangkok. Go back to Surin or Korat or wherever you're from and stay there."

She looked at Calvino like he had said something stupid.

"You don't understand Thai girl. Cannot go back. No job, no money, no food."

Girls like Kwang could never go back to a village; to the family shack made of bamboo and leaves; to the fields to plant and harvest a rice crop under a sun that turned their skin black. She'd had a taste of nightclubs, cars, gold, telephones, and easy money from *farangs* who treated her like a goddess emerged from the earth to save them. Her only chance was to remain in Bangkok and survive the best way she knew how—selling photographs taken by dead boyfriends; selling her gold, if she had to; and selling her body to *farangs* who wore her like a bulletproof vest for a night, thinking she might stop some of the rejections and insults that life had shot at them. It was all the compensation she had for the permanent stain of working late into the night.

As Kwang left, Calvino studied the photograph of Karl and wondered what kind of protection he wore at night, and if it protected him. Calvino had selfish reasons. He wanted the chance to question Karl about the psychedelic green helmet found below Sleeping Dog Mountain. A helmet of the same description Calvino remembered seeing beside the body of one of the executed Burmese students in the video. No one had suggested that this color of green had become standard combat issue among the Burmese students fighting along with the Karen. Nor had anyone told Calvino how psychedelic green had become the color of death for three young Burmese students that the world continued to mourn.

SIX

FRESH START

A soft hand firmly crawled finger over finger over the top of his shoulder. The slender fingers did a spider's dance across the nape of his neck, and then followed a line down his spine to his hips, where the nails drummed the beat of a famous Morse code sequence. There was no mistaking the kind of SOS being telegraphed. A hot flashed signal of passion. The messenger had launched a full-blown sexual assault. Calvino lay with his face away from the intruder. He smelled her perfume, felt her hair, and saw sunlight through the curtains. It was morning. He had shut his eyes for a moment, or so he thought. He had awakened with an erection. His mind raced through the possibilities fueled by the touch of her skin. Then something inward rose up inside: the photographs of Hutton, Roland May, and the 'roid warrior named Karl who had gone to the front line of a dirty little war. Two of the men were dead, the third in hiding. She planted a wet-mouthed kiss on his neck. Shivers surged through his body, raising gooseflesh down his back.

"Kwang, who taught you Morse code?"

Kiko lowered her head, sweeping her hair over Calvino's back.

"Five thousand baht was the deal. For the photos and the monkey-cock," said Calvino, slowly turning over on his side. "And . . ."

Before he could finish he was looking eyeball to eyeball at Kiko, who had shed her clothes.

"Shit," he said.

"Who is Kwang?" she asked, her eyes retreating into small bored holes like the kind bullets make. "And what photos and what monkey-cock?"

"Kiko, I thought you were . . ." He buried his head in the pillow.

"Kwang. Sorry to disappoint you." She rolled off the bed and began slipping into her underpants.

He unholstered his .38 service revolver, pressed a finger to Kiko's lips, and leaned forward, using both hands to clasp the revolver in the firing position. The form of a heavyset person was outlined through the curtained screen door to the bedroom.

"Khun Winee, you come eat breakfast now," said Mrs. Jamthong, Calvino's maid, who turned and walked away from the door.

He caught sight of Kiko, her black panties wrapped around one knee. She stood in front of the mirror, looking over the bedroom and her man, and from the expression on her face not much in her survey was a cause for happiness. Her hands dug into her hips. She reached down and untwisted her panties, then stepped into a red sundress.

"If you didn't drink so much you wouldn't pull a gun on your maid five mornings a week when she calls you for breakfast," she said. "The poor woman deserves combat pay working for you, Vinny."

"I had a bad night," he said, waving his .38 like it was a magic wand and he could reenter dreamland with a pass, saying it was all a bad dream.

"I've had a bad morning. So that makes us even."

Calvino looked sheepishly at the .38 Police Special.

"You're right about pulling the gun. I knew it was Mrs. Jamthong. And I knew that you knew. You understand what I'm saying?"

One thing he admired about Kiko was her profound, practical understanding of how badly he manufactured lies. Nothing could salvage the situation but the truth. He leaned back for his holster, with a wraparound grin, and shoved his gun inside.

"They say you have to kiss a lot of frogs before you find a prince," said Kiko. "But since this is Bangkok, I'd settle for a frog who doesn't sleep with a gun."

He fingered the leather holster. "Maybe you picked a dangerous corner of the pond to catch your frog."

"Someone was here last night," she said, not even bothering to make it a question.

He nodded. "I had a visitor. A woman visitor. But it's not what you think," he said.

"Unless you tell me who Kwang is, then you will have all the time in this world to think without me," said Kiko, with a depressed look.

"Kwang's a dead man's live-in whatever," he said.

Kiko smiled. "And you were her customer?"

Calvino nodded. "A couple of times a few years ago. And not since. You gotta believe, last night was strictly business. And without the usual sexual component, in case you're interested." He swung his legs over the side of the bed, groaned, then walked over to a dresser and unlocked the top drawer. He pulled out the photographs and the wooden phallus. He dumped them on the bed beside his gun, and sat down on the edge.

"Recognize this guy?"

Kiko looked away with a blank expression.

"Jerry Hutton," said Calvino. "And this guy with the diamond earring next to him? Roland May. He was the guy who tried to whack me with a sniper's rifle. And this guy with muscles on his earlobes— he's evolution's answer to climate change in two thousand years— his name's Karl. I'm looking for Karl. Unless someone whacked him for his paws in which case I'd like to talk to the people who can tell me what happened. What I really want to do is talk to Karl. Just to check out if he knows something about the hit on Jerry."

The anger had gone out of Kiko, and she was relaxed enough to sit on the edge of the bed and look at the pictures. He held the wooden phallus between his thumb and forefinger, twirling it back and forth like a cigar.

"Ever see one of these? Some Thais think if you wear this monkey riding a cock, you're guaranteed a hard-on."

"And what should I believe, Vinny?" Kiko asked.

"Bangkok's got an army of hard men. Killing is just another line of work." He tossed her the wooden phallus and she made a one-handed catch.

Her expression softened, her eyes returned to normal size, and she leaned back on the bed, her hair falling around her shoulders. She pressed her teeth down on her lower lip as she examined the monkey, turning the object over between her fingers. "I think that you never stop working. That you are bullheaded. That you never stop looking for an answer to something that doesn't concern you.

That you are selfish sometimes—a lot of the time. That you never stop believeing that understanding all the facts matters. That I'm just another fact you think about sometimes. But not flesh and blood. Just another data entry in Vinny Calvino's database of interesting facts."

Calvino grinned and pulled Kiko into his arms.

"So what can I say? You're wrong? I can't say that. But what you gotta understand is, sometimes when you find yourself deep in something, with people are coming at you for reasons only they know, how can you stay neutral? The answer is you can't. You take a stand. Maybe you get killed in the process. But that's okay, and I'll tell you why. I don't have a lot of choice. Hutton was trying to get by, do the right thing. I liked him. He was a nice kid. I'm sorry he's dead. But I've been around Bangkok long enough to know that people get themselves killed every other day. I can't take on every murder case in this city. Or try to right the wrongs of the world. What makes this different is that I'm involved. Someone tried to kill me. I can't raise my hand and say, 'I'm sorry I killed the guy you sent to kill me, can I leave the room now?' It don't work that way. I've got their attention. So either I run away or I find out what this is about. Not just because I liked Hutton, but because I want to stay alive. And I know that makes me sound selfish. But I've got a few questions I'd like some answers to starting with—who are these fucking guys? Will they be coming back to finish their business? When I walk out the door, are they going to be waiting for me? You can't watch your front and back at the same time. It's called a limitation."

Calvino, his arms wrapped around Kiko's neck, pulled her down and kissed her on the nose. "And that's all I gotta say. So if you think I'm another Bangkok *farang* asshole, then that's for you to decide."

Kiko kissed him back. "I don't think you're another Bangkok *farang* asshole," she said in a bad imitation of a Brooklyn accent. "But you have to admit, Vinny: It takes a special person to find pleasure in being shot at."

"It's happened before," he said. He held out his open hand, then squeezed it shut. "But what do I know? Forget everything I said. I'm just another Bangkok slum dweller. A guy who fishes his *farang* neighbor out of a lake and finds that he's gone to heaven wearing a wooden dick necklace. There's a Catholic priest in Klong Toey I gotta raise this theological point with."

She reached behind her back with one hand and unfastened the buttons, her eyes sparkling, as she pushed Calvino, rolling him onto the bed.

"Shut up, Vinny. You talk too much," said Kiko, following after him and kissing him on the lips.

"You can get killed in Brooklyn telling someone to shut up," he said, looking up as Kiko balanced above him on her hands. "Because it doesn't show respect."

She lowered herself, flicking her tongue on his neck.

"Bangkok's not Brooklyn, Vinny," said Kiko, her breath more irregular and hot now. "And respect is the first thing you give up living here."

He liked the texture of her skin. There was that shiver sliding down the base of his spine, as if his vertebrae were charged with electricity. The current flowed like two hundred volts connecting. As he moved inside her, Kiko sighed, her eyes shut. She moaned, parting her lips and taking his tongue in her mouth. Like two conductors facing one orchestra, long practice and genuine intimacy meant an instinctive means to co-ordinate each movement. Sex was like a symphony with the pleasure only as good as the players working in complete harmony. Neither one broke away with a long solo riffs, leaving the other behind; instead, they made sure the other played the same melody, with each movement, smooth, wild, graceful like a note looping and darting like a swallow. Afterwards, they lay quietly, two indistinct body surfaces cooling down under the table fan opposite the bed. Hearing applause inside their head.

She nibbled his ear. "I came this morning to tell you something. I'm going to be in a movie."

At first he didn't understand what she had said. She repeated it again and he looked hard at her, as if he was seeing her for the first time.

"What movie?"

"The one being shot in Bangkok. *Lucky Charms*. It's not a big part. But the director has promised at least two thousand dollars for Klong Toey. With another three grand bonus after the movies comes out. That will mean a lot to the Foundation."

That was Kiko, he thought. She ran a drug rehab center for the children of the thousands of displaced Isan peasants who lived in a shanty town at Klong Toey. She was always thinking about ways to help the slum kids, raise money, make a difference. He wanted to tell her to forget about the movie. Tyler was using her and the kids. The money was a cheap way to buy good publicity down the road.

"Hutton was hired for a second-unit shoot on that film. And he's dead."

Kiko pinched Calvino's nose like a mother playing with a child.

"You worry yourself. But you don't have to worry about me, Vinny. I'm a big girl. Not a bargirl."

He rolled his eyes and groaned. "So what kinda part did Tyler give you?"

"You know him?"

"His bodyguards and I worked out together."

"You really want to know about my part?"

"I wanna know."

He could feel the pride swelling up in her. "The part of a fertility specialist. An IVF doctor. She examines Anne—that's the name of the character. Anne's rich. An American girl who has been told that she's sterile but wants a baby. A baby at any cost. And has been to every quack doctor in America and Asia. Only I'm not a quack."

He couldn't put his finger on it, but something told him unknown people weren't cast in films the day filming started. He looked at Kiko's body next to his. Why wouldn't anyone want her in a picture: Her hair, skin, firm upturned breasts, smooth tapered legs, small ass, and English were perfect. And no one could push her without getting shoved back. He liked that about her. She had enough intelligence not to let her role go to her head, or to get sucked in by the glamour, he told himself, but without a deep, certain conviction. Movies made sensible people into something else. He went through the script inside his mind, visualizing each scene playing out.

"Chorat—that's your doctor character—points at a lab report and says, 'Your test came back negative. The fertility treatment isn't working. Professionally, I think your American doctor was right. Science says you can't conceive. But some people believe there are powers beyond traditional medicine. If you want, I can give you a name.'"

She looked surprised. "That's right. How did you know?"

"After my workout, Tyler gave me the script to read."

"You two are close?"

"Not close enough to exchange jewelry. He wanted Hutton's monkey necklace of wooden cocks. I said I'd hold on to it."

❖

CALVINO understood Kiko's determination to play a Thai doctor in *Lucky Charms*. What woman wouldn't want to star in a movie? But why she had been cast in an American movie left him puzzled: Of all the possible choices for the role, why Kiko?

His options were quickly narrowing. Either he could accept that she was going to get the part or convince her to turn it down. His best card was to drive home the reality that her last-minute casting was connected with his continued interest in Hutton's murder.

"Tyler is doing something other than shooting a movie. I want you to phone him and tell him you can't take the part. Robert De Niro wants you for something else," said Calvino.

"I won't."

He clasped her wrists and held her down.

"I won't let you up until you promise."

"I would rather die first. And you're heavy. I think you're putting on weight."

Calvino sucked in his stomach. "You'd rather die first? What kind of crazy talk is that? Tyler and this Oxley and I don't know who else are up to their ass in bodies. These guys are dirty. They are using you to get at me. For two grand they're roping you into something so far over your head you'll never see the moon or the stars or the sun again. You are letting yourself be used, Kiko."

"'Used' is the right word. And I'm looking at the usual suspect. If all you want is a dependent bar *ying* with a number pinned on her bikini, then go out and buy one out. But get off my case. And don't tell me what I can or can't do."

Calvino released her wrists and rolled over on his side.

She sighed. "Did anyone ever tell you that you were a great fuck but a lousy lover?"

He raised an eyebrow and grinned. "No, but my ex-wife said I was a good lawyer and a bad motherfucker."

She laughed and cried at the same time. "I hate you. And I hate you all the more when you make me laugh when I'm hating you. It's not fair."

Less than two minutes later she was in her dress and out the bedroom door. He heard the murmurs of conversation between Kiko and Mrs. Jamthong. Then in the sitting room the phone started to ring. He heard the door slam. A minute later, Mrs. Jamthong, dragging the snarled rat's tail of a ten-meter cord, delivered Calvino the telephone, tugging and pulling, working up a sweat to bring him his phone call.

"Kiko go now," announced Mrs. Jamthong. "She very nice woman." This was a veiled reference to the women he used to bring into his apartment. He waited until Mrs. Jamthong left his bedroom and closed the door behind her before putting the phone to his ear.

"Across from the National Museum in thirty minutes." The line went dead. It was Pratt.

Calvino slipped into his chair at the breakfast table and toyed with his fork at a piece of watermelon in the chipped dish Mrs. Jamthong had laid beside the *Bangkok Post*. He had fought with his girlfriend and his best friend had given him a five-second message before slamming the phone in his ear. He sucked on a piece of watermelon, spit out a seed, headed to the shower like a relief pitcher who had walked two consecutive batters, and sent his maid to Sukhumvit for a taxi. In the *Outlook* section of the newspaper was an article about filmmaker Jesse Tyler and the crew of *Lucky Charms*. The reporter called Tyler a filmmaker in the tradition of Hitchcock. Calvino wanted to vomit.

❖

PRATT had received a handwritten note from one of the police officers guarding Calvino's residence: "Find out this villain, Tyler; it shall lose thee nothing; do it carefully." He'd recognized his friend's writing. Calvino had played a clever substitution game which he knew Pratt would enjoy. He'd switched Tyler's name for that of Edmund in a passage from *King Lear*. "We have seen the best of our time: machinations, hollowness, treachery, and all ruinous disorders, follow us disquietly to our graves," Gloucester had said to his bastard son Edmund. Sanam Luang was a place to contemplate such ruminations of Shakespeare, Pratt thought. An appropriate place for meeting and planning. If Tyler, the film director, was the bastard son in the Shakespearian drama unfolding in Bangkok, then who was Tyler's father? That had been Calvino's question. Given Tyler's role it was likely no father would step forward and claim him.

Calvino, if he had any precise ideas, had not yet shared them. Pratt, for his part, had more than an idea. A major general who commanded Unit 113 of the Internal Security Operation Command—ISOC, which was assigned to gather information on anticommunist forces— had sent an order down the chain of command. Pratt was ordered to leave Tyler alone. Pratt was also ordered to control his friend Vincent Calvino, to keep away from the film production of *Lucky Charms*, and to arrange for Calvino to meet with an American colonel named Sam Hatcher. An officer's duty was to obey his superior. *Tham taam poo-yai*. That was the Thai way. The beginning and the end of the chain of command of order givers and order takers. Pratt was on the receiving end. No one asked or cared about his opinion; his duty was to carry out his instructions.

Pratt played babysitter as he waited for Calvino. His charge— Colonel Hatcher—was on the Sanam Luang, a large open field in front of the Grand Palace, watching the kite fliers. The colonel had felt his distance, the weight of his silence, and had finally got up from the bench, bought a Coke, and walked onto the field.

Pratt watched Colonel Hatcher and wondered about the colonel's connection with the retired ISOC officers who had formed ultra-right-wing groups to hunt down the enemies of the state. Enemies they knew when they saw them. The orders came backed powerful men, invisible to the outside world, a collective force, assembling, watching, looking, and knowing when and whom to strike. These subterranean alliances and networks, working old loyalties and bringing fear to any who would threaten, were part of the reason Pratt had taken a stand, part of the reason he had been attracted to the pro-democracy movement in Bangkok. If democracy meant anything, it meant people should be free from reprisals because they held to a different view. Someone like Dex. Someone like Calvino, who had a right to raise questions when Hutton, his own neighbor, was pulled dead from Lumpini Lake.

The ISOC had labeled Dex's political activities a threat to the security of the Kingdom. A confidential ISOC report had called Dex a troublemaker—it was the new code word; too many had laughed at them when they called someone a communist or terrorist and the press reported how out of touch the right-wing had become with

world politics. The problem was easily contained by labeling someone "in the pocket of a terrorist." That stopped all debate and reflection, driving straight to the conclusion. The last Pratt had heard, Dex
had been playing before standing-room-only crowds in Tokyo. The
Japanese were hearing that soft, velvet sax in the night; they weren't
hearing a siren call for the overthrow of the military government. The
colonel had mentioned the names of several of these retired officers,
names Pratt recognized, and the utterance of which carried sound
waves of pure fear.

Pratt sat back waiting for Calvino's arrival. This was one of his
favorite spots in Bangkok—a bench behind a line of trees which ran
straight and wide like a Parisian boulevard on the west side of Sanam
Luang. He tried not to think of the ISOC order, or what he was going
to say to Calvino. Dex was off the death squad list and Calvino was
about to be put on it. When the time was right, Pratt would know
what was right and what was possible. Meanwhile, he relaxed near
the enormous expanse of Sanam Luang; he could watch someone
approaching for a hundred meters. The flat, open field was a place
where a hundred thousand people could gather. Crowds came for the
annual plowing ceremony, a political demonstration, a royal crema-
tion. Thais came to Sanam Luang to observe and participate in the rituals of life and death. Pratt imagined this place as inspiring Shakespeare
—its vast unpopulated emptiness seemed to beg for words to fill
the void. And Pratt liked the presence of the tall, perfectly spaced trees,
with coconut shells cut in half and belted around the trunk by wire.
Orchids climbed from the shells, the skinny green veins racing snake-
like, sending the eye in an upward spiral until it found the patch of
mauve and white blooms piercing the skyline.

In the flat, green field, two children were flying kites. Hatcher
sipped his Coke through a plastic straw and watched the children. In
the trees were order, beauty, and continuity which ran in both directions as far as the eye could see. A light wind buffeted a kite, kicking
out the long tail. He looked closer at the pattern on the kite. It was a
reproduction of the Canadian flag: a red maple leaf on white. Another kite had a Pepsi commercial on it. Hatcher dumped a handful
of coins into the open palm of the kid, who passed him the string of
the Pepsi kite. To his left, upcountry peasant women in straw hats
hawked soda, rice cakes, and fruit. Their faces and heads wrapped
with scarves, they peered out through slits and swept the promenade

with the slow, measured gaze of sleepwalkers. It was hard to think of them swallowing the communist line; it was harder still to think the ultra–right wing would allow a group to speak publicly of their plight. A line of tour buses passed the museum on their journey to Wat Phra Keo and the Grand Palace.

For a moment, a sharp feeling, an emotion like regret and sorrow, seized Pratt. So much had changed, but the change was surface-deep. Most of upcountry Thailand had remained unchanged from the rural backwater mentality of his childhood. Bangkok was a different story; there change accelerated, overcoming the old ways. But there was no going back to the days before the Vietnam War or before the effects of globalization turned lives upside down. There was no rolling back to a time before cash became the measure of worth. As a holy refuge, Sanam Luang, a place connected to the past, reminded him of the half-forgotten values—such as compassion, or the command to cause no harm to another living thing: lessons from Buddhism. What would be the fate of those whose lives would be affected by his decision? Fates interconnected like a tightly woven web where the action of one vibrated down every strand, forever shaping the destiny of all.

Pratt watched Calvino cross behind a group of monks from the east side of Sanam Luang. He saw from the way Calvino walked that he was trying to delay his arrival. Normally, Calvino would have steamed past the monks like someone focused on catching a taxi in the rain. This wasn't Calvino's New York walk; this was Calvino's wishing-the-monks-wouldn't-walk-so-fast walk. The kites flew overhead, and for a moment it seemed as if the day might freeze like a stop-action frame in a film.

❖

CALVINO sat on the bench a couple of feet away from Pratt. He was eating chicken pieces from a wooden stick and watching Pratt, who continued looking up at the kites. After Calvino finished swallowing the last of the chicken, he threw away the stick, leaned back, took a deep breath, and cupped his hands behind his head. He sensed it was time to bring things out into the open.

"Why do I get the feeling you got something to say, and you ain't saying it because you feel in your guts it's not right? And I'm probably not going to like what you are going to tell? To make matters worse you ain't going to like telling me, am I right?"

"We know Jerry Hutton was murdered," said Pratt. "A professional hit covered up to look like an accident."

"Who is this 'we'? You're talkin' to Vinny. So what is this thing you can't say straight out? Pratt, it's Vinny. Level with me. Who hit Hutton?"

Pratt smiled and looked as if he was carefully choosing his words. "It's in an intelligence report. Your military people to our military."

"What's this 'yours to ours?' Military and intelligence should never be used in the same English sentence. If a man's got intelligence he doesn't need uniforms and guns to convince you or me what is good and right for us and our kids. You understand what I am saying?"

"Stop playing the tough guy from Brooklyn, Vinny," said Pratt. "That's not going to go down. ISOC is involved." At the end of Sanam Luang, a large balloon was anchored to a string; it advertised fried chicken.

"Hutton may have lived like a communist but he was a capitalist. He wanted to breed dogs. German shepherds. I thought the right wing liked attack dogs," said Calvino.

"It doesn't matter if he voted Republican. He got in someone's way. Some American's way," said Pratt.

"Don't tell me some genius at ISOC found out who whacked Hutton."

Pratt was silent. His mind worked back through a text. He knew there was something to say, a response, that Calvino would latch onto and that would kick him hard until he let go. He remembered a quote from *Henry V,* and spoke it: "'In peace there's nothing so becomes a man as modest stillness and humility: but when the blast of war blows in our ears, then imitate the action of the tiger . . .'"

"This ain't King Henry's France," said Calvino. "And Shakespeare wasn't a member of the crew who hit Hutton."

Pratt turned around on the bench. In the distance, on another bench, was a *farang,* feeding pigeons from a brown paper bag. Hundreds of birds were at his feet. He wore a white shirt and black slacks, and had a neatly trimmed brownish-gray mustache.

"See the *farang*?"

"The guy flying the Pepsi kite? Yeah, I see him."

"That's Colonel Samuel E. Hatcher, Pacific Command, Hawaii."

Calvino stared hard at the *farang*, who yanked hard on the string, sending the kite into a dive, and then brought the nose of the kite up before it smashed hard into the ground.

"Uncle Sam's returned to Bangkok to fly a kite?"

"He wants to talk to you," said Pratt.

Calvino looked away from Colonel Hatcher and half-turned, facing Pratt. "You're sayin' this colonel got something to say to me?"

"Talk to him, Vinny."

"About flying kites?" asked Calvino.

Pratt waited, letting Calvino have a second look at the middle-aged *farang* man who was looking at them.

"I don't like this any more than you. And I don't like this colonel any more than you. But orders come down a chain of command. You aren't in the chain. So all I can do is ask. If you say you won't then that ends it."

He had read Calvino's mood right—he would have needed a gun to stop him from talking to Colonel Hatcher. The man had arrived for one reason and that was to contain the situation. And Calvino was the situation which had to be contained. The last time Pratt had his balls cupped in a sling, Calvino was the one who came around and cut him free. He got Dex out of the country, saving enough faces to fill a large room. Pratt also knew that he couldn't bullshit Calvino, lead him along because a long time ago a favor had been done. Calvino didn't think or work that way; and neither did Pratt.

"So I'll talk to him," said Calvino.

Pratt rose from the bench and signaled to the colonel. And Colonel Hatcher touched his forehead with a two-fingered salute. Pratt watched as the men stood like two boxers in the middle of a ring being briefed by the referee. Calvino never broke eye contact. Colonel Hatcher continued to gently tug on his string, then called over one of the Thai boys and gave him the kite. Calvino stared at the colonel like someone who didn't belong on his turf.

"So you're living in Hawaii, and kiting in Bangkok?" he asked.

"Kite flying was an ancient Chinese form of military warfare. It steels the mind," said Colonel Hatcher.

"'Flying a kite' is slang for masturbation in Thai," said Calvino, watching Hatcher's eyes narrow. "To get a Thai permanent residence card you take a written test in Thai. One question is, 'Discuss your

68

favorite sport.' My friend didn't have a favorite sport. He had to write something so he wrote about how he loved flying a kite. He also didn't know this was the Thai slang expression for beating off. That's my point. A lot of people are thinking one thing when they're saying something else. I look up at your kite and I wonder what kind of question you're asking and kind of answers you're looking for."

"Did your friend pass the test?"

Calvino nodded. "Grins all around. The examiners liked his answer. They gave him points for being original. They didn't say anything about it steeling the mind."

"I'll take that as an original insult."

Calvino smiled. "Take it any way you like. You are the guys who are in the business of original stories. I hear you wanna talk to me. I'm ready to listen. I'm assuming you didn't ask me hear to talk about the history of kites."

Colonel Hatcher didn't smile, and his cold blue eyes betrayed no emotion. "Our colleagues in ISOC have confirmed our own intelligence reports—Jerry Hutton was killed by a two-man Burmese team. The two suspects have left Bangkok. Roland May, we have solid evidence, had staked out Hutton's residence in Bangkok with the intention of stopping the Burmese suspects from ransacking Hutton's residence. You shot him. That, of course, is neither here nor there, Mr. Calvino."

"You can call me Vincent," said Calvino, turning as the Thai kid with the Pepsi kite crashed it into the ground.

"I'm not finished," said the colonel in a military command tone.

Calvino raised an eyebrow. "Unfortunately the same can't be said for your kite, Colonel."

The colonel displayed a slight hint of emotion: It was hard to peg, but it fell somewhere between annoyance and disdain. As if Calvino was someone he had been assigned to deal with, and then he could return to more important, pressing matters of military policy. The colonel seemed like a man in a hurry; he had his mission, his brief, and his schedule. Civilians were always interrupting. That was the nature of the nonmilitary world. He fitted Calvino's law of the well-balanced man—he had a chip on both shoulders.

"I haven't come to Bangkok in order to waste my time or your time, Mr. Calvino."

"Vincent," insisted Calvino.

"Vincent," said the colonel through clenched teeth. "I am a soldier. I gather you never were. But that doesn't matter to me and it shouldn't matter to you that I'm in the military. I am authorized to say that a certain consideration has been accorded you. You might call it a fresh start. Some time ago you were disbarred from the practice of law in the State of New York—wrongfully, we believe. Should you wish to return to New York and resume your practice of law, then your membership in the bar gets reinstated." Colonel Hatcher paused, trying to assess the impact of his statement on Calvino, who betrayed no emotion. "Vincent, let me be blunt. I'm giving you a way to go home. Take up your profession. Maybe get back with your wife and daughter; I understand wife hasn't remarried. Your life has dead-ended in Bangkok. You don't belong here. And you never will. You'll always be 'that *farang.*'"

"You've done a major amount of homework," said Calvino. "And I'm flattered. Sam—if I can call you Sam—the United States Army sending a colonel like yourself all the way from Pacific Command in Hawaii to Bangkok, and telling me I can practice law again, is real decent of you people. You know what I'm saying, Sam? Nine years ago if you had showed up, I might have said, 'Justice at last.' And now you know what I'm saying to myself, Sam?"

Colonel Hatcher glanced over at Pratt, twenty meters away. Pratt knelt beside the young Thai boy with the broken kite. The kid had been crying, his face all wet with tears. Pratt consoled him, thinking about his own son, who was about the same age. He turned the kite over and decided the broken frame could not be mended. Calvino waved at him. He didn't look like he might need some moral support, thought Pratt. Calvino could fly his own kite.

"Poor little mushroom," murmured Colonel Hatcher, looking at the kid.

"Mushroom?" asked Calvino, picking up on the strange expression.

This pleased the colonel. He wanted to catch Calvino out with a piece of American street slang. "You've been away from America too long, Vincent. Things change. Language is one of those things. A mushroom is what the Colombian drug dealers call innocent bystanders who get cut down in a street shoot-out. You see, the street is like a jungle, and mushrooms explode from the floor, and just as the man with the Uzi swings around to take out a big jungle cat, he pops a few mushrooms which get in the way. Sometimes when things get out of hand, mushrooms are imported. Mushrooms which the jungle cat is real fond of and doesn't want to see hurt, and so what does the cat do? He flees the jungle."

"Guys in the army should never use metaphors. What you're saying is, I should go home. And if I don't go home, then something bad is going to happen to some people I care about. Is that about it?" asked Calvino, trying not to lose control of his voice, to let the anger flood through the gates.

"We have a ticket—first class, of course. One, two weeks, whatever you need to settle your affairs in Bangkok," said Colonel Hatcher, avoiding the question.

"You're talking, Sam, you know what I mean? But you're not listening. I figure that comes with giving orders all the time. You don't listen to what someone is saying to you unless they got stars on their uniforms."

"What do you want?" asked Colonel Hatcher. "Is that direct enough for you?"

Calvino looked at Colonel Hatcher and smiled. He touched his hands to his chest the way his uncle used to do in the '50s on Mulberry Street when some wiseguy would make a crack about his gambling. "Sam, I don't think we're seeing this the same way. I didn't ask you to come from Hawaii to give me lessons on kites and mushrooms. But you're in Bangkok saying you got a first-class air ticket for me and that you have real good news about my right to practice law in the State of New York. And I am saying to myself, What if I don't want to go back? Jerry Hutton died in Bangkok. He was a neighbor. I helped him out once. So I'd like to know who whacked him. And that's gonna be a problem. Is that what you're saying?"

"It's a problem. We are dealing with a matter of top security. What I'm telling you is classified and in the possession of those with top security clearance. There were two men. Hutton and May. They're dead. The case as far as Washington is concerned is closed. There is nothing else to check out, Mr. Calvino."

"Washington? Since when has Washington ever given a second thought to a third-shift guy like Hutton getting himself killed in Bangkok? And then you fly in from Hawaii—Pacific Command—talking to your colleagues at ISOC and then you have a message for me. Classified information limited to people with top security clearance. And to let me know Washington's decision about

71

Hutton's murder. Just to emphasize how important it is I understand where everyone's coming from. And a gardening report about mushrooms," said Calvino.

"I think we understand each other, Mr. Calvino."

Colonel Pratt sighed as he rejoined the two other men. He had avoided the confrontation; such conflicts were ugly, potentially violent, messy. *Farangs* seemed to enjoy such conflicts. For a Thai a raised voice, a mean stare, a rough way of speaking was a form of violence. It was intended to cause injury, and as a direct attack could be repelled with physical violence. Despite himself, Pratt waded in on the only side which made sense to him—the side where his personal loyalty lay.

"Mr. Calvino is a personal friend. I don't believe threats are appropriate."

Calvino, sweat streaking down his face in the open field under the oppressive sun, shrugged his shoulders and smiled. "It's okay, Pratt. Sam's doing his job. He's not making any threats. Nothing personal. Sam just told me all is forgiven and I can go back to being a lawyer in New York. After nine years. Think of all those billable hours," Calvino said, snapping his fingers. "And the United States military has dispatched a colonel to bring me home."

"Then it's settled," said Colonel Hatcher.

Calvino betrayed no expression. He watched the kites darting above the flat, open field. "I am curious," said Calvino.

"What about?" asked Colonel Hatcher.

"You army intelligence guys ever get involved in the movie business?"

SEVEN

THIRD SHIFT

THE first thing Jerry Hutton wanted after walking out of his cell at Tonglor district police station was a public phone. He found one with dirty phone books at the far end of the second-floor office area. Hitting up Calvino for one baht, he punched in numbers that he knew by heart. His mouth twisted, his arms folded around the cord, as he spoke in a whisper. Then Hutton slammed down the receiver and leaned against the stained wall and looked like he wanted to cry. What Calvino saw in Hutton's face was more than a look of disappointment; he saw that worst of things on *farang* faces in Bangkok—defeat. After the call, the weary way Hutton lowered himself into the chair at the processing desk confirmed that he was carrying a ten-wheeler-load of bad news.

"What happened? Did your live-in find a rat in your sock?" asked Calvino.

Hutton shrugged. "I blew the appointment," he said.

"There is no 'the' appointment. There is 'an' appointment, which means you set up a new one. Is this guy from out of town?" asked Calvino.

Hutton nodded.

"Then it's easy. Blame it on the traffic. The full moon in February," suggested Calvino. "That means Chinese New Year celebrations on Sukhumvit."

"This guy doesn't give a rat's ass about the Chinese or their fucking New Year. You can't understand how important this was for me. I

73

let someone down. You can't do that in the film business. They never forgive you."

Calvino leaned forward. "What's he gonna say, 'You'll never work in this town again'? This is Bangkok. You want a film you buy a pirated video for four bucks on the street."

Before the police had finished processing the necessary paperwork Hutton had already been hinting about a serious problem and the lack of any hope for redemption. Jerry Hutton's ride on the sidewalk, dumping Khun Sompol's Chinese New Year banquet, had sent bad vibrations pulsating from the world of hungry ghosts to the world of Hollywood filmmakers.

They left Tonglor district police station around noon. Hutton smelled of pumpkin and rice and sewage. He was still in a slump and looked depressed as hell. Down the street, Calvino pressed another baht into Hutton's hand and told him to make a second phone call. He watched Hutton inside the kiosk, shifting from one foot to the other, his shoulder leaning against the glass. When he pushed out of the kiosk, Calvino asked him what was wrong.

"He doesn't like accident-prone people. It's bad luck."

"So he told you to get lost," said Calvino.

"He told me I fucked up."

"Screw him," said Calvino.

"It ain't that simple."

❖

A bus belched a large trail of black smoke—it looked like a soldier had thrown a smoke bomb in one of those old World War II movies. The bus driver sped away from the curb, passengers weaving inside the bus, and cut through the traffic lanes as if some hungry ghost was gunning for him. The oily fumes stung Calvino's eyes as he reached for the wooden handle on the beer-barrel-shaped door. They entered the small, dark, air-conditioned restaurant, Der Braumeister, which was around the corner from Calvino's office. Hutton offered to buy Calvino lunch until he remembered that he had had to borrow money to make his phone calls.

"I know the owner real well," said Hutton.

Sure enough, he was on first-name terms with the German owner. Inside the narrow restaurant were rows of empty hardwood tables.

The owner, a lean, bony man with a large forehead, stood at the bar, his glasses extended on the end of his nose. He was reading a German newspaper, licking his fingers to turn the pages; a cloud of smoke rose from a cigarette sticking out from the yellowish knuckles of his other hand, which rested on the bar.

"Jurgen, this is my friend Vinny," said Hutton.

Jurgen, who was in his fifties, looked up, sucked on his cigarette, and nodded. He looked Calvino over.

"You still interested in that dog? Or have you changed your mind?" asked Jurgen in a matter-of-fact, German-accented voice.

"My mind's made up. I'll have the cash soon, Jurgen."

Jurgen shrugged and shuffled his newspaper.

"Dog? Yum-yum. What else is on the menu?" asked Calvino. "Goldfish in a nice cheese sauce?"

A Thai waitress dressed in a milkmaid's outfit, including red apron, yawned as she came over to the table. Popular German music played in the background: a deranged, shrill coffeehouse-from-hell music piped in from an old half-inch tape deck with a couple of dusty speakers in the back.

"You're a funny guy," said Hutton. "I mean funny like you make people laugh. Not funny like people laugh at you."

Hutton had calmed down enough to order a steak and fries. Calvino decided not to stray from his liquid diet, ordering a Mekhong straight up and wondering if Hutton had recovered as much as he pretended.

"What was this life-and-death appointment?" asked Calvino.

"I can't tell you." Hutton chewed off the end of a bread stick. "I know that is an asshole thing to say. You get me out of jail, and convince Sompol to back off, and I'm saying that I can't tell you about the film. Vinny, these guys are obsessed with secrecy. They make Woody Allen appear like a talkaholic. And if you knew the stuff I filmed, you would understand. The footage I shot is unbelievable. It's worth a fortune. When you see it, the film will knock you over. Okay, okay. I've said enough."

"Jerry, you ain't said dick shit."

"Other than I am working on a movie."

"What kind of footage?"

"Heavy-metal, death and rock-'n'-roll stuff. I've already crossed the line. Silence is golden. Oxley said that."

"Exactly who is Oxley?"

"An L.A. film guy. He's been around the block."

"And this heavy hitter hired you as DP for his film?" Calvino said, letting the irony fall on "his."

Hutton grinned like a kid who had been caught with his hand in the cookie jar. He sized up Calvino with a new sense of respect.

"I hired on as their second-unit camera. Five hundred bucks cash plus expenses. Five hundred-dollar bills."

"Except you haven't been paid?"

"The check's in the mail," said Hutton.

"You said five hundred-dollar bills."

"That's what they promised. I had this appointment, see. I'm supposed to pick up the cash. But I ended up in jail instead. So maybe they will fuck me out of the cash? Who knows? All I can tell you is their finance guys in L.A. would go crazy if they knew I was a local hire. You have to be on a list. That's the way it works in L.A. If you're on the list, you work. If you're not, you park cars. But what I brought them will put me on the list. Even Oxley said so. A fresh start. Maybe I'm gonna be on the first unit in their next film. Who knows?"

"Yeah, who knows? So what kind of movie are you talking about?"

"One about war. There's this mercenary, an ex-'Nam vet who sides with the Karen. He witnesses a heavy war crime. His buddy gets shot to shit. So he goes for the big 'R'—revenge. He kills the bad guys with all kinds of cool weapons. Special effects are gonna be done back in Hollywood. Anyway, he wastes some Burmese lethal warrior types, then gets shot in the nuts in a firefight. He's flown back to Bangkok and a beautiful Thai doctor with big tits turns him on to some black magic so he can get an erection again. He falls in love, goes back into battle, kicks ass, and in the end his squeeze joins him at the front. But what I've told you is confidential, Vinny. If it gets back that I've been talking to you, I'm in deep shit."

"For instance, they might not pay you," said Calvino. "Now tell me what exactly did you film that's gonna put you on the Hollywood A-list?"

Hutton thought for a moment, waging a battle of loyalties.

"Some realistic action. Close-range visual stuff," said Hutton. "No one on the A-list ever got as close to the front line as I did. You have to know what you're doing or you can get dirty real quick."

"What are you afraid of?" Calvino looked at him hard.

76

The question caught Hutton off guard. It wasn't the kind of question people normally asked, even in Bangkok, and he had to think a minute before he knew the answer himself.

"I guess that it won't get picked up," said Hutton, looking away. He stopped, rolled his eyes, pierced some French fries on his fork, and looked up at Calvino. "That I'll get screwed out of a paycheck. That I can't figure out how the special effects was set up. That Oxley was bullshitting me about working on the next film."

"Heavy-league fears," said Calvino.

"Yeah, I'd guess you're right. But this jail thing has thrown everything into a weird spin. It wasn't supposed to work out like this."

"It never is, kid," said Calvino.

The first reply had sounded as convincing as a laugh track on a sitcom; like something Hutton had said before, and probably had used to get the job in the first place. What would an L.A. producer have to lose on taking a chance on a local hire like Jerry Hutton who'd work way under union scale? The answer was it was a good move, leaving open the possibility that Oxley might have stiffed Hutton, kept the money for Patpong bar *yings*. But money anxiety wasn't at the heart of what was eating at Hutton. Hutton's second reply was more honest, real. As if Calvino had caught him off guard; as if he hadn't thought about it, or if he had, it hadn't given him much trouble.

There was something about Hutton's greasy hair, the dirt under his nails, the rumpled clothes, and the slight stutter that stumped Calvino as he ran through the possible reasons why a Hollywood production team would have placed faith in him to get the front-line action shots. Calvino had no experience in the film business, but his time in Bangkok had convinced that there were hundreds of *farangs* who'd ransom their mother to be part of a Hollywood film team. Hutton wasn't the only third-shift *farang* with camera experience willing to hire out for the day or week for a cut-rate fee. Third-shift *farangs* elbowed each other, scrambling for crumbs left along an underground labor network, pushing and shoving to cut in front of a long line of other social rejects. Everyone playing the same soundtrack in their head: take me, take me. Fucking take me.

Third-shift *farangs* arrived in Thailand because the third-shift workers' rumor mill had hooked them with the promise they might advance into a first-shift life in a tropical paradise. These *farangs* had walked away from their third-shift factories, taxi companies, police

77

forces, newspapers. Or their jobs had walked away from them. The geographically ignorant lived as homeless people on the streets of New York, Chicago, and L.A. Guys like Hutton knew the time had come to flee the American scene. They arrived as walk-ins, extras looking to make a buck in the sun, and to fuck all night. Southeast Asia— they couldn't find it on the map before they arrived—was their second chance, their fresh start. Even to other *farangs* this troupe of newcomers stood out on the street, in the buses, department stores, and bars. They looked, talked, walked, and acted like attic people. That's what Calvino's uncle Bosco the Fuss called them.

Uncle Bosco the Fuss said, "These are the kind of people in the old days people hid in their attics when relatives and friends came to visit, or ended up in institutions if the home lacked an attic."

Third-shift people were products of bad schools, bad neighborhoods, bad homes, and bad genes; they started at the bottom of a hole and never got a rope to pull themselves out to see the surface of life. Third-shifters slept all day and ate breakfast when it was dark and everyone else was going home for the night. Stooped, grayish figures sloping from doorway to doorway, bald or with receding hairlines, consigned to a world which hated the sight of them.

In New York, you caught a glimpse of one at six in the morning limping home like someone who had been mugged for his crutches. If they weren't in Uncle Bosco the Fuss's attic, they lived alone, avoiding fellow zombies. Hutton wasn't one of those. He was in the upper class of third-shift types—the small fraction who had enough brains to understand that anyone could leave the United States with a passport, airplane ticket, and pocket money and no one would arrest you. In Bangkok, you could start over and no one would suspect, except the old hands, that you were a third-shifter. Calvino picked them out of a crowd. The short list of shared characteristics of these *farang* males included one or more of the following: They were overweight; ugly; tattooed; crippled; had a defective personality; were a borderline alcoholic, a speed freak, or a heavy smoker; and/or were on the run from someone or the law. After being disbarred from the practice of law in New York, Calvino had joined the ranks of the third shift. It was one of the reasons he liked Hutton; they looked at each other and saw "third shift" printed all over the other.

The only jobs Hutton had ever held back in Chicago were on the third shift. No one wanted him in their face. He was a no-hoper. He had no social graces. He ate his French fries off his fork with his fingers, and then licked them clean. Capitalism had invented the third shift to keep guys like Hutton off the streets, sleeping in their beds, as the first- and second-shift people ate dinner out, watched a boxing match on TV. When Hutton came to Bangkok he lived like a prisoner on a forty-eight-hour sex furlough. Then he met Kwang in a Soi Cowboy bar. Calvino had had her, as had a couple hundred other guys. But a born-to-the-third-shift kind of guy didn't know that. He thought Kwang loved him. She called him her special friend, her stud. No woman had ever called him special or a stud before. His friends back home, with the recession closing down the third shifts, lived in cardboard boxes or old cars. His old man lived on a disability pension. His mother was in another rehab program because of her drinking. In the luck of the draw, he had drawn third-shift parents. In the luck of the draw, he had drawn Calvino as a third-shift neighbor in the same Sukhumvit Road slum.

"I'm buying a shepherd for Kwang. Did I mention that?" Hutton looked up at the wall.

Calvino followed his eyes, thinking that was Little Bo Peep's dream come true. There was a calendar with a German shepherd standing rigid, like a reborn storm trooper in the point position. The long tail was combed; not a hair was out of place. The large, long snout, showing tongue and teeth—no foam, no rage, no angst. The animal hardly looked German, thought Calvino. But here was an animal that would charge a machine-gun nest if given the order. The kind of first-shift dog any third-shift guy in the world dreamt about owning. Control, power, and authority in a hundred compressed pounds that would lick your hand and bite a wiseguy's balls on command. So this was the dog Jurgen had been asking Hutton about as they were about to order from the menu. A German shepherd with an attitude. Calvino figured Jurgen was probably working on a commission. Jurgen had been in Thailand long enough to know the value of personal connections; that value could be squeezed, commissions claimed, from ripe connections. He must have needed to die before being reborn with a Thai-Chinese shophouse mentality.

"There aren't enough fucking dogs roaming around for free on Soi 27?"

"Man, are you out of it. This isn't just a dog."

"It works a computer?"

Hutton let out a third-shift giggle, his large stomach rolling, and belched in his hand. "This dog has lineage. Major relatives going back a hundred and fifty years. These dogs are the best of the best shepherds in the world. Its mother and father were grand champions; grandmother and grandfather, and on and on."

The dog's upper-class roots were going to enhance Hutton's third-shift status. Calvino got the picture.

"How much this kind of Chivas Regal dog cost?"

At first Hutton wasn't going to tell him. His neck stiffened like someone had grabbed him from behind. "About a grand," he finally said, looking up at the calendar.

"A thousand U.S. dollars? Jerry, this is Thailand. You don't pay a grand for one year of rent. What are you doing with a thousand-buck dog in a ten-buck back-soi slum?"

"You won't laugh?"

Calvino hated it when someone asked him that question. He was curious. Calvino shook his head, understanding that Hutton's decision was likely based on third-shift deranged logic. And Hutton didn't disappoint Calvino with his answer—though it was the last one Calvino would have guessed.

"I want Kwang to breed shepherds."

That was it; he wanted his ex-whore, who had screwed for a living, to go into the dog-breeding business. He wanted Kwang to become a German shepherd *mamasan*.

Calvino swallowed hard twice, sucked in his breath, tongue between is teeth; telling himself if he didn't break this habit, he ended up an old man with his tongue tattooed with rows of teeth marks.

"What does Kwang know about breeding pedigree German shepherds with a lineage that goes back about one hundred years further than her own?"

"She can learn. I have books in Thai. It's all set out, Vinny. None of this requires any more than common sense."

Kwang had served a great apprenticeship in common sense, thought Calvino.

"Two litters of pups a year; eight pups to a litter. That's more than three hundred thousand baht a year. And she loves animals."

You couldn't beat that third-shift upward-mobility logic.

"The best part is I got a fifty percent discount," said Hutton in a whisper. He leaned forward so Jurgen couldn't listen in on the conversation. "No one ever gets a discount on a purebred shepherd. Vinny, listen to me. This kind of dog is like gold. There's one price. You don't bargain; it's take it or leave it. But I took a chance and let a guy tag along over the vents. He saw some action. He got what he wanted and loved every minute of it."

This was typical soldier-of-fortune talk, thought Calvino. To third-shift guys in army-surplus flak jackets, "crossing the vents" was in-talk for getting within a mile of some muscle flash from gunfire on the Burmese border.

❖

AFTER Hutton had wiped out the Chinese feasts for Chinese New Year, and he'd ended up in the Tonglor district police station slammer, someone had wheeled Hutton's motorcycle around the corner into Soi 27 and parked it beneath a large, overhanging tree. Then, according to the security guard that Calvino interviewed at the car lot, a couple of Thai guys had wheeled it farther down the soi. The two men then parked the bike inside the front yard, which was boarded up with corrugated metal; inside the yard were small mountains of raw garbage and rats as large as cats. By the time Calvino and Hutton had arrived to find his beloved motorcycle, it had been moved a couple of times more—by whom and when, the security guard didn't know or wasn't saying—until the bike had been rolled through the gate of a huge empty old house where the windows had been smashed four, five years earlier and weeds grew through the front porch. The haunted house was enveloped in an overgrown jungle.

Hutton had started to cry.

His motorcycle had been stripped clean. Only the silver frame remained intact; his imported motorcycle had been reduced to bare metal. The only difference between Bangkok and Brooklyn lay in the tipped-over silver frame: In Brooklyn the thieves would have taken the frame and sold it to a junkyard for scrap value. They would have left Hutton, the third-shift, hotshot biker, with nothing to remind him that he'd ever owned a pair of wheels. But in Bangkok, with a thousand eyes watching who passed in and out of the soi, the thieves had dismantled and carried off the bike like meat—a line of ants stretching from a dead frog to some distant slum, with the small bits handed down the line without anyone seeing what was in the hand. The frame didn't fit the hand; the frame stayed behind.

"Who would have done this? Sompol? You think that Chinese asshole did this because I wouldn't pay him the fifty thousand baht?" asked Hutton, walking around his bike.

"Look at the bike, Jerry. Pros broke it down; took it apart."

Hutton kicked the toe of his boot into the dirt. He had the same look of frustration and anguish as when he had returned from the phone call over the broken appointment. The Year of the Monkey was not turning out to be a great year so far.

"You have insurance?"

Hutton shook his head. It was a dumb question. What company would insure a *farang*'s motorcycle in Bangkok?

"I will kill the sonofabitch who did this. I will find and kill the fucker." It was the kind of threat a kid makes when someone has tapped him on the head too hard. Hard enough to know it wasn't intended as a joke. But Hutton was that kind of guy who almost never committed murder. Calvino's law: Professional killers prefer working in silence. They never warn; they never brag. They just get on with it. Silence is the language of death; threats are the language of impotence and fear. Hutton, who wanted to buy a thousand-buck dog to rehabilitate his whore, wasn't a killer. The kid didn't have that savage touch in his soul. Calvino was sure of that.

EIGHT

A BRIDGE TOO FAR

AS close as Pratt was to Calvino—he thought of him as his best friend—there remained a barrier in understanding. Something that translating from Thai into English filtered out; and it wasn't just a question of language, it ran deeper than that. The problem Dex had with the right wing, and again in the Hutton case, arose over the fight to control the sacred fire of violence. Guys like Dex who believed in accountability made enemies among those who believed power never accounts except unto itself. Not every member of the tribe was created equally. Protection and safety had one source—powerful patrons. Cross a patron, and anything could happen. In return for protections patrons demanded absolute personal loyalty.

An ISOC officer had once explained that this feeling of loyalty was like the roots of a thousand-year-old tree: It went deep, mostly underground, overlapping, weaving, woven around and around connecting families and clans and institutions. Pratt understood the fear of those on the right—society was in transition, and the changes threatened to cut down the tree and rip out this root structure, destroy the fine network of loyalties spanning and linking generations.

The officers had asked, "How do you trim the loyalties without killing the tree?"

Another ISOC officer had said, "Democracy is about as useful as an ashtray on a motorcycle."

That was the dilemma and no one had figured a way out. This most basic, gut fear was of chaos arising from the destruction of the old patronage system. You were loyal to the one who protected you.

This childlike fear of losing a secure world is what kept Pratt from hating the right wing. Most of them were decent, good people who needed reassurance that in the new world they could survive without their traditional patron's protection. The world was changing fast, and the ways of the past were blocking the new wave of the future. Pratt knew that men like Dex—who had not been born in the right family—would no longer sit quietly on the sideline. They were politely knocking on the door. It was time to let them in. And men like Calvino had a right to ask questions.

❖

"COLONEL Hatcher asked me whether you would go for his plan," said Colonel Pratt, as he turned a plastic page in the menu. Behind him on the Chao Phraya River, a long-tailed boat fishtailed, executed a sharp turn, and reversed under the bridge.

"And what did you say?" asked Calvino.

"Maybe that's a problem."

"Typical Thai understatement, Pratt. Hatcher have any reaction?"

Colonel Pratt glanced up from the menu. "He wanted to put you away. Typical American overstatement. 'Put away'—I believe that was the expression he used."

"And Hatcher asked you what you thought of his idea?" asked Calvino.

Colonel Pratt nodded, running his forefinger down the list of seafood dishes. Calvino glanced at his watch, making a mental note of the time. Colonel Pratt called over the floor captain, who wore a black coat and tie. The floor captain executed the command and stood at attention beside the table.

"I told him that he would have to put me away, too," said Colonel Pratt. He turned to the young Thai waitress and ordered the sweet and sour sea bass.

Each time they came to this open-air restaurant off Phra Atit Road, they sat at the same semiprivate table overlooking the brown, choppy Chao Phraya River, and each time Colonel Pratt ordered the sea bass. Two steps below the elevated platform, on the main floor, a dozen or more tourists squeezed around half a dozen tables, getting served a set menu.

84

"You took one minute longer than usual to order the sea bass," said Calvino.

Colonel Pratt said, "I saw you look at your watch. I didn't want to disappoint you."

Last time they'd had lunch at the restaurant and Colonel Pratt ordered the sea bass, Calvino had told him about Calvino's law: Senility means you keep going to the same restaurant and order the same food but take longer and longer to read through the menu.

Calvino ordered a small bottle of Mekhong, a bucket of ice, and a cheeseburger with French fries. "And if I had gone back to New York, how much time you figure they'd give me? Two, three months," said Calvino, making his forefinger into a pistol barrel and his thumb the hammer. "Then one night going out the door someone pops me. Good night, Irene. Then Hatcher and his fellow Little Leaguers have the perfect alibi. 'What? Us touch a guy like Calvino? After what we promised? No way. Hey, you guys in Bangkok have read about New York City. It's a dangerous place. Junkies. Drug dealers. Crazies pushing secretaries in front of trains. Guns everywhere. And wasn't Calvino's family connected? Didn't he have an uncle up on a RICO charge a few years ago?'"

"Or they phone our old friends in the Chinese triad and say, 'Guess who we saw on Canal Street today,'" said Colonel Pratt.

Calvino liked Pratt's attempt at a Brooklyn accent.

"Yeah, the triad would do the job for free."

"One thing, Vincent, you should keep in mind."

"What's that?"

"Colonel Hatcher knows the right people in some of the fringe groups."

"What are you saying?"

"Hutton's film of the execution has stirred things up in certain circles. Maybe military advisers might be sent to help the Karen. It's possible."

"Hatcher didn't say he wanted to win the hearts and minds of the villagers?" asked Calvino, watching the long-tail boat cutting a line straight toward the restaurant.

Colonel Pratt saw Calvino's hand move inside his jacket.

"We got a problem?" asked Colonel Pratt.

"We got a problem," said Calvino.

He pulled his .38 Police Special, rolled out of his chair, and with one knee on the cement floor, arms extended over the table, drew a bead. "I hate gunmen in boats."

Colonel Pratt tipped his chair over, drawing a Colt .45 handgun. The driver of the boat had already opened fire with an automatic weapon. One, two bullets tore through the throat of the floor captain, who collapsed into a tableful of tourists. Calvino returned fire, but he was out of range and the boat closed in. Colonel Pratt swung onto his belly, clasped the .45 with both hands, and killed the driver with his second or third shot. The boat spun out of control and crashed into the retaining wall, showering debris across the restaurant.

Calvino sat up, reloading his .38. He looked around at the crouching tourists and the dead floor captain. "Hatcher calls them mushrooms. Popping mushrooms, he told me."

"His Thai friends will drop him."

"Hatcher has played it smart. No one knows his friends," said Calvino.

"Not yet," said Colonel Pratt.

"My guess is Hatcher sees they make a bundle from commissions on arms sales. They owe him. Now he called in some chits. They'll be back. Believe it."

"You don't understand how Thais think," said Colonel Pratt.

"I'd say they lost some face. Or maybe they wanted to miss—it allows them to double their commission on what's in the pipeline."

"'These words are razors to my wounded heart,'" said Colonel Pratt, quoting *Titus Andronicus*.

❖

THREE hours later, Colonel Pratt slammed the door of his unmarked police car and stopped at the side door of a nondescript concrete building. Calvino looked up at the four-story shophouse on the edge of Chinatown. The metal gate was pulled down on the ground-floor entrance. Pratt pressed the outside buzzer according to a prearranged code, and the metal gate clanked noisily as a small boy cranked it up from inside. Pratt nodded to the owner, who looked at the *farang*, his old, watery eyes showing no reaction. The owner's wife served them tea in small Chinese cups with red dragons painted on the outside. Fong, the Chinese owner, was in his late fifties, a dozen wild hairs shooting out of a brown mole to the right of his chin; he wore small green silk slippers and shuffled like a cross-country skier as he walked. His head was shaven. One of Fong's eyes was smoky gray and the other yellow. His powder blue silk shirt clashed with his slippers, and when he smiled he displayed a set of teeth that looked like an aerial photo of a napalmed jungle. The black ridges shone behind the grin as he examined Calvino's .38 Police Special. He sighted the gun, cocked it, pulled the trigger. It made a dull thud.

"No good," said the Chinese man. After a long, hacking cough, Fong leaned over and dropped a load of spit which fell like a bomb from a plane.

"It never jams," said Calvino.

The Chinese owner chuckled, wiping his mouth, then turned the .38 around and stared into the barrel. "Shoot pigeons. Close range. Maybe kill, maybe not," said Fong.

Colonel Pratt stayed in the background, drinking tea. But his eye never left the door. He had known Fong, a Malaysian Chinese, for twenty years. Fong had the best supply of AK-47s, RPGs, mortars, and handguns in Bangkok. His prices were fair and he never cheated his customers. He delivered to your door—wherever that door happened to be—and that gave him a reliable value in an unreliable business. Given the general temperament of his clientele, his honesty may have arisen more out of fear than a deeper moral vision of right and wrong.

"What are you sayin'? I'm out of date or what?" asked Calvino.

"Your gun's out of date," said the owner. "I don't know about you. Maybe you're not with it either."

Score a five-shot bull's-eye cluster for the Chinaman, thought Calvino.

"How many of your shots hit home at the restaurant?" asked Colonel Pratt.

"My gun's a piece of shit. I'm a disgrace; out of date. What've you got for river rats?" asked Calvino, hunching his shoulders over a case of handguns. "Show me that one." He tapped the glass top above a Browning Hi Power handgun.

The Chinese owner nodded his approval and carefully lifted out the two pounds of Browning. He set it on top. Calvino turned it over in his hand.

"Nine-millimeter, and holds thirteen rounds," said Colonel Pratt. "Single-action, semiautomatic, seven-pound pull."

"Why you know so much about guns?" Calvino asked.

"It's my business."

"I don't recall that line from Shakespeare."

"Shakespeare ran with a better set of friends."

"So I have a few flaws," said Calvino.

He squinted as he sighted a Mekhong calendar on the wall. He aimed at the right eye of the naked girl for February, the start of the Year of the Monkey, then lowered the gun. He liked the weight and the feel.

"How much for the Browning?"

"A special price for Colonel Prachai Chongwatana's friend."

"So what's the friendship price, Khun Fong?"

"Twenty thousand baht," said the Chinese man, staring at Calvino with watery, unblinking eyes.

Calvino smiled and laid down the Browning. "What about a Year of the Monkey discount?"

"Twenty thousand," Khun Fong said again.

Calvino wasn't sure he wanted the Browning. It was easier trading wives than guns. He'd developed an attachment for his .38 Special, and packing the monster replacement with the big hips and large bang was not exactly what he'd had in mind. But at the same time, if he didn't buy the gun, Pratt was going to lose face. A *farang* who didn't know about face wasn't worthy of friendship. He tried one more line of attack.

"For that kinda money, I can get a pedigree German shepherd that can trace its lineage back more than a hundred and fifty years," said Calvino.

"For this price, Khun Winee," said Fong, "you can stay alive so your lineage may last one hundred and fifty years. It's up to you."

Calvino bought the Browning and two boxes of 9mm ammo and a new lease on Pratt's face. Colonel Pratt, smiling, advanced him the cash. Calvino examined the new Browning. It was an arranged marriage, he thought, looking at the gun. Khun Fong bowed his head and silently slipped out of the room, leaving the two men alone.

"It's okay, he won't be back for a few minutes. We can talk here. What about the script?" asked Colonel Pratt.

"My problem is the script for *Lucky Charms*. Hutton told me about the script he read. The story was about a merc, a *Rambo* flick along the Thai-Burma border. But Rambo wasn't in the script Tyler showed me. There was nothing about Burma, nothing about the conflict. You know what a second unit is in the movie business?"

Colonel Pratt shrugged, watching Calvino load the magazine of the Browning with thirteen rounds of 9mm ammo. Till death do us part, he thought as he clasped the gun. Or a mutual divorce.

"Second unit for what?" asked Pratt.

"I didn't know either until I phoned Tommy in L.A. Tommy said a second unit has a few guys who shoot visual wallpaper. Some exterior shots of Paris or London. In this case, the Thai-Burmese border. It costs too much to send everyone. So they send in a stripped-down crew. Or often they hire a local camera and sound guy. The director and even some actors might go along. But it's lean and mean. Afterward, in the editing room, they layer in the footage. When you see it, no one could tell it was second-unit stuff. The magic of film."

It had been worrying Calvino that Tyler's script of *Lucky Charms* was totally different from the story Hutton had told him over lunch at Der Braumeister. When he phoned Tommy about how second-unit teams worked, he got an answer about double scripting.

"It sounds like two scripts. Sometimes in foreign countries they run double scripts. They show one to the local censors and the other script is the actual shooting script. In this case, it's hard to say what the fuck is going on," Tommy had explained.

Pratt listened to this explanation. "A backdoor script?"

"That's what I'm saying," continued Calvino. "There's gotta be another script of *Lucky Charms*. The one Tyler showed to Hutton, and got Hutton to take the job along the border."

"If there were two scripts, it will take a miracle to prove it now," said Colonel Pratt.

"It would be a perfect way to get Hutton upcountry, and cover their ass if things didn't go right," Calvino said, flicking on the safety of the Browning. "Tyler will deny it. Or even if we did find the script Hutton saw, Tyler would say they had it rewritten. We've got nothing to connect him to Hutton's shoot or Hutton's death. He's clean and he knows it. Then I ask myself, why is this guy so worried? He sics two bodyguards on me. That doesn't work, and Hatcher arrives in town. Kiko is given a role. Hatcher pops some mushrooms as a warning."

Colonel Pratt groaned. "Kiko's in a movie?"

"And Tyler, being the gentleman he is, will give enough money for the Foundation at Klong Toey to buy a new water pump."

"Has she ever acted before?"

"Not outside of our sex life—as far as I know," said Calvino. "I'm trying to understand why anyone would hire someone off the street who's never acted before? I'd go for a star. Wouldn't you? I tried to talk with Kiko. But it didn't work. She thought I was nuts. That I was power-tripping. Making a scene."

"They may have a script where she's the hostage."

"A mushroom hostage. That was Hatcher's message, delivered to me personally at Sanam Luang," said Calvino. "I think that I will talk this over with Jesse Tyler. Let him know some background about Bangkok that Hatcher may have left out. Who knows, Tyler might think it's just like Hawaii."

Calvino pushed back his jacket, removed his .38 Special, raised it to his lips for a kiss. He slipped the .38 into his jacket pocket. Then after he holstered the Browning, Calvino showed Colonel Pratt one of the photos he had bought from Kwang.

"That's Hutton. And Roland."

"And this one?" asked Colonel Pratt.

"With the cute haircut and muscles? The steroid freak is Karl. I wanna buy him a beer. Get to know him. Soften him up. Ask him who his barber is. Ask him about the snuff film Hutton shot along the Moei River. A few details in Hutton's film are starting to bother me. Karl could have witnessed the execution along with Hutton. And if Hatcher knows about Karl, then he's gonna be an unhappy warrior. Guys like Hatcher don't like loose ends. It's the mentality of either tie a knot or burn the rope. Chances are about a hundred percent Karl would burn."

"Colonel Hatcher wants to burn you. But he isn't sure how much you really know, Vincent."

"About the U.S. Army intelligence involvement in the movie business? He came straight at us because he's giving dirty business a bad name," said Calvino. "Someone inside your neck of the woods must have given him the okay. That way they get two for the price of one. A cop who helped a certain Thai pro-democracy sax player escape the country, and a *farang* who thinks some guys named Hatcher, Tyler, and Oxley might know who killed a kid named Hutton."

Colonel Pratt lingered over the image of "woods," thinking who under his charge, who inside ISOC, or which right-wing group might be waiting with Hatcher and planning the next move. It was less "woods" than a vast forest of possibilities. He had been reading from *Titus Andronicus* the night before. The overhead light was on above the bed. Manee was sleeping on her side. He picked up the telephone on the second ring. Manee stirred and cuddled up next to him. The call was from ISOC, a high-ranking officer asking him to help with a meeting between a Colonel Samuel E. Hatcher and a civilian named Vincent Calvino which was scheduled to take place at Sanam Luang. It was a matter of national security. Colonel Pratt was to report back after that meeting with a full, detailed written statement regarding the outcome of that meeting. After he hung up the phone, he returned to Shakespeare, and knew at once that the passage he'd just been reading would form the report he would file after Calvino met Hatcher.

"'The woods are ruthless, dreadful, deaf, and dull; there speak, and strike, brave boys, and take your turns.' I was reading that passage when the phone rang last night."

Colonel Pratt's lips tightened into a frown as he handed the picture back. Khun Fong pushed through a bead curtain with a tray containing three glasses of whiskey. Calvino watched the tray like a man unable to look away from a snake. Colonel Pratt waved off the offer of the drink. Calvino stared long and hard at the black lacquer tray, and shook his head, squaring himself with the door to the street and feeling the weight of the Browning press against his side. He took two steps forward.

"Where are you going?" asked Colonel Pratt.

"To see a man about a dog," said Calvino.

❖

CALVINO found Kiko sucking on an ice cube at a back table in Der Braumeister. She didn't look all that happy to see him. Above her, nailed to the wall, was a calendar with a German shepherd and a dog breeder who looked like a Colombian drug dealer in a business suit and sunglasses. He recognized the calendar—Kiko had taken the same table he had shared with Hutton on Chinese New Year's Day when the rest of Sukhumvit's restaurants had been closed. Not much had changed, including the month—February.

"Why the sour face?" asked Calvino.

"You're late."

"There was a boating accident," said Calvino.

"That's a good one. Anyway, I saw Ratana near Villa supermarket. And she acted, well, very odd. Does she have a problem with the Japanese?" asked Kiko, crunching the ice cube and swallowing hard.

"What's this racial sensitivity?"

"With all the newspapers filled with horrible stories about comfort women for the Japanese Army during World War II, I feel—I know it's crazy—that people here think I did something wrong."

He leaned over and kissed her on the forehead.

"Ratana loves you. So forget about it."

He had phoned his secretary from the street. When she picked up the phone on her end, he heard a click. It figures Hatcher would run a tap, he thought.

"I'll phone you back in five minutes," he said, and hung up.

He waited five minutes, giving Ratana enough time to run down the two flights of stairs, through the Finns' real estate office, and sprint up the street to a phone booth. She was out of breath when she picked up the receiver on the seventh ring.

"I'm not coming back to the office. And I don't want you to go back. Take the rest of the week off. Phone Kiko from this booth and tell her to meet me at Der Braumeister in thirty minutes." Then, with no further explanation, he hung up.

Kiko explained, "I said hello, and she pretended not to recognize me."

"Okay, if you want to know, Ratana suspected that she was being followed. She did the right thing."

"What's going on, Vinny?"

Jurgen had been watching them from behind the bar, sipping beer from one of those fancy German mugs where you press your thumb down on a hinge to raise up a silver lid. A thin foam of suds covered Jurgen's upper lip. A solitary Thai waitress in the same milkmaid's outfit shuffled to the table; only the bodice seemed cut lower this time and when she leaned over the top of her breasts were exposed like ripe melons. The waitress smiled at Calvino and silently laid down two photo albums. Inside were faded, slightly out-of-focus Polaroids of sausages, steaks, soup, and hamburgers.

"Pratt and I had a small problem at lunch."

"I know, a boating accident."

"I'm still here. And Pratt is back in his office, more than likely reading Shakespeare and thinking about the meaning of democracy in a city with thirty-mile traffic jams."

"I don't believe it was an accident. Someone wanted to kill you." The color had drained out of her face.

Calvino shrugged, ignoring the statement. His silence had no effect. She looked like she might be ill with fear. Her memory flashed back one year before to the sound of gunshots, an eruption of sudden violence and death; she had been with Calvino when it had happened. She'd been bloodied, but, unlike in the movies, it was over in a few seconds. She had listened to him joke at the hospital. He told her one of Calvino's laws: A good day was a day when you didn't call someone an asshole and escaped the label yourself. Even though he had been shot at, he was having a good day.

"What are you going to do?" she asked now.

He turned around in his chair. "Jurgen, you remember me?"

Jurgen nodded. "I remember," he said, lowering his drinking mug to the bar. "You wanted goldfish in a nice cheese sauce."

"Vinny, you didn't?" asked Kiko.

Calvino ignored the question and waved for Jurgen to join the table. "Come over here. I want to show you something."

Jurgen lit a Lucky Strike cigarette, moved to the end of the bar, and came out the far side beside their table. Inside the photo album menu, Calvino had inserted the snapshot of Jerry, Roland, and Karl. He opened the menu and turned it around. A cloud of gray smoke coiled out of Jurgen's nostrils.

"What is it you want to show me?"

"Next to the picture of sausage and chopped sauerkraut. You see the kid with the Mohawk hairdo? You wouldn't happen to know Mr. Universe from Outer Space here? His name's Karl."

Jurgen furrowed his brow, knitting his eyebrows together, looking at the ceiling as if trying to remember. He sucked in hard on the cigarette. "A lot of tourists come. I can't remember them all."

"You see guys like this coming in every day? I've been here twice. And I ain't ever seen anyone else. So why don't you level with me, Jurgen."

"You seem to be forgetting this is my restaurant. I don't see why I have to do anything other than ask you to get out."

Calvino had one weapon left in his arsenal. "Hutton said you were making a big commission on the dog deal. You brokered the deal with Karl. So why don't you cut out the bullshit, and tell me where I can find this guy."

"Or what? You are going to shoot me?"

"You're watching too much TV, Jurgen. I'm not threatening you. I'm trying to help Karl before some pretty rough people start looking for him. You know what I'm saying?"

"You come back at six, and maybe I can help you. Right now, I'm busy."

Calvino shook his head and gestured with one hand around the restaurant. "I don't see any reason to wait. I look around, but I don't see customers pounding their fists on the table."

Jurgen shrugged, smoked his Lucky Strike, and walked back to his position at the bar. His cigarette had the shakes. That was a good sign, thought Calvino. Jurgen was coming apart.

NINE

SACRED FIRE

EARLY on the evening of Dex's farewell party, Calvino was alone in his bedroom dressing himself for the Yellow Parrot. He reached into his closet and fingered an imported Italian necktie, which was a dusty peach color; he rejected it, and selected the smoky gray one instead. It fitted closer to the sound of Dex's sax, he thought. Silky, smoky gray jazz—kinda sad, like the sax registered an inner pain and turned it into music. Not that the jaded crowd who inhabited the place would appreciate a tie which was tailored to the music. For a second he had the rare twinge—he missed New York. In the Village people would notice the tie. He flipped it around his neck, running it under his shirt collar. About the only guy in Bangkok who could relate to that spasmodic feeling of inexplicable loss was Pratt. And Pratt was gonna be at the club, thought Calvino with some comfort.

He untied the tie and made a face at himself in the mirror. Then he thought about how most of the photos of executives in the local business magazines showed them wearing a power red necktie—the Chinese favored red partly because it was the color of gold shops. It was good to be associated with gold. Red ties did the job. He wore what should have been a power red tie in some half-assed knot, but in place of power it displayed the grace of a hangman's noose. The executives appeared like stragglers struggling to catch up with a re-treating army of white-collar workers. A necktie advertised their class but any *ying* could smell a false advertisement; revealing once the shirt and tie was removed, a *farang* one generation away from his own peasant roots.

95

He studied himself in the mirror on the inside of the closet door as he retied his necktie. Great necktie, nine-year-old designer trousers—bought in New York when he was still a lawyer—a symbol of his downward mobility into the peasant class. "Who doesn't have peasant stock lurking somewhere in their background?" he muttered to himself. "I'm just working myself back the long way around." He was half-listening to an old tune about nesting with a woman. That afternoon, after Kiko's daughter Lisa had come home from school, he had given her a one-hour English conversation lesson. Lisa was seven years old and always greeted Calvino with, "Give me five, Vinny." He liked Kiko's kid. And he liked it that Kiko never made a big deal out of being a single mother abandoned by her husband in Bangkok; she never felt sorry for herself—she just picked herself up and went on with her life. As he left her suite, Kiko had slipped the tape into his jacket, leaning forward on tiptoes, kissing him as if she meant it. She knew that he loved jazz. As he finished dressing, Calvino was thinking about some lyrics to the song: "Safe and together . . . we'll shelter in each other's arms forever." Kiko was sending him a message without its actually seeming like she was sending him one. She was subtle. He liked that about her.

Then someone hit the front door buzzer. He turned down the volume on the tape deck. He waited a couple of seconds and the door buzzer blared again, making that echo one hears inside public school corridors and prisons, a crude sound; an echo bouncing deep off the memories of Calvino's childhood. He answered the door in his tailored white shirt, the imported Italian smoky gray tie, and beige-colored Armani trousers that matched the jacket still hanging in the closet. His .38 service revolver fitted snug inside the leather holster behind and below his left arm and didn't move as he walked. He had been wearing it the last couple of weeks—ever since Dex's threatening phone calls had spilled over onto his own phone line.

"*Farang* go home or have bad accident in Thailand," said the voice on the phone. Then bang, down slammed the phone.

He hadn't told Pratt, figuring the calls were nothing to worry about. Just a little psychic harassment to let him know they didn't like him helping Dex. But Dex was on his way out of the country, and the calls, he reasoned, would stop once Dex landed in Tokyo.

He opened the door on the third long buzz.

"Hey, Jerry, you wanna borrow a jacket and tie?" asked Calvino, looking at the dirty jeans and Saigon T-shirt.

"I have to cancel, Vinny."

"Just don't stand in the door. Come in before the killer cockroaches rush the place," said Calvino.

Hutton, his hands in the front pockets of his jeans, walked in, kicked off his shoes, and moved over to a broken-down rattan sofa.

"You want a beer? There's beer on ice."

"Yeah, that would be great."

Calvino brought him back a Singha Gold and a glass. Hutton set the glass on the table and drank straight from the bottle, then shook his head and let out a long sigh.

"You see, I gotta take a meeting," said Hutton.

Calvino watched him take another long swallow from the bottle. "Jerry, this is Bangkok. No one uses that Hollywood bullshit about taking a meeting. You take a girl. A girl takes you. You take an air-conditioned bus. You take a visa run. But what you don't take in Bangkok is a fucking meeting."

"You know what I mean," replied Hutton, a hurt expression creeping over his face like he was someone whose confidence was easily eroded.

"Okay, I remember. It's something do with this film you were not telling me about. So after you meet whoever it is you're gonna meet, then come over to the Yellow Parrot and listen to some jazz. It's the last time you'll hear Dex for some time—he's off on a tour to Tokyo and then Europe. But it's up to you. Just because I helped you out of a jam doesn't mean you owe me. You understand what I'm sayin'?"

Hutton didn't say anything as he put his thumb in the top of the bottle to make a dull, popping sound. He looked far away, like a man absorbed in memories and thoughts. His eyes displayed an emotional weather pattern filled with storm clouds and pelting rain.

"I feel like an asshole," said Hutton, removing his thumb from the hole, tipping the bottle back against his lips until he had finished the beer. He belched and set the empty bottle down.

"I owe you three thousand baht, and that doesn't include your fee. And I come in your home, and the first thing you offer me is a jacket, tie, and beer. And you don't say anything about wanting the money."

"You need some pocket money for the club? Is that what you're saying?" Calvino pulled out his wallet and peeled off two purples—five-hundred-baht notes—and held them out.

Hutton shook his head and waved his hand. "I'm sorry. I can't take the money; it wouldn't be right. I gotta stand on my own feet. And I'm trying but the film is driving me crazy. I got a ton of pressure from my work. You ever feel like you had so much pressure that you couldn't breathe?"

"Pressure doesn't come from work, it comes from the assholes you work for. And it seems from what you said, you're working for assholes."

He looked like he might start crying but at the last moment stepped on the brakes. His eyes were still watery when he took a second Singha Gold from Calvino. "You know how *farangs* sometimes say Thais will do anything for money?"

"Only *farangs* who think in slogans and drool in their cornflakes say that kinda bullshit," said Calvino.

"Well, I did something for money. Something pretty bad. Beyond any shit a Thai would ever do. I was stupid. I acted like a sonofabitch and it's eating me." He leaned back, his neck resting on the rattan rail, tearing the paper label off the Singha Gold with his thumbnail. "And I'm gonna put it right."

"I don't know what you're saying. Or if you're saying anything. Maybe you're talking to yourself out loud. But let me give you a piece of advice: If you fucked up, ninety-nine percent of all mistakes can be put back together like Humpty Dumpty with enough time and money. It's the way things work."

"This is the one percent case. All the king's horses and all the king's men can't buy enough fucking glue to fix this broken egg," said Hutton.

The telephone started to ring, and as Calvino answered it in the bedroom he slipped *Hollis Gentry's Neon* into the tape deck.

"How did you like the tape?" asked Kiko.

"Nowhere is safe and nothing lasts forever, but other than those minor objections, I liked the song, if that's what you mean."

There was a long pause.

"You still there?" asked Calvino. He walked into the sitting room, carrying the phone. He cupped his hand over the mouthpiece.

"Get yourself another beer, Jerry," he shouted.

When he came back on the line there was a cold wind blowing. He could feel the chill in Kiko's voice.

"Vinny, I'm a little busy," she said. "I don't think I can make it to the club tonight."

He watched Jerry Hutton open the third Singha Gold and drink half of it in record time. There was definitely something eating away at the kid. Kiko was saying something but he wasn't concentrating on her words.

"I've lost you. What were you saying?" he asked her.

The line went dead. She had slammed the receiver down. It was the same moody, dead sound he heard in the aftermath of the threatening callers. It was an angry, hostile old world, he thought.

"You were saying something when the phone rang," said Calvino as he laid down the phone, turned up the music.

"Before when you got me out of jail, you asked me what I was afraid of," said Hutton.

"And you gave me a bullshit answer. Something about your second-unit stuff making its way into *Lucky Charms*."

Hutton leaned over the sofa, watching Calvino opening another Singha Gold on top of the small fridge. "You have a good memory. But if I read you right, I knew you didn't believe it."

"You read me right."

"You want a straight answer?"

Calvino raised an eyebrow and tossed the beer cap into the trash. Several small house lizards scattered across the wall, their lightning-fast tongues darting through space, bagging mosquitoes and ants. He poured himself a double Mekhong on ice, and brought back the rest of the beer for Hutton. He sat in a rattan chair opposite Hutton, who showed the effects of the three earlier beers.

"Anytime you're ready."

From Calvino's angle, Hutton's eyes looked a little misty.

"After I'd been laid off a couple of months, I rode around all day on the subway in Chicago. One day two yuppies sat across from me. You know the type: fancy suits, leather briefcases, good-looking. That real confident, 'I've got a real job and you don't'. One of them is looking at me like I'm scum or something—like straight *at* me. He turns to his friend and says, 'Another organ donor heading downtown.' His friend got a big laugh out of that. It wasn't until they got off the train that I started feeling like shit. What right did these guys have to say that, man? And what kinda country was I living in where just riding in a train, some total stranger just comes out and says you're nothing? Just fucking nothing. After a couple of years in Bangkok, I can't stop thinking about what that guy said. And you know what

I'm afraid of? Maybe he knew something I didn't. Sometimes people can see you the way you can't see yourself. And I started to think, Does Kwang see me this way, too? An organ donor? Then I start to worry she might go back to Soi Cowboy and get her old job back as a go-go dancer at the Love Nest Bar. Then I start thinking, I'm over the edge; I'm starting to bullshit myself. I say some shit to get you off my case. Then the next thing I know I'm saying some shit to get myself off my own back. Does any of this make sense?"

"Kid, you make sense. I understand that kind of fear. Anyone who tells you they never felt it is lying," said Calvino. "It's the human condition. Everyone's on the run. It's like they think there's this contest and a finish line somewhere out there. And some people win the race and others get left behind. But when you stop to think about it, you find out the contest is with yourself. And you can't ever win it."

"Tell it to those two guys in Chicago," said Hutton.

"There's no need. Reality catches up with wise guys first. It's the unwritten rule of the universe."

"And what's that reality?"

"That no place is safe, nothing is permanent, and we are born and die alone. And, of course, never donate your organ to a woman whose troubles are greater than your own."

Hutton started to laugh. He drank from the beer, and seemed more relaxed. He wiped his eyes and smiled.

"Deep down, I was afraid you would laugh at me. Everyone I know in Bangkok would laugh at me if Kwang went back to working the bars. They would say, 'Jerry Hutton fucked up like a million other asshole *farangs*.' They would say, 'Jerry Hutton couldn't keep her satisfied.' What was the way out? There had to be an angle. I knew a guy who knew a guy who hangs out at the Washington Square bars. He was talking about breeding dogs over the forty-baht lunch special. I listened in on what he said. He talked about how much money you could make right out of your home. So I thought, Bingo. It makes business sense. Kwang could make all the money she needs. And, looking after the dogs would keep her occupied at the same time. Keep her mind off Soi Cowboy and fucking around."

"That's it?" asked Calvino.

There was something Hutton was holding back. He wrinkled his nose, and set the beer down. He shivered and rubbed his hands together.

"There's something else. Kwang told me about you and her. That before I took her, you bought her out a couple of times. I was afraid if things didn't work out she might want you again."

He was silent. Calvino took the empty beer bottle from his hand. "Let me tell you something, Jerry. Don't lay down the tracks for your life on some wild guess that someone else is watching or cares. It's a waste of time. If Kwang goes back to the bar, I am not gonna laugh at you, or think you are stupid or an asshole. I am thinking, There is a guy who cared enough to try. A friend of mine works at Klong Toey and she tells me there are people who think they can change lives. Turn street kids around and make them into citizens. Most of the time nothing changes. Except money changing hands. She says to me that each time it doesn't work out, you don't feel stupid. You keep on trying and trying. You never give up. And Kwang would never come back here. That was a business transaction, not an emotional connection. You've been around long enough to know the difference."

For the first time that day, a smile crossed Jerry Hutton's face. He pulled himself off the sofa, walked over and gave Calvino a bear hug. "Thanks, Vinny. You know, for everything."

"Hey, you're messing up my tie. It's imported Italian Thai silk. Only a guy like me would buy such a tie. But it's one of my weaknesses."

"You're all right, Calvino. For an old guy baby boomer."

Calvino smiled. So that's what the generation behind him really thought in their heart of hearts. But "an old guy baby boomer" had a certain ring to it, like cradle to grave except it was backwards—grave to cradle.

"At thirty-seven, if I am lucky, I've got another twenty years," said Calvino. Making a living by opening the door to other people's private lives, learning their secrets, their crimes, their betrayals and exposing them wasn't the kind of activity that correlated with longevity.

"I didn't mean it that way."

"Then in what way did you mean it?"

Hutton shuffled his feet, looked at his fingernails. "Most guys like them traded away their family for a pile of money."

"Exactly what are you trading?" asked Calvino. "And what are you getting in return?"

"For guys my age having a family is everything. My parents are divorced. Almost every one of my friends back home had parents who are divorced. I want a marriage that lasts. If Kwang and I can breed dogs, then we'll have more in common than my parents ever had. Something to talk about. We will have time together and enough money to start a family."

"Tonight, just talk with these guys, find out what they want."

Hutton got up to leave.

"I thought of something. This wounded vet who comes to Bangkok in the movie—what happens to him?" asked Calvino.

"He is taken to a place where there is a sacred fire . . ."

"What is this, a Disney picture?" asked Calvino.

"And if you bathe in this sacred fire nothing can hurt you."

"That's magical thinking. But people like that kind of bullshit.'"

"The hero brings this flame from the Burmese front lines. He doesn't know what he has found. It's his cure. His . . . what did Oxley call it . . . yeah, his redemption."

"Sounds like movie talk. 'Taking a meeting' and 'redemption' should never appear in the same conversation." But, then again, thought Calvino, this could have passed for third-shift-people talk: Bangkok was a step on a new path to some personal redemption that the old religion of home never offered.

From the detached expression on his face, Hutton appeared to be thinking about something else. It was getting late, and Calvino got his jacket from the closet and was putting it on when he came back into the living room. The screen door was wide open and Hutton was outside standing on the balcony and looking through the trees and over the roofs to the lights coming from his slum. Kwang was inside one of the rooms. What he was doing was for her, as if he wanted to program her dreams so that they matched with his own. With enough seed money he might have the sacred fire, an irresistible force to shape those dreams and salvage them from the slum.

"I'm telling them straight-out," he said, as Calvino stepped onto the balcony. "For the stuff I delivered them, I want more money. Without me on the front line, they would have come back with nothing. I know it wasn't right. But you look after your own."

Calvino had a bad feeling. Breaking contracts in Bangkok was viewed as a personal betrayal: a violation of trust, the equivalent of challenging someone to do something about it. It rarely involved the courts. Gunmen were cheaper and more effective—you didn't have to worry about appeals. Hutton had been around; he knew the rules, thought Calvino. But he couldn't help saying, "Hey, watch yourself."

"They owe me, Vinny."

"It makes people real nervous when you tell them they owe you something. So do yourself a favor, don't tell these guys they owe you. Why don't I tag along. A silent observer who says nothing."

"No dice. Besides, I'm a combat veteran. You'll see what I mean when the movie comes out."

Calvino backed off. Pressing the point would make him come across as an asshole. Hutton finished his beer as the *Neon* tape ended. Calvino listened to the background silence which swallowed the soi. Then a dog barked in the distance. Mrs. Jamthong's birds started singing in their cage below. Another dog entered the chorus. The silence was gone and so was Hutton. He had gone inside to the sitting room, shuffled over to the door, slipped on his tennis shoes without bothering to lace them up or tie them, and disappeared into the night. Old guy baby boomer, thought Calvino. That's how his generation was going down in the minds of the new kids on the block.

TEN

QUEEN BITCH

CALVINO realized before Kiko and he left the restaurant on Sukhumvit that it made no sense to push Jurgen any harder. He made him for the kind of guy who for whatever reason had decided not to talk unless he knew who he was talking to. It was a hangover from the attitude that kids learned growing up in war zones. Jurgen could have been scared, though he didn't *look* afraid. Hutton was dead. He must have remembered seeing Calvino the day he walked in the door with Hutton fresh from Tonglor district police station jail. That gave Calvino the smell of death.

Besides, giving information out to strangers in Bangkok was more than likely to get Jurgen into the middle of something that he couldn't see his way out of. After the waitress brought back the change, Calvino left Der Braumeister with Kiko but without the information he wanted. Jurgen, pretending to read his German language newspaper, watched him from behind the bar. Chances were Jurgen kept a gun under the bar. Chances were he had never used it but the gun made him feel more secure when the smell of death walked in the door.

Outside on Sukhumvit Road, Kwang, wearing skintight shorts and no bra under her tank top, bicycled past him, pouted her lips, and threw him a "Longing to see you back at the hotel" look. She mouthed the words "*Hum hiaw.*" Then she broke out laughing as she pedaled on the odd-numbered side of Sukhumvit. This was the *ying* hit-and-run trick, a bar *ying* hustle on the run—a glance thrown instinctively at an old customer passing her on the street. If the old customer had another *ying* in hand but had a good heart, she'd go easy on him (that was good business); but if he'd been Cheap Charlie, it was a good chance for a little revenge. She looked at Calvino, then at Kiko, registering that she wasn't on the game. The body language said they were a couple. An unwritten bar *ying* code—born more out of fear than honor—was that a john with another girl was off-limits. Kwang was hard-core enough to break the code to flush a little street excitement into Calvino's life; after all, he had cut her price on the photos—he deserved it.

Calvino pretended to read the double bill on the Washington Square cinema marquee across the street. But the ploy didn't work. He turned and headed in the same direction as Kwang had been riding. He took Kiko's hand.

"She knows you," said Kiko, picking up on the way Kwang and Calvino had exchanged a certain knowing look, and stood her ground. She wasn't moving from the location of the visual exchange.

"That's Hutton's widow," explained Calvino.

"And is that a mourning dress?" snapped Kiko.

"Let's say she appears to have coped well."

"She's the one who was in your bed," said Kiko. "The one you confused me with the other morning."

Calvino stopped, turned and put his hands on Kiko's shoulders.

"What do you want me to say? I was fucking Hutton's girlfriend? I didn't."

"What did she say to you?"

He stalled, his teeth biting his lower lip. Then he said it. "That I have a limp dick."

"Why do you always have to joke about everything?"

Kiko's eyes filled with tears. She didn't know what she wanted him to say, or what she believed or felt. Kwang had disappeared among the fruit and flower vendors selling from stalls in front of Villa supermarket. Calvino took out a handkerchief and dabbed her eyes.

"Your eyes are watering. It must be the pollution and dust," he said.

"It's just hard. And I don't mean your dick. I mean to trust any man who lives in Bangkok. You always have women throwing themselves at you. It would drive any woman's self-esteem into the ground."

Kiko's husband had run off with a nineteen-year-old bar *ying* to Tokyo a couple of years earlier. But the hurt still came to the surface now and then. Kwang's performance had touched that nerve. The pain flooded through her; she couldn't stop it. Finally they both left it alone. Walking on sealed inside that man-woman envelope of silence, they crossed the soi.

Someone had tried to kill him a few hours earlier. It had felt so good to be alive, thought Calvino.

I had so looked forward to seeing Vinny, she thought.

Then the celebration of surviving was over before I had a chance to enjoy it, thought Calvino.

He didn't ask me a single thing about my part, she thought.

Calvino marveled with wonder how quickly the day-to-day bullshit made him ask himself the question, Survived for what?

When he paid the bill, I saw he had a different gun, she thought. Why does he hide these things from me? A gun, a girl—what next? Am I in his life or not? she thought.

Trying to explain to Kiko the bar subculture that Kwang worked in would, despite Kiko's experience in the slum, have only deepened the trench of misunderstanding and suspicion, he thought. Why do women have to worry about everything? he wondered.

Why can't men talk about what is going on inside them? she thought.

Surplus thoughts, like surplus beautiful, available women, were not something that surrendered to precise answers; there were emotions, events, theories, and beliefs which lacked rational explanation. Take love, money, democracy, and death—which had to do with faith. Take away faith and the whole lot separated from reality and fell into the deep trench doubt had opened. Calvino took her hand and gave it a squeeze. Some of the emotional heat dropped. She gave a crooked half-smile and squeezed his hand in return.

"Better?" he asked.

"I think so."

He made a face and pulled back his shoulders, then relaxed them and worked his neck from side to side. "One of Pratt's friends—a Chinese version of E.T.—sold me a new space-age weapon. It weighed like a ton, and it's giving me a sore neck."

She stopped and kissed him in the middle of the street.

"Thanks, Vinny."

"I should talk about guns more often."

"You should phone me more often, too," she said.

The image of Colonel Hatcher handing him his card flashed into his mind.

❖

THERE had been that distance which had fallen between Hatcher and Calvino at Sanam Luang. Even with the chill between them, it could not have been a brighter day to fly a kite. The wind punched the kite, lifting it high in the sky. He remembered the expression on Colonel Hatcher's face as the Pepsi logo had smashed into an accordion when the kite crashed to the ground. Colonel Pratt had stayed back, watching them from the bench. Hatcher talked, walked, and gestured like brass. Someone who naturally assumed that an order was given to be followed. Calvino was thinking that the big mistake guys like Colonel Hatcher made was believing that they could take anyone apart either by offering them a lot of money or by roughing them up. He was always thinking about his own big mistake—not connecting Hatcher with the people who had been making the death threats to Dex and himself, until Hatcher made the connection for him.

"Pratt says you've been getting threats on the phone," Colonel Hatcher had said.

Calvino glanced back at Pratt, who sat on the bench. He hadn't told Pratt about those calls. The only way Hatcher could know was if someone who knew the organization behind the calls had been in contact with Hatcher.

"I told him to keep it confidential," said Calvino, lying, covering Pratt's tracks.

"Take it from an old Asia hand, there are certain Thais who can make it dangerous for a *farang* to live in Bangkok," said Colonel Hatcher, handing him a name card with an embassy phone number. "In case you change your mind, give me a call."

That's how it had been left. He had the feeling he would be receiving more phone calls. Hatcher was of the school that anyone who fell between those loyalty cracks was the enemy. Hatcher hadn't waited for Calvino to phone; he knew when he handed the name card to Calvino that someone was on his way to kill him and Colonel Pratt—not for the usual personal reasons of revenge or betrayal,

107

but simply because it was the most efficient and economical way to escape a dangerous situation with people who proved to be difficult and who would sooner or later cut you down and hurt you.

❖

AS they crossed Soi 31, Calvino saw his secretary waiting near a street vendor; Ratana was looking over her shoulder, then pretending to express interest in a raw silk skirt on a metal rack. She saw her boss but pretended that she didn't recognize him. She turned her back quickly before Kiko recognized her. Calvino picked up his pace, clutching Kiko's hand as he walked past Ratana and reached out with his free hand, into which she stuffed a piece of paper. After she passed him the paper, without saying a word or looking at him or Kiko, she walked to the curb, waved down a taxi, climbed inside, slammed the door, and was gone.

"Why did she do that?" asked Kiko.

"She's afraid that being seen in public with me might spoil her reputation," said Calvino, reading the note.

Ratana had written down a name—Khun Rolfo—and his telephone number. He was a dog breeder. He bred German shepherds— Calvino was betting with a pedigree that could be traced back about one hundred and fifty years.

"I can believe that," murmured Kiko.

He looked up from the note, lost in his thoughts.

"Now you're in the business, I'm hearing new lines. You're not going Hollywood on me?" asked Calvino.

"Not as long as you don't go Bangkok on me."

"I like that. We share something in common. I'm in the business, too. Only it's Bangkok style. Which means I've got a problem."

"Which is?" she asked cautiously.

"I can't figure out how many versions of *Lucky Charms* are floating around. I'd like to get my hands on the script Hutton saw."

"Ask Mr. Tyler."

"Yeah, right. Or Colonel Hatcher. Or this guy I'm dying to meet, Oxley."

"Mike Oxley. He's cute," said Kiko.

That stopped Calvino like an elephant gun.

"You know this guy?"

"I met him. He suggested me for the part. Why are you mad?"

"I'm not mad. I'm thinking about German shepherds and Mike Oxley."

The late afternoon heat blazed down on the street. No trees, no shade broke the sun as it slanted like a laser gun on low voltage, zapping, stunning, but stopping short of outright killing those at ground level. Groups of students—girls in white blouses, blue, pleated skirts, white bobby socks, and black shoes—passed drinking soda and eating snacks, making remarks about the large *farang* in the funny suit, sweat dripping off his face. "Mushrooms," Colonel Hatcher had said, his jaw cracking into an evil shape as he said the word. Calvino still had that mad look on his face as they walked passed Villa supermarket. He was still thinking.

Then he saw the notice Rolfo, the German shepherd dog breeder, had posted. Calvino thought that what made Ratana a first-rate secretary was her basic instinct of knowing when to appear and vanish with a gesture; and where to look for something that had been right under his nose. She knew how *farangs* bought and sold their cars, TVs, cameras, washing machines, transformers, pets, and record collections. They used the supermarket windows as a community bulletin board. Typed and handwritten notices papered the window. Expats who arrived in Bangkok were looking for a maid, and expats on their way out were looking to unload household goods before fleeing the scene. Among the notices was one about six days old advertising a litter of German shepherd pups for sale.

"You ever wanted to own a dog?" he asked Kiko, nodding at the notice.

Kiko read the advertisement, wrinkling her nose in disapproval.

"German shepherds are huge. Too big for the city. Unless you want it as a guard dog."

"Are all the Japanese so practical?"

"Right down to the last kamikaze."

❖

CALVINO stood in front of a bronze plaque bolted on four sides to the front gate. It read in raised lettering:

"Rolfo Stadler—Stud Service."

Underneath the English words, in smaller type, was the Thai translation. As he read what appeared to be a boast, Calvino, his shoulder sore from the Browning, was thinking about how he missed his .38 Special and about his uncle Mario who had retired to Florida. Uncle Mario carried around a key chain on which he had paid someone on Coney Island to inscribe the words "stud service." Whenever Uncle Mario dumped his change on a checkout counter with a good-looking cashier, his key chain was mixed in.

"Eat dirt and die," Uncle Mario would say, counting nickels and dimes as the checkout girl went into turbo overdrive, calling him a dirty old bastard, sometimes bringing in the manager. He had been banned from three Gravesend supermarkets in eighteen months.

"I'm putting 'Eat dirt and die' on my tombstone," he told Calvino a couple of years after he retired to Florida. "The human species is no different than a garden-variety earthworm. The dirt we eat is different dirt but it's dirt all the same. I left out something. Eat dirt, fuck, and die." Then Calvino's aunt, who lay on a recliner rubbing sunblock on her flabby upper arms on the other side of the screen door, shouted, "Mario, stop with that dirty talk. Vinny didn't come all the way to Miami to hear you talk dirty." The old man sniggered, relit his cigar, and under his stale, smoky breath, leaned over and grabbed Calvino's arm. He winked; it was the same wink Calvino remembered his uncle giving after he beat the RICO rap.

"Eat dirt, talk dirty, fuck, and die," said Uncle Mario.

"Mario, you're gonna need a tombstone as tall as the Empire State Building to get all those words on," said his aunt.

Calvino pushed the outside bell. Out of sight, behind the wall, the sound of large dogs, snarling, snapping, and barking, kicked up in the night. Another sound was partially masked by the gnashing of teeth. It was the sound of high-heeled shoes, clicking, the *clicky-click* growing more distinct on the driveway. Calvino had expected that the sound was of a pair of basic plastic flip-flops as a maid shuffled slowly to answer the door. But this woman was dressed to kill.

One hand rested on her hip and with the other she removed the joint from her lips and smiled. Her meter had clocked more than a few miles; but she was still roadworthy as she turned the last corner on her thirties. Somewhere in the fast lane she had acquired a discolored eyetooth and an African haircut of tight ringlets. Calvino imag-

110

ined that her picture was used by customs officers around the world as the profile of a drug smuggler. She smelled of Mekhong, and staggered a little, her wheeling grin forming a sexy pout as she looked Calvino up and down and picked a piece of weed off her outstretched tongue. She balanced one round hip against the door frame, her hand-rolled weed held between a couple of long, tapered fingers sporting red polished nails. The ash fell off. She laughed and swung her hand up, looking at the damage.

"Got a light?" she asked in English with a trace of an Italian accent.

Calvino flicked his Zippo, a long tongue of flame illuminating her face; she wore a set of false eyelashes that could have been used as minesweepers.

"Thanks," she said, folding her arms and blowing out smoke.

She had a tattoo of a black cat curled into a ball on her right shoulder and each of her fingernails was painted blue. She wore rings on each finger, and a small watch was set inside one of the rings. Her hair was frizzed and set with a reddish rinse.

"My name is Tom," she said.

He cracked a smile, thinking how "Tom" was a generic word for a *katoey*—transgender, third gender, a ladyboy—but this person appeared to possess one hundred-percent factory original female equipment.

"I've got an appointment with Khun Rolfo," said Calvino in Thai. "The Italian dog breeder."

"You mean the German dog breeder," she said, slurring her words.

"A German with an Italian name," said Calvino.

"His real name's Rolf. But I called him Rolfo years ago. Now he calls himself Rolfo. You see, he is an old friend of mine. I'm a married woman. My husband's Italian. Next month I fly back to Roma. You understand, Rolfo is an old, old friend. Just so you don't get the wrong idea."

"What kind of wrong idea?" asked Calvino.

"I didn't know there was more than one."

She smiled and licked her lips, with a wild-eyed, catlike expression that went with sharp claws and the loyalty to match. Tom drank him in like a saucer of warm milk, looking him over, up and down, and around, then stood to the side and gestured him in, throwing back with a flick of her hand some loose hair which had fallen over her face.

"You don't look or talk like one of his customers. You know, a dog person. People who don't mind the smell of dog shit," Tom said, gesturing like an Italian with her hands, the movement rattling a kilo of silver bangles like mobile wind chimes on both wrists.

"What do they look like?"

"Like Italians. Did I tell you my husband is an Italian?" she said, in Thai. "And my name is Tom?"

"You told me."

"It's okay, sometimes when I drink, I repeat myself."

"I have the same problem," said Calvino.

She threaded her arm through his, hugged him, and walked alongside. "You like to drink, too? Then you must be Italian, too."

"Half."

"Which half?" she teased.

The dog breeder's large Thai-style house was set back in a garden, with overgrown banana and mango trees, the odor of fruit rotting on the ground, and fifteen-foot stalks of bamboo arching over the drive. Lights shone through the windows of a room lined with bookshelves. To the right there was a walkway, in the shadows, and Calvino could make out the form of three large wire holding pens with coils of barbed wire on top: in the shadows they looked like the tiger cages the Vietcong used to warehouse prisoners. The barking echoed, split into deep, husky shards of noise, something so violent and coarse that it could only come from an animal trained to enjoy the kill. Slathering, frothing jaws with blood and foam mixed, he imagined.

"The dogs bark like this every night?" he asked.

"No good. Bark, bark, all the time. I tell Rolfo too much damn noise. It makes me fucking crazy. He bitches new girl comes here, she's scared and she won't come back. Rolfo, he says, never mind; no *kamoey* come to rob him. He has an old friend like me. Did I tell you Rolfo is German? I once lived in Germany. Before I lived in Italy. Next month I go back to Roma."

He took a second look at Tom. She was the woman his uncle Mario had been looking for to show his key chain, and never found. Tom had lost her Thainess; she didn't bother to use "Khun" before Rolfo or his name. As her long, painted fingernails clawed playfully at his sleeve, she stopped before a pool of light and pulled down the strap of her blue, pink, and white top.

112

"You see this tattoo?"

Calvino looked at the black cat.

"Rolfo says his dogs would eat me alive if they saw this tattoo. Why? Because a dog doesn't know it's a tattoo. I think Rolfo is bullshitting me. What do you think?"

"I'm in here, Mr. Daniels," said a German-accented voice from inside. "Daniels" was the name Calvino had used over the phone to make the appointment.

Then Rolfo was at the door holding a green bottle of Kloster beer. He was barefoot and knobby-kneed in a pair of shorts, and his badly faded blue Isan rice farmer's collarless shirt was half untucked, spilling over one side. "Take off your shoes and come inside."

"I have this feeling I've interrupted you in the middle of something," said Calvino.

"Never mind. I am always running a little late." Rolfo leaned out the open door and stuffed a five-hundred-baht note in Tom's shirt pocket. She pulled it out, looked it over, as if it might be counterfeit or a smaller bill he was passing off. Convinced it was a purple, she jammed it into the hip pocket of her jeans.

"Next week, Tom. Same time."

She brushed against Calvino and whispered. "You phone Tom at Star Hotel. Room ten."

"If I decide on a cat instead of a dog," said Calvino.

Tom threw him a playful punch and then disappeared along the walk and into the night with snarling dogs snapping jaws in the background; a moment later the side door slammed shut. Rolfo shouted in German at the dogs. On command, the barking stopped. From a nightmarish violent chorus of bloodcurdling yapping, he had created complete silence.

"German shepherds are very smart dogs," Rolfo said. "My queen bitch has the equivalent of a master's degree from obedience school. She's pretty good. You have two choices. You breed in discipline or you train a bitch in discipline. An untrained bitch will take advantage of you, Mr. Daniels."

"Unless you train her to understand German."

"That's a good joke. I like that one. And an untrained bitch only understands American. You must really see my queen bitch to appreciate the meaning of discipline."

"A master's degree?"

"She's very smart."

Rolfo Stadler's skull had the appearance of a deforested globe. His gray stubble was the kind that always looked two days old. The strong, craggy, pockmarked face put him in the range of an abused fiftyish. His narrow shoulders were slightly stooped. He rarely smiled as he spoke but when he did, along the edges of his puffy eyes spikes and canals ran like incisions left by a sharp instrument. A knife or a stick. He led Calvino into an air-conditioned room lined with books. On the coffee table were albums of German shepherds and pedigree papers in a neat pile. Rolfo took a cigarette from the table and lit it. A mat was rolled out a couple of feet away next to a fake fireplace. The room had the clammy smell of fresh sex.

"How long you stay in Thailand, Mr. Daniels?"

"Long enough to know it attracts breeders of all kinds."

"I think you liked Tom. Am I right about that?"

Calvino nodded. "She told me how she added the 'o' to your name."

Rolfo smiled. "One of my fiancées. She's a talented girl. You should try her sometime. But she needs more discipline."

From the pedigree papers on the table Calvino picked out the German word *Zuchter* in front of "Rolfo Stadler."

"What's this word?" asked Calvino, looking up from the paper.

The question distracted Rolfo.

"It's German for 'breeder.'"

"I've got another question. You wouldn't happen to know a Karl Stadler? Jurgen over on Sukhumvit gave the impression he might be staying with you."

Rolfo tensed in his chair, and then quickly snuffed out his cigarette.

"I thought you came to discuss my dogs, Mr. Daniels."

"I did. I'll get to that in a minute."

Calvino stayed in his chair, legs crossed, watching Rolfo Stadler. He tossed him a photograph of Hutton, Roland, and Karl from the Burmese border. Rolfo glanced at the photograph, quickly looking up at Calvino with an expression signaling confusion.

"Perhaps you could get to it now."

"Hutton was a neighbor of mine," said Calvino, seeing the nervous way Rolfo fingered his cigarette and figuring that a few facts might calm him down. "Jerry liked German shepherds. But he was probably here a couple of times so you already know that. Hutton and his girlfriend planned to breed shepherds. He had a business deal with Karl for one of your dogs. Only Hutton ended up dead. Maybe you had him killed. The newspapers say ninety percent of murders are a result of gambling debts or business conflicts. If Hutton started breeding dogs, then you would lose business."

"My uncle didn't kill Jerry," said Karl, appearing suddenly from a nearby door. Wearing a pair of workout shorts, he entered from behind where Calvino was seated. Calvino turned around slowly; no jerky or rough movements. Karl held a Colt .45 in both hands, but there was a slight wobble, like that of an old man or a junkie. He was even bigger than in the picture, thought Calvino.

"Karl, put away the large argument," said Rolfo. He used the same tone he had used with his queen bitch.

"A good description of a .45," said Calvino, staring at the barrel end.

"No," said Karl. His deltoid muscles tensed to the size of trolley car cables.

"Appears we have a breakdown in German discipline," said Calvino, sitting very still so as not to spook Karl.

"Discipline works better with animals," said Rolfo with a sigh, lifting himself up, stepping across the room, and holding out his hand, waiting for Karl to hand him the .45. Rolfo snapped his fingers. "Animals can be trained. Sometimes I think man is untrainable. Would you agree, Mr . . . ?"

"Calvino," said Karl. "His name is Vincent Calvino. He's a private eye who puts his nose into other people's business."

"I investigate other people who cause a problem for a client. You cause a problem, you invite someone like me to look at your business," said Calvino.

Discipline was more than a simple virtue; it was a necessity, thought Calvino. But what mostly passed in the name of discipline was an oppression to keep the herd going in one direction. It's what Dex had found out when he kept on attending pro-democracy meetings. Democracy was messy; it violated the old ways of maintaining discipline.

"How do you get lats like that, Karl? Those are painted on, aren't they?"

From the look on Karl's face—rage and frustration—Calvino guessed this was not one big happy family. Karl's size dwarfed his uncle's. The body mass was at least 25 percent larger than seemed suitable for the bone structure; the upper torso heaved in a kind of rolling action as Karl's anger reached a critical point. For some their body is their temple, but for Karl it was a bunker.

"Easy on the trigger," said Calvino.

"Why are you here?"

"Jerry Hutton was a friend of yours," said Calvino.

Rolfo kept his eyes on the .45.

"Some friend. He almost got me killed."

"And pointing a gun at me makes you feel safer?"

Something dispersed the fear and anger, and Calvino saw that Karl was relenting, though still keeping up a certain front. No one said anything for a moment. He studied Karl. His Mohawk hairdo was longer than in the photo, and the word "BERLIN" cut into the hair around his head looked as if weeds were taking it over as a new growth of hair blurred the letters. Karl hadn't been to a barber lately, thought Calvino. Still, his frame cast a dinosaur-like shadow against the wall, and he blinked his watery eyes, looking from his uncle to Calvino. Then the toughness drained from his expression; his chin dropped as Rolfo snapped his fingers again. Karl obeyed the order and lowered the Colt .45 into his uncle's hand. Calvino watched Rolfo stick the gun into his waistband.

"That's much better," said Rolfo, patting his nephew on the shoulder. He turned and looked at Calvino. "He wouldn't have hurt you," said Rolfo.

The transformation was immediate and radical. It was as if something in Karl had collapsed in defeat. One extremely washed-out-looking steroid warrior slid down the wall and onto the floor, his hands covering his face. Karl had been on the edge, on the run, not sleeping much, appetite gone ever since he had come back from the trip with Hutton. He knew something bad was going to happen. Then Hutton died. He held himself together by shooting steroid and heroin speedballs. It helped fight the constant fear of waiting. He sensed someone was hunting him, coming after him. The only uncertainty was how long it would take them to find him. He went everywhere with the .45; he slept with it as well. Out of the shadows, he figured, they would jump into his face. But he was ready. He had been ready for days, pulling iron two hours in the morning, two more hours in the afternoon, and injecting his steroids. His supply of Deca-Durabolin was running low.

He had switched over to Parabolin, saving the Deca for the big event. He wanted them to come. He had his training, his gun, and the dogs. It would take a commando team to take him out. Only he wasn't happy that it was Calvino. Not that he was surprised it was the private eye. Hutton had hero-worshipped Calvino.

"What do you want?" asked Rolfo. "You want money? Okay, no problem. I will give you money, then you go."

"You look like an intelligent man, Rolfo. Do I look like someone who has come to shake you down?"

Rolfo lit another Lucky Strike cigarette, the match shaking in his hand as he put the flame to the tobacco. Through a thick column of fresh blue smoke, Karl rose to his feet and edged around a table in the corner. As he passed Calvino, he glanced down at the photograph with Jerry and Roland. He had the shakes, as if he were coming down.

"I know who you are," said Karl, beads of sweat layered on his upper lip, his voice shaking. "Hutton talked about you, liked you a lot. You helped him get out of jail. Jerry told me about the Chinese guy and going to jail. He shouldn't have ever got involved with the film. The whole thing was stupid. I should have seen it. You know they killed him?"

Calvino nodded. "Yeah, I know."

Then Karl turned to his uncle Rolfo. "He's okay. This is my uncle Rolfo. Hey, I'm not really fucked up. It's just . . . you know." Karl's voice trailed off as his brain started firing blanks where there had been words.

Rolfo stared with the cigarette pursed between his lips, pretending not to notice as Karl pulled a syringe from the table drawer. He sat down hard on the floor, pulled up his right leg, leaned forward, and slowly slid the needle into the flesh between two of his toes. This was not a place police looked for tracks on a junkie. Karl removed the syringe and sighed. The effects of the heroin were almost immediate.

Rolfo stubbed out his cigarette. "You an American?" he asked, then saw the answer in Calvino's smile. An expression of old wounds and hatred appeared in Rolfo's eyes.

"You Americans bombed Munich, Frankfurt, and Berlin. Bombed and bombed. These scars on my face came when one of your bombs hit our neighbor's house. I was standing near the window. Whoosh, the glass blew out. I was seven years old in '44."

Calvino leaned forward, looking Rolfo Stadler straight in the eyes with a degree of concentration that set Rolfo back. "My mother was eighteen in '44," said Calvino. "She was Jewish and fortunately for her she lived in Brooklyn. Not so lucky were about nineteen, twenty of her relatives, my relatives, who went up an oven chimney as smoke. What I'm saying, Rolfo, we all carry some scars. So don't start feeling sorry for yourself or lose your perspective. Fifty years ago, we weren't bombing seven-year-old kids but a Nazi war machine. As far as I know, American pilots didn't set out to bomb seven-year-old kids. On the other hand, I had a nine-year-old cousin a concentration camp guard tossed into an oven. Your face got smashed up. But you're still here. Remember that. Now we've settled the last war, let's talk about Karl's war adventures along the Burmese border. If I had to guess, you have talked and relived World War Two more years than it lasted. Maybe Karl felt he needed a taste to prove he was a man. So he found a way to get himself in a battle zone. He tagged along with Jerry Hutton. He wanted to come back and say he understood how you felt in '44. Only it didn't quite work out the way he thought it would. Karl thought it was from a script someone had made up. He didn't understand until too late what really was planned to happen on the Moei River. But he had already got involved. Way in over his head. You see this picture I'm seeing? Jerry's dead. Roland's dead. The main thing is to see that Karl doesn't become a casualty of war."

"You can help me?" asked Karl. His voice quivered as if he were cold. But there was this hunting dog loyalty, snout-forward, pointing-to-meadows-and-fields aspect to Karl which Calvino hadn't seen at first. The kid had been hiding behind his bulk, the .45, the dogs, his uncle, but no matter how many controls he had constructed he didn't feel they were enough to keep away the men who had killed Hutton. Whatever was out there was beyond his control. Calvino didn't know how to answer Karl's question. But he understood the meaning of the question: Please help me control my fate which I can no longer pretend is in my hands. Someone like Colonel Hatcher would take Karl and three cages of German shepherds out with a single round from an RPG. They wouldn't see or feel anything.

"I can give you the answer you want to hear, or an honest answer. It's up to you."

Karl swallowed hard. "The honest answer, of course."

"That answer is I dunno if I can help you. But if you level with me: tell me what happened along the Moei River, how things really went down when this famous documentary got shot, then maybe—no promises—but maybe there is something I can do to figure a way out of this."

"That's the best you can offer my nephew?" asked Rolfo.

"It's either that, or he takes his chances hiding out with the queen bitch."

This made Karl laugh. "I see very little humor in this, Karl," said Rolfo, reaching for another cigarette.

"You're right, Rolfo. There's nothing funny about a bitch with the master's degree in obedience being edged out by an undisciplined bastard from Brooklyn."

ELEVEN

SLEEPING DOG MOUNTAIN

KARL'S father had devoted his life to working as a local civil servant in a small German town near Frankfurt. His mother was employed as a part-time school librarian. His parents had worked extremely hard after the war, managing to acquire a quiet, normal, and uneventful family life. His father said he'd had enough surprises to last a lifetime. The purpose of life, like the grandfather clock in the hallway, was the regular, predictable *tick-tock*. To Karl the *tick-tock* was like being condemned to death. Rolfo, his uncle, had, for as long as he could remember, fed him on a steady diet of travel and adventure on the road in Southeast Asia. His uncle told stories of elephants, wild monkeys, temples, jungle trails, witches, and magic amulets. He told of war and death, too. His father's younger brother Rolf (his father refused to call him Rolfo) talked for hours at the dinner table about life in the wild.

When Karl turned twenty-three years old he was working in a photography studio near Frankfurt. He was an apprentice sent to help photograph weddings, birthdays, and anniversaries. Late at night he hung out at emergency wards in local hospitals and photographed accident victims. People who had been shot or knifed. His brilliant photos of the late night carnage and violence largely went unnoticed. He taped the photos to the walls of his bedroom, listened to heavy-metal music, pumped iron, and shot up on steroids. He was doing heroin. He was planning something. He wasn't sure what. Maybe an escape. Sometimes, he'd get a 'roid rush, and think about killing himself. His uncle Rolfo was the first relative who had been to his studio apartment. His uncle had always delighted in shocking the family. Karl had a test waiting for him: his private collection of late night photos.

"Not bad," said his uncle with faint praise. But it was still praise.

"This one—a Turk—had been hacked to death by neo-Nazis," said Karl, pulling one of the photos off the wall.

Rolfo's expression didn't change as he looked at the photo. He handed it back to his nephew with a shrug.

"It's okay. But you should come to Bangkok. You will see photos much worse displayed in public. The body snatchers tape them in the window each day."

His uncle had passed the first level of security. Next Karl opened the drawer of a night table.

Rolfo stared at a half-dozen syringes which had rolled to the side. Rolfo watched Karl pick one out, prepare some white powder which he then injected. His uncle never acknowledged Karl's ritual-like preparation of the heroin or his injection. Instead he mechanically launched into his standard rap about exotic adventures—elephants, jungles, and hill tribes. Southeast Asia was the place where many, many things could be had in the pure form, his uncle said. This was what Karl had been waiting to hear. Rolfo didn't have a difficult time convincing his nephew that there were opportunities for him should he wish to settle in Bangkok. He would have the advantage of Rolfo's years of experience. But Rolfo's real motive was to find a successor for his German shepherd breeding business. He left out a few details, such as that the jungles had become office furniture, the elephants had become handbags, shoes, and belts, and the hill tribe women had become street beggars in ragged, dirty clothes. And that shared needles had spread AIDS rapidly through the heroin users in the city.

After eighteen months of working in the kennels, helping to train the dogs, Karl received a bonus from his uncle and immediately went out and bought a fire-engine red 400cc Yamaha motorcycle. Not long afterward, through word of mouth—a *farang* motorcyclist with rippling muscles stripped to the waist stuck out in Bangkok traffic jams—Karl became friends with Jerry Hutton, who had invited him to drink with several dozen other *farangs* who called themselves The *Farang* Angels. Each Friday, the members of the informal club met at Buckskin Joe's Village, a vile strip of outdoor hole-in-the-wall bars shoehorned under the Expressway. The strip was in a no-man's-land beside rail tracks marking the border between the Tonglor and Lumpini police districts. At the entrance was a large neon arch with a cowboy in a saddle on a bucking rodeo horse. After a few Fridays of drinking and whoring, Karl got Hutton to join him in a workout. Hutton showed him video footage he'd taken a year ago of civilians killed by land mines on the Cambodian border. They struck up a friendship based on photography, war, and body counts. Karl showed Hutton around Rolfo's house and grounds. A month after they met, Hutton fell in love with Joy, a fourteen-month-old German shepherd bitch. The name was Rolfo's idea. A Thai girl named Joy had been one of his fiancées. All the female dogs had been given bar *ying* nicknames.

"Uncle Rolfo gets weird with women," said Karl.

Hutton had looked up from patting Joy, staring at Karl's Mohawk haircut and tattooed biceps the size of tree trunks. "A little weird? I guess it's in the genes."

"How much does he want for her?" asked Hutton.

"With the discipline training, Uncle Rolfo wants thirty thousand, maybe forty thousand baht."

"How about a trade for something instead?" asked Hutton.

Karl thought for a moment. "Like what?"

"I take you across the vents into Burma. We can pick up shots on the battle scene near Sleeping Dog Mountain. The Karens are across the border in Manerplaw. They got the Burmese Army trying to kick their ass. And I've got an assignment to take some shots. What do you say? Isn't that why you said you came here? I mean, no offense to your uncle, but it doesn't look all that different from how you said your parents live in Germany. I see a middle-class house and lifestyle. But I don't see much adventure. Karl, if you're up to it, I can guarantee you some mean-assed armies, live bullets, jungle bombings, and rivers with bodies. Fresh kills. And sixteen-year-old Karen girls with AK-47s and M16s."

"Big talk."

"Only one way to find out," said Hutton.

He had baited the right hook. "Fresh kills" replayed in Karl's brain, giving him a little shudder of excitement. He brushed Joy's coat, thinking as he worked the fur.

"You ever seen anyone actually blown away?" asked Karl.

"It goes with the territory. So what do you say? You in?"

"Tell me more," said Karl as Joy nudged her nose under his arm and flipped it back on her head.

"This is secret information. Can I trust you?"

The muscles in his chest flexed. "Yeah, 'trust' is my middle name."

"You don't get it. I'm taking a personal risk. But I want the dog. Here's the deal: Your uncle Rolfo sells me Joy for ten thousand baht, and you can come along. Try your luck at being an aficionado. Or stay home with Uncle Rolfo and breed dogs."

❖

OVER pint mugs of beer at Der Braumeister, Hutton had showed the junior Nazi about twenty pages of a film script. The first page included the director's name plus "Confidential and Private" written in large font. On some pages there were only a few lines and the rest of the words had been blacked out with a Magic Marker. It wasn't clear why the copy had been censored or who had done the censoring. Hutton hadn't a clue, didn't really think much about it; making a copy on the sly had been a proud achievement.

EXT. DAWN BREAKING OVER THE BURMESE HILLS

ANGLE on young Karen soldiers marching along dusty path with rifles slung over their shoulders. Some are teenage girls. Others are singing and laughing.

EXT. DAY. KAREN BASE CAMP

ANGLE on wounded Karen soldiers on cots. More stretchers are brought into the cramped quarters. Doctors attach IV drips. Everywhere is the sound of human pain and suffering. The room is a primitive bamboo structure with broken glass in the windows. Flies and mosquitoes buzz round the bandaged faces of the wounded. The dying are pulled off cots and replaced with the new arrivals from the front lines.

EXT. DAY. THE MOEI RIVER SLICING ALONG THE THAI-BURMESE BORDER

ANGLE on several old wooden boats ferrying Karen soldiers into battle. C/U of the soldiers—boys and girls—huddling uneasily inside the boats. Their young, frightened, anguished faces look to the horizon. They clutch their weapons and look at the shoreline on the Burmese side, knowing that death waits for them there.

Karl Stadler quickly flipped through the balance of the script. "There's no dialogue. No one says anything? And, look at the page numbers—they're out of order. Page 14, then 27, 77, 43, and on, and on. What is this?"

"You don't know the business," said Hutton, proudly. "I'm the second unit—well, at least part of it. This is the script for the second-unit shoot. Producers and directors don't want the second unit wandering around Indian country with a full shooting script; it could get lost or stolen. Film scripts are handed out on a need-to-know basis. Later the director works with an editor to put everything together," said Jerry.

"How many days will it take?" asked Karl.

"We go on our bikes. We take three, maybe four days shooting. Then back to Bangkok. Then we can hang out with the film crew coming in from L.A. Young actresses, Karl. Alone in the big city. They're into bodybuilders. Double your action, double your fun. You in?"

Karl nodded. "I'm in."

"One thing. The producer is an old guy with an attitude about secrecy. He would go ballistic if he knew I had shown you the script."

"Let him. You think I'm afraid?" Deep shadows formed on Karl's face as he sucked in his cheeks, holding in his breath as his neck muscles popped out like special effects flesh.

"Jesse Tyler and the guys working for him are people even you wouldn't want to fuck around with."

Hutton couldn't tell Jesse Tyler that Karl was going to tag along, so he invented a backup story—Karl Stadler was a German freelance photo-journalist he'd bumped into on the shoot. The border area had journalists coming in and out all the time. Stadler liked the idea. He was no longer the nephew of a German shepherd breeder and son of a civil servant, but a war correspondent.

"I'll give the word to my uncle about Joy. Maybe ten thousand baht."

"Not maybe. I want a firm deal."

Karl Stadler watched the absolute concentration with which Jurgen worked the wooden handle, drawing down a pint of draft beer. He thought of how precisely and meticulously his uncle examined every detail of the dog breeding business. Dogs were his business. But Rolfo had a weakness in his knowledge—it was about drugs. Joy was his bitch to sell and he had set the price. But Karl had it in mind that the price could change if he placed Joy on a steroid treatment program. He figured injections of Deca-Durabolin in the hip would do the trick. There would be swelling. Rolfo would think the animal had a deformity. Karl would offer to take Joy to the vet for a checkup and X-rays. He had it all planned. How he would take out a purple banknote and lay it on the table. The vet's assistant—someone his own age—would write whatever Karl wanted on the report. Rolfo would discount the dog. Unload her for a bargain price. Like Karl, he hated defectives. The plan excited Karl because it was so perfect. But he wanted to string Hutton along a little.

"We can work something out. A good price, the right price." Karl saw that Hutton still wasn't satisfied.

"Ten thousand baht, or no go," said Hutton.

Karl wanted to see the fresh kills. That was one reason he had come to Thailand. He wanted a war zone littered with the dead. Instead he had a job cleaning up dog shit. This was a good day, he thought. The first day he had felt really good about anything for a very long time.

"It's a firm deal," said Karl.

They shook hands and Jurgen set down two pints of draft beer on their table.

❖

ONLY what Karl found on the front line was not in the script Hutton had showed him at Der Braumeister. That was no surprise, for a couple of reasons. Producers never put anything that might be even a little controversial into a script that needed approval for shooting from Thai authorities. And Hutton's brain was already wired to believe his mission was to shoot real war footage to give that edgy authenticity. Karl, in the back of his mind, wondered if Hutton had been caught up in a line of bullshit.

Roland May rolled up in a battered jeep with two Karen armed soldiers sitting in the back with a mortar tube. May was dressed in army field olive green. On his hip, he packed a Colt .45. His blond hair was tied back into a ponytail, and the late afternoon sun threw brilliant shards of light from his diamond earring. The jeep skidded to a halt, kicking up a wall of dust. May climbed out and walked over to Jerry Hutton, who squatted down with a wrench, working on his motorcycle.

"You Hutton?" asked Roland.

Hutton stopped working and looked up at the man standing above him. There was something in Roland's tone of voice that suggested anger and violence.

"I'm Hutton."

"You're one day fucking late, Hutton."

"Shit. My bike broke down."

"We've been waiting for you for twenty-four hours. And we don't like to be kept waiting. Not by you, Tyler, or anyone else. I've got a job to do. I want to get it done."

"Who the fuck are you?" asked Hutton, rising to his feet and clutching his wrench.

"Roland May, asshole."

"Tyler said you were an American."

"Born in Detroit."

"Shit, yeah, that explains the stupid Australian accent."

Roland May landed a sharp hooked elbow into Hutton's midsection, knocking him backward. He crashed hard into his motorcycle. He lay flat and stunned on top of his overturned bike. May walked over to him, glancing back at the soldiers, and thrusting a raised victory fist into the air. But the moment of glory was short-lived as Hutton kicked as hard as he could, catching Roland May square between the legs. Roland's eyes appeared to boil from the force of the kick, his knees buckled, and he tipped forward into the dirt.

A dusty yellow pickup truck with a bashed left door pulled up alongside the jeep. The driver rolled down the window and stuck out his head. Seated next to him was Karl Stadler.

"Boys, boys. What's going on?" There was no mistaking the nasal American voice. He was out of the truck and crossing over to where Roland May, rising to his knees, had unholstered his Colt .45.

"Roland. Put the fucking gun down, Roland. Before I shoot you in the balls." He nodded at Karl, who climbed out of the truck and slammed the door.

"Who are you?" Hutton looked away from the Colt .45 and saw a late fortyish American with short-cropped pepper gray hair and a broad, friendly grin. He was muscled like someone who had been an all-American halfback two and a half decades earlier. And he dressed like someone who had beamed in from the '60s: Hawaiian shirt, gray slacks, white socks, and penny loafers. A boomer, thought Hutton. One of those guys who had never left college in his dress or speech. Someone whose eyes turned wet when they heard the Beatles or other dinosaur music.

"Mike Oxley," he said, extending his hand and placing himself between May and Hutton.

Oxley was packaged with a jock's winning smile, a head coach's ability to demand respect, and a team owner's authority to control the situation. He cocked his head to one side, whispering, "Come on, we need a demonstration of team spirit." Roland jammed his Colt .45 into his holster.

Stepping back from May, Oxley addressed all of them. "Now, that's better. We are working together, boys. A team has to pull together. So let's get started, okay, guys? Tyler wants this second-unit film in Bangkok. And fast. You know how directors are? Pressure, pressure twenty-four hours a day from the money guys. Besides, I want to be in Bangkok myself. This place makes me nervous. The Burmese are about to launch a new offensive. The health conditions leave a lot to be desired. Even the mosquitoes are dying from malaria."

As Oxley spoke Hutton tried not to catch Karl's eye. Hutton thought this was an old guy's way of trying to be funny. He wondered exactly what story Oxley was able to get out of Karl. The German's mind sometimes misted over; he forgot things. Maybe it was drugs—Hutton didn't know or care. He was worried, though, that Karl might have blown the whole assignment. There was something in the way Karl hung back, staring at the ground, which told him that something was wrong. Hutton thought it was better to avoid eye contact with Karl until they had a chance to talk. Only one thing: Oxley wasn't going to give them that opportunity. It was as if Oxley was waiting for Roland or Hutton to comment on the size and haircut of the *farang* who had climbed out of the pickup.

"Who's the freak?" asked Roland, gesturing to Karl, whose huge arms and chest were visible through the photojourno vest.

"Dustin Hoffman's brother," said Oxley.

"Why has he got 'BERLIN' carved into his hair?"

"My name's Karl," he said, looking directly at May.

"It fucking talks, too," said May.

"Karl flagged me down and said there was a *farang* up the road having mechanical problems with his motorcycle. And I said to myself, That's got to be one of my boys."

"Oxley, this is getting complicated. The plan was for one guy. Now we have a crowd. And I don't like crowds," said Roland May, brushing the dirt off his trousers.

"Crowds. I count one, two, three, four. Yeah, four of us. I wouldn't call that a crowd."

"Tell that to the Burmese snipers," said Roland. "If they stand on their toes, they can see Karl from Rangoon."

It was the first joke Oxley had ever heard May crack. Humor was a dangerous sign; it translated into a loss of authority and command in the field. Laughter destroyed discipline.

The Moei River was more than two hundred meters away. "Fifty bucks to any Burmese sniper who can hit you standing here. Three months playing merc-slash-Rambo has turned you into a crazy warrior, my friend. After twenty-five years you see things a little differently." Oxley was hitting at him hard. A right hook to the ego. He slapped an arm around Hutton.

"You look like you could use a beer, my boy."

Jerry flashed a smile. "Yeah, that would be real good."

"Then get in the pickup. Don't worry about your bike; Roland and his friends will load it in the back. Then I'll arrange to get it repaired tomorrow. A second-unit AD has to be a jack-of-all-trades, Jerry."

As they drove on the dirt road toward the base camp, Oxley chewed gum and tapped his fingers on the steering wheel of the Honda pickup. Hutton felt nervous as he squeezed in between Oxley, who was driving, and Karl, who rode shotgun.

"So you two guys know each other in Bangkok?" asked Oxley.

Neither Hutton nor Karl knew what to say, or who should go first. After a long moment, Oxley stopped chewing his gum, and glanced around at them. "I saw you on Soi Cowboy," Hutton said.

"Yeah, I was sitting on a stool outside the Lamb and Kitten Bar," Karl said.

"But I never actually met you until today, when you stopped to help me with the bike," said Hutton.

"I think the world is very small," Karl said in stiff English.

Oxley grinned. "Stop the clowning, guys. So you're friends. I mean, who gives a ripe shit? You think I'm gonna rat on you to Jesse Tyler? What for? When I come down to Bangkok maybe we can go for a beer. Where you staying, Karl?"

"Khao San Road. Charlie's Guest House," he replied.

"I have an apartment off Sukhumvit," said Hutton.

"In '69, Bangkok was Phetchburi Road." Oxley spoke with an easygoing, friendly manner, as if he went back years and years with those listening to him. "You slept, drank, ate, and fucked on Phetchburi Road. You know, when I was in 'Nam, I was interviewed by journalists far more than I was shot at by Charlie. I was stationed in Saigon. It was a great, perfectly ordered city. All the women in the bars; all the men in the jungle getting their asses shot off. But that's the past, and tomorrow, as they say, is another day. Let's say we get started about six."

"Is that asshole coming?" asked Hutton.

Oxley threw his head back, laughed, and bumped the steering wheel with the heels of his hands. "You worried about that dickhead? He's a teddy bear once you get to know him."

"What's with his fake Aussie accent?"

Oxley shrugged. "It matches his fake diamond earring. Guys like him last about three months before a real sniper gives them a nugget-sized hole in the head. Figuring the averages, May's living on borrowed time. So he's uptight, edgy. A little crazy. I saw it all the time in 'Nam."

"I thought you spent the war in Saigon bars," said Hutton.

He didn't reply for several seconds. "I got out in the field once or twice," said Oxley. He was thinking Hutton was sharp, a smart kid. Karl he hadn't figured out. Karl reminded him of some of the guys in 'Nam with bulked-up bodies. Guys who thought muscles made them indestructible. That they were immortal. Those guys, when they got hit, always looked surprised; and they died with that shocked, "You gotta be fucking joking" expression on their faces.

Hutton was thinking how much Oxley seemed to live in the past, an ice-age warrior who hadn't noticed the world had thawed out. Oxley looked a million miles away. It was an old guy look that reminded him of his father nursing some memory of when he was young.

"Those field guys during the war, they ever come down with fake Aussie accents?"

Oxley smiled, cranked his head to the side, and flashed Hutton a wink. "One or two of the military intelligence boys would get a sudden attack. Just before they perished in the jungle."

❖

TWO days later, Hutton was asleep under a mosquito net when Oxley stuck his head in the door of the shack.

"Rise and shine, Jerry."

Hutton groaned, opened an eye. In the corner, Karl fooled with his camera equipment, sitting upright on his bedroll and loading film. "Weren't you the guy who got us drunk at the second-unit wrap party? Or whatever you called it?" said Hutton.

"I like second-unit wrap parties. No one's looking over your shoulder. But I have a message from Tyler. Some twenty-three-year-old asshole who has never been outside of L.A. was brought in to polish the script."

"I thought you polish gems," said Karl.

"Very good, Karl. But this is Hollywood talk for fucking around with someone else's script that ten other guys have already gang-banged to show the boys that your dick is bigger than everyone else's. This new guy belongs to the distributor, though, and if Tyler tells the twenty-three-year-old asshole to go fuck himself—which mind you is what he should do—then the distributor might kill the deal. No distributor, no money; no money, no film. So Tyler has to let the kid do his thing. Tyler caved in on some action footage. But— and this is a big 'but'—on the basis we can get it without anyone getting their ass shot off. Are you with me?"

"You want combat footage."

"Tyler is satisfied; the fucking distributor wants combat footage. So I checked with Karen intelligence and told them our problem. They have information on some troop movements."

"I am not getting paid to get my ass shot off," said Hutton.

"Tyler will take care of that. He said you had his word on that."

Hutton thought about it, glanced over at Karl, who took several shots of Hutton and Oxley. "Crossing the vents," said Karl.

"Okay, okay," said Hutton.

"You ever do any duck hunting, Jerry?"

Hutton shook his head.

"The theory is simple enough. You build a blind along the edge of a pond, float a few decoys, hide, and wait for the ducks to circle overhead and land, and then you open fire. Roland has set up a kind of 'duck blind' on the other side of the river. I told Tyler we would stake out the clearing for a couple of days. If Jerry Hutton sees no ducks, then we head for home. And Tyler gets the twenty-three-year-old asshole from L.A. to haul his ass up Sleeping Dog Mountain to film what Tyler tells him he needs. You understand, we are all pulling together to make this film something we can be proud of. Otherwise, what's the point?"

"I've been to Sleeping Dog Mountain before," said Hutton, pulling on his jeans. "Why don't we go there? I can get some good stuff. Incoming. The shells knock chunks of rock off the mountain. The Karen scramble off the other side."

Oxley held up his hand, lips closed tightly.

"Next trip I'll let you take me up Sleeping Dog Mountain; I know it's a rite of passage. But for this film the answer is no. Like I explained, Karen intelligence has tipped us about some Burmese troop movements. Maybe you can film an ambush. Only one thing: Whatever comes, you go with it. Just roll the film. Get the action down no matter what the hell you see happening. You got that?"

"Fresh kills," said Karl, slamming the back shut on his camera.

"Rambo, you stay put."

Karl flashed an angry look at Hutton. That hadn't been their deal.

TWELVE

COVERT UNIT

"DAMAGED." That was the word Rolfo had used to describe Joy and her hip condition. He showed Calvino the vet's report, confirming a rare muscle formation disease. It was probably better to destroy the dog; but his nephew had insisted the dog be sold to his friend. Then the friend had died. Calvino saved Joy from a lethal injection. Karl had no intention of telling his uncle about the deal he had cooked up with Hutton. It was pointless. Karl was glad Calvino had taken the dog; every time he saw Joy, he felt guilt, and she was a constant reminder of how bad things had gone ever since he met Hutton. The American had been bad luck; so had the dog.

Her ears stood erect, she cocked her head to one side and then shifted it to the other, and her mouth closed until the last moment, when she snapped a mosquito out of a midair flight pattern. Joy's jaws clamped shut, then opened again, the tip of her wet tongue curling out of her mouth. She scooted forward, nuzzled her large black snout into Calvino's naked shoulder. The wet nose pressing into his flesh gave him a shiver.

"You do that?"

"Do what?" asked Kiko.

"Joy, sit."

"I thought she was trained."

"She is," said Calvino. "But she likes affection."

"Who doesn't?"

Joy lifted her head, backed away, and sat erect, watching as Calvino kissed Kiko, running his lips down her neck. He opened one eye—

there was Joy, her alert eyes watching his every move. Waiting for Calvino's command. Calvino worked his tongue down to Kiko's nipples. He tried to concentrate. But he was thinking, his tongue on Kiko's nipple, that Joy had not moved since he had given her the command for "sit." She had grown bored, he thought. Part of her enormous head overhung the side of the bed as she exhaled a steady stream of bad breath across his pillow. For a mouth-breather she was a class act, thought Calvino.

"What are you doing?" asked Kiko, feeling his distracted touch.

"You don't know?"

"You're looking at the dog."

"I saw her head."

"How can we make love if you're looking at the dog?"

He didn't have an answer. Despite himself, he was dog-proud. He liked looking at Joy. She wasn't like the dogs in the soi or like the mutts he remembered from Brooklyn. Brooklyn street gangs and drug dealers had gone into designer Pit Bulls and Dobermans. Not so much designed as psychologically trained to kill—dogs turned into lethal weapons. He stared at Joy, wondering what Rolfo had imprinted inside her brain. How much damage had he inflicted to shape the will of the dog? Calvino locked eyes with the Joy. She didn't seem any more damaged than he was. He smiled to himself, thinking that assessment was paying Joy no favor. She had been trained for a job, and conditioned to execute commands without question or argument. She was the perfect employee. Calvino couldn't imagine Joy being called an Italian or French shepherd. She was German. As Rolfo would say, "A furry big argument. No need for bullets."

Kiko rolled on her side, pulling the sheet around her. She propped on an elbow and locked eyes with Joy. The dog cocked her head to the left.

"Hello, competition," she said to Joy. "Other women are jealous of Thai women. That a woman can deal with. But a German shepherd . . . I'm not so sure."

Calvino slipped his hand under the sheet and ran his fingers over the curve of her ass.

"Last life what animal were you?" she asked.

Calvino's hand stopped. "A sea turtle. The kind that lives six hundred years at the bottom of the sea."

"But sea turtles breathe air," said Kiko.

"So I discovered when a Japanese trawler hauled me up in a net."

"You probably fed a lot of Japanese."

"Or was fed to their dogs."

"Why did you come back this life as Vincent Calvino?"

"I got tired of being wet. Six hundred years is a long time in the shower."

"Sometimes you can be funny."

"Last life what kind of animal were you?"

Kiko grinned. "That's easy. An earthworm."

"You're stealing Uncle Mario's line."

"Did he have 'Eat dirt and die' carved on his tombstone?"

Calvino pulled Kiko on top of him. Joy growled and barked once, then twice. "Stop," said Calvino in a sharp voice. Joy stopped barking. Then he turned to Kiko. "I didn't mean you. We were talking about my uncle Mario. The man who coined, 'Eat dirt, talk dirty, fuck, and die.'"

"Your aunt told him to 'Stop!'" She used the command tone, watching the German shepherd's head twist to one side, then the other.

"You're right. But Uncle Mario won in the end."

"What makes you think that?" asked Kiko, reaching over and stroking Joy's neck.

"Uncle Mario was reborn as a sea turtle eating small fish off New Zealand. Floating near the surface. Trying to get laid. Missing only one thing from his last life."

Kiko wrinkled her nose. "Yes."

"His old 'Stud Service' key chain." Calvino started kissing Kiko's neck, but she pulled herself away.

"I can't do it while Joy's watching."

Calvino looked at Joy, who sat less than an arm's length away.

"Joy, close your eyes," he said.

Joy blinked and kept on staring at Kiko and him.

"They're not closed," said Kiko.

"If you met Rolfo, her trainer, then you wouldn't risk closing your eyes either." Calvino swung his legs over the side of the bed and called Joy into the living room. He rolled out a mat, and pointed. Joy cautiously moved forward, circled the mat twice, then lay down, her eyes waiting for Calvino's next command. He patted the dog, then rose up and walked over to the screen door. He stepped onto the balcony where he had stood with Hutton and saw the lights in the slum where Kwang and her relatives lived. Calvino had custody of the dog which Hutton had dreamed would change their lives. Joy was their escape from the slum to a better life outside of Bangkok, and once they crossed to that other world, everyone would be warm and safe. Like the words in the song Kiko had given him. Safe and warm was always just across the way, a ray of light and nothing more. But what did he know? he thought. He was an old guy in Hutton's brave new world where everyone aspired to become an escape artist.

❖

CALVINO remembered how the *Lucky Charms* script had been laid out. Tyler kept a stack of three copies in his suite. The scripts had blue covers like a book but the inside wasn't anything like a book. There were shorthand expressions like "POV" for point of view, "C/U" for close-up, and "INT." for interior. A short description of the scene—what the characters were doing, like driving a car or running down a street—was followed by dialogue. The effect was more like reading sheet music and deciding in your own mind what the music would sound like. Calvino sat at his office desk in front of his word processor. Joy sat a couple of feet away, her eyes never leaving Calvino. At the top of the page he had written *War Crimes*. He had phoned L.A. and for the last five minutes had sat listening with the phone wedged between his ear and his shoulder.

"A film treatment is the story," said Tommy Loretti. "Then once you get the green light on the treatment, you go to script. Or if they say 'pass,' then you may never go to script. Or you can just go ahead and write the goddamn script. There are a hundred ways to do this, Vinny. And at two bucks a minute long distance, you are gonna run through a film budget before you know what you're doing."

"So you're saying, I should write it?"

"I'm saying, this is crazy. Someone already has rights to the Hutton story."

"But this is a better story," said Calvino.

"What's 'better' mean? I'm saying, you are gonna get your ass sued by Jesse Tyler for starts. Remind me, didn't you use to practice law? Graduate number one in your law school class? You've been living in Thailand too long. In case you forgot, in the States you can't steal intellectual property."

Calvino laughed.

"You think that's a laugh line? Forget it."

"I'm adding a part for a dog." Calvino looked over at Joy on the floor.

"Rin Tin Tin is dead."

"So is Hutton," said Calvino. "Tommy, I need a favor. After I finish the treatment of *War Crimes* I need your help."

"For Christ sakes at least change the title."

"*Covert Unit.*"

"They'll sue you for infringement."

"Believe me, Tommy. These guys aren't gonna sue me."

"Since when did you go into the film business?"

"I've been thinking about it. I'm going to do a treatment for *Covert Unit* and send it to Colonel Sam Hatcher, Pacific Command, Hawaii."

"What's an army guy supposed to do with it?"

"He's into making films."

"You don't know dinkshit about the film business, Vinny. The army? You're nuts. Or are you reading *Catch-22*?"

"Just help me out on this one, Tommy."

Covert Unit
A Treatment
by
Vincent Calvino

EXT. JUNGLE. DAY

The midday heat shimmers off the river as the surface breaks with a water buffalo slipping into the mud to cool down. A thick canopy of jungle foliage obscures the far bank. There are jungle birds and monkeys along the tree line. On the Thai side of the river there is a C/U of OXLEY and HUTTON near a trench. HUTTON is all sweaty, and setting up his camera equipment. OXLEY is dressed like an Atlantic City hustler. Two Burmese students climb out of the trench with shovels and join a third student who is kneeling almost out of sight in the elephant grass. A breeze bends the grass. Each of the students is dressed in combat gear.

OXLEY

We want you guys positioned about twenty meters ahead. See that clearing? There's where we do the shot.

HUTTON

Are you directing the shot?

OXLEY

Tyler wants authenticity. An action piece. You wanna get your ass shot off going across the river?

HUTTON

I thought the writer wanted documentary-like footage?

OXLEY

Does it really matter, Hutton?

ANGLE ON HUTTON as he slaps film into the camera. He looks at the students and then over at OXLEY and shrugs.

HUTTON

So let's do it.

OXLEY

That's what I wanna hear, Hutton. Teamwork. Cooperation. Come over to where I'm standing. See where my feet are? You stand here. Okay. You over there. And now, you follow me. There. Don't move. When the bad guys arrive I want you to look scared. Real shit. Terror, fear, hatred. You have to make it look, sound, and feel real. You'll get roughed up like in the movies. You're going to be a star. You'll get fan letters from girls who will send you naked pictures with their phone numbers. One more thing, Jerry.

HUTTON
>Yeah, Mr. Oxley.

OXLEY
>We've got some neat special effects. Blood and shit. Don't let it freak you out. Sometimes special effects look more real than the real thing.

CUT TO:
Two Burmese soldiers crouch, looking around nervously as they enter the clearing. One is smoking a cigarette. They both look tense as they shake hands with the students. OXLEY, an arm wrapped around ROLAND MAY's shoulder, walks him over, talking to him like a coach to a quarterback.

ANGLE ON OXLEY and MAY as they walk out of the shot.

OXLEY
>When I say action. I want you guys to pretend that you have been captured by the Burmese. And the Burmese, as you know, never take prisoners.

HUTTON
>Can you move them over about ten feet to the left. I'm picking up shadow lines.

ANGLE ON OXLEY clapping his hands and shooing the students and two Burmese officers over to the left.

OXLEY
>How's this, Jerry?

C/U ON HUTTON looking through the camera.

HUTTON
>Okay. That's far enough.

OXLEY
>You still got the river in the shot?

HUTTON
And a water buffalo.

CUT TO:
Aerial shot of AWAC military operations plane in flight.

CUT TO:

INT. of AWAC. COLONEL HATCHER is seated at the communication center in the rear of the aircraft. He is wearing earphones. From the window it is a blue-green carpet of jungle and mountains. COLONEL HATCHER looks at his watch and marks time. As the secondhand hits twelve, he presses a panel of buttons.

HATCHER
Fox-trot 1, do you read me? This is Tango 8.
There is a crackle of static from the radio communication as he waits for a reply.

OXLEY
Tango 8, this is Fox-trot 1. We are ready to dance. Authorize or cancel mission.

ANGLE ON OXLEY beside a jeep with ROLAND MAY seated on the passenger side. Ahead of them, HUTTON is stretched out near the camera. In the clearing, the students are squatting in a semicircle, looking bored and slapping mosquitoes. The two Burmese officers are alone, off to the side, tense, not smiling, clutching their rifles.

HATCHER
Fox-trot 1. Proceed to dance. Do you copy?

OXLEY
Affirmative, Tango 8.

CUT TO:

INT. AIRCRAFT. DAY

HATCHER takes off his earphones. He sips from a West Point mug with steam rolling over the top, and looks out the window at the jungle terrain below and wrinkles his nose.

HATCHER
Too much sugar. It leaves a bad aftertaste.

EXT. AIRCRAFT. DAY

ANGLE ON AWAC aircraft with American military markings on the wings and tail. The aircraft banks to the right and disappears into the clouds.

CUT TO:

INT. JUNGLE CLEARING. DAY

C/U of Burmese soldier, 22nd Division patch sewn onto the shoulder of his uniform, pistol-whipping one of the students. Blood flows from the boy's nose and he spits out blood and teeth. An officer kicks his boot into the student who had fallen to his knees. Next the officer slowly lifts his .45 service pistol from his side holster, extends his arm, aims, and fires into the student's forehead. The student's head jerks back, and he collapses; the blood squirts from the wound and onto the ground. The soldiers stand with rifles held in the firing position, waiting for orders from the Burmese major—this officer, also of the 22nd Division, wears a gold star on each olive green epaulet. The officer nods in the direction of another student.

CUT TO:

POV OXLEY, who is watching HUTTON film the scene. He turns to ROLAND MAY.

OXLEY
(*Sound of AK47 rounds*) That's one down. Two to go.

CUT TO:

POV HUTTON, looking through the camera lens. HUTTON zooms in for a C/U on second student who is savagely beaten and kicked by the Burmese soldier. He looks terrified. The camera zooms in on the white death mask of the dead student, and as the camera pulls back the remaining students cry and plead for their lives. The Burmese officer gives a sharp command to fire and the soldier's rifle cracks and a second student drops hard into the dirt and is still. A soldier moves forward and rams the toe of his boot into the dead student's face. There is no reaction. The soldiers smile.

C/U of the last student on his knees, his hands raised above his head as if trying to surrender, then he slowly joins his hands into a *wai*, a gesture of grace, respect, and devotion. The Burmese officer screams at him in Burmese and then pumps three shots into the boy's face.

OXLEY (VO)
     Hutton, hold the shot of the guy eating. Pull back when the other soldiers come within five feet. (*beat*) Fox-trot 1 to Tango 8, do you read me?

HATCHER (VO)
     I read you, Fox-trot 1.

OXLEY (VO)
     We've got a take. Oscar-winning performances.

HATCHER
     Good job, Fox-trot 1. Over and out.

POV HUTTON as the camera follows the officer lighting a cigarette and sitting in the clearing. He looks satisfied. Before him are the clump of bodies in the clearing. The Burmese soldier opens a tin of fruit with a knife, and together the two men eat pineapple slices as if they were on a picnic. A minute later, the soldier and officer are on their feet and have been joined by another half-dozen soldiers, who look at the bodies, joking, laughing, and rolling the bodies over, looting the dead of watches, wallets, amulets.

ANGLE ON OXLEY laying down the radio set and walking through the tall elephant grass, where HUTTON continues to shoot.

OXLEY

Cut. Pack up. We're out of here, Jerry. Let's go.

HUTTON

(*Pushing a path through the elephant grass. He hands equipment to OXLEY.*)
Those were some special effects.

OXLEY

Go, go. We just got a call on the radio. Karen intelligence reports a Burmese patrol is moving this way. We gotta move, and quick.

ANGLE ON HUTTON climbing into the jeep behind ROLAND MAY. OXLEY is riding shotgun. He's bouncing up and down, happy as a pig in clover. He has the camera and is unloading the film.

HUTTON

What are you doing, man?

OXLEY

This film goes to Bangkok tonight. By plane.

C/U ON HUTTON, who looks frustrated, disturbed, but says nothing as the jeep passes along a jungle trail.

HUTTON

Bullshit. No one takes my film.

C/U ON ROLAND MAY finding OXLEY'S eyes in the rearview mirror and giving a knowing glance.

OXLEY

Hey, Jerry. We're making a film here. You did a good job. I'm letting Tyler know you came through in the crunch. That means more work. So lighten up.

CUT TO shot of two motorcycles at full throttle cutting through a path in the jungle.

C/U ON HUTTON and then of KARL STADLER, who catches up; they slow down, riding side by side.

HUTTON
Fresh kills. It was something you had to see, Karl. Oxley said it wasn't real. He said special effects look more real than the real thing.

KARL
You believe Oxley?

HUTTON
No way. Those guys were dead. I've seen dead people. I know what real blood looks like.

KARL
What are you going to do?

HUTTON
Fuck. I dunno. Maybe talk to Tyler.

KARL
Tyler works with Oxley. How does that help anything?

HUTTON
Maybe it doesn't. You tell me. What would you do?

KARL
Leave it alone. Keep out of their face.

HUTTON
They offed those guys. Three of them. Just like that.

KARL
Shit. I'm in this too.

HUTTON

That's what I'm trying to get through your thick skull. Why in the fuck did he bring me into this?

KARL

I dunno except what you promised in Bangkok. About seeing action. Crossing the vents. I haven't seen anything.

HUTTON

Maybe that will keep you alive. Something bad is happening that Oxley's not talking about. I'm part of it. And I'm scared, Karl.

KARL

They aren't gonna fuck with you. Not with me around.

HUTTON

Tell me one thing, Karl: Do steroids make you bulletproof?

❖

TOMMY LORETTI made that kind of noise that comes from the throat of a driving instructor one icy morning when his student jams the brakes, sending the car fishtailing into the oncoming lane of traffic.

"Nooooooooo." Calvino got a howl of despair over the phone in reply to his question as to whether Tommy liked the treatment.

"It's all wrong," said Loretti after a moment.

"Like what?"

"Everything. For a start, you've got no hero."

Calvino thought about that for a second.

"But there isn't one," said Calvino.

"Maybe in the private dick business. But in Hollywood without a hero you've got nothin'. Tyler went for *War Crimes* because he knew Hutton was a hero working people could relate to. The kid was someone you can root for. Relate to. Give a fuck about. Hutton isn't a hero in this. He's a sucker."

"What else?"

Loretti sighed. "All the dialogue between two guys on motorcycles. You ever been on a motorcycle in the jungle? I haven't but I can't believe you can have talking heads. It's like Bing Crosby and Bob Hope on the road. Besides, Vinny, you're wasting your time. You don't have a story."

"How can I? The story's not finished. It's still happening. I don't know how it finishes until it finishes."

An associate came into Loretti's office and he put Calvino on the speakerphone.

"Here's how it works. You figure out the beginning, middle, and end. You write them down. One, two, three. Act One, Act Two, and Act Three. It's like throwing rocks in a lake. Act One you watch the guy throw the rock. Act Two you watch the rock splash into the water. Act Three you see the ecological damage of his action, he repents, runs for Congress as a Green. But you. All you've got is the splash. People would ask where did it come from? Outer space?"

"I'm working on that part," Calvino said, and hung up. He hated being put on a speakerphone with people he didn't know listening to the conversation.

THIRTEEN

JAO MAE THAPTHIM

An attractive *farang* woman with long, white-blonde hair and pale blue eyes danced, dipping and turning, making ritualistic-like movements in an area beside a spirit house. She brushed the end of her red, gold, and white silk wraps over the bucking head of a goat wild-eyed with fear. From her left a bearded shaman stabbed the air with a long-bladed knife. The steel edge flashed a circle of reflected light, cutting the spirit house in half. A spiritual mugging. The *farang* woman stopped dancing, raised on her tiptoes, and kissed the blade, taking her time as her tongue slid down the shaft. She hurried through the shadows, then suddenly stopped dead in her tracks as a long-tail boat roared past on the opposite side of a four-meter-high chain-link fence. A deafening noise splintered the silence. It came from a V-8 engine which powered the propeller blades through the narrow *klong*.

"Cut," said Tyler, who wore an L.A. Dodgers baseball cap with the bill facing toward the back of his head. He waved his hands. "Cut the shot," he yelled.

Carol Hatcher turned around, covered her ears with her hands, and screamed, "I fucking hate this scene."

The engine sounds had ruined the scene. But Tyler could read his leading actress's lips. With open arms he approached her, gave her a hug, and stroked her cheek with the back of his hand.

They stood in front of an ancient teak spirit house at the front of which was an altar flanked by two small, weathered wooden elephants and festooned with jasmine flowers and pink and white lotus. Smoke coiled from the burning incense sticks and a dozen lighted candles.

146

Rising to the right and above the altar was a massive unsheathed Styrofoam black penis which pointed at the night sky like a Patriot missile. It was in the five-meter range, higher than the chain-link fence. This physiologically correct penis—with every vein etched in vivid detail and a hood like an agitated cobra's head—made a visually impressive, warlike cone on a launch pad.

The script called for Carol Hatcher to dance in a long transparent white silk scarf, light the ritual candles, embrace this symbolic male structure. She had lit the candles seven times. But somewhere during the scene, Tyler had always stopped the action. This time she had danced within range of the penis and was about to embrace the structure when the long-tail boat screamed past on the *klong* no more than ten meters away. She had pounded the penis with her fist, denting the Styrofoam. Circling around each of the penis props, the set designer had red, brown, pink, yellow, green, and gold silks, and the prop man moved one of them to cover the holes.

"I can't stand the stink in that dick garden," said Carol Hatcher, turning and marching through the set. She punched another hole into the penis, a perfect right jab. It gave her pleasure. She stared at the indentation left by her knuckles, then walked away.

"Carol, no one likes the smell, darling," said Tyler, chasing after her into the parking lot.

"She punches it again, the dick's gonna fall in the *klong*," said the prop man, adjusting another silk scarf to cover the latest piece of damage inflicted by Miss Hatcher.

"He can't talk that way to me," said Carol Hatcher. "He has no right."

"Take a hike, Eric." Tyler pulled the prop man to the side, and he soon disappeared, shaking his head.

"Vampire bitch," he said under this breath as he walked off the set.

"Carol, it's okay, let's set up the scene again." He saw her crinkle her nose as she stared toward the *klong*. "I know the smell is bad. Don't lick the knife blade this time; it's not working. Just brush your lips against it. Not tongue. Lips are reverence. And tongue is . . . well, is something not exactly spiritual."

It was as if she hadn't been listening to him. She was trapped in a world in which the nose was overwhelmed.

"Jesse, that's not just any smell. Nothing in the world has ever smelled like this. Bad liver. Rotten eggs. Dog shit. Where in L.A. have you ever smelled anything remotely like that river? No sewer in the world smells like that. It's like breathing acid fumes. My face is breaking out. My eyes are bloodshot. I'm soaked in sweat. And this heat is driving me crazy."

Tyler turned to the American and Thai crew. "Crew, listen up. We're taking a ten-minute break. Everyone back in ten minutes."

No one among the crew objected. The tension drained off as Carol Hatcher left the set.

A hot breeze swept off the *klong* behind Jao Mae Thapthim—a ritual garden which Carol Hatcher had aptly translated as a kind of "garden of dicks." Local legend was that the garden was a spirit house for a spirit which lived in a *sai* tree. The spirit had renown throughout Thailand for bestowing fertility on women who came to Jao Mae Thapthim and paid homage to the spirit with a certain kind of offering—flowers, yes; incense, yes—but this spirit wished to be honored with reproductions of the male sexual organ. In a cramped space located behind a garden shed, fenced off from the *klong* on one side and from a parking lot in front, there was an overgrown, haphazardly maintained garden. Tyler's film set crew had taken photos of the garden, made computer models, run storyboards based on the garden. They rearranged certain elements Tyler had announced were the heart of Jao Mae Thapthim.

Believers—and they were from everywhere in the world—arrived at night with an offering of incense, silk scarves, and penises in various shapes and fashioned from wood, stone, and plastic. Suspended beneath the spirit house were dozens of small wooden penises threaded on strings. Piles of weathered wooden penises lay scattered around a kind of specialized lumberyard. White marble penises. Plaster penises in the image of a pig had tails sculpted in the form of a penis plus a long penis touching the ground like a parked plow.

The parking lot was closed except to the film crew. From two large trucks thick black electrical cables snaked across the cement to the film set. Booms and cranes were erected and Jesse Tyler was working with the gaffer, who was adjusting a large overhead series of lights. More than a dozen members of the film crew were at work, some in the vans and others on the set.

The lead role in *Lucky Charms* was played by an American actress in her early twenties, Carol Hatcher, who had obtained a cultlike following based on a short-lived TV series. The TV series was about a college vampire, a five-hundred-year-old junior who played quarter-back on the college football team. Carol had been cast as his younger sister and knew his secret, having hung around as he drank the blood of young coed cheerleaders from a rival college. But the series was canceled after six half hours. *Vampire U* had never risen above fifth from the bottom of the ratings. Hatcher had delivered her lines to the vampire in a *Gone with the Wind* southern belle accent. After the series was canceled, she continued to talk in the same clipped south-ern accent, as if the Civil War were still being waged. She hadn't worked in the fourteen months since the series had been canceled.

She was frustrated and upset in Bangkok. This was supposed to be her comeback, but she had hated every minute since arrival. Noth-ing had gone right. She blamed Tyler, as she had for *Vampire U*. Now there had been another delay in the shoot. Time had been wasted, for a hundred reasons. There had been trouble with the lighting equip-ment. The continuity guy had overslept—he had been with two girls the night before. Then an American boom operator who wanted a roll of electrician's tape had pointed his foot at a Thai. This nearly led to a fistfight and death threats. The electricity had gone out for twenty-five minutes, and the weather report called for a heavy thun-derstorm to dump rain on Bangkok. Tyler followed his star into the trailer.

"Carol, I want you to help me, okay?" He put an arm around her shoulder. "You need to hang in a little longer. I know this take is a bitch."

"I'm boiling hot. I'm tired. My legs hurt. And my skin—Jesus, Jesse, that shit in the *klong* is peeling away my face," said Carol. "I don't know if I can stand to go back out there. I should see a doctor. I need a professional medical opinion."

"We've almost got the shot. You're doing great. Tomorrow you'll see the dailies and you'll say, 'Jesse, this scene paid off the whole movie. Thank you,' you'll say. Reviewers will say that Carol Hatcher in the ritual garden is a classic. Believe me, no one will ever forget that scene."

She was softening. Enough time had passed to allow the air-conditioned van to cool her down. She had stopped sweating. Her breathing was regular again as she poured a glass of wine, sipped it slowly. He watched her throat as she swallowed—soft, white, vulner-able—and at the same time heard the words of agony, complaint, and condemnation which continued to spill forth and cause Tyler no end of headaches. She was the boss's daughter. Or he would have fired her from the set the first week. No such luck, Tyler thought. He had never had much luck. But he was working in a town where 90 percent of the directors, actors, and writers were looking for work—any work.

"Tell me again, Jesse: Why do I have to hug that ugly foam cock?"

Tyler smiled. "Okay. I know that's bothering you. I'm sensitive to that. But it's a ritual embrace. It's not about sex. It's fertility you want. The local witch doctor gives you precise instructions what you must do. We've already shot that scene. You saw the dailies. You love it. So remember your motivation. You want to get pregnant but every doctor has told you that's impossible. So you descend into the hellish, nightmare underground world of rituals and magic. That's why you came to exotic Bangkok. You've heard the legend of Jao Mae Thapthim. It's your last hope of conceiving the child you so desperately want."

Carol lit a cigarette. "Bangkok's not exotic. It's just a big, dirty, hot city where the traffic never moves." After she exhaled, she looked at Tyler. She crossed her legs, her silk dress falling open to her thigh. "I want back into the business."

She needed a little reassurance. Tyler looked past her as the door to the trailer opened. Colonel Hatcher, wearing a sports shirt open at the neck, stepped inside.

"You okay, honey?" asked Colonel Hatcher.

"Just great, Daddy. Your little girl has punched a few holes in the world's biggest foam dildo. But that's showbiz."

❖

COLONEL Hatcher walked, with Tyler at his side trying to keep up, across the parking lot and entered the lush, green, tropical, manicured garden behind the Hilton. Palm trees and flowering bushes illuminated by lights looked airbrushed—not a thing out of place. Tyler had moon-shaped sweat marks in his cotton shirt. He trailed a step behind as Hatcher led the way along a winding flagstone path to the swimming pool. On the patio the reclining chairs and tables were empty. Tyler had been moaning about the difficulty of foreign location shots and about the skin reaction Carol had been experiencing in the heat and pollution. And about how the stench coming off the *klong* had caused both crew and cast to complain, and how if one more long-tail boat ruined a shot he was going to ask Colonel Hatcher to mine the *klong*. Hatcher had listened, saying almost nothing, letting Tyler ramble through his troubles.

They sat in deck chairs beside the pool. The water was an eerie misty blue—floodlights recessed into the bottom of the pool had been turned on. Hatcher was thinking how he half-admired Calvino's straight-ahead, no-bullshit attitude; Calvino wouldn't have been whining about smells and boat noise. But Calvino, whether he had style or not, was causing trouble, and the time had come to stop him.

"We have a situation, Jesse," said Colonel Hatcher, playing with his West Point ring.

"What kind of a situation, sir?"

He looked scared, unsettled, thought Colonel Hatcher. Oxley emerged from the lower rear lobby of the hotel and called out from the opposite side of the pool. He raised his Bloody Mary and rattled the ice in the glass. His face was tanned, and he was grinning a boyish smile. Oxley approached in a thin white jacket, faded jeans, Hawaiian shirt, and highly polished penny loafers with pennies in the leather slots. He had the tailored look of a producer about to give an interview.

"Colonel," said Oxley, pulling up a chair. He turned to Tyler. "You look hot, Jesse. Bangkok weather can get kinda hot this time of year."

"I thought you were back in L.A.," said Tyler.

"I was. But as I told the colonel, I had this feeling there was a problem with *War Crimes*. You have the option. It's been written up in *Variety*. A lot of money rides on this one, Jesse. And what do I hear over lunch with some close friends in Malibu? Some guy living in Bangkok is selling the Hutton story."

"Calvino," said Tyler.

"The one who helped two of your assistants gain an education in Thai medical care," said Oxley.

"You didn't handle that with much intelligence," added Colonel Hatcher.

Tyler was feeling the heat. The moons beneath his arms had gone wet again. Hatcher and Oxley were beating up on him, he thought. "Look, I'm making a film. Calvino's not my problem. He was never my problem. Making *Lucky Charms* is my problem. That is our deal."

"Okay, okay. You're getting all excited, Jesse. Don't play a hard-ass," said Oxley, still smiling. "You lack that thing which makes it work. A hard-ass guy never talks about 'That is our deal.' He does something definite."

"Like Calvino," said Colonel Hatcher.

There was that fucking name again. In my face, thought Tyler.

"Jesse, don't worry about it," said Colonel Hatcher, reading his mind. "Calvino is nothing a small rewrite of the script can't fix."

Oxley leaned forward. "We had a short conference on the phone, Jesse. I know you're in the middle of a shoot and outside guys coming in to fuck with your script is the last thing you need. But we got to be realistic. We have a two-picture deal. Unless we make a few small changes, we could have some trouble down the road."

❖

TYLER leaned back in his chair, yawned the way a dog does when it's bored, and folded his arms defensively at chest level. He felt cornered, and kicked himself for not seeing before that these kinds of back-end financing deals were a nightmare. In all the years he had worked with Hatcher and Oxley, he had called himself an independent. The word "independent" was such bullshit; in Hollywood it meant sucky-fucky with assholes you wouldn't trust to return your telephone book. Independents were money junkies. They did what was necessary to raise the budget. Hatcher never let him forget who he worked for, who provided the money. He was on a string; and if the string broke—well, there was what happened to Hutton. "Creative financing" was how Hatcher had gone on record to describe his involvement in the film business. "As long as the movies get paid for, Jesse, that's all you need worry about. Your end is the creative thing. That's your baby." It was the same bullshit line of every money guy in the business.

Tyler was part of the Unit. That was the name Hatcher and Oxley and a few other longtimers used. The Unit. Once he had seen a document with "104 Unit, Pacific Command" and Colonel Hatcher's name on it and stamped "Top Secret." It had been a budget estimate for a film. He'd pretended he hadn't seen it. Tyler pretended enough to create the illusion that he was a filmmaker and not a guy fronting a covert military operation. Sam Hatcher was operational head of the Unit. The scripts had been written to be filmed on location in exotic places; on the surface, they read like any other script. The crew's presence was often marked with an item running in a local newspaper about a guy with his brains blown out, stabbed in the throat, or, as with the Hutton thing, drowned. Hatcher had Oxley doing other things as well—blowing up bridges, buildings, cars, depots; or stealing documents, computer data, government files. Sometimes Tyler had been invited to speak before groups of film people or would-be film people.

"Mr. Tyler, how do you recommend getting a film financed?" He would swallow hard, smile.

"If you have the right property, the money comes," he always said. He never defined "the right property."

Lucky Charms was a Bangkok shoot. He hadn't asked the right questions when the project came up. He hadn't worked for the Unit for nearly three years. He had parted ways with Hatcher on a friendly basis. Only one thing he'd overlooked—parting with Hatcher was like a homeboy dropping the flag, quitting a street gang: It wasn't all that easy. Tyler had convinced himself that he had done his part, kept his bargain; as far as he was concerned, he had made real films. Money people had their own lives, their own involvements round town, and if Hatcher's people happened to spend time blowing up things and killing people, it merely confirmed that money people had some other agendas. But everyone in the business knew that.

Then Carol Hatcher's agent had phoned his office. He had his secretary say he was in a meeting. He kept in "meetings" for four days. Finally Carol showed up at his office and wouldn't leave until he saw her. Talk about too much personal package—Carol would have filled the *Queen Mary* to the gunwales, he thought. He had done a TV series with her. Since then she had been the butt of one-line jokes on late night TV. Jay Leno had even had Carol on his show dressed like a vampire. Tyler told himself he was being paranoid. The assignments had always come directly from Colonel Hatcher; and one of the ground rules was that the Unit and his daughter were in two separate orbits and Hatcher intended to keep it that way. So Tyler assumed if Carol was pitching something, it was without daddy's money and connections.

Hollywood was a place never to make assumptions about money or connections.

Carol Hatcher had played her approach real smart. She waited until after her appearance on Leno's show. She was an item in the news again. *People* magazine wanted to do a feature. She wore Tyler down. She had development money for the project—what the fuck did he want? All she wanted was a credit on the script and the possibility of becoming an associate producer. She got two more meetings. He kept telling himself, "Jesse, don't take the money. Jesse, don't even read the script."

He didn't bother reading the script; he went straight for the money. Cash was always the paramount motivation. Scripts could always be changed; money couldn't always be found.

Even kept waiting for her to spring the backstory. Scripts always came with a backstory you found out about later on. Who had been shopping it around, and to whom. And who was attached that no one had mentioned at the meetings. But it had seemed like a straight deal with Carol Hatcher. Hey, she was on Leno, she was gonna be in *People* magazine. Her old man swore death to anyone who dragged his baby into a film done by the Unit. A clean deal, he thought. But in Hollywood even a clean deal had a roll of toilet paper hanging from the back end.

After the financing was arranged, the rest started to fall into place. She was going to bring him a surprise. He hated surprises. They gave him stomach cramps and clamped his bowels for forty-eight hours. She moved straight to the kill. She could guarantee him financing on a two-picture deal. She knew he had been trying to get a pilot done called *Satin Nights* about a jazz group, composed of ex-'Nam vets and two Vietnamese, who were looking to take the reconciliation tour. Everyone had passed on the idea. Now Carol Hatcher was in his office telling him she had the money for the project.

He had smiled as she laid that one on him. But he let it pass. She had brought the money, hadn't she? This was his chance to get *Satin Nights* made. The Unit had given it a pass. Her money made him feel renewed confidence in the film. But he warned himself against getting pulled headfirst into her illusions. Did she seriously believe that he had the power to breathe life into a dead film project? He'd been around long enough to understand that false confidence was a danger signal. It meant you'd crossed into the territory of agents, whose job was to convince poeple like him to believe in the resurrection of the lifeless deals. Even a hooker who had faked a climax knew the difference between a dead horse and one that still have one more kick left in him. Tyler wanted to believe he heard the distant sound of a hoof thumping against the barn door.

He nibbled at the offer without biting. Carol hadn't let up, she kept coming in his face; she plunged on with the second element which he would never have guessed in a million light years—the *Satin Nights* script had to be rewritten, the action moved from L.A. to Bangkok. He had to think for a minute; he couldn't remember for sure where Thailand was other than somewhere in Asia near Vietnam. She would pay for the rewrite; he could choose the rewrite guy, that was okay with her. He swallowed it hook, line and sinker.

"You want me to shoot a film in Thailand?" he asked, trying to find an atlas on his bookshelf.

"Both films. Why not?" she asked.

He stared at her long and hard. In working for the Unit there were two kinds of film projects Tyler had learned to fear and hate—those involving either Middle East-based stories or any locale with an active group of Muslim extremists. Those guys were over-the-top crazy. But in Bangkok, he reasoned, Muslims never had a history of extremists. They were a quiet, content community and seemed light-years away from the billion Muslims who had wanted a ticket to heaven by killing Salman Rushdie, the English author. Thailand was a Buddhist country where although people got killed for all kinds of reasons, no one ever argued that killing was a passage to paradise.

"This drug money you're bringing to the deal, Carol? And don't bullshit me."

"Jesse, you've been in this town a long time. Have you ever heard a single story about me doing drugs? I was just on Leno. He's gonna have a drug addict on his show?"

He had to admit she had a point. She had a reputation for clean living: if not exactly a prude, she was an actress who would appear on a religious TV program and talk about the importance of her belief in a drug-free lifestyle. She had once done a public service antidrug commercial which ran four times longer than her TV series. This had led to some of the late night humor: Carol Hatcher likes her blood straight. Don't drink and drive, and don't drink and offer her your neck.

"It's up to you, Jesse," said Carol.

"Any ayatollahs attached?"

At the door she smiled and said, "Don't be silly. Call me."

Tyler had hit a dead end with *Satin Nights*. Oxley asked her if she had any interest in a film called *Lucky Charms*. If so, then he could help. But she had to keep quiet about the project. "Do you want in? Think about it."

She didn't have to think about it.

She fucked Oxley that night in his office.

It had been up to Tyler. If he wanted his film made, he had a real offer on the table, or he could take his script and find financing somewhere else. But he had nowhere else and she knew it. So what was the catch? Tyler had asked himself after she had gone. He phoned everyone he knew in town that had ever worked with Carol Hatcher. Straight as an arrow, they said. He bought a map, and after confusing Taiwan with Thailand for about five minutes, he convinced himself that changing Latino street gang members into Thais was not a real problem. Two members of the band were Vietnamese. He had checked out there was a guy named Dex in Bangkok who was real good. He told Carol about Dex's reputation in the jazz world. Only one thing: Dex ended up leaving town, and putting *Satin Nights* on hold. A bad piece of luck, sending karma into a wobbly spin.

That moved *Lucky Charms* up to the plate. When the witch doctor from casting appeared, Tyler knew. They had worked before. The guy was a member of the Unit. He had been had. The deal had been locked up; there was no way out.

❖

AS he sat around the Hilton pool with Colonel Hatcher and Oxley, Tyler wished the scene at Jao Mae Thapthim were in the can. He wished the Thai actor had slit the throat of the goat, and Carol had done her dance around the base of the five-meter-tall penis. But, he comforted himself, though things had turned bad, at least there were no terrorists.

"Maybe your decision to bring Carol into this wasn't such a great idea," said Tyler, as he caught Colonel Hatcher's eyes clocking him.

"My decision, was it?" said Colonel Hatcher.

This caught Tyler off guard.

"It's just. . . ."

But Colonel Hatcher put up his hand.

"Oxley tells me you went to Carol."

Now he was in it. He looked at Oxley, then at Hatcher.

"Oxley should be writing scripts," said Tyler.

"That's exactly what I want to talk to you about. The script," said Oxley.

FOURTEEN

LOVE NEST BAR

LOVE was not something anyone found in the bar.

As for nest—it was more of a pit than a nest.

Bitter Bob slumped over the bar, his arms collapsed around his head as if he had heard an air raid siren. He squirmed on the bar stool, shivering with the cold sweats. His pants were wrinkled and soiled, and he smelled like he hadn't had a bath in a couple of days, which in the tropics amounted to a month of neglect.

"I knew that kid. Hutton. And one more thing: I used to know his whore. I think I even used to know you, Calvino. From the old days. They fucking killed him," said Bitter Bob. "And you wanna know why they killed him? Because Hutton was a *farang*."

In Bitter Bob's mind "they" were unknown people, mostly Thai thugs, always out on the edge, waiting like toilet flies to attack a *farang* with his dick in his hand. If they got Jerry Hutton, the way Bob's mind reasoned, then they might have targeted him next. And they were waiting for him outside the bar, lurking in the back of tuk-tuks or slouched over a motorcycle in the shadowy areas in between street lamps on Soi 23.

"Bob, did you get a look at the guy Kwang left with?"

Bitter Bob raised his amber bottle of Singha beer. He sucked on it long and hard, not taking in any air, until he set the bottle back on the counter and ordered another round.

"Some fool," said Bitter Bob.

"What country was this fool from?"

"If you're asking me whether this fool was a foreigner, then I guess I'd have to say he was. Foreign, I mean. He didn't speak English like an American."

"Was he French, Aussie, German? Think, Bob." Calvino was thinking that Bitter Bob had about as much ability to identify the nationality of a *farang* as did the average upcountry *ying*.

"I'm thinking but nothing inside my mind. I ain't good at spotting accents. He was just another shitfaced fool. A stranger, and that's all I know."

Calvino had walked into the Love Nest Bar around ten. He had missed Kwang by fifteen minutes; she had been bought out for a shorttime. When Calvino came back after eleven Kwang still hadn't returned. He looked at his watch and ordered a Mekhong and soda.

"You might be in for a long wait," said Bitter Bob.

Calvino bought him a beer.

"The mamasan said she went short-time," said Calvino.

"In my opinion that could mean just about anything from ten minutes to ten days in Bangkok. The Thais got a different way of telling time. I've got a theory about that," said Bitter Bob.

The waiter set down Calvino's Mekhong and Bitter Bob's beer. Calvino wasn't in the mood to hear Bitter Bob's theory. So he took his drink and sat alone on a long bench in the back. He liked having his back against the wall. A waitress in high heels and a bikini top brought him two chits stuffed in a bamboo cup and put it on his table. He nursed his Mekhong and soda. Kwang was a businesswoman, he thought. For her a short-time averaged one hour and that included travel time. As he drank his Mekhong he saw Bitter Bob clocking him in the bar mirror. Bob's bloodshot eyes stared as if wondering whether Calvino might know who "they" were, and he was toying with Bitter Bob, trying to egg him on, draw him out; he was part of the plan for the Thai bikers who waited outside. The moment ended when Bitter Bob lifted his hip on the stool and farted, making the sound of a tire at high speed hitting a nail on the road. He chuckled in his hand, then Bitter Bob's attention moved back to the TV screen, where his favorite film was playing.

The video was one Calvino thought was tailored for Karl's specialized interest—vivid color close-ups of smashed, burned, and punctured human bodies. Bodies pulled from cars, planes, rivers, lakes, sandpits, and streets. Doctors in white frocks performed autopsies, using a workshop worth of tools, scalpels, tongs, and a special stainless steel saw. Calvino watched as the saw cut through a skull and the brain fell out with a nudge from the doctor's gloved hand. The video was an all-time favorite of the leftover drunks who floated on alcohol vapors through Soi Cowboy. *Farang* zombies—the third-shifters gone paranoid—sucking down drinks and trying to hold it together watching teams of doctors ripping out hearts, lungs, livers, and miles and miles of guts. Hutton's video of the Burmese executions of the students was a sweet piece of innocence compared with this.

Calvino drank inside the dead zone of a Soi Cowboy night, that period between the end of happy hour and the run-up to midnight. In that concourse, *farangs* cut adrift from all moorings applied alcohol to their pain of losses which could never be recovered. Their energy level fell to the basics of breathing, eating bar nuts, drinking, and watching videos. During the nightly downtime the *yings*—who had done one or two short-times—got their second wind and began moving in for another kill before the night ran down. All that flickered during this period was the same video repeating how messy it was to open and disassemble the organs of the human body.

Seated at the bar with Bitter Bob were a couple of dark, hunched-over figures looking like they were shaking off the effects of a tranquilizer gun. Their expressionless, yellowish faces, glued to the tube, looked the same as what was left of the faces on the bodies in the video. Hard-core credentials were earned by witnessing one gory video autopsy after another and never breaking into a sweat or throwing up on the bar. They gathered at the Love Nest, and dozens of other places like it, these men of indeterminate age who carried their emotional dart marks in public like war wounds which never properly healed.

But this night Bitter Bob had the cold sweats, and it gave Calvino a bad feeling. He kept thinking of what Tommy Loretti had said about his treatment's not having a hero or a linear story. It was the Bitter Bobs who longed for a hero. Someone to look up to, someone who could tell him who "they" were, and show him how to protect himself when they came at his face. He was thinking Tommy had a point when he suddenly felt an overpowering urge to see Joy.

"I want to see the dog," said Calvino to the waitress in tight jeans and a red knit shirt that clung to her breasts. "And don't tell me Joy's gone out on a short-time."

The waitress replied to his request with a fake smile and then studied Calvino's face, trying to remember where she had seen him before. Was he a Cheap Charlie on the make, or could she squeeze him for a few baht? A light came on somewhere in the back of her eyes. Yeah, yeah, she remembered Calvino. He had taken Kwang a couple of times some years ago. And this was the same guy who had given her the German shepherd. She had scored. One *farang* was dead and another had taken his place in less than a month, confirming that the universe of Bangkok bars was perfectly ordered. The girls had taken bets that Calvino would come checking after the dog; *farangs* had that way of not letting something go. *Farangs* had a strange relationship with dogs, always patting and kissing them, forgetting they were animals, talking baby talk to them. No wonder they believed just about anything a girl would tell them about her mother's broken leg, her brothers and sisters with the unpaid school fees, and the water buffalo about to die unless a vet was called in.

"Joy's upstairs," the waitress said. "Sleeping. She not go out with *farangs*. Her pussy too small."

Not because Joy was a dog; it was simply a question of weight class. It came down to a practical question of size. If a *farang* wanted to buy out Joy, then there would be a price. So far there had been no request, but the possibility was left open.

"Joking," said the waitress. "Why you want to take dog? Take girl. She's much better for you. Look there and there." Her finger stabbed the air as she circled around the bar, pointing out the girls in red rayon Chinese housecoats with white piping along the collar and the front. "Love Nest Bar" was printed in big white letters on the back.

"Fifty baht, you go upstairs, wake up Joy, and tell her an old friend has come to scratch her ears," said Calvino, taking a fifty-baht note from his wallet and holding it out.

The waitress slipped away—no, not slipped . . . she skipped, pranced away, because she had scored, and when anyone scored she clutched the money and did an end-zone victory dance across the floor to alert the other girls that money had gone through the goalposts and landed right in her pocket. Without a hug, a kiss, or a fuck. Lucky money, free money.

A few days had passed since Calvino had delivered the German shepherd to Kwang. He had changed his mind a couple of times, but had finally walked over with Joy, knocked on Kwang's door, and walked home with an uneasy feeling that he had been thinking American in the gesture when he should have been thinking like Kwang in Thai. She'd looked out with a pack of relatives at the door and shrugged her shoulders, as if to say, "What are you saying? I gotta pay to feed this fucking monster? Look at all my hungry relatives behind me. And you're saying this royal dog has more right to food than them?"

He had given her money for the dog food but he was certain the dog would only get leftover rice, fried grasshoppers, and chicken bones. He had been smart enough not to tell her the dog was worth at least forty all-night pump-and-grind sessions in some cheap hotel or run-down guesthouse on Soi Ngam Duphli where the geeks and shitkickers who shot up with heroin hung out. The "Croaks" who unlike Karl didn't pump iron or shoot up steroid chasers. The "Croaks" never worried about AIDS because they were already dead. "Buying this dog meant a lot to Jerry," Calvino had tried to explain to her. "He thought you could change your life. Breed the dog. Sell the puppies and make money. Enough money to stay off Soi Cowboy." He was talking to stark cold stone, something talk never could blast through.

She'd stared at the dog and thought about what Calvino was saying, working it over in her head, trying to figure out what was in it for him and how to get some cash. "Jerry's dead. Never mind. Everyone *taeylaew*. Jerry not help me now. So what you say I do? I sell dog pussy, no problem. Sell, can. But I cannot sell my pussy? I think very stupid. Jerry think like you. *Farangs* don't know how Thai girl think."

"Don't let anything bad happen to the dog," said Calvino. "You know what I'm saying. The dog gets hurt, then there is gonna be some trouble. And I know you don't like problems. I'm trying to help out here. Do the right thing. All I'm asking is that you do the right thing. What Jerry would've wanted." After he finished his little speech he knew that basically he had wasted his breath; but he owed it to Hutton to try. Kwang's relatives shrank into the shadows as Kwang tensed her entire body in the doorway.

"Jerry buy the dog for me. None of your fucking business. I eat dog. Can. I let *farang* fuck dog. Can. I sell my pussy. Can," said Kwang, as if she had earned an MBA degree in supply-side economics.

In a buyer's market, a smart seller like Kwang knew that fast money was the only money worth getting up for, or going into the sack headfirst for. It had ended in direct confrontation. The worst of all

161

sins in Thailand: He had challenged her, implied she was less than trustworthy, and suggested she would be accountable for her actions. Calvino had been in Thailand long enough to know Calvino's law: Never tell a bar *ying* that she's accountable for her actions unless you are prepared for tears and a knife.

With Kwang, he had broken the cardinal law. Sooner or later, he'd have to pay the cost of his violation. Kwang was patient; she understood that in revenge timing was everything.

❖

A couple of weeks later, Calvino found Joy sitting near a mosquito net with several of Kwang's relatives crawling over her. He realized that he'd made a mistake. He had heard that Kwang had returned to her old bar. What disturbed him was the rumor that the German shepherd had entered what the Japanese called "the Water Trade"— the nightlife. Joy was being kept at the bar, where she had become a star attraction.

"I dunno if it's true or not. But some fool said that German shepherd cost more than two of these girls. You know, if you go upcountry you can buy a girl for twenty, thirty thousand baht. That's what some fool said Joy cost."

"Where would you put your money, Bob?" asked Calvino.

"Well, that's a tough one. For good balling you'd have to go for the girl. For loyalty the dog. You can't really piss off a dog. A girl gets pissed off and she's liable to take a knife to your cock. So I guess the best thing is just to keep drinking and not think too much," said Bitter Bob.

The *yings* at the Love Nest Bar liked Joy. They cuddled, teased, kicked, hugged, kissed, and ordered Joy around the bar. There was more than a little sadism when the girls pounced on Joy. Some deep anger that the life of the animal was more highly valued than their own. The customers such as Bitter Bob liked Joy, and the mamasan decided Joy was good for business. Customers were buying drinks for the German shepherd. The first night on the job, Joy got drunk on beer. The Love Nest was one of the few remaining single shophouse bars left on Soi Cowboy where the girls slept like firewood stacked in cords; the others had become large entertainment centers for tourists.

The waitress who disappeared upstairs with Calvino's fifty baht had been gone ten minutes. Enough time for Calvino to have a good look around the bar. In the two years since he had stopped coming around, little had changed. He recognized most of the half-dozen hard-core customers who mixed with nearly two dozen *yings*. The customers and girls were the same old faces from before.

It was a time-warp kind of bar. He had paid the bar fine for Kwang a couple of times in those days. A year later, Jerry Hutton had bought her out, fallen in love, and made the traditional *farang* one-man rescue mission into the never-never heartland of the Bangkok sex world. If Hutton had lived long enough, he would have understood that the kind of people who worked and camped out in the Love Nest Bar could never be saved; they always returned to the same old grind. Calvino's law: Cinderella doesn't hit up a customer to pay her bar fine because she's bored waiting for Prince Charming to arrive with a glass slipper.

The Love Nest had no Cinderellas or Prince Charmings. What the bar did have was a pedigree German shepherd which was a cheap drunk and drank beer, scotch, and gin chasers. Joy had provided a diversion from the go-go dancers, the mirrors, and the autopsy video.

Calvino drank, stared at the go-go dancers and the mirrors behind them, concave wraparound mirrors constructed inside a cylinder. The *yings* rarely danced; they hung motionless like commuters, a hand grabbing the floor-to-ceiling silver metal pole. The only rotation of hips occurred as they shifted position to better see the TV screen at the opposite end of the bar. The mirrors reflected *yings* whose minds and bodies had detached.

For guys like Bitter Bob who glanced between the dancers and the autopsy video, the special effects of the mirrors confirmed their view of the world in three time frames: a hostile past, a hopeless present, and a bitter future. They didn't care about the mind; it was the body they wanted to buy. And in the center were two beautiful dancing girls who were half in the present and half somewhere else— more guts dropped into the bucket on the screen—and in this Bar Jerry Hutton had thought he could change one life.

❖

JOY bounded across the floor and jumped over a *ying*, landing on Calvino's lap. Her paws resting on his shoulders, she licked his face and pushed her head against his neck. Then her head whipped around and she stuck her snout into his Mekhong and drank, her tongue splashing the beverage over the table. She sneezed a couple of times. Calvino stroked her long, thick brown and black coat. The fourteen-month-old puppy pulled away from Calvino and swung her large front legs and their enormous paws onto the small oval table in front of the bench. The mamasan came over and sat on the bench a few feet away from Calvino and made sloppy kissing sounds. Calvino knew a power play when he saw one. This one worked. In a reflex action, Joy leaped over Calvino and nuzzled the mamasan, her jaws gnawing gently on the mamasan's large, floppy breasts. The mamasan, half drunk, pretended to punch Joy's face with her fists. As she laughed and turned her red face away, Joy chewed on her hair in its bun.

Joy lurched and snapped off one of the mamasan's long, dangling earrings. This caused near panic. Bar *yings* and the mamasan grabbed at Joy, pulling open her mouth, searching her throat for the earring. A teenage *ying* pulled down the top half of her bikini and offered a breast to the dog—she pinched her pinkish nipple, sticking it in Joy's face, then pulled back. She returned with a cigarette lighter, flicked it under Joy's nose; Joy barked and playfully chewed on the *ying's* arm. A pimp at the bar leaned back from his stool and patted Joy, fed her a handful of peanuts. He reached back to the counter, then returned with a lighter. Joy barked as the flame came close to her face. On the second sweep of the lighter Calvino came across from his table and grabbed the pimp's wrist, then raised the flame to touch a cigarette clenched between the man's lips, saving the pimp's face from Joy's wrath and making his point with a single gesture. At the same moment, there was a further diversion, as one of the *yings*, on her hands and knees, found the mamasan's earring on the floor.

The obedience school graduate was regressing fast. Joy was acting like any young girl brought in from upcountry and put in a bar. It wasn't a ride downhill; it was being dropped off a cliff. Calvino wondered what Rolfo would have thought, seeing the German shepherd with papers getting sloshed on bar scotch in a place called the Love Nest. After he'd given Rolfo ten thousand baht for Joy, Rolfo had said there was one confidential piece of information that as Joy's new owner he was entitled to receive. He said it was a code word.

"What kind of code word?"

Rolfo wrote it down on a piece of paper, tore it off the pad, and handed it to Calvino. The word was—Bismarck.

164

"If you say that word in a sharp, firm tone, this dog will kill. I trained my dogs for the special forces. And when I finish they are no longer man's best friend. They are one man's friend. The owner who controls and disciplines the animal."

Calvino patted Joy on the head. "A killing machine?"

"One hundred percent guaranteed," Rolfo had said. "So you must be careful never to use this word. Not even as a joke."

The pimp gave every indication of not backing down. Big mistake. Calvino thought the word to himself—Bismarck.

The girls beat up on the dog; the customers cuffed her on the ears and flicked lighters in her face. These weren't wanton acts of cruelty as much as acts of pure boredom.

"It ain't right, I told Toom," said Bitter Bob, nodding at the mamasan. "If she doesn't watch that dog, the girls are gonna kill the poor bitch. You give booze to a dog and it ain't gonna live long. You ever see a dog liver? It don't amount to a hill of beans."

❖

THE Bangkok police didn't arrive at the Love Nest Bar until about half past one. Colonel Pratt had been looking for Calvino for nearly two hours when he remembered the matter about the dog. Bitter Bob and most of the dead-zone characters had fled into the night, alone and in the broken-down condition which made neither sex nor sleep likely alternatives.

"We found her at Hotel 99. She had been dead two, maybe three hours," said Colonel Pratt.

"And you're not telling me the rest." Calvino stroked Joy, her large head on his lap. The girls in the bar were huddled in a dense clump at the far end of the bench, crying.

"There is some rough play, Vincent," said Colonel Pratt.

"Hatcher had Kwang killed."

"Nothing points to Hatcher. It all points to you."

"Of course. That's how he works," said Calvino.

"I'm doing the best I can, Vincent."

"What happened?" asked Calvino, wishing a waitress would take his order for another drink.

The operators who ran the short-time hotel had reported the murder to their contact in the force, who passed the information along, until someone who worked for Colonel Pratt saw that a connection was being made between Kwang's death and Calvino. Kwang had been found dead in a short-time hotel—the kind with white plastic curtains which drop behind a car so no one can see the license plate. Hotel 99 was located deep inside Soi 11. An attendant had checked out the room after he knocked a couple of times and no one answered the door. He used a master key and let himself inside. He had called out in Thai. There had been no answer. The sheets on the bed were in the usual tangled state and the scent of bodily fluids circled in the air. Kwang was found in the bathroom. More precisely, she was inside the bathtub under the taps, which had been left on. The bathroom was flooded. Kwang's hands were tied behind her back. She had been held down with some force. When the attendant looked over the edge, Kwang stared up with dead eyes.

The attendant had identified the john who arrived with Kwang at the short-time hotel. It was a photograph of Calvino. Kwang's relatives had already given a statement about the conflict between Calvino and Kwang over the dog. Most murders in Thailand were the result of a gambling debt, a business conflict, or a failed love affair. Circumstances pointed to Calvino being guilty on at least two counts.

"I was here at ten, and then again at eleven and never left. Bitter Bob was at the bar. Toom was here. That waitress over there was serving me drinks," said Calvino.

"And between ten and eleven?" asked Colonel Pratt.

He had gone to Rolfo's house and talked with Karl again.

"Talking to a German about dogs," said Calvino.

"The attendant at Hotel 99 has fingered you, Vincent."

"How much you figure Colonel Hatcher paid him, Pratt? Two thousand baht? Maybe five thousand?"

"I can handle the attendant for now," said Colonel Pratt.

"But sooner or later this asshole is going to take us, Pratt."

"Did you hear the news?"

Calvino shook his head; he didn't want to admit that he had been watching the bar blood and guts video.

"The army has sent a thousand more troops to the Burmese border, and the air force bombed the Burmese about an hour ago," said Colonel Pratt.

"I guess I missed that part when I read Oxley's script."

Colonel Pratt leaned over and patted the dog.

"'I blame you not; for you are mortal, and mortal eyes cannot endure the devil,'" said Colonel Pratt, quoting *Richard III*.

It was the most Thai of answers wrapped in the most elegant of Shakespearian prose. Calvino was not accountable under either Thai or English emotional sensibilities for searching out the devil while avoiding the blame laid at the feet of mortals. What Colonel Pratt didn't tell his friend was the bargain he had made or the devil he had made that bargain with. He would be attending no more pro-democracy meetings. Nonaction was the Thai way of trading something to fix a problem. Personal loyalty trumped the card of official duties. The Italians were using a parallel system when they greeted each other using the word *paisan*. There was no other choice in Colonel Pratt's mind but to help Calvino. It was the Thai in him. Just as it had been Calvino's decision not to tell him about the threatening phone calls he had received for helping Dex. Calvino's law: Learn when to stop talking when you have nothing to say. Pratt had his own law of silence: Don't start talking about threats received unless you need to be rescued.

There was nothing that Calvino as a *farang* could do or could be expected to do about the phone calls to Dex. There was no rescue mission Calvino could work or blanket of protection he could offer. Dex had invited the threats through his actions; and Pratt, by going along to the meetings, thought he might be able to create a shield from harm. Only it didn't work out that way.

FIFTEEN

BUS DANCING

AROUND five P.M. an air-conditioned bus lurched forward, the wheels slamming against the curb. Passengers—young, old, crippled, blind—pushed past Calvino as they got off the bus. Inside, the blue curtains were drawn over the sealed windows, creating a dimly lit semisecret chamber. All the seats, in rows of two, were occupied by sleeping passengers, their heads rolling from side to side as the bus accelerated through the traffic. The narrow corridor between the seats teemed with dancers. The rules of engagement were always the same. No one talked. No one established eye contact. The bus conductor shouted for the *farangs* to move to the rear of the bus. That was the signal. The Thais backed away, leaving a space between themselves and the foreigners.

Calvino's knees felt rubbery, as if they had been fitted with double-density truck shocks. The bus driver hit the train tracks at full speed. His body dipped, and he bounced forward. The ticket taker, a uniformed woman, rattled the silver cylinder containing the coins, telling Calvino to keep to the back. She had long, straight hair which touched her waist, smooth, pale skin, and the kind of front-line eyes which had captured the afterimage of battlefield flares—the burning stars which floated to earth on tiny white parachutes. She had no name. When he tried to protest, he couldn't find the words. The rule was to never open your mouth or acknowledge what you saw; a *farang* stayed in the back, the whole journey made in silence.

As the pneumatic doors opened, he recognized Joy's bark. The barking seemed distant. Calvino missed his stop and made another three trips around the city, going for miles and miles.

Soon the bus had emptied and no one was left except the driver and conductor—and Calvino.

He tried to raise his hands but couldn't. He tried to move from the back of the bus but nothing happened, as if his brain function had cut out from his body. The conductor and driver turned on the dog, kicking her in the hindquarters. The dog screamed in pain. Calvino looked on helplessly, watching, and then he recognized the conductor's face: It was Kwang. Instead of the silver money container, she held a gun, pointing it at Calvino's head, her finger pressed against the trigger.

"End of the line, asshole," she said in perfect English.

"Bismarck," he screamed, as he heard the sound of the gun explode in his face.

❖

CALVINO awoke with his face resting on a filthy concrete floor smelling of piss. He rolled over on his side, crashing into a mountain of blubbery raw stomach; the flesh was spotted with dozens of mosquito bites. Cockroaches raced over his hand. He shook off the bugs and opened his eyes and slowly looked up until he was eyeball to eyeball with Ron the Strange, a regular of Bangkok's Washington Square watering holes, someone who had once called him "a fucking Jew pretending to be a wop." Calvino had dropped him with one punch to the midsection—the same midsection he now found himself staring at on the cracked concrete floor of a jail cell in Tonglor district police station.

Ron groaned, scratching his mosquito bites, and turned over on his side. He lay there quietly for a moment, then leaned up on one hand and stared at Calvino.

"It ain't a fucking dream. It's you," Ron the Strange said, his voice thick with smoker's phlegm. He coughed with a loud hacking, like someone trying to bring up a fish bone. He tried to spit in the open hole in a corner which served as the toilet. But he missed, and it hardly mattered.

"Look at my belly. I've got no blood left. The mosquitoes sucked me dry. I could die here."

Calvino definitely was not in a number one air-conditioned bus.

He remembered the layout of Tonglor district police station jail— four holding cells on each side with an oblong common area in the center. The smell from a squat toilet in the far corner overpowered all other smells; *Klong* water would have smelled like air freshener by comparison. The cell was a bare room, no mats or benches, just grimy concrete floors. Screwed into the ceiling was a single naked lightbulb which burned day and night.

"What are you doin' here?" asked Ron the Strange.

"They say I murdered a bargirl," said Calvino.

That impressed Ron the Strange.

"No shit. You killed someone?"

He looked at Ron the Strange.

"What do you think?"

"It ain't up to what I think," Ron the Strange said, and rolled over on his side, curling his knees up to his chin. "A crime of passion. I gotta admit, that's hard to believe about a guy like you, Calvino."

"Yeah, I'll call you as a character witness, Ron."

"I just got drunk and blacked out," said Ron the Strange. "This morning they said I beat up Linda. I don't recall laying a hand on that girl. But if you ever do decide to kill a bargirl, she's one you oughta think about putting number one on your list."

Calvino turned away from the fat slob and looked around the cell. About tens guys—Thais and *farangs*—bunked down on the floor. No more than a couple were sleeping. Some were wrapped in blankets, teeth chattering, blue-lipped; their heroin fix had worn off, leaving them looking like larvae locked halfway between two worlds, beings stalled in a transition taking them into the pupa stage.

Calvino remembered Hutton inside Tonglor police station jail, holding on to the bars, looking like grim death. Now it was Calvino's turn: Only this time it wasn't running over a Chinese New Year banquet—he was being held on a murder charge. The previous night he had listened to his cell mates talk. Big talk in a small cell. The stinking, cramped cell contained self-confessed drug addicts, con men, B&E specialists, tough guys picked up for causing serious bodily harm—it was like being back in his old neighborhood in Brooklyn.

"You guys are making me homesick," Calvino had told them.

One *farang* with hollowed-out cheeks, sunken eyes, and a shaved head broke out in a smile as he looked at the ceiling. "The light never goes out. Light attracts mosquitoes. This place fucks up your mind. You can't get food. You can't get out. You can't take a shit in private. You can't get help."

Thumbtacked against the wall was an official document listing the amount of bail required to be posted, according to the offense. Murder was broken down into before nightfall and after nightfall. To kill someone at night doubled or tripled the penalty of a noontime slaying. Ron the Strange followed Calvino's eye line.

"I know what you're thinking," said Ron the Strange.

"What am I thinking, Ron?"

"You'll make bail."

"Just checking the menu." What Calvino was doing was conceiving a law for Asia hands like Ron the Strange—a *farang* who had spent one year in Asia twenty times. He'd never learned much beyond the lessons of that first year, and each experience that followed afterwards confirmed that life was a matter of simple repetition.

Ron the Strange giggled and shook his head. "*Farangs* aren't entitled to bail. Not on a serious charge."

Calvino turned around. Ron the Strange was standing downwind from the toilet. The vomit stains on his shirt left a mustard streak from his collarbone to his belly button.

"Why didn't you let Linda wear the dress you bought her?" asked Calvino. It was an old, running story on Washington Square. Ron the Strange had bought Linda, a Thai bar *ying* in her thirties, a dress in Singapore but beat her up every time she tried to wear it outside his room.

"Because I know what she'd do," said Ron the Strange.

"What were you afraid of, Ron?"

"That dress made her look good."

"A dress is supposed to make a woman look good."

"Linda's a whore. If you make a whore look too good, then her price goes up and you can't afford to keep her."

"You're a real economist, Ron."

Linda had left him after he no longer had money for the room and started sleeping rough under bridges. When he left, he took the dress with him.

About nine o'clock an NCO entered the corridor between the cells with a large bucket of rice and boiled pumpkin. He stopped in front of each cell and dished out the food. The prisoners pressed against the bars, holding out a tin plate and spoon. The NCO dumped rice and boiled pumpkin on each plate. One of the drug addicts dropped his plate and vomited before he made it to the squat toilet. He had been eating rice and boiled pumpkin for five straight days. Moments later his mess was crawling with cockroaches. Calvino took his plate and sat in a corner, watching the other prisoners spoon the rice into their mouths.

He thought about Colonel Hatcher as he turned the rice over with his spoon. Calvino's law: The romantic dreamed of a tolerant world, the objectivist an ordered world, and the cynic knew both of them were fools. Colonel Hatcher was no fool. He had played it smart. No more ambushes that might go wrong. That was disorder. It created chaos and the litter of mushrooms being popped. It was much better to throw Calvino headfirst into the system, and let the system digest him. But Colonel Hatcher had made one mistake, a flaw in judgment about the system: It was less ordered than he ever imagined.

Thanks to Colonel Pratt's personal intervention, Calvino wasn't being held on a murder charge. No matter how much Calvino tried during the ride to the police station, Pratt would not respond to his questions as to the cost he'd had to pay for the favor. Finally, as the car stopped and the driver got out, and they were alone, Colonel Pratt turned to Calvino.

"'My ransom is this frail and worthless trunk,'" he said, quoting King Henry in *Henry V*, his hand touching his left breast.

"Hatcher's wants war. I can't see it any other way. Do you?"

"'The sum of all our answer is but this: We would not seek a battle, as we are; Nor, as we are, we say we will not shun it,'" said Colonel Pratt.

Shakespeare could've passed for a Thai, thought Calvino. "The do not shun part works for me."

"I thought that might appeal to you," said Colonel Pratt.

❖

FOR a farang to be granted bail, they were two possible paths: the hard and medium-expensive way, which required the accused to have some juice with a person of status, or the difficult, mortgage-his-balls-house-and-kids way, which demonstrated that he was unaffiliated with anyone who had influence. Being a *farang* living in Thailand was like being an invited guest at a Masonic lodge dinner. Everyone was beautifully dressed, polite, smiling, and accommodating. Everything on the surface looked friendly and normal; but the guest remained aware all through dinner that the real decisions, the power, the rituals, the initiations, and the order of rank lay out of view.

After his assistance to Dex, the brothers had moved Calvino to the left of Pratt at the dinner party. Only Pratt's guest had got himself in trouble: spilled soup down his shirt, splattered a couple of brothers sitting nearby. Bad form and all that. Colonel Pratt had gone behind the closed door to find a way to salvage the situation.

All the usual factors came into focus—status of the brother, the seriousness of the guest's crime, the social position of the guest. Being a private eye with a gun made Calvino an unusual guest. But Pratt's power and standing as a brother allowed him to arrange for Calvino to make bail. Colonel Pratt was able, through his connections on the force, to arrange for Calvino to make bail the hard, medium-expensive way. He had made a crucial phone call from Hotel 99, letting the right person know that he would withdraw from any further involvement in the pro-democracy group connected to Dex. After that call on behalf of Calvino, Pratt had trapped Calvino's arresting officer, Lieutenant Narong, into riding to Tonglor district police station in his car. Just the two men—senior and junior officer—riding inside the police car. Once he climbed inside the car, Lieutenant Narong sensed that he had made a mistake in judgment; he had stepped behind a curtain where chants, oaths, rituals, and the like would drag him into the mess created by Colonel Pratt's friend.

The Thais have a saying: *Nee sua pa chorake*—Flee the tiger only to face the jaws of the crocodile. The saying rushed into Lientenant Narong's consciousness as he sat beside Colonel Pratt. He wasn't under arrest. He hadn't committed a crime. He was a police officer trying to do his job in accordance with his training and the orders of his superiors. But despite all those objective facts, he knew that basically he was fucked. He tried to figure out what he had done in his last life that such a thing would happen to him in this one.

Lieutenant Narong had formulated his escape plan. He would go into hiding at his mother's house, the default setting for Thais, who were taught from knee high that their mothers were the source of all goodness and protection. Lieutenant Narong looked over at Colonel Pratt, who broke eye contact first; he wanted to tell Narong how important it was for him to go into hiding.

Narong knew Calvino had been picked up on the orders of someone with influence, a high-ranking insider with connection to ISOC. Nothing had been said outright; the system of interlocking loyalties and obligations didn't work on the jackhammer principle. An indirect word, a subtle hint—that was enough. Whenever ISOC became involved in a civilian case the red flag was raised—under the surface was a political claim which overrode any criminal action. When his superior said a certain person would appreciate assistance, the hint was enough. The second hint silently sealed the coffin lid shut: Another superior officer stopped by to say how a certain highly influential person whose picture often appeared in the newspaper stories about right-wing groups had phoned to say how important it was to rid Thailand of undesirable foreign elements. The superior office suggested that Lieutenant Narong investigate a murder charge involving a *farang*.

Lieutenant Narong stiffened in his chair. He could say nothing but "Yes, sir." The body was at the Hotel 99. The attendant had identified a *farang* named Vincent Calvino, a private investigator, as the principal suspect in the murder.

Lieutenant Narong discovered shortly after his arrival at the murder scene that Calvino had a well-developed personal relationship with Colonel Pratt. With the colonel at the scene of the arrest, Narong had to be careful.

It was a no-win situation for Lieutenant Narong. He knew that his decision came down to a choice between arresting the *farang* for murder or acknowledging the colonel's friendship with the *farang* and helping him to dig into the case. Whichever side he came down on, there was the distinct possibility that someone on the losing side would seek revenge. He was in the middle of a bigwig pissing contest and there was a danger his face would be stuck against the urinal. On the ride to Tonglor district police station in Colonel Pratt's car, Lieutenant Narong's hands were shaking as he formed them into a *wai*. Fighting against a feeling of panic, he requested that his *pii*—older brother—provide guidance to help his *nong*—younger brother—find the middle path.

Colonel Pratt knew that with ISOC officials, there was no middle path. A line had been crossed beyond which someone like Lieutenant Narong couldn't step back even if he wanted to. Nothing Pratt could say or do—other than lie—was going to give him much comfort. But although there was no middle path for Lieutenant Narong, there was the chance of a safe passage.

"You have two choices," Pratt said. "You can be compensated with a quarter of a million baht. And resign from the force." With enough money, Lieutenant Narong might save his face and establish another line of work after being reassigned to a jungle border post scattered with land mines near Burma or Cambodia.

"You said two choices," Lieutenant Narong said, swallowing hard and trying to maintain his professional composure.

"Or I have you transferred to the Crime Suppression Unit. You will work with me. No one will touch you. But if I fall, then you will fall, too. So I must warn you of that risk. It is up to you to decide."

Colonel Pratt had offered cash enough for a fresh start, a new life out of Bangkok, the pollution, noise, and corruption. He didn't call it a bribe—this would have robbed Lieutenant Narong of his dignity, and destroyed his face. He had called the money "payment": "compensation." Lieutenant Narong liked that. The figure Colonel Pratt had quoted was sometimes called "disappear money" or "flee-the-scene funds." Lieutenant Narong could leave Bangkok with sufficient respect and capital to buy a new life upcountry. Colonel Pratt felt sorry for Lieutenant Narong in his indecision. He waited for him to choose.

"I committed a sin in my last life," said Lieutenant Narong.

It was the ultimate scapegoating reflex to lapse into magical thinking, where it was natural to blame a sin committed in a previous life for the troubles experienced in the present. He was putting off a decision, avoiding the exposure to danger which came from favoring one faction over the other.

Colonel Pratt said nothing and let the young officer think it through at his own pace. "You are not to blame for what has happened. This incident is my direct responsibility. You are blameless."

This was a strong statement coming from a superior officer. Colonel Pratt was behaving like someone Lieutenant Narong had thought was nonexistent—a superior who did not let his junior take the fall.

"But I suffer because I did a bad thing before," he said, searching Colonel Pratt's eyes, wondering if this was an elaborate trap, a test of his Buddhist faith.

Pratt took this response as Lieutenant Narong's astrologer talking through him.

"Take the money or work for me. I cannot blame you if you take the money. Because to work for me may hurt your career," said Colonel Pratt. "I must be candid. I have gone to pro-democracy meetings. There are those who believe that was disloyal. I believed what I did was in my personal capacity as a citizen. So you must understand that your superior—if that is your choice—is not supported by certain quarters. I can't lie to you. It is too important for a young man such as you."

There were tears of relief and admiration swelling in Lieutenant Narong's eyes by the time Pratt had finished. The young lieutenant had secretly attended such meetings himself. He had felt a coward for not telling those at the meeting he was a police officer. He thought he had stood alone. No more.

"I don't think the case against Calvino is strong enough," said Lieutenant Narong. "The gun charge will hold him in Thailand. If we later find that Calvino killed the girl, we have his passport. He can't leave."

Colonel Pratt didn't reply, as his car turned into Tonglor district police station. The man who would fill out the day book—Lieutenant Narong—had made his decision.

"And I would be grateful for the opportunity to work in your unit, sir," said Lieutenant Narong. He waited several moments, collecting his thoughts, and working out how he would say what was in his heart. "I read in *Thai Rath* that Dex's tour in Tokyo has gone extremely well. Dex is a hero to a lot of us, Colonel Pratt."

"A hero is someone who knows a price has to be paid, and pays it," said Colonel Pratt.

❖

SHE remembered the girl. "Kwang," he had said was her name.

She also remembered what Kwang had said to Calvino that day on Sukhumvit Road as she rode her bicycle in a skin-tight pair of red short-shorts: "*Hum hiaw.*"

Not all Cinderella stories had a happy ending. Being murdered in a short-time hotel breached the unwritten rule that the *ying* is always rescued. But in the real world children's stories rarely played out. If Kiko knew one thing, it was that Kwang was the last person in Bangkok Calvino would have wanted to kill. He had tried everything in his power to help the girl. Out of his own pocket he had bought the dog—the one Jerry Hutton hoped would change her life—and it had made no difference.

Calvino was in trouble, and when she took the phone call from Colonel Pratt's wife, Manee, telling her that Calvino was in jail, Kiko needed about thirty seconds to make up her mind as to the right thing to do. She parked at the at Tonglor district police station and walked inside. Rows of officers sat behind battered metal desks, filling out paperwork. Complainants leaned over and told their stories while officers took down their statements. She waited her turn until an officer called her over and gestured for her to sit down. He pulled out a file, turned the pages, sighed, his lips pursed as he read the contents.

"Are you Thai?" he asked. He knew from her accent that she wasn't.

"I am Japanese," she said.

He frowned and flipped through more papers. "Let me see your passport."

She took it from her handbag and handed it to him. He looked through the pages, finding her visa. "Work permit?"

She reached into her handbag and removed the blue work permit book and set it on the desk. He put down her passport and leafed through her work permit. "If he runs away you understand that your forfeit the bail?"

"I understand."

He swiveled around in his chair and pulled out papers from a filing cabinet. "Fill these in."

"They are in Thai," she said. "I don't read Thai."

He sighed, clinched his jaw. "Twenty baht if I fill in the form."

"What if I make that five hundred baht? Is that possible?"

The officer smiled for the first time. "I can only accept twenty baht." He filled in the forms and handed them to Kiko. She signed a document pledging her condo to secure Calvino's bail bond of one million baht. He had already surrendered his American passport. A few minutes later, two officers escorted Calvino into the room. He nodded, said, "Good to see you." He smiled, his hands still cuffed. She passed him a copy of the morning newspaper with his picture inside. Calvino sat at a long wooden table with two police officers on either side, his handcuffed hands stretched atop the table. On the table no more than six inches away was his Browning revolver. The 9mm bullets were lined up in a semicircle on their shell castings like miniature missiles ready to be launched. There was a news story along with the photograph. The caption under the photo ran: "Vincent Calvino, aged thirty-seven, an American citizen was arrested on Soi Cowboy for possession of an illegal weapon."

"I look tired, beat-up, thirty-seven," said Calvino, looking at Kiko over the newspaper.

"You've looked worse," said Kiko, laying down the pen.

"How's Joy?"

"I fed her half a kilo of prime rib last night. She belched. She's no longer a puppy, Vinny."

Calvino looked up from the paperwork.

"What do you mean?"

"Joy started her first period. Blood everywhere."

Lieutenant Narong looked up, sliding Calvino's watch across the desk.

"It's okay, Joy's our dog," Calvino said to the police officer.

"You can go now," he said, nodding to Calvino.

Calvino slowly slipped the watch onto his wrist, taking a long look at Lieutenant Narong. Kiko rose from the chair and walked beside Calvino through the doors, down the stairs, across the concrete yard to Soi Tonglor.

"Safe and warm," hummed Kiko.

Calvino remembered the lyrics of the song.

"One million baht bail buys a pass from jail. It doesn't buy safe and together."

"What does it buy?"

He pulled her close to him as they stood on the curb.

"I dunno. I wanna think of it as rent on a dream. The kind of dream where you can kiss a woman and it means something. Where you can trust a woman and she never questions that trust. You know, when you go to jail, she bails you out without ever thinking about it twice."

"I like that kind of dream," said Kiko. "But we should start with reality. There's something you need to know."

This caught him off guard, and she saw a kind of hurt expression cross his face.

"What kinda reality?"

178

"Janet's in Bangkok."

He drew a blank as if to say his mind was trying to place with some difficulty this woman named Janet. It was a normal case of expat confusion. It was a name out of context, from his past life in another country. The reality didn't immediately register. A taxi stopped and Calvino negotiated the fare through the rolled-down window. He opened the door for Kiko.

"Your ex-wife. That Janet," continued Kiko. "She's here with Melody and they are staying in a suite at the Dusit Thani."

"I don't think I'm gonna like what you're going to tell me next. Am I right?" he asked.

Kiko waited until they were both inside the taxi and the door had closed off the heat.

"Melody's got a part in *Lucky Charms*."

"I told you I wasn't gonna like that part."

"She has a *great* part, Vinny."

His mind raced through the script. There wasn't any role in the script for a thirteen-year-old kid. Besides, they were in the middle of a shoot. He broke out into a cold sweat. These guys were good. They had gotten to Karl Stadler, the steroid Nazi, who'd refused to provide Calvino with an alibi. But for Colonel Pratt working an angle, he would have been charged with murder. Colonel Hatcher and Oxley were clever, dangerous, and connected operators, Asia hands who knew how to push the buttons and keep one step ahead of anyone who tried to circle around to ambush them from behind. It would have been easy enough to have killed Karl—get him some spiked heroin or egg him into a confrontation in the street—but why go to the trouble when Calvino was flushing him out, doing their work without knowing it. Then once they had Karl, it was in their interest to keep him alive. They had brought Calvino's family to Bangkok as insurance.

"Where are we going?" asked Kiko.

He shrugged his shoulders. "The safe-and-together place. Where else?"

"Which is?"

"Which never was," he said, looking out the window as the taxi turned right onto Sukhumvit Road. "We are going to my apartment. Then I'm going to the Dusit Thani."

"Janet said she won't see you until after Melody has done her part."

Calvino shook his head. "She phoned to say I shouldn't see her. That's Janet."

"I'm in the scene with Melody," said Kiko. "Tyler sent over a revised script. Funny coincidence, isn't it?"

Calvino touched his empty holster like an amputee trying to scratch a severed limb. He had this itch. Some might have scratched this itch with the claws of revenge. But Calvino thought he had a better idea.

SIXTEEN

MELODY'S PART

CALVINO had never thought he would have a long, difficult discussion in Bangkok with his ex-wife over spending some time with his daughter. But it turned out that way. Janet stood her ground. Earlier battles during the divorce years had created emotions which had not cooled with time. Maybe there was never enough time to heal the blowout caused by divorce, he thought. It should have been simple. Calvino wanted to see Melody, his daughter. He thought about the logical, reasoned steps of how to "get to yes" with someone who hates your guts. In this case his ex-wife made him sweat that hostile journey. When he finally succeeded, he felt the satisfaction of having won a class action—something major in scope, like a massive toxic waste case with thousands slowly dying of cancer. What he got was a few minutes alone with his daughter. Victory enough, he thought.

"You can take a fifteen-minute meeting," Janet said. She had already picked up some of the L.A. insider lingo.

"She's my daughter. You don't take a meeting with your daughter."

"Fifteen minutes, Vinny."

"Does that include travel time?"

"Starting now." She looked at her watch.

He knew the territory of the Dusit and opted for spending the time alone with Melody in the lobby restaurant. Janet had looked unhappy about the idea he was taking Melody out of the suite. Calvino sat on the sofa in the suite eating an apple and making it clear to Janet that he wasn't leaving until he had a chance to talk to his daughter.

She watched him chewing and staring out the window. He finally got to yes by saying nothing.

The restaurant was one of those place where two scoops of ice cream cost the same as a taxi to the airport and Japanese and Hong Kong Chinese sat together with mobile phones. Calvino and Melody sat at a table below a huge potted bird-of-paradise plant. A waiter brought them two soda glasses filled with ice cream and topped with whipped cream and a cherry. He watched his daughter twirl her spoon in the whipped cream. She had been quiet, standoffish since they got out of the elevator.

"Daddy, are you really a criminal like the newspaper says?" asked Melody. She popped the cherry into her mouth and chewed.

"What do you think?"

"Mummy says she wants to change my name because you're going to jail in Thailand for a very long time."

"Your mother is misinformed."

Melody shrugged her shoulders. "But that's what she said."

Such discussion created a no-hope situation. He shifted ground: putting her outside the zone of danger where she would have to choose between her mother's version of events or his own.

"So you're going to be a star?"

"That's what Mr. Tyler says." she sighed. She made a face as she licked the chocolate ice cream on the edge of her spoon.

"I think that's just great, honey. So you auditioned or what?"

"Well, you see, I was discovered."

"Discovered?"

"Mr. Tyler said most actresses are discovered. It's ordinary in show business."

"Then it was Mr. Tyler who discovered you?"

"Well, not exactly."

"Who then?"

"His associate. Mr. Oxley, who is an important producer. He saw my picture in the school yearbook. And then I had an interview. I never thought he would pick me. I'm so ordinary. I hate my nose. I have your Italian nose, you know."

"When did you get discovered, honey?"

"Oh, about a week ago."

"And now you're in Bangkok."

"With my dad and mom. And Carol Hatcher. I bet you never saw

182

Vampire U in Bangkok. She was great. Now I'm going to be in a movie with her. Leslie—she's my best friend—she just wants to die to change places with me." She stuck her spoon in the ice cream. "Dad, can I ask you something?"

"What's bothering you?" he asked, noticing she had breasts. His daughter, his baby, had grown breasts in the eighteen months since he last saw her. Before she could answer his question, he asked a second one: "Are you wearing a bra?"

"Are you upset with me? I mean you don't seem very happy to see me or excited that I'm here. I thought you would want to see me. Mom says that you're selfish and only think about yourself."

"What do you think?"

She didn't answer, playing with her spoon in the ice cream.

"Dad, if I tell you something will you promise to keep it a secret?" she asked, without looking up.

Making such a bargain was always a mistake, he told himself.

"It's hard making a promise about something I don't know about."

She made a disapproving face. "It's about Mom. But you've gotta promise."

"She's got a new boyfriend and he's a cannibal, right?"

Melody laughed. But the joy was soon shed and replaced by a serious mood. "You're half right. I saw Mr. Oxley coming out of her room early this morning. I think maybe they slept together. In New York I think they had sex, too."

He didn't have a chance to respond before Janet arrived and sat down beside Melody. She nervously smoked a cigarette and glanced at her watch several times. She stroked Melody's hair back from her forehead.

"Hi, Mom," said Melody as if she had been talking about the weather.

"You said fifteen minutes," Janet said to Calvino.

He tried to remember Janet the way she was about the time she had broken out of her twenties. She had been something. She stopped traffic with her long legs, her sensual smile; and those large eyes as blue as the sky. But the years don't let you keep your beauty any more than death lets you keep the stuff you accumulated in life. It wasn't a Calvino law—it was the universal law. The woman at the table was a newly minted forty; she clenched her jaw, working the muscle like someone resisting a breakdown in her ability to control the situation.

Time had worn her down. Oxley, the Asia hand, was screwing his ex-wife. And she was feeling like she was back in her prime; Oxley had found her addiction—that ego surge that came from stopping traffic and turning heads when she entered a room.

In the lower lobby of the Dusit Thani she looked out of context: too large, too old, and too tall against the Thais. Only Oxley hadn't seemed to mind. Calvino regretted that she could never accept what had happened in New York, and now she was in Bangkok, screwing her brains out with a guy who was more than likely trying to kill him. The Hutton murder had nothing to do with her or Melody. But they were right in the middle of it without any idea what they were involved in. Janet lived in a world where nothing happened which wasn't directed either against or for her. She lived in a world where nothing had ever been neutral. He didn't know how to crack that shell.

"There's a problem with Melody and you staying in Bangkok," said Calvino, knowing immediately he had said the wrong thing.

Melody shot him a knowing stare, and mouthed, "You promised."

He winked at Melody and waited for the blast. He wasn't disappointed.

"When it comes to me or Melody there was always some problem," Janet said. " Now your daughter will earn more in six months than you've made in the last nine years. And that hurts your ego. So you tell me there's a problem. And you're right. There is. The picture of Melody's father wearing handcuffs in the newspaper. Sitting in front of an illegal handgun. Her father is a criminal and he's going to prison."

He studied her for a moment. She was coming apart.

"You've been in Bangkok for what? Twenty-four hours. And you think it's no different from going from Brooklyn to Manhattan. Nice hotel. Great suite. Out of nowhere some guy bangs on your door and says Melody should be in the movies. Says he saw her picture in some school yearbook. And it never occurs to you this is too easy, too fast, maybe a little strange? A guy pushing fifty grand into your hands. Probably in hundred-dollar bills. And you made a couple of phone calls. Oxley checked out as a guy with credits in Hollywood. No problem. It's a done deal. You could fly first class with all expenses paid to Bangkok. And you would show me that you had life by the tail. Only you didn't check with the one person you should have checked with."

"Who?"

"Me. And I would have told you that those are bad people and they are trying to mix you up in something dangerous because they know you are my family."

She pushed back the table, and pulled Melody up.

"You can't stand it that we have made it. And you—look at you in the newspaper. You were a fucking criminal in New York and you're the same in Bangkok. I hope they throw your ass in jail and throw away the key."

"Janet, you know, being the mother of a future star, you really should clean up your language. Fuck this, ass that. What kinda image are you projecting?"

She didn't answer him. He watched them circle around the tables and walk to the lower lobby entrance. He caught up with her in front of a brand-new red Mini Minor rotating on a small circular platform —it was the prize in a raffle. Melody started filling out one of the cards. Janet stopped and snarled. "Forget that, Melody."

"I'm almost finished," said Melody, scribbling on the card as fast as she could write.

"Janet, I'm serious. If you don't go home now, you and Melody are in real danger."

Her mouth dropped open and she raised her hands. She addressed the people in the restaurant. "Did everyone hear that? Vincent Calvino has threatened me. His picture is in the newspaper. He is a criminal." She stormed over to the bank of elevators and pushed the buttons.

Melody dropped her card in the transparent plastic box stuffed with cards, and as the car came around, she cocked her head and read the sign again. Someone had added a word. The word "wife" had been written in bold letters. She tugged on her father's jacket, and he looked around.

"Dad, what does it mean?" she asked, pointing at the sign.

He read the sign as amended—"Free Red Mini Minor Wife."

"It's a kind of joke someone like Oxley would like. An old hand joke."

"Thanks for not telling about him, Dad."

The elevator door had opened and Janet was screaming for Melody.

"Gotta go. Bye. Love you."

Then his daughter was gone.

The sign had rotated back around on the car.

"Free Red Mini Minor Wife."

This violated The only free sex was the sex you paid for law.

❖

CALVINO took a taxi to Rolfo Stadler's house. He was greeted with a chorus of snarling, yapping German shepherds with that big-dog gnashing of teeth. The barking ended with one shouted command. Calvino recognized Rolfo's voice. The real maid in plastic sandals shuffled to the gate and let him in. She led him to the back of the house, where Rolfo, stripped to the waist, was cleaning out the holding pen of his queen bitch. Half a dozen shepherds, muscles tense, watched him approach, ears pointed up, eyes waiting for any sudden movement. Rolfo Stadler had told him the first night they met that the German shepherd was the perfect breed: Its instinct had been refined through breeding to produce an animal absolutely loyal, an animal which would protect his owner from harm. A dog sensed trouble; the smell rose like heat waves in the sweat of strangers. The outsider had to deal with the dog before ever getting to the owner. Owning a shepherd was subtle intimidation. Rolfo had started to sound like Kiko's song about staying warm and safe: The dog never relaxed; the stranger never relaxed. But the owner was warm and safe.

"Joy started her first period," said Calvino, eyeing the dogs. "My maid saw blood on the floor. I spent the night locked up. And she got emotional. Started to scream, thinking something bad had happened."

"She probably thought it was yours. But logically, it was impossible because you were in jail. In Bangkok, who has a logically thinking maid? Cause and effect are meaningless. Even if she saw your picture in the newspaper this morning, she wouldn't have connected your being in jail with your not being at home. By the way, that was a nasty-looking large argument. But Americans like large, nasty arguments," said Rolfo.

"You keep them. Who knows when Poland might be persuaded to merge with the fatherland again?" replied Calvino.

"Naw, no one wants Poland. Not now. Not even the Poles," said Rolfo Stadler, laughing at his own joke.

"I see you sold the pups," said Calvino. The four pups which had been bundled together with the queen bitch were gone.

"An American buyer. He said he was a friend of yours," said Rolfo, pointing the nozzle of the hose onto the floor of an empty cage.

"Let me guess. Tyler?"

Rolfo shook his head no, not looking up as he hosed down the pen.

"Colonel Hatcher?"

Again Rolfo shook his head.

"Oxley?"

Rolfo turned off the water. Of course it would be the guy who was bonking Janet, he thought.

"In Germany we go on facts and proofs. We analyze the situation before we make a judgment. We don't go around guessing our way through life like the Americans."

"You could've played Dr. Spock's German brother in *Star Trek*."

"What is that?"

"A TV program. It's world-famous."

"Never heard of it. But then I don't watch TV."

Karl came out of the house, slamming the door hard. A couple of the dogs jumped and barked; Rolfo silenced them immediately. Karl's hair was punked stiff and high on his head with wax, and he wore jeans with rips in the knees and a shirt which looked like it had been made from an old fishnet. He didn't acknowledge Calvino's presence.

"Karl, I just heard that Joy had her period," said Rolfo, as his nephew picked up a broom and began sweeping the water across the drive and onto the garden.

Karl turned angry. "You told them where I was," he said. "I thought I could trust you. But you're no different from the shits who killed Jerry. You're an asshole and I hate you."

"This might not make any difference to you, but once they arrested me I knew you were no longer in danger; it made no sense to hurt you. Because you really had nothing other than what Hutton had told you, and Hutton was dead. Looking at the facts, what could you have done to rock their boat? So when Oxley came around for a little talk you were scared. He saw that. He knows you'd left a helmet behind. But he bought the fact you weren't with Hutton when the footage was shot. You're in the clear. He bought the pups for the full price, right? And he told you not to talk to anyone, including me. We were living in dangerous times, and bad things were happening. He probably said he was sorry about what had happened to Jerry and he was doing everything in his power to find the murderer. Meanwhile, he told you I was getting in the way of the investigation: I was causing confusion and trouble. And if anyone from the police

187

should ask if you had seen me last night, then you were to say I hadn't been around. Is that about it?"

Karl calmed down; he knew that Calvino had hit a number of points. Oxley had warned him that Calvino was using him as an alibi. Calvino had been at the house. Then killed the girl and returned to the bar. It had been a clever trick, stopping by the house. Karl should be able to see that much, Oxley had told him.

"He said you had been using me. That you had something to do with Jerry's death."

"What do you think, Karl?"

"It doesn't matter what I think."

Why should he have expected Karl to stick by him if a better offer came along? And Colonel Hatcher and his sidekick, Oxley, were making better offers right down the line.

"I sold him the dogs," said Rolfo. "Military types love the shepherds. The French Army trained German shepherds to sneak through enemy lines; the dogs are very quiet. Then when the dog had reached the destination, the French handler pushed the button."

Rolfo's eyes flashed.

"And after the Frenchman hit the button?" Calvino could see that Rolfo was dying for him to ask.

"The bomb the dog was carrying detonated. It was a good way to kill lots of the enemy without risking your own men. It does seem a waste, I told Oxley. To live in a world where you have to use such a beautiful, loyal animal for such a terrible thing."

"What did Oxley say?"

Rolfo reached into the cage and stroked the queen bitch on the head.

"He said it was a dog-eat-dog world out there. But like most Americans he didn't exactly know where 'out there' was located."

❖

CALVINO found Prakash stylishly dressed in a midnight black outfit—a fashion statement: a black T-shirt under a black jacket rolled up to the elbows. His hair tied back into a ponytail, Prakash had features that suggested Indian, Burmese, and a brushstroke of Mongol. His high cheekbones and suspicious eyes gave him the look of someone who had reinvented himself for heavy-duty operation in the night world of

Bangkok. The age curve rose or fell somewhere between thirty and fifty depending on how the shadows played over the crevices around the eyes, cropped his brow and cheeks. Prakash could have passed as the proprietor of a New York art gallery, the owner of one of those very chic restaurants with no name on the door, or a Muslim terrorist leader plotting to kill the hero in a Hollywood action-adventure film.

In fact Prakash worked as a journalist for several Middle Eastern publications that reported on current affairs in Southeast Asia, and he had connections in the region that went back twenty years. There was something about him that indicated a deep mine shaft, the sides of which were slatted with a lifetime of pain and scars. As he sat at the Foreign Correspondents' Club bar, Prakash appeared to have emerged from this underground of memory, drinking and waiting until his day arrived. He had a connection with the owners of the bookstore in Rangoon that George Orwell wrote about in *Burmese Days*. His family had adapted to exile life in Bangkok, but Prakash had been waiting to return for nearly twenty years.

Prakash nursed his gin and tonic at the bar, and caught Calvino in the mirror as he came up from behind. He raised an eyebrow of acknowledgment in the mirror. Calvino eased onto the stool next to him.

"You look at the clip?" asked Calvino.

"Look, man? I studied that clip frame by frame."

"What do you think? Was it a setup?"

Prakash smiled and raised his gin and tonic.

"No doubt about it. The Burmese guys doing the killing did a pretty good job of it, man. But they still fucked it up."

This was what Calvino had been waiting to hear.

"How? Give me an example."

"I can give you many," said Prakash.

"Start with one."

"You remember the Burmese officer's uniform?"

Calvino remembered.

"On his shoulder he had a gold star," continued Prakash.

Calvino slumped. "It checks out. I found the major's gold star in an old Burmese military book."

"Sure, the gold star checks out if you're looking at formal dress. When an officer is going on parade or to some fancy dinner party. Then you see the gold star on his shoulder. But never in the field. A gold star would catch the sunlight. A sniper could pick him off at five hundred meters. Officers always wear brown insignia in combat. You wouldn't see it unless you were right on the guy."

Calvino thought about the star, and wondered if it was enough. It seemed more the kind of lawyer's technical argument which made juries yawn and stare at the floor and shake the blood which had collected in their feet and legs.

"Anything else?"

"Sure, man. Relax. You seem on edge or something. Jail life obviously didn't appeal to you," said Prakash, grinning. "Just a joke, don't take it serious. Okay, take the Burmese officer. The guy who pulled the trigger of the .45. He did a convincing job. Only one thing: I know how those guys work. The badges on his uniform said '22nd Division.' The guys in that division are real killers, man. Orphans and hard-core street kids taken in by the army and trained to be killers," Prakash said. "They'd kill you just like that," he said, snapping his fingers. "And they'd feel nothing. Except maybe some pleasure. Maybe they've got no normal emotions. Maybe they're the perfect killers."

"So the Burmese soldiers in the TV clip are 22nd Division?" asked Pratt.

"Don't make me laugh. I recognized the one guy, man. His makeup job was pretty good, but I know his face. If it's who I think it is, his name's Ali Ahmad."

"You know him?"

Prakash smiled. "Sure, man. I drank with him. Just like I'm drinking with you. But that was a few years ago."

"Can you be more specific?"

"Ten years ago in Afghanistan when he was killing Russians. Or so he said. People say a lot of things."

"He was fighting with the Mujahideen?"

"You got it, man. He hung out with the Mooj."

"A fellow traveler working to move the jihad forward," said Calvino.

"The Mooj don't have sidekicks or fellow travelers. Either you're in or you're not," said Prakash.

"Get tailored for a suicide vest or take a hike."

"No one takes a hike once they've signed on." Prakash lit a cigarette. "Ali Ahmad and I got drunk in a Mooj safe house. Then after the Russian withdrawal, I heard he had gone to work with the Wahabi."

"The Saudi faction," said Calvino. "He have any connection with the Islamic Party—you know, the one they call Hezb-i-Islami?"

It was starting to make sense. The Wahabi faction of the Mujahideen were rumored to be on the CIA payroll. The same rumor surfaced from time to time about the Hezb-I-Islami. There was enough misinformation put out to cast a doubt about who belonged to what faction and who was the real paymaster. Showing a connection between the CIA, Hutton's tape, and the Unit would be a journalist's dream story. A secret unit staffed with a bunch of Hollywood people had "Pulitzer Prize" written all over it.

"Last I heard Ali Ahmad had showed up along the Bangladesh-Burma border, where the Burmese Army is slaughtering Burmese Muslims. The Rohingyas. These people have lived in Burma hundreds of years. You think the army cares about that? More than a quarter-million Rohingyas were forced into Bangladesh. They didn't go over as tourists. The Burmese Army is right behind them with mortars, flamethrowers, and rifles, kicking ass. They just threw them out like they were yesterday's trash."

"But Hutton's tape was shot in Manerplaw. There are no Muslim communities for hundreds of miles. The Karen are Christians. The Holy War is on the other side of the country."

This brought a slow shake of Prakash's head.

"You don't know how guys like Ali Ahmad think. You open a new front where no one expects you to be operating. Thailand has a big problem with the Muslims in the south. If you expand it to the north, the Thais will lean on the Burmese, go easy on the Rohingyas. Ali Ahmad's what you'd call a true believer in spreading Islam across borders. He'd like nothing better than a new Muslim community flanking northern Thailand, and to link it up with the insurgency in the south. That would be a perfect storm. It might cause a fracture in the cozy business-as-usual relationship between the Thais and Burmese, but Ali Ahmad's mission is to kill people with dirty hearts in order to stop them from contaminating those with clean hearts. If the dirty hearts are inside the chest of Burmese students, then kill them. It doesn't matter. Someone sends you. You go. Saying no isn't an option."

"Could it have been someone else shooting the students in the TV clip?"

Prakash set his jaw, and his teeth gleamed as he smiled.

"I sat as close to him as I am sitting to you. If I saw you with some weird makeup shooting people in New York, I would remember your face. I'd say, 'That's Calvino, man. A well-oiled killing machine.'"

"Makeup," said Calvino. "It didn't look like makeup."

"In movies makeup ain't supposed to look like makeup."

"It was that mud-colored shit snipers slap on their faces to hide in the trees," said Calvino.

"Only this guy was an officer, not a sniper. Burmese officers don't walk around with mud on their face. They're too proud, man."

"If Ali Ahmad were a true believer, wouldn't he want all his friends in the jihad to see that he had scored a big one, earned his glory spur? He was riding toward paradise."

Prakash liked that. "Maybe. I ask myself, Why is Ali Ahmad hanging out with the Karen around Manerplaw? There aren't any Rohingyas on that border; it's Karen and students from Rangoon."

"Say some of his old buddies from his Afghanistan days made him a deal he couldn't refuse," said Calvino. "They say you help us in Manerplaw and we'll help the Wahabi settle some scores with the Burmese. Maybe they slip him into some action with the Karen, let the Muslims exercise some power where no one would expect to find them. The heat's turned up on the Burmese. Maybe Rangoon pulls troops off killing the Rohingyas and throws them against the Karen."

"Only one thing, man. These true believers aren't that complicated. You say, 'Go, kill, come back.' But what you're saying is high politics. Guys like Ali Ahmad wouldn't get it," said Prakash.

"Unless he were a political guy," said Calvino.

"You think he knew he was gonna be on TV?" asked Prakash.

This was a question Prakash had been building up to. The thought had also crossed Calvino's mind. What kind of deal had Ali Ahmad made with "the boys"?

"I dunno," said Calvino. "But I am thinking about some old Asia hands who might know. Military intelligence from the States who are working with the Thais. And I'm thinking these guys—let's say he knew them from Afghanistan—wanted to create an image. Maybe send a message."

Prakash's smile widened. "Maybe. But what kind of message?"

"Maybe . . . some kind of a mutually beneficial deal," said Calvino.

"The Mooj like benefits. It was the 'mutual' part they had trouble with."

As Calvino left the bar, he had a question he was unsure whether he could answer: Why would Colonel Hatcher and Oxley blow the cover on a long-term operative?

SEVENTEEN

SCREEN CREDITS

TOMMY Loretti sat at his desk, his feet propped on the edge, holding the remote control and looking at a giant TV screen in the corner of his office. He cradled the phone between his neck and shoulder and pushed the fast-forward button. Then he switched to play as the camera moved forward for a close-up of Carol Hatcher's breasts—firm, pointed mounds warm and safe inside a cheerleader's outfit. The Razorback football team ran out on the field as fans cheered in the stands. Her vampire brother, the team captain, number 12 on his back, jogged through the shot with a cunning smile. He gave his sister the Winston Churchill victory signal—only the cigar was missing. Through the goalposts a large Halloween moon shone as the brother's tongue licked his lips, a sly lizardlike flick of the tongue.

"I'm looking at it now," Loretti said. "Carol Hatcher ain't bad-looking. Each show opens with a medium close-up of her erect nipples, her chin upturned as she stares longingly at the full moon. It was the best part of the series. It's all anyone remembers. When she was on Leno they showed it and someone cracked, 'One small step for mankind, two nipples for the moon.' And then someone else said, 'Isn't that what Neil Armstrong said?' And Carol said, 'No, Armstrong said the Eagle has landed.' And Leno said, 'If Armstrong had seen this moon he would've said, 'The Beaver has docked.' He got a lot of negative mail for that."

It was Calvino's dime. And Loretti was starting to get into these long-distance conversations with Calvino about the business.

"I'll send a copy of *Vampire U* overnight. You don't need all six. If you've seen one, then you've seen them all. And a copy of something called *Teheran*. It's weird. Like Hitchcock dropped LSD. A special treat. Also, I have a couple of other B films you might want to see."

"You find out anything else about these guys? Military records, that kind of thing?" asked Calvino. He knew Tommy had, otherwise he wouldn't have been sending all the films and suddenly sounding serious and contemplative.

Tommy Loretti had said Calvino was paranoid, that checking military records was an expensive waste of time. But he'd made a search and, bingo, Calvino's instincts had been right.

"Hatcher, Tyler, and Oxley served in Vietnam," said Tommy. "Roland May was too young for 'Nam."

"Doing what? Repairing plumbing in Saigon brothels?"

Tommy Loretti knew he deserved that one.

"Okay, you were right. Look, they don't give Oscars for being right—what do you want from me? Anyway, these guys were part of a military documentary film unit. Stationed in Saigon, so the records say."

Calvino thought out loud on the phone. "And the unit never got disbanded. The band just kept playing on. Doing what they had been doing in Saigon. They planned it well, Tommy. Hutton goes up to the border. Does the dirty work, they kill him, make him a hero, buy the rights to his story for another film deal."

"You're jumping to a lot of conclusions, Vinny."

"What do you call it? A coincidence? The screen credits, the locations, what happened in Thailand?"

"If you're right, then maybe you should back off. It's like the mob guys and their thing about *omerta*. Violate the code of silence and you're dead. These black-bag guys are just like the mob."

"Send me the cassettes, Tommy."

"Sometimes I think your friends would have done you a favor if they had left you in jail."

❖

COLONEL Pratt pressed the reverse button on the remote control, reeling all the characters backward through time, with the team running in reverse off the field, wiping the smile off the quarterback's face until he reached the opening credits.

Jesse Tyler had two screen credits: one as director and the second as associate producer. Calvino leaned over the wet bar, emptying the last of a Johnnie Walker Black bottle into a glass. He dumped in a handful of ice. He rattled the ice against the glass, staring at the screen. His head hurt from watching so much bad television. Tommy Loretti had run a search of a Hollywood data base. Screen credits matched up for Tyler and Oxley. But no credits turned up for Hatcher.

Together with Colonel Pratt, Calvino had gone through part of list of films that had gone into DVDs. Hatcher's most memorable titles had been: *Vampire U*, *Teheran*, *Weapon Man*, and *Friendly Danger*. B-list movies fit one category but these movies defied category, falling off the opposite end of the alphabet. Hatcher's films occupied a small niche of failed entertainment that not even the local pirates in the back of their Sukhumvit Road luggage shop were able to unload. No other producer had film credits that included both an anti-Soviet three-hour endurance screed set in Afghanistan and populated with actors no one had ever heard of and a low-grade recycled vampire film. Artistic integrity wasn't the mission. Location shoots provided cover. Their track record supported the conclusion that these filmmakers would take on anything for money.

The fact that Tyler made feature films that went straight to the video bin hardly mattered. No one could deny he was a film industry man. It was his name that was attached to all of the films. The computer printout listed the feature films Tyler had received a major screen credit—most of the time as director. One of the listed features was entitled *Weapon Man* set in Belfast circa '78. The synopsis said it was about gun smuggling, with the American Irish funneling weapons to the IRA. Another film, *Friendly Danger*, had second-unit work from Kabul circa '82. Not one of the film titles or stories had clicked for either Pratt or Calvino. What did click were the coincidences between the films and the headline trouble spots where they had been shot.

"You ever see *Weapon Man*?" Calvino asked.

"Maybe it didn't play in Bangkok," said Colonel Pratt.

"I think it probably didn't do *any* business."

Colonel Pratt cocked an eyebrow.

Calvino grinned. "That's Hollywood talk, meaning it probably didn't play anywhere for more than a couple of days."

Calvino had never heard of Tyler's work. Neither had most people, Tommy had said on the phone. But as Melody said, and Hutton had implied, Calvino's generation was out of touch with reality; better yet, they were frozen solid in the ice age where old hippies never rotted, they just turned blue and fish-eyed. Tyler's feature films were the small-budget, no-name-cast films which received a limited release, meaning—according to Tommy—they had played in a couple of downtown New York and L.A. theatres and had then been put to bed in the back bins of video shops, where they slept without being disturbed.

"You seriously think American intelligence would use a TV series about American college vampires as a covert operation?" asked Colonel Pratt, shaking his head.

"I asked Tommy the same question," said Calvino, staring at the screen. "How did *Vampire U* ever get on the air? You know what he said? Forget about vampires. The series pitch was a fish-out-of-water story. Two beautiful young college kids coping with a social disability and supernatural powers. And you've got college football and cheerleaders. And there is a brother-and-sister team with sincere, sweet personalities, and they each suffer from a strange eating disorder."

"It still doesn't add up, Vincent."

"Maybe it's not supposed to," said Calvino. The same questions had troubled Calvino. "Maybe Tyler wanted to try it on his own. Or maybe Hatcher and the others wanted to create that impression. These guys have a history that goes way back. Why not let Tyler do a TV series without Unit money? When they need his services again, he has more credibility. It would be good for Tyler's ego. Why should the Unit crowd the guy? He was an important asset."

"Or it might mean the Unit had ended operations. Twenty years is a good run for any covert group," said Colonel Pratt. "The series might have been his way of establishing himself."

"Those guys never go out of business. I figure given a history of all those shared screen credits, Hatcher decided some distance wouldn't be a bad thing. Let Tyler establish outside TV credits. Only Tyler's solo flight into TV-land crashes."

Colonel Pratt, the first time he met Colonel Hatcher, had the distinct feeling he was meeting a man carrying some heavy emotional baggage. *Kang won jai*—worried heart; that is what Pratt had felt about Hatcher at the time. And Colonel Hatcher all but confirmed it when he said, "I retire at the end of this year. I was planning a little golf this winter. Then in December I was planning to play a lot of golf. Sometimes I wish it were December rather than February." It was enough to draw an emotional sketch of an unhappy, worried man.

"Colonel Hatcher said he was retiring at the end of this year," said Colonel Pratt. "And he wasn't all that happy being here."

"Maybe it wasn't his idea," said Pratt.

"While his daughter might not be up to Rosalind in *As You Like It*, *Lucky Charms* might still show she had some minor talent. Just enough to justify casting her for another TV pilot," said Colonel Pratt.

"Isn't that the Shakespeare play where the girl pretends to be a boy?" asked Calvino. "Carol Hatcher pretending to be a boy. You should be in the casting business," said Calvino.

"Only my explanation fails to explain why he tried to kill us at the restaurant," said Colonel Pratt.

"Because the movie isn't a real movie. It was shot as cover for his unit's operations. Each film drops an action story into a current political hot spot, giving it a nice propaganda twist along the way. On every movie, they're killing two birds with one stone: supporting the Shah, stopping gun smuggling to the IRA, blowing up Russian tanks in Kabul, setting up Burmese Army as cold-blooded murderers. We've looked at the earlier stuff. You recognize any of those names in the credits?" asked Calvino.

"None."

"Each of his projects was part of a covert operation. But who can tell? They look like bad *Rambo*. Like *Lucky Charms* and the Burmese. So why would he want his daughter in the middle of something like that? It doesn't make sense."

"Unless someone else cast her," said Colonel Pratt.

It made sense, and stopped Calvino cold in his tracks.

"Why didn't I think of that?"

Calvino flipped through the thick folder of computer printouts Tommy had sent with a scorecard of credits going back to 1973. There were many overlaps in the crew—gaffer, best boy, key grip, electrician, set designer, and director of photography. There were also overlaps in the casts. Tyler and Oxley were listed. Roland May was given screen credit in three feature films. But there no mention of Hatcher, the silent partner who didn't officially exist in Hollywood.

"You study the screen credits and a pattern emerges, Pratt."

Colonel Pratt looked over the figures.

"Carol Hatcher's name doesn't appear in a single production outside the vampire series." Colonel Pratt looked through a separate screen credit sheet on Carol—TV commercials, walk-on appearances in sitcoms, summer stock theatre. It was nothing much different from what he imagined were the records of thousands of women looking for the chance to break into the big time.

"Tommy says screen credits are like a battlefield. People sue over credits, whose name is on top. It's like sexual positions. But your screen credits determine how close your restaurant table is to the kitchen," said Calvino.

"So Tyler is seated at a reasonable table in L.A.," said Colonel Pratt.

"Carol Hatcher's is better. She was on Leno. But that's good for about two, three weeks. Oxley gets seated two tables closer to the toilet than Tyler. But Hatcher is in the lobby behind a line of tourists from Des Moines, Iowa. Did I mention he had one credit? He was listed as a technical adviser in one old film no one ever heard of and that wouldn't get him past the table captain. Unless, of course, he was wearing his uniform."

"And Roland May?"

"His table got canceled in Bangkok," said Calvino.

They watched a sequence of the '73 film entitled *Teheran*. It was shot during the final days of the Shah in Iran. Unlike the later films, *Weapon Man* and *Friendly Danger,* which were Chuck Norris like action-adventure films, *Teheran,* which was in black and white, had the feel of an avant garde NYU student film, the look and feel of a French film *noire voir*. The dark, dreary, stark textures of the interiors were somber. Powdered white limbs at strange angles dangled from chairs, beds, and windows in the twilight. The gritty characters, faces dipped in sexual tension and frustration. There were long shots of rain-drenched Teheran streets, the alienated urban landscape littered with surreal figures smoking cigarettes. One character was talking about the meaning of life, addressing his speech to a couple of naked women in their twenties, coiled on the bed and peeling oranges from a wooden bowl.

"Stop it there," said Calvino.

Colonel Pratt pressed the still button.

"Back up to the bedroom scene. More. There. Hold it on the girls, the knife, and the orange."

The remote control froze the peeling action of the two naked women in the background and the actor, head cocked to the side, looking straight into the camera with dark, hooded eyes and a brooding mouth, an orange in one hand, a knife in the other.

Teheran had been Tyler's first feature film. In a 1973 issue of *Variety, Teheran* had been called a small work of genius and the director one to watch. *Teheran* had played in three movie houses and died an obscure, lonely death. Tyler was quoted in an article about how unrecognized genius would one day be recognized. Hatcher had earned his sole screen credit as technical adviser in that film. The screen credits listed the actor who made love with a whore in an alley as "Frank Horn."

Calvino had underlined the name "Frank Horn" several times on his notepad. He walked over and sat in the chair, studying the face of the actor.

"You recognize him?" asked Colonel Pratt.

"I get this strange feeling I'm looking at someone twenty years younger. Ali Ahmad. Our Burmese officer. The triggerman in the Moei River executions. It's got Hatcher worried, with his retirement coming up. He's got a screen credit under a phony name for *Teheran*. He used the name 'Frank Horn.' That was almost twenty years ago. Do you get the feeling that Hatcher not only knew about the executions but that his unit planned them? That's why he was so jumpy at Sanam Luang and sent a team to shoot us by the river. He's unhappy that we found out his movie history. Look at the credits for *Teheran*—Oxley, Tyler, and Frank Horn. Guess who's working in Bangkok on *Lucky Charms*."

At first Colonel Pratt did not share Calvino's excitement. Calvino was jumping around the room, clapping his hands, doing a little victory dance. He went to the bar, opened a new bottle of scotch, and poured himself a drink.

"But to use him doesn't make sense," said Colonel Pratt, as Calvino lifted the glass to his lips. "Why risk his own daughter, Vincent? She was never involved in any of these projects. It seems strange. And just as strange to risk using Frank Horn or Ali Ahmad or whatever his name is. The man's face is recognizable. Even I see that." Pratt appeared amazed as he looked at the actor on the screen and then over at Calvino, who lowered his freshly poured scotch to the bar.

"Film people always talk about what the motivation of the character is. And the answer is almost always the same: They do what they do on the screen for money. None of the films and TV sitcoms Tyler made ever earned any money. I read Tyler's script for *Lucky Charms*. It's certainly not *Moby Dick*. *Vampire U* is Shakespearian by comparison."

"What do you think their motive is?"

Calvino ran his finger around the rim of the scotch glass, then licked his fingertip. "The same reason they made the other films. They are in the covert operations business. The films are collateral to their main business. A film that's any good would get noticed. These guys don't want publicity for their mission; they want to be seen as struggling to get their third-rate movies on more than three screens worldwide. They have agents pounding on doors of critics and anyone else in the industry. No one pays them any attention. That's what they like. Their movies didn't just drop out of sight—most people never noticed they existed in the first place. But they accomplished what they wanted. They've covered their asses, and so long as egos were kept in check and they remembered their real job, they could go on and on forever. But I think you're right about Colonel Hatcher and his daughter: There's something not quite right, some personal thing that doesn't make sense. Carol would get the film noticed. Why would they want that after twenty years of producing consistent bombs?"

"You read the script, Vincent. But you said almost nothing about it." Colonel Pratt sounded slightly hurt, as if Calvino hadn't trusted him enough to level with him about the film. And afterward, learning Melody had a part in the script, Calvino had clamped up even tighter.

"I read one version of the script; Hutton saw another. God knows how many other versions are floating around and which one they're shooting. But you're right—his daughter could have come as an unpleasant surprise."

"Like Melody," said Colonel Pratt.

Calvino stared hard at his glass. He didn't want to look Pratt in the face. "Oxley's screwing Janet," said Calvino.

Colonel Pratt remembered Rosalind's passage on love, "'Love is merely a madness, and deserves as well a dark house and a whip as madmen do; and the reason why they are not so punished and cured is, that the lunacy is so ordinary that the whippers are in love too.'"

❖

COLONEL Pratt felt compassion for his friend's pain, the circle of fire that had enveloped Calvino and led to his exile to Bangkok. The fire had returned. He was back in the center of the flames with his daughter and ex-wife watching him sweat as the heat moved closer. It was Vincent's nature to make jokes about what had happened. From his student days in New York City, Pratt had learned that certain kinds of Americans dealt with pain and suffering by using humor. "Full of tears, full of smiles," as Shakespeare had said. Pratt's own wife, Manee, and their two kids had gone to the Dusit Thani. They had had lunch with Janet and Melody. A decade before in New York City, the four of them had shared the close bonds of a common friendship. He also knew that Janet partly blamed him for the breakup of her marriage to Calvino. That Calvino had put his career, reputation, and family on the line for him; and that, in the end, he had lost all three. He had struck out: lost the game, the home, the wife, the kid, his profession. For what? Loyalty to a foreigner who was in trouble with Chinese triad drug warlords. That foreigner had been Pratt. The Chinese in New York City would have killed him if it hadn't been for Calvino.

Calvino finished his scotch and looked around Colonel Pratt's house. He saw that Pratt was thinking hard about something and figured it was the connection between the film script, Shakespeare, and the war on the Thai-Burmese border. Calvino thought that if he were looking through a camera, bringing the sitting room into focus, it could have been almost anywhere. But if the camera picked up a few revealing details, then the room could only be in Thailand. The fresh-cut orchids in a crystal bowl of water. A copy of *The Nation* opened to a piece on Dex's jazz tour in Japan, comparing him to Miles Davis, John Coltrane, and Herbie Hancock; next to it an item about the democracy movement—nice positioning for those who knew the relationship between Dex and the movement. In the far corner, a small shrine with a golden Buddha seated in the lotus position, and candles, flowers, and incense decorations. By the

201

sliding glass door which led out to the garden, the rows of shoes neatly lined up, and beyond, a spirit house. With every camera angle, the mood, feeling, and personality of the room created the overwhelming impression that the location was not just Asia and not just Thailand but an upper-middle-class house in Bangkok. And that the people who inhabited the room marched to a different beat from the one in America.

Watching anything Tyler had directed was low-grade torture: a hundred and twenty minutes filled with cultural stereotyping, bad lighting and crazy angles, and a travelogue of images running from interiors of old warehouses to jungle camps and deserts, mingled with big-city aerial shots taken at night. It was like a series of postcards that had no apparent connection. The good guys always had a mission to kill terrorists and rescue a woman or child. The audience watched the heroic slaughtering and cheered as the body count mounted. Close-ups of blood gushing out of an open wound were Tyler's signature shots. Calvino had had the same feeling when Tyler let him read the script of *Lucky Charms*. Take the goat. No Thai in Bangkok would ever participate in the ritual goat-slaughter scene at Jao Mae Thapthim. The shrine was a small, cramped place where a woman might go with flowers, incense, and candles and perform a ceremony in private. But she would never arrive in a see-through silk wrap like ex-vampire Carol Hatcher. Nor would a Thai woman ever dance around the grounds and sensually embrace the five-meter-tall penis. The script said everything about Hollywood and almost nothing about Thailand or its people, their beliefs and rituals. The pictures reflected the agenda of the men who made them. They weren't gathering intelligence—not even close. They were running covert ops, killing people for real, and that had been their game from the time they made their first feature.

Calvino understood Colonel Hatcher's motivation in coming to Bangkok and making this film at this time. Like any father Hatcher wanted to do all that was humanly possible to help his daughter. Calvino felt a strange sympathy for him. Hatcher more than likely suffered from guilt at having ignored her, having been stationed overseas most of his life, having always had another tour, assignment, mission before coming home. Then one day, he came home and she had grown up and they were strangers. He was a typical boomer who had put his family on hold, or changed one family for another, always putting his career first. By the time he realized what had happened, it was too late. Hatcher felt a sense of panic. He wanted his daughter back; he wanted his youth back. Both had flown away along a stream of time he couldn't stem.

Hatcher was an old hand. Bringing his daughter into the eye of this storm didn't fit. Calvino kept thinking about "obligations" owed. The word "obligation" crept back into his mind. Pratt had said Hatcher hadn't been happy to find himself in Bangkok. By bringing Melody to Bangkok the Unit was sending Calvino a very personal message: *You are a father so we will use the one thing which matters to you—your daughter—as leverage. You abandoned her once by taking the outbound path; will you abandon her again in Bangkok? Or is this your chance to make amends for having been away?*

Save your daughter; save yourself.

Had Colonel Hatcher done what an Asian father would have done? Had he used his official position to help his kid's career? Carol was Hatcher's flesh and blood. Calvino knew the impact Melody's arrival had had on him. It had stopped him from thinking about Jerry Hutton's murder, and feeling he had some responsibility to find who had killed him. If it was Colonel Hatcher's move, then he had acted brilliantly. He had diverted Calvino from his goal simply by inserting his family before his eyes, and implicitly asking: *What is really important to you, Vincent Calvino? Or have you lost sight of the meaning of such a question? Because if you have, then you must live with the fact that your searching has estranged you from the very thing that defines the lives of most people: their family.* Maybe Janet was right and he was a bad father, Calvino thought. In ten years Melody would be the same age as Carol Hatcher. Maybe Hatcher had brought in Melody not as a hostage but so that Calvino might understand what he had done. Hatcher was a family man trying to help a daughter whose career was in free fall.

But in the back of his mind, Calvino had this doubt.

He had measured Colonel Hatcher that day on Sanam Luang. He came up short as the kind of man who would put his own daughter at risk.

Oxley had been the one who had brought Melody and Janet to Bangkok.

If he were a betting man, he'd bet Oxley was the one who had brought Carol Hatcher to the City of Angels as well.

❖

THE wall of steam gathered above their heads. They were naked and alone. Kiko had locked the door to the hot tub and left on a side light. It was cozy, private; a relaxed moment for both of them.

"One piece of good news. The pimp who identified me as Kwang's customer has fled the scene," said Calvino, breaking the long silence. "Pratt told me tonight. That ends the murder case."

"What if the police find him?" said Kiko, pushing her hands through her wet hair.

"I'm not sure the police are looking for him," said Calvino. "The gun charge did the job."

There was something in his tone of voice that struck her as uncharacteristic of Calvino.

"It's not like you to feel sorry for yourself, Vinny," said Kiko. There was a slight echo effect. The acoustics of the small bathroom amplified the hint of his sorrow.

"You're right. What's there to feel sorry for? My thirteen-year-old daughter is wearing a bra. My dog had her first period. My ex-wife calls me a criminal. Hutton is drowned in the lake at Lumpini Park. Kwang is killed in a short-time hotel bathtub. And in the course of a murder investigation, I stumble onto a major American covert operation using the cover of a low-budget feature staring my daughter and girlfriend. Other than that, I'm having a great day."

It was three in the morning and he sat with the water jets of the hot tub pulsating against his back. Kiko sat with her arms stretched out on the plastic molding. She slid closer and began to rub the back of Calvino's neck.

"That's better," he said.

"There's something else, Vinny."

"Manee had lunch with Janet and Melody. When Pratt and Janet were in New York we were all friends. Did I ever tell you that?"

Kiko shook her head, her hands working over his shoulders.

"Manee had a talk with Janet."

"You mean Janet listened to her?" asked Kiko. "And now she understands that you're not a criminal?"

Calvino smiled, thinking how quick and smart Kiko was about people; and how much longer it had taken him to reach the same conclusion. "Something like that . . ."

"And what else did Manee say?"

"That I can spend tomorrow afternoon with Melody."

Kiko hugged him. "Vinny, that's wonderful."

As her arms wrapped around his neck, he was thinking, Yeah, though she's got her own reason. It gives her the afternoon off to bang Oxley. But he didn't say it; it wasn't the right time or place. There was a moment for anger and there was a moment for passions other than anger. He had to choose. And anger lost out.

"I want you to come along, too. And bring Lisa. Melody should meet her." He imagined their daughters' feeling each other out. Two kids who didn't know one another yet whose parents slept together; it was the kind of world which Hutton had wanted to change with a German shepherd named Joy.

"You don't need a crowd, Vinny. You need that time with Melody. Just the two of you alone. Talking about things," said Kiko. "Melody and I are in the same scene—we can talk on the set. Funny, isn't it?"

Her eyes were hot on him, circling his face like a fly looking for a discreet place to land. He gave away nothing. Slowly the fragments were coming together in his mind, forming an image of the tapestry woven by Colonel Hatcher. He saw the setup put in place by Hatcher and Oxley; it was a perfect trap. Using his daughter and girlfriend as bait. He read his fears as if they were neon scrawled across a billboard. There was little for him to do. Everything was in motion just as Hatcher and Oxley had planned it. He felt despair in being drawn along for a ride he didn't want to take.

"Vinny, I said Melody and I are in the same scene at Jao Mae Thapthim. You look so far away."

"Tyler doesn't have you drinking blood?"

Her eyes sparkled as her hand moved between his legs. "We're not vampires—not yet. But I think being a vampire could be a great advantage. *Hum hiaw.*" She showed her white teeth and wrinkled her nose.

The *hum* was anything but *hiaw*. He felt his erection growing; the form of his body changing underwater. A corridor in his mind split off, as if some dense dose of brain chemicals had discharged tracers through his thoughts, piercing them and leaving them motionless, lifeless starbursts. In the steamy mists he found her lips. His tongue slipped into Kiko's soft, wet mouth. The water drained off her breasts as he lifted her and lowered her gently down on his erection. Then her lips were moving, but nothing issued from them. No lines of script, no sweet talk, as if the data readout in her brain had been wiped clean. She straddled him, rocking back and forth on her knees. Twisting and splashing in the water, she moaned and stroked his cock, guided it back inside, spreading her legs and wrapping her arms around his waist. She slipped up and hooked her ankles together, pulling her body in against his. They were locked in an embrace that comes from trust and is fueled by animal passion. The fate of relationships was woven from two kinds of threads—passion or commitment; only the fool thought both could co-exist long-term. Passion was good for the temporary stitch but commitment was signing on to the whole unchanging wardrobe. Forever. No man ever seemed satisfied with having only one.

They slid deeper into the water until it came around their necks, spinning and bubbling against their chins; and their bodies were a blurred pinkish silence below them as if they were shells attached to some other time and place. Calvino dropped his mouth below the water level and blew bubbles. Her eyes smiled. She lowered her head underneath the water and rolled forward, playfully biting his nipple, and then came back up for air. He nibbled on her neck, thrusting deep inside her, pushing her against the plastic edge of the hot tub, until her eyes closed, her teeth catching her lower lip.

"Vinny," she whispered, her arms around his neck, her head on his shoulder. "I'm scared. Hold me."

"Afraid of what?"

She held on tight as he worked her arms loose. She was crying a little.

"You might go back to Janet."

"Hey, look at me."

"I'm looking. But I'm still scared."

"You gotta understand how people use the past. Some people try to convert it into a gun. Others bribe you with it or manipulate you into feeling guilt."

"Others run away from it," said Kiko.

"You think I'm on the run?"

"How do you remember it, Vinny?"

"With Janet?"

Kiko nodded and touched his face. The water beaded on his cheeks and mouth. She leaned forward and kissed him; then she waited, looking at the way his mouth had gone tight after the kiss, which meant he was thinking.

"You wanna know the truth? Sometimes people find themselves on the wrong side when they really want to do the right thing. It's hard to admit that you're wrong, that your actions are causing damage to other people. People need to feel they are on the right side. It's hard to get them to see that what they are fighting for is wrong and that they should find the strength to walk away. Janet wanted something important to her, but I couldn't give it to her. If I had given what she'd wanted, then I'd have walked away from what I saw was the right path. You can't do that, can you, Kiko?"

She didn't want to cry. She didn't like it when her throat swelled up, and she hoped the steam and mist would hide what was falling from her eyes.

"No, baby, you can't." And she held him tight.

She knew what had haunted him all these years—at least the outline of the story of a Chinese triad working out of Canal Street that had tried to hook Pratt into their drug operation. He'd slammed the door in their faces. Big mistake. New York City Chinese weren't Bangkok Chinese. Pratt had been in major trouble. He was alone in New York City, and Calvino had the choice of removing the threat or walking away. He didn't walk away, and neither did the Chinese. They came after him, and after they finished Calvino no longer had a licence to practice law in the State of New York. But he had done the right thing.

"You wouldn't go back for Melody?" asked Kiko, as she buried her face in his shoulder. She was crying now. Despite herself she shuddered against him. Now there was no confusing mist and steam for what was in her eyes.

He pulled her back from his shoulder and raised up her chin.

"Say your ex shows up tomorrow from Tokyo. He's got two suitcases ready to move back because he misses Lisa. What are you gonna do?"

"It wouldn't work," said Kiko, shaking her head, then fishtailing around and thrusting her hips against him.

"Because the trust is gone," said Calvino. "Passion is never enough. You know what I'm saying?"

With her back turned, she swayed her hips, grinding them against his cock. Her hand plunged through the waterline as she reached around and caressed him again.

"Janet said to me then, 'You're fucking insane. It's not your goddamn business. You think Pratt would put his ass on the line for you in Bangkok?' She was wrong. He's done that, Kiko. More than once. He's paid back and paid back. I wish he knew he didn't have to keep on paying back. The debt is paid." His voice became a sound in his head, the words tearing up into sounds, some with meaning, some way off in another patch of his head. Her hand was working his flesh like underwater dough.

"Some debts never get paid off, Vinny."

❖

ON the bench across the room, Kiko's shortwave radio was turned on and the *BBC News* signature tune came on. Calvino turned slightly to hear the news. More than four thousand people had crossed the Moei River into Thailand. Burmese artillery from the top of Sleeping Dog Mountain was chewing up Manerplaw, the Karen stronghold, blowing their headquarters to pieces. Manerplaw had been deserted. There was no place to hide; no place was safe from the mortars and artillery the Burmese were shooting from the top of Sleeping Dog Mountain.

He lay back in the water and closed his eyes, listening to the radio. He splashed in the water with his leg like a kid. Kiko was a foot away drying off with a large, fluffy towel. A sense of peace had settled on them. It wasn't Janet who was on his mind. It was Melody. Why suddenly did he feel awkward at the thought of spending an entire afternoon with her? He wished he knew the answer. Melody's face shifted in the fog of his mind, which drifted back to the news, then reeled back to Colonel Pratt's sitting room and all the VCR tapes they had watched. The entertainment business had swallowed almost everything whole: parenthood, schools, politics, and the intelligence business. He remembered Ali Ahmad's brooding face in *Teheran* and the hard lines on the same face in the student execution scene. What had been Ali Ahmad's motivation to make those films and work for guys like Hatcher and Oxley?

Ever since he had talked to Prakash, he'd sensed Ali Ahmad was playing more than one role. But what role was he playing in Thailand? It bothered him. Had Pratt been right—that Hatcher had burned his operative? What had they promised Ali Ahmad? That Sleeping Dog Mountain would never fall into Burmese hands? Because if it did, then the Burmese could reinforce their troops along the Bangladesh border. Maybe Ali Ahmad was the consummate actor. He was a Unit regular. He memorized his lines, fitted himself to the character, and collected his paycheck. He had played the role of Mooj well—even taking in Prakash. Why was the Unit working on the Thai-Burmese border? Americans had no political or economic interest in Burma. The Burmese battle with the Karen had been going on for forty years—every dry season. The battle had almost nothing to do with religion. The Karen fighters were Christians and the Burmese Army claimed to be recruited from Buddhists. But generals signed off on the murder of Buddhist monks, the sacking of temples, the burning of Buddhist texts. The Burmese Army's religion was terror and murder.

The BBC newsreader said, "The Burmese have committed ten battalions to capturing Manerplaw." The day before, the Bangkok newspapers had reported that the Thais had agreed to stop the Burmese from using Thailand to attack the Karen from behind. Otherwise, nothing. No air support. Nothing. Zip. The American government was saying nothing. Behind the scenes, Colonel Hatcher and Oxley were back on the border, slipping in and out of Bangkok as Tyler filmed *Lucky Charms*.

Colonel Pratt's sources told him that every shaft and well they had shouted into echoed back that Colonel Hatcher was running a high-level covert operation mission in Thailand. This was the way the world had operated for half a century. Guys like Hatcher been running around Planet Earth since 1948, when Truman brought in the CIA. The New World Order was tailor-made for the Unit. With the fall of the Soviet Union, the far right everywhere had been robbed of their enemy, their basis for existence. They'd dreamed up new targets, new goals, new visions to justify themselves, new methods to entertain the mass audience. Colonel Hatcher's unit and his right-wing allies in Thailand had seemingly targeted Burma. But why? Burma was on friendly terms with the powerful the "dark influences," as the newspapers called them—and had cultivated long-standing friendships with local officials and police and, of course, politicians; sweetheart logging and fishing deals were the fruits of such power, and were distributed along the line to the right people in the right positions of power. Why would the Thais allow a covert operation inside their own territory? Calvino could think of several reasons—among them that the Thais were business allies of Burma. And there would be the usual weapons contracts with commissions to gain cooperation. Another hint was buried in a news report on the BBC.

The BBC reporter said, "Muslim guerrillas in the south of Thailand have reportedly received training from an Arab country. A local leader was quoted as denying the rumor. At the same time, the secessionist movement in the south is once again causing the Thai military problems."

Calvino climbed out of the hot tub. "Of course, that's it."

"That's what?" asked Kiko.

"I've gotta phone Pratt."

"And then?"

Calvino reached over and kissed her. "Watch me."

She wrapped her arms around his neck.

"Come back into my corner of the pond where I can watch you."

EIGHTEEN

THE SHAMAN

CALVINO gave Melody three choices for their afternoon outing in Bangkok: a long-tail boat trip along the Chao Phraya River with stops at Wat Arun and the floating market, a tour of the Grand Palace and the Temple of the Emerald Buddha, or the National Museum and Sanam Luang for some kite flying. Melody chose a fourth alternative, one that had not occurred to Calvino. One that she had set her heart on as they walked out of the lower lobby of the Dusit Thani Hotel. She had wanted to go to McDonald's.

"I mean, it's so hot outside, Dad. And I'm so hungry," Melody said. "Mom is so worried about my weight. She thinks if I get fat that Mr. Tyler will fire me because I won't look like the picture in my school book anymore but just like some dumb fat girl living in Queens, New York." She was nearly out of breath as she finished.

"But there are McDonald's all over New York." He sounded hurt. "The food is always the same. Don't you want to do something different?"

"But you said it was up to me. That the Thais always let the other person decide." She was a quick study.

"McDonald's. Yeah, why didn't I think of that?"

"Because you've got a lot of worries. Being in jail on gun charges and all that. Mom and Mr. Oxley. You know."

Oxley was making it all very personal, he thought.

Outside the lobby, Calvino stopped a taxi and gave directions for Robinson Department Store on Sukhumvit Road. As the driver turned right on Rama IV Road, Calvino didn't like the way he kept staring at Melody in the rearview mirror, and saying how beautiful she was. They sped through the corridor of exhaust fumes, the driver showing off as he veered between lanes, laughing and practicing his English. "Where you from? Where you go? How old you are? You like Thai people? Can you eat hot food?"

Melody liked the attention, and leaned forward with her hands perched on the headrest of the passenger's seat. She giggled in the way her mother did when she was being coy; one generation had passed lessons down the line. Melody was growing up—whether Calvino wanted that to happen or not. Others were telling him what he didn't want to hear—his baby was no longer a child. She had entered the phase of half child and half woman; the advertisers' dream entity where taboo and product commingled, sending a thrill charge all the way to a cabdriver in Bangkok.

Finally they arrived at McDonald's, ordered, and carried their plastic trays in silence to a table near the bank of windows overlooking Sukhumvit Road.

"These people are so cute, Dad," she said.

He didn't say anything. She had also remained locked inside the state of innocence where things were cute or ugly, good or bad, right or wrong. It was a phase most people never grew out of; and sometimes it led to their destruction. For a second, Hutton crossed his mind. And Kwang.

Melody unwrapped her Big Mac, sipping her Coke at the same time, her eyes focused on the street outside.

"Dad, that building across the street. You see the Lacoste sign? And the Pizza Hut and Esprit? This is so neat. Mom said Bangkok was like going to the jungle or something. I didn't know what to expect. But it's just like home."

Calvino pointed to the brass letters on the front of the building. "See the name of the shopping center?"

Melody chewed her hamburger, searching until she found the sign.

"I can't believe it. My God, no one at home will believe me. Times Square," she said, her eyes growing big. "This place could be New York. You know, if you forgot a few little things."

For nearly two years the shopping center had been one of those little things people had forgotten—a concrete ruin, an unfinished bunker with rusting iron rods curling out like incense sticks that had burnt down in an offering bowl. Then someone had taken over the project and the glass high-rise had gone up; and in the basement a Pizza Hut was spawned like a little shop of horrors to compete head-to-head with a McDonald's. Times Square was part of the New World Order that Hatcher and Oxley and the others had been defending since Vietnam. He thought about *Teheran* and Frank Horn eating an orange slice. Then he saw his daughter eating a Big Mac.

"Remember when we went skating at Rockefeller Plaza?" asked Calvino, thinking about a time four years earlier when he had been home around Christmas. They had walked on Fifth Avenue checking out the Christmas displays in department store windows.

"Yeah, you fell down and hurt your knee."

Of course, that was what she would remember.

"And we bought hot pretzels and drank hot chocolate."

"*You* drank whiskey. I drank hot chocolate. Mom says I can buy a new car when I turn sixteen. A red sports car. And if I become a star, then we can move to Los Angeles and I can have a house with a swimming pool. Mike is a good swimmer."

"Mike?" asked Calvino.

"Mr. Oxley. The film producer. You don't remember?"

"I'm out of it."

"It's okay. Take a deep breath and think positive. That's what Mom always says. And. . . ." She stared at a *san phra phoom*—a spirit house—on top of a pedestal in the driveway. It was white like a Christmas crèche, with a series of three sloping red roofs and decaying garlands of flowers which had been looped over the tiny fence surrounding the house. Small figures were seated on tiny chairs inside the doorway. And below the pedestal were two wooden elephants with more flowers hung over their tusks.

"Is that a dollhouse? And why does it have Christmas tree lights on it? God, I can't believe anyone would put a dollhouse in a parking lot."

"Some Thais believe that spirits live on the land. So they keep spirit houses and give offerings. They think that the spirits will bring them good luck. Protect them," said Calvino.

She sucked her Coke until it made that scratchy dry sound signaling that nothing liquid remained along the plastic-coated bottom of the cup. As he explained the spirit house, she frowned as if she didn't understand him.

"You mean ghosts?"

"Like ghosts."

"And the ghosts like hamburgers?"

No one had ever asked him that question.

"I never thought about it."

"Can I have another Coke?"

Melody left the table and joined the crowd at the counter. Outside the window Calvino watched a blue Toyota truck inching ahead in the inside lane. It was a medium-sized van with the sides open. Squeezed inside were about thirty Isan peasants. He counted ten seated peasants, who were crunched as if joined at the hip, moving like spectators doing the wave at a football game. Except they were on a hard wooden bench, stuck in traffic, exhausted. Another fifteen were standing, and he guessed another ten or so seated on the opposite bench. Six or seven of the passengers were girls about Melody's age, wearing plaid cotton shirts hanging out of their pants and scarves wrapped around their heads; some wore bamboo hats. Peasant sunblock. They were construction workers returning to a slum for the night, for a bowl of rice and some sleep on a bamboo mat, before the Toyota returned at dawn to cart them back like cattle to the building site, where they would carry bricks and mortar on wooden planks suspended around high-rise office blocks and condos rising above the world of McDonald's and Pizza Hut. Seventy percent of the country had the same education and background, and about the same amount of hope as these construction workers. Democracy was as remote from their lives as the fast-food restaurants. The wall of glass between those in the van and those in McDonald's was several lifetimes thick. Melody slipped back into her seat, sticking the straw into the fresh Coke. She followed his eye line to the street.

"Those people look real hot, Dad," said Melody. She thought for a moment. "I would die without air-conditioning. God, look at that girl. She looks younger than me. Don't they have to go to school?"

"It costs money. Books, uniforms," said Calvino.

"But if they don't go to school, what will they do when they grow up? Work in a place like McDonald's?"

"If they could work here, it would be like dying and going to heaven," said Calvino.

"Then they should stay in school," said Melody.

"Tell me about your part," said Calvino, shifting the subject away from the peasants. There was no explanation of what the blue Toyota truck meant that would have satisfied Melody. It was better to veer away from those young, exhausted, expressionless faces and the notion of how remote school was for them, or the fact that what life had in store for them was a series of seamlessly boring days stacked one after another, with death waiting to claim them at the end.

"Can I tell you a secret?"

She was feeling comfortable.

"What kind of secret?"

"You have to promise not to tell anyone. Promise?"

They were back at the same standoff, he thought.

"Is it about Oxley and your mother?" said Calvino.

She nodded.

"No promises," he said.

"Dad, but I want to tell you."

"It's up to you," he said.

"Mike wants Mom and me to move in with him. He has this really neat place in the Valley. I could have a horse."

"What's your mother say?"

"That she doesn't trust me very much after what happened with you. And I've got something to show you."

Melody slipped her shoulder bag off and removed an object, then quickly lowered her hand under the table without showing what it held. Then a fist appeared at table level. She opened her hand one finger at a time. Inside was a necklace of small wooden penises, of the same style found on Hutton's body. There had been a second necklace, too. He had not seen that one. Colonel Pratt said the police had found it around Kwang's throat in the room at the short-time hotel.

"Isn't it gross?" asked Melody, making a face.

The blue Toyota truck moved ahead a couple of feet in the heavy traffic.

"What are you supposed to do with it?" he asked, taking it from her hand.

"I have to wear it, of course. Like this," she said, putting it around her throat. "I wear it in a scene with your girlfriend. Kiko. Or whatever your girlfriend's name is."

"Kiko. That's her name."

"Whatever. And I think if my teacher saw this, I would get kicked out of school."

"When do you wear it, Melody?"

"Dad, why are you upset?"

"Just tell me, sweetheart. It's important."

"Not until Friday night. It's no big deal," and she put the necklace back in her bag. "It's not like I have sex or something in my scene. The necklace is a prop. I thought it would weird you out, that's all."

"I'm weirded out," said Calvino, thinking it was Wednesday, when Friday night was coming up fast.

❖

CALVINO'S maid, Mrs. Jamthong, flew across the room and swung open the ancient fridge. One hip resting against the door, she poured a tall glass of water for Melody from a plastic bottle.

"*Suay*," she repeated several times.

"That means beautiful," explained Calvino.

"Thanks, Mrs. Jamthong. It's so hot. Oscar Wilde said, 'It's better to be beautiful than to be good.'"

"Where did you hear that?"

"Mike said it, I guess."

"You're spending a lot of time around Mike," said Calvino, trying not to sound jealous but not quite pulling it off.

Mrs. Jamthong cut up yellow watermelon, pineapple, and bananas. She unwrapped sweet buns from the fridge and carefully arranged them with the fruit on two big plates, surrounded by orchids carefully laid out around the edges.

Melody held the glass and walked around Calvino's apartment for a minute and a half, which seemed to her like an hour in hard-currency judgmental time. She opened the fridge to refill her glass.

"Dad, you've got ants *inside* your fridge. I have never ever seen ants living in a fridge before. But if it doesn't bother you, then it doesn't bother me. I guess." Mrs. Jamthong had whisked away the glass and refilled it with water. Melody's eyes cautiously roved around the apartment.

He followed her inspection. He began to see his apartment through his daughter's eyes as Melody digested the cupboards, walls, floors—the cracked floor tiles, the flyblown curtains, the rips in the cushions on the rattan furniture. Pasted to the walls above the stove were six grease-splattered sheets from an old calendar with stylized drawings of seventeenth-century Japanese women, their hair done up, smiling behind fans. Below the calendar pages were the discolored green pages of a glossy advertisement for a real estate development project on Bangna-Trad Road. She sipped her water and moved back into the sitting room, running a finger over the cracked glass panel in an old, dusty bookcase. She swallowed the water and stared at a white chalky line. These white lines zigzagged everywhere: over the walls, door frames, cupboards, sometimes forming circles, then shifting into a kind of ancient script like cave writing.

"Why do you write stuff on your walls, Dad?"

Calvino looked at the chalklike marks. "It stops the ants."

"Killer ants?" said Melody, swallowing water. "Like the ones in the fridge?"

"No, these are different ones. They only bite." He left out a description of how the small red ants attacked any region of the body—shoulder, arm, thigh—their signature being a large, swollen, irregular bump rising like a blistery mound on the skin. Four or five bites made in a cluster left a ghastly swelling that went down after several hours. Nor did he tell her about the ants which Mrs. Jamthong was by now too familiar with to notice as she folded and stored his underwear.

As she set the glass down she slowly looked up at the ceiling, where half a dozen geckos—two-inch-long brown house lizards—were catching insects.

"Dad, do you really have to live in the jungle?"

"I've been thinking of fixing it up. You know, painting it. But I've been kinda busy lately."

"Dad, those things on the ceiling. Do they bite?"

"They eat the ants that the chalk doesn't stop. And mosquitoes."

"They give me the creeps. No offense."

He pushed open the door to the bedroom. The fan rotated on low from the nightstand, ruffling Joy's fur as she sat erect on the bed. She had gnawed halfway through a pillow. Thousands of duck feathers hung from the windows and floated in the air. Melody started to giggle. Mrs. Jamthong looked over Melody's shoulder and screamed at the dog and quickly fled the scene. Joy barked, cocking her head to the side. Loose feathers drooped from her mouth. Blood had stained the sheets a dirty red. The bedcover, twisted and torn, had been dragged into the corner as if Joy had decided to make it a nesting blanket.

"This is your dog? Oh, she is so beautiful. I just love her." Melody piled onto his bed and wrapped her arms around Joy's neck. "I want to hug her. Joy, I love you." She kissed Joy's nose and hugged her around the middle. Her hand came across a patch of blood. Melody looked at the blood, and then her father.

"Joy's having her period."

"Oh, that's okay. I have periods now, too. All women get emotional when they have their period. So don't punish her, okay?"

"So long as I don't have to promise."

❖

ON his balcony, Melody had outlined the scene that was scheduled for Friday evening; the location was in what she described as some kind of weird garden.

"Let me ask a question, Melody. Did Oxley have anything to do with your spending time with me today?"

She didn't want to answer, and had that faraway look.

"He told Mom a daughter should have some time with her father, if that's what you mean."

"He didn't make you promise not to discuss the script?" asked Calvino.

She smiled. "Dad, you're being silly."

"Did he made you promise?"

She patted Joy on the head, looking pensive. She kissed the dog's wet, cold nose. "He said it might freak you out. That's all."

The script of *Lucky Charms* must have been rewritten to freak him out, he thought. He knew the scene at Jao Mae Thapthim had been changed to include his daughter. In the new version, Melody was substituted for the goat. He could imagine Tyler explaining that a goat did not provide enough of a feeling of jeopardy for an audience to commit emotionally. "Not enough jeopardy for Calvino," he could imagine Oxley saying, as he cut through the bullshit.

Tyler, as the front man with all the insider's L.A. lingo, had served the Unit well over the years. He actually believed that audiences had an emotional need to lose themselves in films. But how far Oxley and Hatcher took him seriously was another matter. For Tyler, this was a film shoot; he was the director, and it mattered to him whether there was a dramatic buildup to the shaman's unsheath-

218

ing his knife. He'd done the storyboard of Carol Hatcher's dancing near the blade, her caressing the five-meter black styrofoam penis. Hatcher and Oxley had left Tyler's storyboard alone; they had the big scene they had wanted in Thailand—Hutton's footage from the Burmese border. And they had their cover story in place. Hutton had been sent to scout locations for a second-unit shoot and had stumbled upon the execution of Burmese students. Everything had fit together as planned.

But before the Unit wrapped *Lucky Charms* there was some unfinished business with a private detective who had put his nose in where it didn't belong, Calvino thought about the possibilities of how they might try to finish their outstanding business. They had tried to cut off that nose. That hadn't worked. Then Oxley had had a better idea—the daughter. Why not sacrifice Melody? Storyboard that one, Tyler. In the new script, the shaman ceremoniously slipped the necklace of wooden penises around Melody's neck, then the camera zoomed in for a close-up of her throat.

Then the actor had been told to do what the script had not called for the shaman to do—slit Melody's throat.

"I'm in earlier scenes. But when you make a movie the scenes are all mixed up. They put all the film in order later so it makes sense. Got it, Dad?"

After he delivered Melody back to the hotel, he went immediately to Colonel Pratt's house and waited in the sitting room for Pratt to come home from work. Manee made him a drink and he played crazy eights with the two kids. They were beating him four games to two when Colonel Pratt's car pulled into the driveway. Manee dragged the kids away from the cards and took them upstairs to their bedrooms. Once he and Pratt were alone, Calvino explained what Melody had told him about the scene at Jao Mae Thapthim.

"They knew she would tell you," said Colonel Pratt.

"I thought of that, too."

"They want to force your hand. Don't go anywhere near there Friday night, Vincent."

"I want a gun," said Calvino.

"That's exactly what they want. Nothing I could do could help you a second time. And Kiko's bail? It would be gone. They are trying to break you, Vincent. To bust . . ."

"My balls," said Calvino, finishing the thought.

"You think Hatcher and the others would kill Melody on camera? In front of fifty, seventy witnesses?"

"They will have ironclad alibis. Don't you see how they've set it up?"

"How they've set you up, you mean."

"You're not listening, Pratt." He ran a hand through his hair and finished his drink. "Behind Jao Mae Thapthim there's a *klong*. All they need is a long-tail boat waiting. Whoever is the shaman slits Melody's throat. There is probably a couple of minutes' delay. A lot of confusion, screaming, running around. Carol Hatcher continues to dance around the dick garden. The shaman disappears into the background, slips through a hole in the fence, and vanishes. Talk about publicity. These guys could sell distribution worldwide and name their own price. Or, now think of this. I go in and whack the shaman in full view of everyone. The same thing. They have a dynamite angle. 'Killer dad does shaman in garden of dicks.' They would run my picture next to Elvis landing in UFOs for the next thirty years."

"They aren't that smart," said Colonel Pratt.

Calvino picked up the deck of playing cards.

"This ain't a game of crazy eights. Oxley has it locked up. They intend to kill my daughter, Pratt."

He shuffled the cards. The house had gone quiet. Upstairs there was no movement, as if Manee and the kids were holding their breath. Colonel Pratt watched his friend suffering, thinking about the nightmare flashing in front of Calvino's eyes.

"Manee said something interesting about *Lucky Charms* last night," he said.

Calvino looked up, waiting for him to continue. Colonel Pratt knew that he had Calvino's attention and played it out.

"I said to Manee, 'Ask Janet to watch *Teheran*. Ask her if she recognizes the actor named Frank Horn.' And Janet phoned her and said he looked familiar. She had seen him with Oxley."

"Let me guess. He's playing the role of shaman," said Calvino, letting the cards drop from his hand.

"I assigned Lieutenant Narong to track down all the hotels where this guy might be staying," said Colonel Pratt.

"He found him?"

Colonel Pratt smiled. "He's checked in around the corner from Hotel 99 where we found Kwang."

"Lieutenant Narong's watching him?" asked Calvino.

"I know what you are afraid of, Vincent."

"There's an old saying that some of the old hands used in Vietnam. It's real simple: Fear is your friend. It is never your enemy. Without fear your enemy will take the high ground and kill you, Pratt. It's the kind of thing guys like Oxley go around saying to young kids like Hutton."

"You still want a gun?"

Calvino lifted the whiskey bottle. "What do you know about makeup?" Colonel Pratt lifted an eyebrow. "Cosmetics. The stuff they put on an actor's face."

CHAPTER 19

SHOW BUSINESS

"HOW did you know I was in Vietnam?"

That was the first question Calvino heard from Ali Ahmad.

It was a sucker punch; because Calvino assumed that Ali Ahmad was like a black hole—you never saw one, but from the way it sucked light and energy from everything around it, its existence seemed like a reasonable scientific assumption.

With Ali Ahmad it wasn't theory; he was in fact a human black hole, sucking in Hutton, Kwang, the students on the border, and probably enough other people to keep a vacancy sign hung out permanently on a high-rise hotel. From his own mouth—or as it turned out, through his teeth—he had been one of the boys in Saigon. One of the Unit guys who learned the business in the field with an M16 slung over one shoulder.

It was Thursday, the day before Melody's big scene. Calvino had had a sleepless night, and had tumbled out of bed and taken Joy for a run on the back sois at about dawn. His face had turned sallow and his eyes puffy. Pratt had his tenor sax strapped around his neck and greeted Calvino as he dragged himself into the garden. He sat across from Pratt, yawning, his legs stretched out; he closed his eyes and listened to his friend play. Then the music stopped. Before they took a ride over to Ali Ahmad's hotel, Colonel Pratt wanted to explain to Calvino how they should approach the suspect. It was peaceful sitting at the table in the back garden of Pratt's house. Calvino listened, nodding his approval to Colonel Pratt's plan. Then they waited until the phone call came through that Ali Ahmad was back in his room.

"It's sounding good, Pratt."

Calvino sat up in his chair. He was getting his second wind.

"Take a look through the folder," said Colonel Pratt, nodding at a file folder on the table. A lot of the report was in Thai. Calvino immediately flipped to the English version.

The cast and crew for *Lucky Charms* occupied a block of suites on the seventeenth floor of the Dusit Thani. Except for one member of the cast. According to the intelligence report Colonel Pratt showed to Calvino, Frank Horn, aka Ali Ahmad (one of his eleven aliases in the report), had shifted between six different hotels, using a different name to register each time, and then shuttled between the hotels frequently over the two weeks since he had arrived in Bangkok. He came alone and stayed alone. He behaved like someone who didn't want to attract an audience. Film industry people liked to give interviews; spooks disappeared into the night. There was no record of anyone matching his description—or descriptions—staying at the Dusit Thani under any of his known aliases. But Colonel Pratt, with a little help from friends at the Ministry of Defense who had connections with TOT—the Telephone Organization of Thailand—had compiled an impressive record of his phone calls to Beirut, Cairo, Dahaka, Karachi, Riyadh, Hat Yai, and Langley, Virginia. And to Cox's Bazar—the flash point along the Bangladesh and Burmese border where the Rohingyas, the Muslim refugees, had poured across, the Burmese Army giving them a push from behind. Pratt discovered that the ministry had been tracking Ali Ahmad since he arrived at Don Muang Airport on a Lebanese passport stamped with what looked like a forged Thai visa out of the London Embassy. It was a case of the left hand not knowing what the right hand was doing.

Pratt finally traced him to a hotel where he had checked in as a businessman bearing the name "Kent Howlett" and using a Canadian passport.

In Colonel Pratt's garden, Calvino continued looking through the papers inside the folder. The guy used hotel rooms like phone booths, so he could have been an actor. But he seemed to make sure he never placed international calls to more than one city from any one room. What kind of an actor would do that? Calvino asked himself. Ali Ahmad took Patpong prostitutes in combinations of twos and threes to his hotel rooms and ran up large room service bills. He always used credit cards—MasterCard, Visa, American Express. He played musical chairs with the string of hotels clustered around Soi Nana off Sukhumvit Road. A smart move, since this was a perfect location to mask lots of calls to the Middle East. Arabs dominated the area. There was a large concentration of nationals from the Gulf states among whom Ali Ahmad could blend. In Arab dress, they sat in cafes smoking cigarettes and drinking strong coffee. This was the part of Bangkok where Arabic signs hung in the windows and on the doors of coffee houses, money changers, and tailors and restaurants served Middle Eastern food. They had their own local women, who had adapted their ears to Middle Eastern music.

But the Langley calls—all seven of them—were placed from a room at a luxury hotel ("spook central," as expats called it) in mortar range of the American Embassy on Wireless Road. There was a gap of about six days between the sixth and seventh phone calls to Langley —the same period Hutton had been on the border filming the Burmese Army executions. Also, Ali Ahmad seemed to be making contacts in the area; he was seen meeting and drinking coffee with Arabs, heads bent forward, talking.

The way the circumstantial evidence fitted, Ali Ahmad's professional resume had begun in Saigon with Hatcher, Oxley, and Tyler. He had enough skill—about on a par with Tyler's skill as a director— to just pull it off; to get over the hump that it was a movie shot in some kid's basement on a videocam. When the Unit shifted into the feature business, Ali Ahmad, as one of the old hands, never had to read for a part; he was automatically cast. Like some third-rate Alan Arkin or Robert De Niro, he was the kind of actor who could alter his physical size and facial features; he never looked the same from one role to the next. Calvino had watched him as a young mob guy in *Teheran* and on Hutton's film clip from the border. In *Teheran* he played a street-smart tough guy with a Middle Eastern accent. He had a two- or three-day beard and smoked Turkish cigarettes. As an actor, Ali Ahmad had shown some style; he had probably studied some of the European actors of the '50s who snarled into the camera and used their eyes and face to show emotion.

"When Prakash interviewed Ali Ahmad a few years ago, he was in a Mooj safe house in Kabul," said Calvino, laying the report back on the table. "Hatcher's boys must be doing stage as well as film work."

Colonel Pratt smiled. He liked that one. Then he tapped his fingers on the tenor sax. He wetted his lips as if he were about to play a few riffs, but a thought interrupted his intention. A maid arrived with a tray containing a small bottle of Mekhong and a pot of Chinese tea. She knew from long experience who got what off that tray.

"We might have been wrong about Colonel Hatcher," said Colonel Pratt.

"He's running the operation. Ali Ahmad is one of the boys. Like Tyler and Oxley. And Roland May."

"Hatcher ran it in Saigon. He may have run it for a long time. But he's about to retire. You know the Thai phrase, *sakit jai*? It means you have this inkling, like a sixth sense."

"And your sixth sense tells you . . . ?"

"Hatcher's a figurehead. He's not heading this operation. After he found out the gunman in the boat tried to kill you on the river, he went into a rage. He didn't expect it. The way it happened, it was like he was being set up. So that leaves us with Tyler, Ali Ahmad, or Oxley," said Colonel Pratt.

"Tyler never. But Oxley? Ali Ahmad? Maybe. I'm gonna have to rewrite the treatment I sent to Tommy Loretti. I had Hatcher in an AWAC issuing orders to Oxley to kill the students on the border."

"One more thing. I have the feeling. . . ."

"*Sakit jai.*"

"Maybe Hatcher doesn't know he's a figurehead. Maybe they didn't want to tell him since he's so close to retirement," said Colonel Pratt. "But he's not stupid. He must know things are happening outside his chain of command."

"Then from the list of international phone calls, it must be Ali Ahmad who is leading the parade," said Calvino.

"What I don't understand," Colonel Pratt said, "is why the leader of the parade would leave two perfect thumbprints at two murder scenes."

"Unless someone set him up."

Colonel Pratt had an idea of what Calvino was thinking.

"Oxley," said Calvino.

"Maybe you're standing too close to him," said Colonel Pratt.

"What you're saying is, I want Oxley's head because of Janet?"

Ever since Calvino had found out that Oxley had been sleeping with his ex-wife, that had been exactly what Colonel Pratt was thinking. The desire for revenge was understandable. Oxley was breaking Calvino's face; and like breaking a man's rice bowl, that was a dangerous course of action in Thailand. It didn't matter that Calvino was a *farang*; he had been in Thailand long enough to grow a face, as the Thais would say of a foreigner who one day stared in the mirror and saw something he had never seen before. Something that could be lost or broken.

"The question is how Ali Ahmad's prints found their way to Hutton and Kwang," said Colonel Pratt.

"I'm starting to think there is a Unit inside the Unit," said Calvino. "It's like Russian dolls stacked one inside the other. Someone might have found out that Ali Ahmad's gone into something he shouldn't, been turned around, compromised. He's the doll which gets busted."

"They burn him." Colonel Pratt blew a few random notes on the tenor sax. "Whack him, as you would call it," he continued.

Calvino was not certain such a straightforward solution would be used by people whose lives had been twisted, reshaped, and manufactured into instruments of policy. "If they put a bullet in his head, then the game is over. But maybe they don't want the game to be over."

Colonel Pratt looked at a cat stalking a bird, moving slowly, silently, in measured steps over the top of the garden wall. "Vincent Calvino might be their means to that end."

"They set me up to do the job for them. Like they set Hutton up to do the film. So this time out they hire Melody, bring her to Bangkok, and give me the choice," said Calvino, his heart in his throat. He got up from the chair on the patio and started pacing. The pressure had been building all afternoon. Colonel Pratt noticed that he hadn't touched the Mekhong. They had boxed Calvino in— he was one of the Russian dolls and he was angry with himself for not having seen what they were doing all along—they were constructing a scene which would leave him with no way out.

"If you don't stop him, Ali Ahmad cuts Melody's throat," said Colonel Pratt. "If he kills her, then afterward Oxley, or someone else, puts a bullet in his head. And maybe they have a set of your prints on the gun. Everything points to you as the assassin."

Calvino stopped pacing. "He might not . . . harm Melody. He's on camera." He was unable to use the word "murder" or "kill" in the same sentence as his daughter.

"He killed two of the three students on camera."

Calvino saw where Colonel Pratt was leading with his analysis.

"They changed the script as a kind of loyalty test."

"*Ying thi diaw dai nok song tua,*" said Colonel Pratt.

"To kill two birds with one stone," Calvino said aloud.

A small-time, no-name B actor who killed people in the name of intelligence and national security had been scripted to kill Calvino's daughter. Ali Ahmad had killed for the Unit before and Calvino had no doubt that he would not think twice about killing Melody. But for some reason, or some lack of reason, an overriding emotion had intervened along the way. Something was happening off camera, off the script, which suggested that some little birds were building themselves a very large nest.

❖

COLONEL Pratt unlocked the door with a passkey obtained from the front desk. He walked straight into Ali Ahmad's room on the third floor of the Grace Hotel, with Calvino following one step behind. They found Ali Ahmad with a towel wrapped around his waist, smoking a cigarette and watching CNN. On the bed were two naked teenage girls playing cards. A dozen empty beer bottles were scattered on the carpet like bowling pins after a strike. Calvino threw an orange underhanded and Ali Ahmad caught it one-handed.

"Peel again, Frank. For old times' sake, like you did in *Teheran,*" said Calvino.

Ali Ahmad stared at Calvino, at Colonel Pratt, and at the orange. "What do you want?"

"You don't have a knife. Is that the problem?" asked Calvino.

Colonel Pratt said to the girls in Thai, "Get dressed and get out. *Pai reow, reow.*" They were gone in under two minutes.

"We heard you were having a party," said Calvino. "So we invited ourselves. We can all have some fun. Talking about movies, the old times in Saigon, special ops buddies like Tyler, Oxley, and Hatcher. We knew you wouldn't mind."

Ali Ahmad threw the orange at Calvino, who ducked. Ali Ahmad ran back and collapsed on the mattress. Calvino grabbed him by his hair and threw him off the bed. Beer bottles smashed under the thud of his weight. He was unrecognizable as the Burmese soldier who had killed the three students. Lieutenant Narong came through the door a moment later and stood at attention as Calvino searched

Ahmad's jacket, which was draped over the end of the headboard. Calvino pulled out a .357 Magnum from a shoulder harness and showed it to Colonel Pratt and then to Lieutenant Narong.

"You don't peel an orange with a .357," said Calvino.

"It's a prop."

Calvino opened the chamber and dumped out several hollow-tipped bullets powerful enough to blow away a large part of someone's head. "A fully loaded .357 Magnum, my friend, is never a fucking prop." As Ali Ahmad stood up, Calvino reached over and slapped him hard across the face, catching the actor off guard.

"We want to ask you some questions," said Colonel Pratt.

"I have got nothing to say," said Ali Ahmad, tilting his head and rubbing his jaw. Cigarette smoke curled up from the nightstand ashtray.

"I find that hard to believe," said Calvino.

He smacked him with an open hand across the face. It happened so fast that Ali Ahmad didn't have a chance to react. The force of the blow knocked the hot ash off the cigarette, to land on Ali Ahmad's exposed arm. His face was a mixture of surprise and hatred. Calvino stood over him, feet planted on the floor.

"You fucking with me? I hear you got nothing to say? Or did I hear an actor delivering a line that don't fit the situation?"

Calvino hit him again—not as hard as the first time, but hard enough for Ali Ahmad to understand that more was in store, and hard enough for him to understand that neither Lieutenant Narong nor Colonel Pratt was going to do anything to stop this *farang* from beating the shit out of him if that was what he had in mind. Calvino saw blood streaked across the back of his hand as he wiped his nose. Droplets of blood dripped on the white sheets. All that was in Calvino's mind was that this man on the bed had been assigned the job of putting a necklace of wooden penises around his daughter's neck and then slitting her throat. The heat of pure hate roiling inside his belly was more than he had ever felt for any man.

"I don't know who you are or what you want. But you are making a big mistake. Do you know who I am?" asked Ali Ahmad.

Calvino looked back at Colonel Pratt, whose face was without expression, a blank; and the look was not missed on Ali Ahmad, who thought the uniform and gun might be some neutral force to prevent the American in the suit from taking him apart.

"Know who you are? I'm one of your biggest fans in Bangkok. I've probably seen every movie you ever made, Frank. At least since Saigon," said Calvino, shifting his tone. He clasped his hands together and smiled. "You're an actor's actor. You were great in *Teheran*." The remark had the effect of throwing Ali Ahmad off—his expression warped from shy grin, to frown, to terror.

"You saw *Teheran*?"

"Two and a half times," said Calvino.

It was then that Ali Ahmad asked, "How did you know I was in 'Nam?"

"That's not the question. The question is what are you doing in Bangkok?" Calvino shot back.

Ali Ahmad paused as the CNN news reported on Burmese military movements along the eastern frontier, where a huge column of Muslim peasants streamed across the border into Bangladesh. There was a shot of refugees in rags pushing carts, crying mothers with malnourished babies, old men with toothless faces padding along a dirt road in bare feet—the usual horror show of old women and men, children, and hordes of gray, faceless refugees on the run from mortars, land mines, helicopter gunships, small-arms fire. They were herded into a makeshift camp. The TV image cut to the jungle area around Manerplaw. There was a brief replay of the highlights of the execution scene. Ali Ahmad nervously relit his cigarette as he watched himself killing the students. He hit the remote and the screen flashed to a yellowish pinpoint of color.

"You were good as the mean-ass Burmese soldier killing those kids," said Calvino.

"All I have to do is make a phone call," said Ali Ahmad.

Calvino pulled the phone off the nightstand and ripped the wire out of the wall. "Phone's out of order."

Colonel Pratt stayed passively near the door, letting Calvino continue with the good cop, mean private eye routine. As Calvino dumped the phone into the wastebasket, Colonel Pratt decided that the time had come for him to present a few facts, now that Ali Ahmad had been worked over physically and emotionally.

"We ran a check on a set of your fingerprints from a hotel glass, Mr. Ali Ahmad. Your right thumbprint is a positive match to a print from two very recent murders: Jerry Hutton and a bar *ying* named Kwang. Both victims wore certain wooden amulets. Your thumbprint is on both sets. You might explain how it happened your thumbprint turns up on wooden cocks?"

Ali Ahmad sat more erect, shoulders back. "In the presence of two Thai police officers I make the following statement. I wish to speak with the American Embassy."

"Whoa, whoa. But you came into Thailand on a Lebanese passport and you checked into the Grace on a Canadian passport. And now you want the American Embassy," said Calvino.

"You are wasting your time." He passed over Calvino and addressed himself directly to Colonel Pratt as the ranking officer in the room, as if following a military chain of command. "Colonel Hatcher will report this to your superior officer. And he will tell you that you have exceeded your jurisdiction. You are interfering with the national security interest of Thailand."

Lieutenant Narong edged away from the door and pulled Colonel Pratt over to the side, where they spoke rapid Thai in whispered exchanges. That had been Ali Ahmad's training—charge ahead, take the offensive, don't sit still and let the enemy take you. He skillfully pushed back, then rolled forward, pushed back again until the high ground was taken and occupied, and the enemy vanquished.

Colonel Pratt walked over to the edge of the bed. "You are right. This is either a personal or a business conflict. It's really between two Americans to settle this matter in private."

Calvino slowly chambered one round into the .357 Magnum, spinning the cylinder with his hand. "You ever see a film called *The Deer Hunter*? A small footnote: The film was shot in Bangkok. You remember the Russian roulette scene? Christopher Walken and the Vietnamese? He's sitting at the table, puts the gun to his head and pulls the trigger. You're an actor. I think I'm gonna let you play both Walken and the Vietnamese. You understand what I'm saying? I spin for you. I point the gun like this. Then if you hear a click—I spin again, and you can take my turn, too."

"Wait," Ali Ahmad said, calling out to Colonel Pratt, who turned back from the door.

"I'll take care of this and meet you downstairs in the lobby," Calvino said to Colonel Pratt. He pointed the gun at Ali Ahmad's head and squeezed the trigger. *Click.*

Ali Ahmad's eyes enlarged with that "What the fuck have I done now?" look? of someone who had been granted more than he had wished for. The blood drained from his face.

"Oxley killed Hutton and the whore. I don't know how my prints got on those little wooden dicks."

"Why would Oxley set you up?" asked Calvino, as both Colonel Pratt and Lieutenant Narong stepped away from the door and flanked Calvino near the bed. He spun the cylinder and pointed it at Ali Ahmad's head, his finger gliding down to the trigger. The hammer struck with a dull, dead *click*.

"You're fucking crazy. You could have killed me," said Ali Ahmad.

Calvino spun the cylinder again.

"Twice lucky. Wanna try for three?" asked Calvino, pointing the gun at Ali Ahmad's head, his finger on the trigger. "I don't think you answered my question about why Oxley set you up with the fingerprints."

"Why don't you ask *him*?" shouted Ali Ahmad.

"I'm asking *you*." Calvino pointed the gun at Ali Ahmad's head. "Why did you kill those three students on the border?"

"It had to do with the Hezbollah." The last word hung in the air. Party of God. "You've heard of them?" asked Ali Ahmad, looking for a reaction. Calvino had heard of them.

The Hezbollah, ran operations in the Middle East and were allied with the Iranians. They were a revolutionary religious and political organization with strategic cells that worked in Shiite communities.

"They're fundamentalists who are knowledgeable about dynamite and other substances which go boom," said Calvino.

"The three Hezbollah agents killed on the border had been responsible for the death of hundreds and hundreds of Rohingyas. They were infiltrators. Men on their way to the southern provinces of Thailand. They had to be stopped. I think I have said enough. If you don't believe me, check out what I have told you with your own sources in the Ministry of Defense. If I have lied, then you can kill me."

The Unit's mission, under cover of *Lucky Charms*, was to kill the Hezbollah assets and pin their deaths on the military by making it look like an execution of innocent students, a war crime captured on TV for audiences around the world to see the cruelty of the Burmese military government and army.

"Why did you kill Hutton?"

"You must believe me. I did not kill him. And I did not know of any plan to have him killed. The plan was to destroy the Hezbollah assets and involve the generals in a war crimes charge."

Calvino's law: Whenever someone says. 'You must believe me,' the chances are greater than 50 percent he's lying through his teeth.

"Where is the person who identified the Hezbollah?" asked Colonel Pratt. It was a Pratt-like question. Not what is his name or nationality, but where is he—or she?

"In Cox's Bazar."

There was a record of phone calls to Cox's Bazar. Colonel Pratt, his face expressionless, glanced at Calvino, who shrugged his shoulders and lowered the gun.

"He confirmed the names and ages, and gave descriptions before we acted. We are not careless people, Colonel."

"What if your information was wrong?" asked Colonel Pratt.

"And Oxley found out you killed the wrong people?" asked Calvino.

"Or Hatcher," added Colonel Pratt.

"Someone might think you're not playing it straight," said Calvino. "A double check might have turned up three dead students who had nothing to do with the Hezbollah."

"Impossible. We are always, always extremely careful," said Ali Ahmad, looking between Colonel Pratt and Calvino, keeping his eye on the position of the gun, the implication being that both of them—and Calvino in particular with the gun—had been reckless. It was late afternoon early in the Year of the Monkey. In Ali Ahmad's hotel room, they occupied the dead center of the Little Arabia section of Bangkok. And here was a guy with forged passports and credit cards, rolling around on the bed with a couple of whores, beer bottles scattered on the floor, talking about what was and was not possible.

The Burmese had started the trend toward ethnic cleansing. They herded their Muslim population and drove them like cattle out of the country. The Rohingyas were ripe for a power play by various fundamentalist factions. The click of the hammer striking the firing pin of the .357 had dislodged what seemed like a credible story of American intelligence acquiring information from the border camps where the Rohingyas were holed up, and from which anti-Western forces saw an opportunity for some quick gains. The only problem with Ali Ahmad's story was the timing. The Burmese had turned against the Rohingyas after Tyler had started the film in Bangkok.

"You guys started the movie before the Burmese went after the Muslims," said Calvino.

"We knew six months before the media reported it."

So this was the Russian doll coming apart, thought Calvino. Thais stacked inside the Americans, and more Americans stacked inside the Rohingyas. The Unit—which appeared to be the final doll—had players of divided loyalties, if Ali Ahmad was to be believed. Infighting, competition, broken lines of authority, and betrayal: That kind of doll didn't fit inside another doll; it wasn't even a doll, it was a labyrinth of rat runs, and the rodents carried guns.

Ali Ahmad blinked his eyes and nodded. He had given a plausible explanation, one that fitted the facts, assigned the blame, and explained how his prints could have been at the murder scene. It was like a perfectly tailored business suit—only the fly was undone. He had given an answer to what the Unit was doing on the border killing students. So far so good. Calvino was thinking that Colonel Pratt looked satisfied by what they had heard. It had matched the information his own sources had given him. The two-for-one-sale mentality of the shopping mall spilling over to an American covert operation seemed to fit as well.

But Ali Ahmad hadn't made a connection between Hutton's death and the Unit. Or clarified what Roland May was doing trying to kill him that night on the soi running next to his apartment.

The tension was slipping away. Ali Ahmad looked relaxed; the element of surprise and fear had passed. It was a good moment to go for broke, thought Calvino.

"Why did Oxley kill Hutton?" he asked.

He raised the .357 Magnum into the firing position, pointing the weapon at Ali Ahmad's forehead. His muscles flexed and he went rigid. It was Calvino's eyes. The way they had narrowed. Ali Ahmad had seen that look before in Saigon; he had seen it in the eyes of people who had killed.

"I told you I don't know nothing about that," said Ali Ahmad, swallowing.

Calvino mouthed, "Bye-bye."

"For the money. The big time."

"Because Hatcher's retiring," said Colonel Pratt.

"And Oxley found out the Unit was retiring with him," said Calvino.
Colonel Pratt smiled. "How did you know?"

"*Sakit jai*," said Calvino, turning back to Ali Ahmad.

"*Lucky Charms* was Oxley's operation," said Ali Ahmad.

"And the story about Hutton would make him rich," said Calvino.

"Something like that," said Ali Ahmad.

"But a movie needs a larger-than-life hero," said Calvino, remembering what Tommy Loretti had told him. "Hutton was a third-shift kind of guy. So when Hutton's killed in Bangkok, you manufacture a hero and a legend."

"If you know already, would you mind not pointing that gun at my face?" said Ali Ahmad.

"Because I can't prove it," said Calvino. "Knowing something is never enough." Oxley had made a side play and gotten away with it; nothing led back to him. The fingerprints had led a dead-end trail to Ali Ahmad. Oxley had even used Hatcher as cover to send a hit man after Pratt and him. The man was smart, a survivor, an old Asia hand. But he had made one mistake along the way. He had cast a little girl named Melody Calvino in the script of a film called *Lucky Charms*.

"Only you have one problem—it's your prints that got left behind. Not Oxley's," said Calvino. "And the way I figure it, you are Oxley's insurance policy. You have Middle East contacts. You have the looks of a heavy dude. Someone with a face etched with malice, a man who receives pleasure from inflicting pain, the kind of man American audiences cheer when he takes a bullet. Oxley's thinking, For *War Crimes* I need a bad guy. And he says to himself, Why not Ali Ahmad. Only you don't know it. Because he keeps this part a secret. And Oxley is figuring he knows exactly what an audience needs to see before *War Crimes* ends. Some justice for Hutton's murder. And the murder of his girlfriend, too. Without justice the audience is gonna feel let down. Maybe he didn't explain this part he had in mind for you. I could be wrong. Think about it."

Ali Ahmad didn't have to think very long. The bad guy always dies in the end or the audience is outraged, wants to rip up the cinema seats and throw them at the screen. They demand that the bad guy pay in blood—the villain who walked away scot-free with a smirk on his face was too much a reminder of real life, and movies were a means of escape from that cruel reality.

"What do you want me to do?"

For the first time since entering the room, Calvino heard something which sounded like sincerity. The mask had come off. Ali Ahmad had realized he had more to be afraid of than Calvino with a gun. Colonel Pratt wondered about these men who lived outside of any accounting for their actions, and asked himself about the prospects for democracy succeeding. Suddenly he felt depressed. He wanted to be home with his tenor sax, Shakespeare's collected plays open on the table and his children playing in the garden. He wanted out of a world where money came first in men's action.

"An American girl named Melody plays a second-act scene tomorrow night," said Calvino.

Melody's name snapped Colonel Pratt back to this moment, in the room, with Ali Ahmad still wrapped in a towel on a hotel bed, his best friend holding a .357 at the man's head. Calvino wasn't about money; he never had been. He had swung the gun around for one reason: his daughter. Here was a reason a Thai could understand and respect.

"You're the shaman and she's the virgin you sacrifice," said Calvino.

"Right," said Ali Ahmad.

"Oxley took you aside and explained something that wasn't put in the script, right? He told you to cut the girl's throat. Draw the knife across like this," said Calvino, cutting his forefinger across the air a couple of inches from Ali Ahmad's neck.

"It's true."

The man was having an overpowering case of sincerity and honesty, thought Calvino. "She'll bleed to death in a minute, Oxley probably said. And you thought, What the fuck, if Oxley says it has to be done then just do it. Right? Like the three you shot on the border. Line them up, and waste them. *Boom, boom, boom.* In the confusion, the girl's father is killed. Hutton's neighbor in real life. A guy named Calvino. Someone Oxley told you was trying to bust his balls over Hutton. Well, I'm that guy."

"Oxley told me there is a chain-link fence behind Jao Mae Thapthim," said Ali Ahmad. "It will be cut and a long-tail boat will be waiting. I kill the girl and get out on the *klong*. I'm five kilometers away before anyone else on the set knows the girl is really dead."

Calvino smiled and nodded. "Only one problem: No matter what goes down you're dead. You understand what I'm saying? They plan to have you killed. It ain't your fault. You're the bad guy. Oxley has plans for your blood in his film. Hutton is the light, and you are the dark. He wants day and night. That's how you make money in Hollywood, so I'm told by a friend."

The steam went out of Ali Ahmad like air from a balloon.

"We can help you," said Colonel Pratt.

"To stay alive," said Calvino.

"How are you going to do that?" asked Ali Ahmad.

"Rewrite the script," said Calvino.

"Oxley's a professional," said Ali Ahmad, as if having taken full measure of Calvino, he'd concluded, that if he were a betting man, he'd bet the bank on Oxley coming out on top.

"Has Oxley fucked Carol Hatcher?"

There was a long pause.

"Yeah, he fucked her."

TWENTY

THE REWRITE SPECIALIST

JAO MAE THAPTHIM had been dressed as a set. Except for one thing, thought Tyler: That goddamn pink pig was still in the shot. This disturbed him. Tyler was a man who read omens into such objects and events. The pink concrete pig covered with cocks as if they were tubercular sores—it was an evil omen, he thought. Like when Roland got himself killed in a dead-end alley in Bangkok. That hadn't been in the script either. Now this fucking pink pig. He rubbed the side of his face; he had a stubble of beard, and it made that coarse, grainy sandpaper sound against his nails. There hadn't been enough time for a shave before going to the set. He disliked a stubble, the five o'clock shadow. It reminded him of terrorists and Richard Nixon.

It also reminded him how much he hated doing this, for the Unit. This film most of all bothered him. He didn't blame Sam Hatcher but he did blame Oxley, who knew all along about the purpose of the second-unit team on the border. Oxley had lied to him. The intention from the beginning was to kill three members of the Party of God. Fundamentalists mowed down on his film. He would never sleep in peace again. One billion Muslims would be looking to settle the score if the word ever leaked out as to who killed those people, and why. Oxley had told him to stop being nervous. No one had clearance except the usual Unit old hands. Still he had broken a personal covenant with himself, and there he was looking down the barrel of Chekhov's gun. He should have seen it coming. Oxley had lied to him before. He'd should've known he'd lie again.

What had he expected this time out? The truth?

The soundman, a bored look on his face, squatted on the set; it was downtime. Carol Hatcher still had not emerged from inside the trailer. The lights were being set up to the right of the spirit house. Oxley knelt forward, creasing the toes of his penny loafers, as he pulled a knife from his pocket, opened the blade, and scooted to the far side of the black penis. Oxley carved his initials in the Styrofoam.

Tyler carried a clipboard and pen, and nervously checked off items on a list of props as he made his way across the set. He stopped beside the ugly, battered pink cement pig. The cement tail in the shape of a curlicue penis had been partly pulled loose, displaying the wire anchoring it to the body of the pig; its ears were also penis-shaped; and in the region below the hind legs was a grotesque appendage—a pink penis, the tip of which touched the ground. This appeared to have been vandalized by someone who had chipped away the edges with an axe. Nothing about the pink pig was the proper scale or dimensions. The mal-formed piece of cement pork made Tyler explode with anger. He hurled his clipboard against the pig. Then he kicked it—which only further enraged him, because the cement pig did not give way when the foot struck. Tyler screamed at the props person to remove the pink pig.

"Get that goddamn thing out of the shot," he shouted. "Now. Throw it in that stinking river. Throw it in the parking lot. Just get rid of it."

Easy for Tyler to say. Just flip one hundred and forty-six pounds of cement onto a wheelbarrow and park the pig around the corner.

"Why can't I get cooperation, Lewis? Why do you hate me? Why are you punishing me with this awful pig?"

Lewis did not have a ready answer to any of his questions, but that didn't stop Tyler from pushing on.

"Is the pig too heavy? If it's too heavy, then get some of the Thais to help you. But the pig goes. Do you hear me?" His face was beet red. Oxley rose to his feet and walked over to the pink cement pig.

"Jesse, cool down. Some people collect toy pigs. This one has character. More pricks than the average asshole."

"Do you want to direct or do you want me to direct?" asked Tyler.

"You're losing your sense of humor, Jesse."

"It has to go, now."

"You're a perfectionist. I like that. It builds confidence. It's important to know where everything and everyone is on the set. And sometimes off the set," said Oxley.

Tyler whispered behind his hand. "He's here. I can feel it."

"Chill out, Jesse. Everything is under control."

❖

CAROL HATCHER closed her eyes, then slowly allowed the lids to open like damp shutters in an old house. She blinked at herself in the mirror, fluttered her eyes, checking that the bluish tint was even on both sides. Dozens of lightbulbs were screwed in sockets around the sides. She picked up a tube of pink lipstick and unscrewed the top. Melody Calvino was shifting from one foot to the other, as Jesse Tyler had told her it was her lucky night: Carol Hatcher had made a last-minute request for Melody to be sent to her trailer. Melody saw it as her chance to get her autograph. Tyler saw it a different way. He personally delivered her to Carol's trailer, with a request of his own.

"Thanks, Mr. Tyler," said Melody.

"It wasn't my idea. Carol asked to see you. I have no idea why. But it doesn't matter why. She's the star. So you will see her, okay?"

"I want her autograph for my mother."

"Where is your mother?"

Melody screwed up her mouth. "Mr. Oxley said it would be better if she stayed at the hotel. He's taking care of me."

"Mike's taking care of you?"

"So he said."

Tyler shrugged. Kids, he thought. Another of Oxley's casting "judgments," parachuted into the middle of a picture. Sometimes he wished Oxley had never come back from Vietnam; sometimes he wished that he himself had never come back from Vietnam—the boys in Saigon were the best.

"Try and put Carol in a good mood," said Tyler. "Tell Carol she's beautiful and talented. And you can't wait to do the scene with her. Can you do that for me?"

Melody removed her shoulder bag, held it by the strap, and took out her autograph book and pen. "I don't get it," she said.

"I don't want any problems. We want a smooth, smooth time, with everyone wearing their thinking caps. We shoot the scene and go back to the hotel before dawn. You got that?"

Melody thought about what Tyler had said as she sat on a chair with her autograph book open on her lap, watching as Carol pursed her lips in the mirror. Melody watched with her jaw dropping. What she saw was not a star but a celestial vision who had been beamed via satellite to an audience of billions. Or at least millions, before *Vampire U* had been canceled. Melody had seen the series. She didn't think it was that bad.

"I think you're beautiful and talented," Melody said like someone delivering a little speech.

Carol's eyes widened and she caught Melody's bored expression in the mirror. "Did Tyler tell you to say that?"

"Yes."

"At least you're honest."

"He's so out of it. No one says, 'We need to put on our thinking caps.'"

This made Carol smile. She liked this girl whose features twisted into a grin as she finished each sentence.

"Why does it stink so much out there?" asked Melody.

Carol turned around and looked at her directly.

"You always say what you think?"

Melody nodded, then paused, an embarrassed expression wiping the grin from her face and causing her to avert her eyes from Carol's in the mirror.

"Do you ever get butterflies in your stomach?" Melody asked.

Carol turned back to the mirror, and pressed her lips together, smiled, and watched Melody's nervous expression in the mirror.

"Like really nervous. You were so perfect on Leno. Everyone laughing at your jokes. And you looked so natural. I can't believe you've ever been nervous once in your life."

Combing her hair, she watched this strange young girl in the mirror. "To tell you the truth, yes. I get anxiety attacks sometimes."

Carol Hatcher adjusted her outfit of overlapping white silk scarves curving over her full breasts.

"How do you deal with it?" asked Melody.

"I concentrate on the essence of the scene. Whose point of view directs the action. Once you find the action point then you can work the scene. Like the scene with you: When the shaman raises his knife is the action point; everything builds to that point. The audience sees the possibility but doesn't know for sure how it will end. Their sympathy is in conflict. They want me to have a baby but they don't want you killed. It's the crisis point, the emotional dilemma of the story. I must decide what is important: this strange girl—which you play—or my longing for a child. Am I willing to pay the price? How I behave, move, dance, the expression on my face has to reveal the conflict I feel. This puts me at center stage."

"In real life would you choose me?" asked Melody.

Carol thought for a moment.

"Movies aren't about real life, Melody," she said. "Acting is a craft. You make it appear real. How? You define the reality in the moral terms of your character. But your character is not you. Some writer invented the character. You climb inside that creation and breathe life into her."

Melody sighed. "Wow, that's beautiful."

Carol Hatcher lit a Winston cigarette, her lower lip trembling. She threw it in the ashtray, and covered her face with her hands. She started to cry, tears spilling onto the white silk scarves.

"Don't cry, Carol," said Melody, tears in her own eyes.

"Not one beautiful word is something I could ever have said. I read this in an interview in *Variety* last week. I could never think of anything like that. I'm stupid. Don't you know I wouldn't be in this film if it weren't for my father? Don't you think that robs me of what little self-confidence I have left?"

"Why are you crying?"

"Because I hate this film. Bangkok sucks. I can't deal with the heat, the stink of that stupid canal."

Melody wrapped an arm around Carol and hugged her.

"I know how you feel. My mom hates Bangkok, too. I probably shouldn't tell you this. But she's sleeping with Mr. Oxley."

"Oxley and your mom," said Carol, without any hint this news had already found its way to her.

"He asked my mom to move to L.A. and live with him," said Melody. "But I dunno know if he's real. When he's not around all she does is bitch about my dad. He lives in Bangkok."

She knew that Vincent Calvino lived in Bangkok, and she knew he had one of the most beautiful German shepherds she had ever laid eyes on.

❖

CAROL HATCHER found that February mornings around six were perfect for a jog in Lumpini Park. If she squinted her eyes, she could cast herself back in the States in that post-dawn euphoria. She had worked up a light sweat after her first lap. Her long dark hair was hidden under a baseball cap; she wore dark glasses, and a light blue spandex bodysuit with blood red slashes like thunderbolts across her chest. When he saw her, Calvino thought it was the perfect mixed signal—I'm hiding but please notice that I'm hiding. He wore a faded pair of green jogging shorts bought from a street stall, a torn Hash House Harriers T-shirt, and a pair of reject tennis shoes. If the homeless ever took up jogging, they would have adopted Calvino's style. He had Joy on a leash, and as Carol passed the side of Mom's outdoor restaurant in full stride, Calvino started jogging alongside.

"Hi," he said.

No response. She looked straight ahead, thinking, Who is this jerk in the Salvation Army outfit? Is he crazy? Will he hurt me? Does he recognize who I am?

"My dog and I jog in this park every morning. How come we haven't seen you before?"

She glanced to the side.

"Nice dog."

"I got papers showing her ancestors going back one hundred fifty years," said Calvino, quickly running out of breath as he tried to keep pace with the young actress.

She glanced at the dog, and he could see her resolve to ignore him weakening as they passed between the lake on their left and the weight-lifting benches on the right. "Nice dog," said Carol.

"You said that already."

She pulled up to a stop, stretching her arms over her head, still running in place. "What's his name?"

"Her name's Joy," said Calvino.

In California singles used dogs as an opener to meet other singles. She wondered if this guy in the weird clothes was single and trying to hit on her, or whether he was just an older guy running in Lumpini Park with his dog.

"You can pet her," said Calvino, taking the leash off Joy.

Joy sat, ears up, head cocked to the side, watching as Carol's hand started to descend and then suddenly halted. "She doesn't bite, does she?"

"So long as you keep away from the war," said Calvino.

Carol laughed, knelt down, threw her arms around Joy's neck, and hugged her. "Like that *Fawlty Towers* episode where John Cleese keeps telling the Spanish waiter and the staff not to mention the war?"

"And in the dining room John Cleese mentions the war," said Calvino.

After they had left Ali Ahmad at the Grace Hotel, he thought through their plan, looking for flaws, hoping that it would all come together. He also knew how dangerous it was to approach Carol Hatcher in this way. But he had no choice. The tricky Year of the Monkey had made him turn the next corner, to drive the direction of the conversation with this stranger, even though if he lost control, the outcome wouldn't be predictable. He couldn't bring himself to think of the consequences. But the knife, Melody, the setup which Oxley had planned . . .

"Oxley is fucking around on you with Janet Calvino. Melody's mother. The kid who out of nowhere has a role. She's my daughter."

Carol kept patting Joy, kissing and hugging the dog.

"What did you say?" she asked.

"Oxley also killed a friend of mine named Jerry Hutton. Do you think we could talk for a few minutes?" asked Calvino.

She gave Joy one final stroke and stood up.

"That's one of the most creative pickup lines I've heard," she said, lowering her sunglasses.

"Can we talk?" He knelt down and planted a kiss on Joy's head, whispering in Joy's ear, "Roll over."

Joy spread her front feet forward and rolled over, then barked and stood back on her hindquarters.

She thought for a second, watching the performance.

"Five minutes. Tops. Then I'm back to the hotel. I'm a sucker for a man with a dog," she said.

"How would you like to be a star?" he asked.

❖

"I'M sorry," said Carol, dabbing a tissue beneath an eye. She was thinking about Oxley's voice on the tape, and the metaphor he had used about her tits being a couple of slices of badly cut sponge cake.

"But you're a star and I think you are great," said Melody, looking around the trailer. It had nice furniture and vases filled with red, yellow, and pink roses and others with orchids so that it was like a flower jungle. All the flowers and Carol crying reminded Melody of a funeral parlor. But she didn't want to say that to Carol. It might remind her of *Vampire U,* which had died on television.

"Really?" asked Carol, sniffling and then blowing her nose. "You're not just saying that because Tyler told you to?"

"You could do anything," said Melody.

"I hate the scene we're doing."

"Then why don't you change it? You're the star. Stars always control the script, don't they?"

Carol Hatcher smiled, wondering how such innocence could ever survive in the film business. Then she thought about what Calvino had said about the new scene. The one they'd agreed would work. The one which she thought would guarantee Oxley the payback he deserved. The creep, the fucking bastard, she thought. She studied herself in the mirror.

"What if you danced around the garden with all those . . ."

"Stupid pricks. It's okay, you can say it," said Melody.

Carol hugged Melody and kissed her on the cheek.

"You know how many zillion times that scene has been rewritten? Written and rewritten by men who don't know the most basic emotion the character in the movie would feel. They make my character into some half-crazed porno star dancing around in the nude. A she-bitch in heat. No woman I know would do that. It's demeaning. Tyler never asked me, 'Carol, what do you think as a woman should happen in this scene?'"

"How would you write it?" asked Melody.

"Thank you, love," said Carol, squeezing Melody.

"For what?"

"For giving me permission," said Carol. She recalled how Calvino had taken her through the scene like a pro. She really thought he was in the business. He opened up the scene, explained a way of looking at it that she hadn't thought about before.

"I would make the woman character strong and in control," said Carol, repeating what Calvino had told her in Lumpini Park that morning. "She and the girl pull a switch on the shaman. The two women move the action. They are the ones who expose the shaman as a fraud. Which isn't so far from the truth. I've worked with Ali Ahmad—he plays the shaman. He's your basic New York asshole."

"I'm from New York," said Melody.

"Sorry. I didn't mean it that way. Maybe my idea is stupid."

Melody shook her head. "I think it's brilliant. And if you believe in something, even though someone says it can't be done, you never stop fighting for what you believe in."

"Who told you that?"

"My father," said Melody.

"You probably don't know exactly how lucky you are."

Melody blinked, trying to think what Carol Hatcher meant. She guessed it was because she got the part.

❖

CAROL stretched her legs, did several squats; she was warming down, as Calvino watched her from the side of the pavement. He was playing with the tape recorder, the headphones over his head. After he found the right place for the tape to start, he pulled the headphones off and looked out at the lake.

"Hutton was killed about there," he said, pointing at a spot in the lake.

Carol looked around at the lake and kept on stretching. It was a 'So what?' kind of look. She hadn't known Hutton. What did she care whether he had been drowned in the lake or hit by a bus? It wasn't her business.

"I'm gonna ask you something," he said.

And she thought, Oh, my God, here it comes. A fucking crazy after all.

"What?" she asked in a tense voice.

He smiled. "Relax. I'm gonna ask you to trust me for about two minutes. Nothing major. I just want you to listen to the tape."

"Why should I trust you?" she asked, her hands on her hips. She had stopped stretching and was one second away from turning and continuing her jog.

"Because," he said.

"Because of what?"

He leaned down and patted Joy on the head.

"You should know that dogs are a good judge of character," he said.

This one stopped her cold. And she smiled, her hands coming down from the stiff assault position on her hips. She looked at him for a moment, deciding whether she was going to give in to this intrusion or blow him off. It was then that Joy, responding to Calvino's hand signal, dropped to the pavement, shoved her head forward, and wrapped her front paws over her snout.

"If you go, Joy's gonna be real depressed all day," said Calvino.

She stayed and they sat on a bench. He asked her to listen and not say anything as he explained the background of what she was going to hear. After he finished speaking he was going to ask her to listen to the tape without any comment, explanation, or argument. She agreed, and Calvino gave her the basic introduction to the operation of Soi 33 bar life.

Oxley and Ali Ahmad had been drinking heavily. It had been party night at one of the upscale bars on Soi 33 named after nineteenth-century French painters. The *yings* weren't called bargirls but hostesses. They went for a hundred bucks a night. No five-hundred baht run to a short-time hotel—these girls were taken to a good restaurant and then a luxury hotel afterward.

They had been drinking at the Toulouse-Lautrec with the yuppie expat set—the young managers, account executives, and marketing and public relations guys in suits and ties, with a few of the old hand ex-CIA faces with their gray hair, bone-crunching handshakes, pot-bellies, and uneasy appearances of trying to mingle with the new generation and not quite fitting in. The past hung over them like their bellies hung over their belts. They suffered from the knowledge that their best years had passed and that their time was about to come to an end, like men seeing the mist ahead of their canoe as it heads to the waterfall. Colonel Pratt was fifty meters away in an unmarked police car monitoring the conversation. Lieutenant Narong, who had a talent for this kind of thing, had hot-wired Ali Ahmad with a hidden microphone and promised that if the meet with Oxley did not go according to plan, then he need not worry about Oxley killing him—Lieutenant Narong would personally slit his throat.

Oxley had bought Ali Ahmad's pitch that they deserved some down time over drinks even though it meant executing an escape from the rest of the crew and cast. In the Toulouse-Lautrec bar, there was an ember, a trace of yesterday in Oxley's smile. Ali Ahmad could almost remember the kid he had bunked with in Saigon.

Carol heard the dull background drum of people eating, drinking, laughing, and joking. She recognized Oxley's voice immediately; he sounded a little drunk.

"I always thought about fucking Carol. You ever think about fucking Carol?" asked Ali Ahmad.

"Come on. What's this shit about thinking about fucking someone?" said Oxley.

"You fucked her?"

"Of course I fucked her. How else do you think I got the dumb vampire cunt to Thailand in the first place?"

There was a pause filled with background noise.

"Was she as good as she looks?" asked Ali Ahmad.

"I'd take a Thai any day."

"You're joking. Carol's body doesn't stop."

"You must be drinking soda, my friend. Her body stops before it gets started. Believe me. I've tried to jump-start her body. It's not worth the effort. Any day, ounce for ounce the Thai women are the best in the sack. Even better than the Vietnamese," said Oxley.

"You said the Saigon women were the best."

"I changed my mind. Besides, you don't think about fucking them. You just do it."

"She wouldn't fuck me," said Ali Ahmad.

"Who?"

"Carol."

"Are you joking? She'd fuck her brother if she thought it would get her a juicy part," said Oxley.

There was another pause and some static, kissing sounds.

"This one's got a nice ass," said Oxley.

"But Carol's got those huge tits," said Ali Ahmad.

"They're like squeezing sponge cake. That one there. I've had her. There's not an inch of fat on her. She's eighteen. Perfect, firm body. Ten years from now, maybe unlike Carol's tits won't be oatmeal. More like sticky rice." There is the sound of Oxley laughing at his own joke.

"I'd like to pork the kid—Melody something. She's thirteen or something," said Ali.

Oxley could see that Ali got a kick out of mind-fucking Calvino.

"You always liked them young."

"The mother's not bad," said Ali Ahmad.

"Shit, don't remind me. I'll tell you a little secret. I've been porking the kid's mother. She's gotta be forty. I deserve a Silver Star for that. No, I deserve a Medal of fucking Honor for fucking that bitch. She never shuts up. Even when I stick my cock in her mouth she's mumbling on about some goddamn thing."

"Like Tyler with some little boy blowing him."

"You're disgusting," said Oxley.

The tape ended and Carol, stunned, paused a few seconds, then took off the earphones and handed them back to Calvino.

"I want you to help me save my little girl," said Calvino.

Tears popped out of her eyes, and she looked away.

"What do you want me to do?"

"Rewrite one scene."

"It's not that easy," said Carol. "There are many people involved."

"And one little girl's life."

She gasped for a second as he handed her a nickel-plated .38 revolver. For a second, it caught the morning sun, showering the grass with a flash of golden light.

"Take it," Calvino said. "And let me tell you what I have in mind."

❖

TYLER rapped on the door of the trailer and stuck his head inside, smiling at Carol.

"Jesse, I was just thinking about you," said Carol. "Come in and shut the door."

He didn't like the tone in her voice. She wanted something every time her voice went sweet and nice with him, treating him in that

248

typical condescending way of a straight actress seeking a favor from a gay director. "What can I do for you, Carol?"

"We are going to fix the script."

"Carol, sweetheart. You want to fix a line? There's no problem."

"I want to fix the scene."

"I was afraid it might be something like that," said Tyler.

She sounded serious enough for him to sit down at the makeup table. The last thing he needed on the set was an emotionally agitated actress, unable to focus, bouncing off walls, screwing up her lines. The entire crew picked up those vibrations and everything started to fall apart. Also, she was more than capable of refusing to leave the trailer. She had done it before over a wardrobe change.

"Assuming we have time for a minor fix," he said, pulling petals off a red rose and laying them down on her dressing table, "say, change a line of dialogue, for instance, what would you suggest?" It was a power thing. The actress who believed she knew better than the director whether a scene worked. Tyler saw it coming. He used an old Hollywood trick of refusing to acknowledge he had any problem, and called her bluff, knowing the probability was she had no fucking idea how she wanted to rewrite the scene. Tyler smiled and waited.

She blew up and slammed her fist on the table.

"Why in the fuck won't you listen to me?" she asked. "The way the jeopardy works is wrong in the scene. The shaman should not be the one who is in control. The whole point is about a woman's control over her body. Don't you get that, Jesse? So instead of him running the knife across Melody's throat, I shove Melody out of the way and demand that he take some of *my* blood. It's done in the name of fertility. So there's the moral dimension at the center of the scene."

She was excited now, up and walking around the inside of the air-conditioned trailer. At first Jesse Tyler showed no reaction to what he had heard. He continued to pluck rose petals, lining them up in rows as neat as graves.

"Carol. It's a wonderful idea. I love it. But, no."

Someone was banging on the outside door. It was the assistant director. "We're ready, Mr. Tyler."

"Five minutes," snapped Tyler. He shut the door.

"Melody, what do you think?" Carol asked.

"Your idea's perfect."

Tyler swept the petals off the dressing table with the edge of his hand. "Now you're asking the kid? Maybe we should stop some *tuk-tuk* drivers and ask them, 'What kind of scene would you boys like among the land of pricks?'"

"Wouldn't you like to see the name 'Jesse Tyler' on the credits of a film the critics take seriously?" asked Carol. "A breakthrough film, Jesse. It's what you've talked about for years. Hasn't that been your dream?"

Tyler started ripping petals off another rose. And Melody wondered if this was why there were so many flowers in the trailer, with Tyler tearing off petals right, left, and center. Melody fiddled with a tube of Carol's lipstick, pulling the top off and putting it back on. When Tyler looked up from the stripped stem, a drop of blood appeared on his thumb where it had been punctured by a thorn.

"You're bleeding," said Carol.

"I'm not," said Tyler.

He sucked his thumb. Carol knew the anguished expression on Tyler's face. She had seen the look of resignation after Oxley or someone else on the set had bullied him. She wondered if Tyler had AIDS as she saw the blood swell up on his thumb again. So many of her friends—Tyler's friends, too—had died of the disease. There had been so much sadness that the mere sight of blood raised the scary question: Is this blood contaminated? He looked scared, and Carol couldn't stand to see that look of fear. She leaned over and hugged him.

"You all right, Jesse?"

"I hate thorns," he said.

"I know. They're a pain in the ass," said Carol.

"I wish you hadn't put it exactly that way."

Then he smiled and hugged her back with that certain look, one which meant that he would not stop her, felt he could not stop her and that there was no point in objecting to a course of action which would happen whether he agreed to it or not.

"Then it's decided, Jesse. I already gave Ali Ahmad the changes. He loves them. So let's just try it."

"One take, Carol. If it doesn't work, we shoot it the way it's written."

She wrapped his hand with a towel.

"Done," she said.

❖

THERE was a sense of being locked without air in a dead zone with toxic fumes flooding through a vent, when in reality a slight breeze had swept over the *klong,* carried through the fence, and swirled around the Jao Mae Thapthim shrine, kicking up dust. Melody held her nose and breathed through her mouth as she sat below the spirit house out of sight of the camera and director. The camera and director of photography were hoisted on a boom over the shrine. Jao Mae Thapthim had been turned into a film set, with large lights positioned at three points.

"What happened to the hand, Ace?" asked Oxley, who stood to his right.

"A bimbo attack," whispered Tyler, then he stepped forward and raised his hands. "Quiet on the set, please." The last residue of conversation stopped.

The clapboard with Scene 19, Take 1 snapped shut. Tyler, a baseball cap with the bill turned around, shading his ponytail, called out, "Action."

Carol Hatcher wore a smart, tailored business suit with a silk blouse underneath and carried a leather briefcase. Her high heels clicked against the pavement as she walked briskly. She stopped with an expression of surprise as the camera picked up Kiko kneeling before the spirit house. The smoke from Kiko's incense sticks slowly snaked upward as she held them above her head. She chanted, eyes closed. The camera panned back on Carol Hatcher, who looked at her watch, then lit a cigarette, the flame from the lighter illuminating her face. When the camera moved back to the spirit house, Kiko had vanished. Carol Hatcher dropped the cigarette and ground it beneath her heel before walking on. She stood in front of the spirit house, and then paced nervously for two beats, looking at her watch, her teeth pressed against her lower lip.

From the dark void behind the spirit house the shaman emerged as a king of phantoms dressed in a white shroud. Strange ink script was written on the hood covering his head. A couple of beats later, the shaman, his face reshaped with special effects makeup—large veins on his forehead, an enlarged nose, and a mouth that was wide, evil,

251

and menacing—reached down. When he rose again he was cradling Melody in his arms, having picked her up from where she squatted out of sight of the camera. The shaman stepped forward, holding Melody out for Carol's approval. Melody wrapped her arms around the shaman's neck. There were ceremonial rings on four of his fingers, and silver bracelets around his wrists.

"Are you my friend?" asked Melody. "This man said my friend was coming to get me." She had to think hard not to call her Carol, and repeated over in her mind a hundred times that in the movie Carol was playing a woman named Anne.

Carol Hatcher moved two steps closer to the spirit house.

"What are you doing with her?"

"You requested the exact ritual." A hint of anger turned in the shaman's voice.

"You didn't answer my question. The girl has nothing to do with this," said Carol Hatcher.

The camera came in for a close-up of the shaman's smiling face, as he drew the knife from beneath his robe.

"If she dies, you conceive." He laid Melody on the spirit house and pulled out a long knife.

"Put it away," said Carol, pulling a nickel-plated .38 from her briefcase.

The shaman smiled and raised the knife above his head. Carol Hatcher fired once, the shaman staggered, his mouth twisted, and then she fired a second shot, knocking him backward. Melody screamed.

"Cut, cut," shouted Oxley, pushing Jesse Tyler. "Ali, what the hell are you doing? And Carol, why the goddamn gun?"

"I thought Jesse was directing," said Carol, the smoking gun in her hand, an arm resting on the side of the spirit house.

"What you did is not in the script, Carol," Oxley said, storming onto the set.

"Fuck you," said Carol Hatcher, throwing him the gun. He caught it, put the barrel to his nose. He knew the smell and didn't like it at all. She turned and walked off the set, with Melody following close behind.

"Ali Ahmad, stop clowning around. Get up and we'll reshoot the scene, and this time, Jesse, make certain they get it right."

"Bye," said Tyler.

"Where you going?" asked Oxley.

"Carol's right. The movie doesn't need two directors."

"I don't need this shit from you. Get your ass back here," said Oxley, but Tyler had threaded his way through the crew and thrown his baseball hat on the cement parking lot as he stepped over the coils of cables for the lights.

No sooner had Tyler gone than panic broke out amongst the crew. Ali Ahmad was still crumpled up and a pool of blood had soaked through his ceremonial robes. Some of the Thai technical people were running. This violent death in a sacred place had sent a shudder of fear through them. No one wished to be accountable to the spirits of that place for such a death.

"What's going on?" asked Oxley. He grabbed one person, who tore away, and then another. Before he could get an answer, two uniformed police officers approached, and they were not smiling. They went straight onto the set. Lieutenant Narong knelt beside the body near the spirit house. The other officer stood guard, his eyes never leaving Oxley.

Oxley walked over and looked at the officers.

"He's dead," said one of the policemen.

"What do you mean 'dead'?" asked Oxley. "He can't be dead. This is a movie. He's an actor. So if you'll just get out of the way I'll handle this." He pushed one of the Thai police officers, violating a basic rule every old Asia hand knows about dealing with authority figures in uniform.

Lieutenant Narong pulled his service revolver.

"What are you gonna do with that? Shoot me? Don't be crazy. I'm in charge here. Now, if you don't mind, I'm taking over."

"May I have that gun, please?" asked Lieutenant Narong, the other officer right behind him.

"You don't think that I—"

Oxley didn't get the chance to finish his sentence.

"Just slowly hand me the gun."

"What are you saying? That I'm under arrest?"

"Yes," said the lieutenant. "You're under arrest."

"What's the charge?" asked Oxley.

"Murder," said Lieutenant Narong, putting handcuffs on Mike Oxley.

"You're making a very big mistake," said Oxley as they led him away.

253

TWENTY-ONE

THIRD ACT

AN overhead light washed over Calvino's body. He tried to raise his head, but nothing happened. He lay with his eyes open and staring at the ceiling of his bedroom. Mike Oxley, dressed in black, his face blackened, sat with his legs crossed on the edge of the bed. He was holding a syringe, and working the stopper with his thumb.

"You don't live so well. I never took you for a slum dweller, Calvino," said Oxley. "I thought you had some class. But then, I've been guilty of some bad judgment recently. So please forgive me."

Calvino's arms and legs had been tied down and anchored by ropes to opposite ends of the bed. He was naked except for the wooden amulet of penises strung around his neck. Oxley saw his eyes staring at the amulets.

"I guessed your size. I hope you're not angry if the fit's not perfect. I tried. But it's off the rack. What do you expect? The same size as Hutton?" he asked with a grin. "It was a shame about that kid. I kinda liked him."

"How was jail?"

"Now there's something other than Hutton that we have in common: We both served a little time in a Bangkok jail. Though technically, I was never in a cell. I was released after the fingerprinting. But I was never one to stand on technicalities. Not having a legal education like you, counselor."

Oxley unwrapped a piece of gum and slowly stuffed it into his mouth. He crumpled the paper and inner silver wrappers into a ball and tossed it at Calvino. "What do you think I want?"

"Like Peter Pan, life in Never-Never Land and never to grow up."

Oxley laughed the jolly laugh that Calvino remembered from the tape in the bar with Ali Ahmad. It was the laugh of someone in a good mood, someone who had heard a joke. "That's good. I like that. Only one small point. It's showtime. And I've been thinking about the right script for you. I mean, you had your fun with my script. That was a good one; I must give you credit. In one scene you pretty much managed to fuck up a lot of planning. You killed a friend of mine. Roland May."

"You don't have friends. You have interests to protect," said Calvino. "That's why you asked Ali Ahmad to try on a half-dozen amulets. Little wooden cocks. It was your way of getting ahold of his latent fingerprints for what you had planned. He figured that one out himself."

"I think you're trying to hurt my feelings. But am I someone to hold a grudge? The answer is, yes. Then again, you knew that. Where to begin? Ah, now I remember. I want you to tell me where Ali Ahmad has gone. Just name the city, the country."

"I know that with your intelligence sources, you can come up with the zip code," said Calvino.

"You are definitely the life of the party."

"I know, but the party's over," said Calvino.

"After I was released I had a long talk with Carol. Well, it started as a talk. You know that girl has a reputation for remembering her lines. She had this ability to recite a conversation I had in a bar. So I asked her, 'Carol, sweetheart, where did this come from?' And you know that girl is one tough little cunt. I broke her nose and she cried out like a stuck pig, but she wouldn't tell me. Until she saw the knife. You know how actresses have this thing about their looks. The knife made a little cut, really nothing, on her cheek. Then she said something about you and her sitting on a bench at Lumpini Park. She sang me a song about the .38 revolver, the wire on Ali Ahmad, the tape you had her listen to. And I said to myself, Oxley, you dumb sonofabitch, you've underestimated that boy. I had made a serious mistake about Vincent Calvino. But what the hell? Americans believe in second chances. That's what made America great, wouldn't you say, Calvino? And so this is my second chance to do it right."

Oxley pulled a Zippo lighter from his pants pocket, thumbed up the lid, and a moment later a long spike of flame appeared. He moved the lighter toward the soles of Calvino's feet, brushing the flame back and forth. "Joy," screamed Calvino.

"Joy to the world, our Savior's come," sang Oxley.

The German shepherd poked her nose into the bedroom. As he raised his head, Calvino saw that Joy had a kilo-sized piece of meat in her jaws.

"Rolfo feeds all his dogs special beef he gets from a butcher shop on Sukhumvit. The German and the Japs, those guys go way back," said Oxley. "And Joy and I go way back. Did our friend Rolfo tell you I bought four adorable pups from him? I flipped them to a Chinese restaurant owner for a profit. Don't tell the kraut, he seemed a little sentimental about his dogs. They have class or something. That's a good one. He probably knows that his steroid freak nephew, Karl, will never make it as a brain surgeon. But he's in love with his illusions. The world's made for such people. The film industry makes a business model out of illusions. It's cash-rich because people want to believe the unbelievable. They want it to be true. And that's where Hutton comes in. Hutton had a thing about dogs. He had an illusion he could communicate with them like a person. I could never understand how someone could be so confused. His feelings for a dog is what made him take the second-unit job. Come here, girl. Come on, Joy. Come to Daddy." He leaned over and planted a kiss on Joy's brow.

Perspiration beads appeared on Calvino's upper lip as he strained against the ropes, trying to get a better look at Joy. The dog sat at the end of the bed. Oxley stroked her and flicked the Zippo lighter again. The dog growled and barked two or three loud, seriously-armed-to-the-teeth barks.

"She doesn't like fire," said Calvino.

Oxley killed the flame and slipped the lighter back into his pocket, emerging with a penknife. "I kinda hate fire myself," said Oxley. "Now the way the scene was supposed to be played, Ali Ahmad holds the knife to the girl's throat. The script said the shaman cuts the girl's throat and disappears. In which case, we have a world-class tragedy. *Lucky Charms* becomes one of those rare films where you actually see someone killed. The film makes a ton of money. We are in the film business for real. Or, girl's father kills terrorist implicated in death of Burmese students. Again, box office smash hit. A no-lose situation. So how did it get fucked up? Our shaman pretends to be dead, or is he dead? No one seems to be talking. I figured he's taken a hike. And I would like to have a talk with him."

"Look in the yellow pages," said Calvino.

Oxley looked at his watch. "I got time. You've got time. And Joy's not halfway done with her steak. Are you, baby?"

Oxley pointed the knife blade at Calvino's cock. "I've only done this a couple of times. And you know what I hate most about it? The mess it leaves. You think about the people who have to clean up all that stuff. What happened to the jokes? You're not making me laugh anymore. Does that mean you're thinking which city Ali Ahmad has gone to or you're thinking about life without a dick to piss with?"

"Bismarck," shouted Calvino. The word rang through the room.

Oxley's head jerked back a fraction of an inch with surprise. Joy found the target in front of her. Her teeth sank deep into the right side of Oxley's neck, and in a single, awful tearing-and-ripping movement gutted his pharynx and trachea. His hands came forward to Joy's head, but he was too late. The teeth dug in deeper, the teeth, mouth, and jaws leaking blood. The enormous force of her jaws snapped clean through Oxley's external jugular. It was the way special forces were taught to kill with a knife. Quickly and in silence. There was little pain. Blood and mucus gurgled from Oxley's mouth and throat. He made loud sucking sounds like someone drowning. Joy's jaws clamped down with the impact of a ten-wheel truck. Oxley had no strength left in his body. Joy never let up for a moment. Oxley's eyes remained open. Oxley keeled over, the coins and key chain spilling from a pocket and clattering on the wooden floor. His body lay without moving. Joy's teeth plunged into the dead man's neck at the same angle over and over again.

"Stop," shouted Calvino.

Joy released her jaws and sat up erect, her tongue hanging out, her mouth bloodied. She had the kind of satisfied look that a cat has bringing into the bed of its master a dead rat.

He looked at the body. It's a dog-eat-dog world. That's what Oxley had told Rolfo.

❖

IT was early morning when Colonel Pratt answered the phone. Kiko was on the other end saying she was worried. She had had a date with

257

Calvino to go jogging in the morning but he hadn't arrived. And he wasn't answering his phone.

"I thought Vincent was spending the night with you," said Colonel Pratt, cradling the phone against his shoulder, as he slipped on his trousers. Manee watched him from the bed, smelling the fear roll off her husband.

"We had a disagreement. It was the same old commitment battle," said Kiko. "Pratt, Vinny always answers his phone."

"He might have gone jogging alone." He looked around at Manee and tried to give her a reassuring smile, but she saw straight through him.

"I'm going over to his apartment," she said.

"No, don't do that. I'll pick you up."

When he pulled into Kiko's condo complex on Soi 49, she was waiting downstairs in her tracksuit, pacing. She'd grabbed the car door before Pratt pulled to a complete stop. During the drive to Calvino's apartment, Kiko sat quietly in the passenger's seat, rubbing her hands and trying to control her breathing, taking slow breaths. She glanced over at Pratt, who watched the road, betraying no emotion.

"How are Lisa's English lessons?" he asked, trying to find a neutral topic of conversation.

She looked over at him, staring through him just like Manee had done half an hour earlier when he was on the phone.

"Okay," she said. "It's a struggle. How did you ever learn English in Bangkok?"

Colonel Pratt turned onto Sukhumvit Road.

"I went to a school on Convent Road. The teacher was English. I remember she was very stern. One day she asked the class to define the English word 'island.' She kept shaking her head. We felt shaken. It was such a simple English word and yet no one could define it correctly according to her. Then I raised my hand and asked her if she would define 'island' for us. She smiled, and said, 'It's very simple. An island is a piece of land surrounded by the British Navy.' That's how I learned English," said Pratt.

"You ever tell that story to Vinny?" Kiko asked. She liked it that he had her laughing, easing the tension.

"Yes, and he said when he was at school he had a similar experience. The teacher defined an island as a piece of land off the coast of America bought for twelve bucks from the Indians."

She could understand how Pratt and Calvino had managed to cement a friendship across cultural, racial, and language lines. Underneath, they saw the world in very much the same way; when they looked through the other's eyes, it was as if they were looking through their own.

Colonel Pratt's car swung into the driveway. Kiko was the first one out. Doors opened and slammed. Joy barked several times as she heard the steps on the outer staircase. The morning sun had sliced above the horizon as the clock turned to six in the morning. Kiko used her key to let herself into the apartment. Joy stood in the doorway, sniffing her. She reached down to stroke the dog and her hand came up sticky with congealed blood. Colonel Pratt, seeing the blood, pushed past her and through Calvino's apartment and toward his bedroom. But Joy had run ahead and blocked the entrance.

"Vinny, are you okay?" shouted Kiko.

Joy held Colonel Pratt at bay. From the door, he could see Calvino stark naked and tied down on the bed.

"Back, girl," said Calvino.

"My God," screamed Kiko, seeing the blood everywhere.

"It's okay," said Calvino. He gave a signal to Joy, nodded for Pratt to come near, and then whispered. "Pratt, get Kiko out of here. There's something I don't want her seeing."

Colonel Pratt looked over the side of the bed, saw a body on the floor wedged between the wall and bed frame. The body had been brutally savaged. Pratt felt bile rise in the back of his throat and he jerked away, closing eyes for a moment, his brow suddenly wet with sweat. He covered the body with the bedcover.

"Kiko, I'd like a few minutes with Vincent," he said, looking back at the door.

She saw from his face that he had seen something terrible. "I'll be in the sitting room," she said, a tentative smile crossing her lips, as she nodded at Calvino.

"Thank you," said Calvino.

Blood had dried on Calvino's bare chest.

Joy turned, ran along the end of the bed, turned again, made her way along the windows, and took up her position guarding Calvino, her head resting on his chest. Oxley's body lay on the floor beneath the crumpled bedcover that Colonel Pratt had pulled over it. Joy had dragged the cover away from the lifeless face, circled two times, before settling down on the body; ears alert, mouth open, head cocked to the side, as if nothing much had happened.

After Oxley had made one phone call, in less than two hours the authorities processed his release outside of normal channels. When Colonel Pratt found out what happened, he had ordered his men to follow Oxley. Several hours later, Lieutenant Narong discovered that Oxley, with a little help from his Unit friends, had arranged for another *farang* to take his place, and they had been tailing this man for hours without knowing he was a decoy. Colonel Pratt had played a hunch and staked out the airport. Oxley never arrived.

Colonel Pratt pulled the bed back and stepped over Oxley's body, crumpled faceup on the floor. He covered his nose and mouth with a handkerchief. The smell of decay was overwhelming. Black flies had settled on Oxley's throat. Pratt looked away from the mauled neck. Kiko's head peered around the corner and she gasped, her hands covering her mouth, as Colonel Pratt covered the body with one of Calvino's sheets.

"What in the hell happened?" asked Colonel Pratt, cutting Calvino free with a penknife.

"You know how they say a dog is a good judge of character?" replied Calvino, rubbing his wrists, his hands and feet numb from hours of no circulation.

"Joy?" asked Kiko.

"Yeah. She did a number on him."

Colonel Pratt, down on one knee, looked up from Oxley's body. "He's been dead about three hours. My God, Vincent. I've never seen any wound like this. Not ever."

Calvino peered over the edge of the bed at Oxley's body. A column of red ants marched in single file, using his left hand as a ramp. His splayed fingers lay fingernails-down on the floor. The ants had turned his forefinger into a highway from which they spread out over his hand and moved forward to the open wound. Oxley's neck was covered with thousands of ants, their small red pincers working into the flesh. Calvino wondered if these were the same ants Melody had seen inside his fridge. If so, they had developed a taste for human things and were eating Oxley, broadcasting the message that there was a fresh kill on the premises.

"She tore out his throat. It happened before he could react," said Calvino, watching the ants.

He explained how Stadler had told him that German shepherds made good guard dogs, and that he had trained each of his dogs to protect its master against any intruder. Protection must have been one of the reasons Hutton had wanted the dog. Hutton had traveled with news crews for four, five days and left Kwang, the golden flower girl, alone in Bangkok. Having Joy in the house was his way of showing he cared about her safety. Kwang could have taken care of herself in most dark alleys against the best of them. She could have: But not even Joy could have saved her from the professional hit at the Hotel 99.

Rolfo Stadler had trained Joy to be a professional killer. Once her master shouted a code word, she went onto automatic.

"What kind of word could make a dog do this?" asked Kiko.

With a fresh sheet taken from his closet wrapped around his lower body, Calvino stepped over Oxley. He looked back at Kiko, then knelt and for the first time gave Joy a big squeeze.

"A special word," he said, hugging the dog.

He pulled the necklace over his head, dangled the wooden penises above Oxley, and dropped them on the dead man. "So much for *Lucky Charms*."

❖

THE late afternoon breeze off the Chao Phraya River fluttered the dozen hydrogen-gas-filled balloons floating above Calvino's head. Melody was several steps away, buying an ice cream cone from a vendor set up along the wharf in front of Wat Arun. Her tongue curled around the dripping cone as she walked back to join her father.

"It's not as good as McDonald's," she said, licking it again. "But I guess it's not too gross."

"I wish you weren't going back tonight," said Calvino.

She licked her cone. "Me too. But you know, it's the way it is. What can I do? Stay here? You know Mom would just die. I mean it's bad enough that I am not going to be a star and I'm not going to get a red sports car when I turn sixteen. And we're not moving to Hollywood to live with Mr. Oxley. Carol talked to Mom. They both cried and decided that all men are deceitful bastards."

"And what do you think?"

"Who knows? I'm still a child. I'm not required to think yet."

Calvino guided her to the narrow, steep staircase leading up the side of Wat Arun. On all sides were broken pieces of fine—and not so fine—china teacups and saucers, the thousands upon thousands of fragments of imported tea services catching the late afternoon sun and showering the skyline with a carnival of light at diffused angles. He climbed the first couple of steps, holding the balloons with one hand and the stone railing with the other. Melody followed a few steps behind, then dropped her ice cream cone.

"Dad, do we have to climb all the way to the top?"

"Partway."

"I dropped my ice cream cone."

"When we climb down, I'll buy you another one."

"It's okay. Ice cream will make me fat."

They emerged at the first plateau and Calvino swung off to the side, walking along the balcony and looking at the river below. He waited for Melody to join him. She was slightly shaken from the steep ascent.

"I'm going to miss you," said Calvino.

Melody wrapped an arm around his waist. "Why don't you come back to New York and be my dad again."

"In Bangkok, I'm still your dad."

"You know what I mean. It's not the same."

Calvino released one of the balloons. The wind caught it and it sailed toward the river, disappearing behind a row of palm trees. He handed her a yellow one and she let it slip out of her hands, and they silently watched it.

"Everyone has their way of dealing with pain," said Calvino. "And your going back to New York is a larger kind of pain than I normally have to deal with."

"Nothing turned out the way I thought, Dad."

"And it hurts."

"Kind of."

"Some Buddhist teachers say that life is learning to recognize what causes us pain. What makes us suffer."

"Like what?"

"Like wanting stuff, things. Wanting people. The more we want, the more we feel the pain of not having what we want. And even if we get what we wanted, it's never exactly what we thought it would be, so we end up wanting something else and the cycle starts over. If you can let go of what you want, then the thing you want can never own or hurt you. Take this balloon. This is Melody's wanting to be in the business." Calvino handed her the balloon. "Okay, let that one go. And remember you let go of wanting not the balloon but being in movies—the movie business didn't let go of *you*."

She took a red balloon. "The red sports car. Good-bye." She watched it sail toward the horizon.

A single balloon remained.

"You send it, Dad."

"One of the hardest of all wantings is to release. I wish that my daughter never had to leave my life."

He released the last balloon, an arm around Melody. A tug pulled several empty barges down the center of the river. Several riverboat restaurants approached from the other direction. More tourists clicking cameras pushed from the other side. Vendors below were selling silver bracelets, balloons, food, and incense sticks.

Melody leaned forward for a last look, following her father's eyes downward. "Everyone in the world wants something."

"But not everyone understands that the trick is to learn how to let go."

❖

TOMMY LORETTI had put Calvino's international phone call on hold. The fact that it was an international phone call from Bangkok to Los Angeles made no difference. When Tommy Loretti came back on the line he had a bright, cheery voice.

"I just got it confirmed. They abandoned the *Lucky Charms* film because the Thais wanted payoffs," said Tommy. "That's the story in L.A. Tyler, Oxley—these guys had a track record of making foreign films. People are saying if Tyler couldn't do it, then it's a waste of time even thinking about doing something over there."

"What about my treatment for *War Crimes*?" asked Calvino.

"Oxley's deal is down the drain. No one will touch it."

"My treatment is different."

"It's in Thailand. People in Hollywood are still talking about how wild dogs took Oxley apart. That sonofabitch was a navy SEAL. He got cut down by a mad dog and was eaten by soldier ants. What a horror show. What the fuck do you think the average guy in the business thinks? He'd rather sell shoes for a living: That's what he thinks. And how do you bring in financing? Want to put some cash into a movie shot in Thailand? Not even a dog food company is gonna touch Thailand for ten years."

"Why don't you come and hang out for a week, Tommy."

"Me? Fly to Bangkok? You fucking nuts or what? You got jungle, wild dogs, death, locusts, ants, killings. The place sounds more and more like the Old Testament or our old neighborhood. I came to L.A. to escape Brooklyn. You went to Bangkok to find it. That's the difference between us, Vinny."

"I've got a great German shepherd named Joy. After a bargirl."

"Look, I got George Clooney on the other line. I gotta run."

"Thanks, Tommy. You made merit for next lifetime."

"Excuse me, I need to make some bread for *this* lifetime."

Ratana showed Colonel Pratt into Calvino's office. He seemed relaxed, happy; the man had the definite look of someone having a good day. Pratt unfolded a copy of the *Bangkok Post* and laid it on his desk. The paper had been opened and folded to the third inside page.

"You made the newspaper, Vincent."

"Gary Larson's *The Far Side*?" asked Calvino.

"The Thai version," said Colonel Pratt.

He hated having his name in the newspaper. At least no photograph was run this time. His eyes dropped down and he picked up the story under the headline "Gun Charge Against Expat Dropped." The story began.

"Charges against American national Vincent Calvino were dropped yesterday. The prosecutor asked that the case be dismissed on the grounds of insufficient evidence. Mr. Calvino was unavailable for comment."

"I love Thailand," said Calvino. "The world is awash with insufficient evidence and it just so happens to wash up on the shores of Bangkok with the morning tide."

Colonel Pratt laid the Browning automatic on Calvino's desk. "I had a telephone call from Paris," he said. "Dex is coming home. He's had a great tour. He asked me to send his regards."

"I don't know if it's a good idea, Pratt."

"Good or not, he knows his own mind. And, I almost forgot, Sam Hatcher phoned me."

"Hatcher phoned you? More death threats?" Calvino looked amazed as he carefully pushed the Browning into his shoulder holster.

"Not this time. He phoned to thank us for helping out."

"Pratt, I don't like the sound of this."

Colonel Pratt shook his head. "They had been onto Oxley from the start. That your dog made a breakfast of him helped out. If you finish reading the paper, you'll see a report from Cox's Bazar. A faction of the Party of God executed what they thought were two American spies who had infiltrated their ranks from Burma. But they weren't American assets. They killed two of their own people. Figure how they got the names?"

"Ali Ahmad," said Calvino.

"He convinced them those two agents were responsible for the men killed on the Burmese border," said Colonel Pratt. "They bought it."

"What did the Thais get out of this?" asked Calvino.

"Information, names, backgrounds on people Ali Ahmad met with around Soi Nana. The Internal Security Operation Command sent a message to Sam Hatcher. They were happy with the results."

"Muslims operating in the south," said Calvino.

"The information was helpful."

"'Helpful'? My maid is helpful. What does that mean?" asked Calvino.

Colonel Pratt smiled and left it on that note of ambiguity.

"Hey, I know that smile," said Calvino. "'The *farang* can't figure it out smile.'"

"You read smiles well for a *farang*," said Colonel Pratt.

Close as he was to Calvino, one thing could never be overcome— Calvino, as a *farang*, would remain a perpetual outsider. No matter how much he knew or understood, it was from standing outside and looking in. Even if he had been born in Thailand, he would stand outside. The invisible interlocking, overlapping networks, seamlessly buried behind the Thai smiles, were hidden inside bunkers constructed from blood, friendship, social rank and marriage. No one was ever more than a mosquito coil away from someone who felt an obligation to defend and protect them against an outsider. There was only one language worth knowing, and that was the one of loyalty; it was a language a *farang* might learn in a Thai lesson and might if he were foolish enough thought applied to him.

To say the information was "helpful" meant it was useful on the inside, where decisions were executed, plans laid, policies formed. In this nontransparent rice cooker, with the lid on, the temperature could be adjusted, and the rice neither burnt nor wound up undercooked. The information was helpful. In Thailand a *farang* ate the rice; but he had no idea how it was cooked. "You were as good to shoot against the wind," as Shakespeare wrote. When the *farang* left Thailand or died in Thailand, he simply vanished—like the wind which was once strong, even powerful as a storm against the body but one night disappeared. But the art of cooking rice was passed down from generation to generation inside an invisible seam of thought, expression, gesture, and feeling.

"The dog was a real hero," said Colonel Pratt.

"You're right," said Calvino.

Joy sat in the corner of his office, her large head resting on her paws, watching Calvino as he suddenly shot up from behind his desk and called over the partition to his secretary.

"Ratana, get Loretti on the phone, quick. Tell him I got the hero for *War Crimes*. It's the missing link in the treatment. An element that's a secret between Joy and me."

"You're not going to tell me?"

"If I did, Joy would have to kill you."